Double Down

Double Down

TOM KAKONIS

A DUTTON BOOK

DUTTON
Published by the Penguin Group
Penguin Books USA, Inc., 375 Hudson Street,
New York, New York 10014, U.S.A.
Penguin Books Ltd, 27 Wrights Lane,
London W8 5TZ, England
Penguin Books Australia Ltd, Ringwood,
Victoria, Australia
Penguin Books Canada Ltd, 2801 John Street,
Markham, Ontario, Canada L3R 1B4
Penguin Books (N.Z.) Ltd, 182–190 Wairau Road,
Auckland 10, New Zealand

Penguin Books Ltd, Registered Offices:
Harmondsworth, Middlesex, England

First published by Dutton, an imprint of New American Library,
a division of Penguin Books USA Inc.
Distributed in Canada by McClelland & Stewart Inc.

First Printing, August, 1991
10 9 8 7 6 5 4 3 2 1

 REGISTERED TRADEMARK—MARCA REGISTRADA

LIBRARY OF CONGRESS CATALOGING-IN-PUBLICATION DATA
Kakonis, Tom E.
  Double down / Tom Kakonis.
    p.   cm.
  ISBN 0-525-93326-3
  I. Title.
PS3561.A4154D68 1991
813'.54—dc20   90-27039
                                                CIP

Printed in the United States of America
Set in ITC Cheltenham Book
Designed by Julian Hamer

PUBLISHER'S NOTE
This is a work of fiction. Names, characters, places, and incidents either are the products of the author's imagination or are used fictitiously, and any resemblance to actual persons, living or dead, events, or locales is entirely coincidental.

For Judith,
without whom it wouldn't get done.
Also for Jeff Gerecke,
for similar reasons.

After looking at his hole cards,
a player may elect to double his bet
and draw one, and only one, more card.

Definition of doubling down
in Edward O. Thorp's
Beat the Dealer

PART
ONE

1

Tammi, Debbie, Dori, Kristi, Marci, Angie, Barbi—in Florida it was the diminutive all in vogue, never mind the lady's age or true dimensions. Take Tammi, for instance, working the adjoining chair: a crimson-lipped pudding of a woman, had to carry an easy one-eighty on a fireplug frame, sun-creased fortyish face, set of lungs would make a drill sergeant proud. Kittenish, you couldn't call her. Or the one busily snipping away at the shag of hair coiling over his ears and trailing south on the back of his neck. Stood six feet in her working flats. Tack on a good three inches in the killer heels she habitually wore for her other, after-hours employment with Bennie's Key Line Services, Inc. Piecework, she liked to call that supplemental vocation, giggling over her excellent joke. She went by "Steffi," out of "Stephanie," but moving rapidly and, he supposed, inevitably toward an even more truncated Steff ("Hey, Steff," Tammi was braying at her now, "loan me a bottle of that jojoba?"). Give it enough time and she'll answer to nothing more than a sibilant hiss.

And after prison you could give him another thousand years and he'd still never feel right in these unisex salons, all gleaming mirrors and walls of amber-tinted glass and may-I-put-you-on-hold music sedating the chill conditioned air. Pungent perfumes of hair spray, shampoo, perm solution, mousse, jojoba—whatever *that* was. And the voices, the incessant chattery voices—female mostly, at this time of day—quacking about diets, fashions, Caribbean cruises, dinner parties, shiftless domestic help. Wildly amusing anecdotes and general discontents. Like Steffi was doing just then, regaling him with a tale of an obnoxious client who demanded a nostrils trim.

"I'm telling you, Tim, this twink had bristles coming out his nose, looked like a couple Brillo pads. He goes, 'But you do my ears,' and I go, 'Hey, heads, eyebrows, ears—fine. No problem. But no noses. Thanks a whole heap, but no thanks.' "

"You've got to draw the line somewhere," Waverly said. Say anything to keep her moving, get himself out of here.

Wrong approach. Instead, what she did was pause in the efficient circuiting of his skull and stab the scissors perilously close to his face, punctuation to her annoyance. "That's what I said. That's *exactly* what I told him. You don't, next thing it'll be your basic cling-ons they want clipped, right? You know what I'm talking here, cling-ons?"

Waverly nodded, to signify he understood.

"Well, when that happens, that's when little Steff starts looking for another line of work."

She was nothing if not earthy, little Steff.

"Speaking of that," she said, voice descending to a confidential murmur, "when you fellas look to be off the shelf?"

Not your most subtle segue. Waverly said he didn't know.

"What's it been? Couple months?"

"At least."

"Things ought to be chilling out by now, all the juice Bennie's got."

"He hasn't got that much anymore."

"What's he hear?"

"Not a lot."

"Well, when's he coming back?"

Some urgent fishing going on here. He understood why, and he could sympathize. But he wasn't about to reveal Bennie's latest scheme, a strategy born out of purest desperation. "Don't know that either. This weekend maybe."

"Reason I ask is, see, Lonnie got laid off again. And Darryl's tuition's coming up. I could use some action."

Lonnie, he remembered, was the boyfriend of record, Darryl the son, a sophomore at FAU. Nose-packers, both of them, came weighted down with costly habits. They kept her scrambling.

"The fact is," he said, "it doesn't look good for us. Not in this vicinity. You might want to think about going solo."

"Jesus, Tim, anymore that's not so easy."

"I know." He lifted his shoulders in a helpless shrug. "What can I tell you?"

It took her no more than a moment to dismiss that disagreeable notion. "Bennie'll come through with something," she said, re-suming the brisk scissoring. "He always delivers."

An optimist, if Brecht had it right, is someone who hasn't yet got the bad news. Bennie was never one to broadcast disaster, so by that definition Steffi surely qualified. In no other respect, though, was her myopic faith in the happy ending justified. Wa-verly tried to understand the contours of her peculiar reality, but it wasn't easy. She figured to be somewhere near his own age, pushing deep into the thirties and beginning to show signs of fraying at the edges, same as he. Medusa ringlets bleached a star-tling platinum framed the vacantly pretty face of an amiable sheep. But splayed out from eyes hooded with purple shadow was a network of fissures settling under the layers of paint. And blue veins, time's notarized seal, were tunneling visibly through her nimble hands. Alas for little Steffi, clinging stubbornly to a forced girlishness in the face of the departing years. The ultimate Florida calamity. It was sad.

"So how about you?" she asked. "How you holding up?"

The condo gone, car hocked, bank account emptied, living out of a damp-sheets efficiency on the beach, less than a dime on his hip—not so famously was how he was holding up, but that wasn't the sort of thing you announced. That much he'd learned from Bennie. "Doing just fine," he said.

In the mirror her reflected face registered a mild impatience. "No, getting by, I mean."

"I'm keeping my head down, Steffi. Gone to ground." In the wan hope she'd take the hint, speed it along, he added, "By rights, I shouldn't even be here."

"What happened anyway, Tim? All this steam coming down."

So much for hints. What happened? Ah, there lies a melancholy tale. But not one he was disposed to share with her. "You got me," he said.

"But out of like nowhere like that. And why just Bennie? You know Armand Zender, operates out of Pompano? Look at him. His people are still working."

She had this pressing need for answers. Couldn't leave it alone. "Maybe it was our turn in the barrel," Waverly said.

"It still don't add up."

Not unless you had all the numbers, which she didn't. Missing for her was the pivotal half of the equation. The Michigan half: another stiff to his credit (or shame, depending on your perspec-tive), this one gone up in flames with half a mil worth of sniff, and a hardballer name of Dietz dogging his heels ever since. "You got any idea who it is you was fuckin' with up there in Michigan?" Bennie had demanded once he heard that name. No idea. "Where you been, boy?" Sheltered, evidently. But not for long. "Just Dietz is all," his dismayed partner had been quick to inform him, letting the squawky monosyllable hang ominously in the air a moment. "Gunter Dietz. Lemme fill you in on his weight. It ain't fly." And now this Dietz—deep pockets, long memory, a weight something heavier than fly—now he was come to collect. And there was no skating out of this one. Their turn in the barrel indeed.

But to Steffi all he could say was, "It's a mystery." Best he had to offer. Thinking about it made him edgy, so he added, in gentle prompting, "Listen, are we about finished here?"

"Hey, you come in looking like the Wolfman, it's gonna take some time. Relax. Almost done." A few more quick passes with the scissors and she was satisfied. She stepped back and studied the results of her art critically. "So what do you think?"

Waverly gazed at the likeness gazing back at him out of the polished mirror. In contrast with the black cape drawn up around the neck, the face looked extraordinarily pale. Also worried, older. But not, he was obliged to conclude, one snippet wiser, to which his very presence here testified: out in the world in the pitiless light of day, careless of Bennie's sound advice to stay buried till the heat got lifted. The now neatly barbered hair seemed to have more gray in it, and the vertical cleft between the brows and the lines of parentheses around the nose were deep as trenches. Distress furrows of a man nursing a persistent grinding headache. Which in a figurative way is what he'd been, these past months. "You do good work," he said, for something to say.

Steffi gave him an impish look. "Yeah, that's what all you nasty men tell me. I know you." She removed the cape with a grand flourish, whisked the stray hairs from his collar and said, "Ta-da! Welcome back to the human race. Next time don't wait so long."

More advice. Everybody's a counselor these days. He got his wallet and counted out some bills, laying a fifty on top of the standard charge. It wasn't much. Most he could manage.

The look turned to genuine gratitude. "Thanks, Tim. I can use it."

He put a hand in the air. "Nothing, forget it."

She followed him to the front of the salon. At the door she glanced about quickly and whispered, "Any buzz comes down, you let me know, will you?"

"I'll do what I can, Steff."

"You're a good shit, Waverly. Always was. Take real special care now, y'hear?"

He stood there a moment, filling his pallid face with the late afternoon sun. Good shit Waverly, nowhere to go but a scummy apartment in Roach Arms, and nothing to do but watch and worry and wait. Taking some care, if not the kind that qualified as real special. At the other end of the small strip mall was a tavern with a sign that laid immodest claim to the world's coldest beer and finest burgers. It was almost five o'clock, and he supposed he was hungry. Or ought to be. Thirsty, maybe. Okay, stalling.

He scanned the parking lot cautiously. A scattering of vehicles, Bennie's pink Seville among them, last flagship of a forfeited fleet. Some shimmery pools of water standing in the seams of the asphalt, remnants of the routine midday downpour. A few shoppers hurrying here and there, fleeing the muggy heat. Over to his left, traffic streaking down Old Dixie Highway. And to the right, along the line of storefronts, no one even remotely suspicious-looking. Nothing out of order anywhere, as far as he could tell. He stepped out into the lot and headed for the tavern.

When he was no more than halfway there, an urgent, upward-inflected voice summoned him: "Timothy? Timothy Waverly?" Instinctively, he ducked behind the nearest car and spun around and discovered an owner to go with the voice, a woman coming through the door of the salon, sprinting toward him. And across some forty yards of south Florida parking lot and the considerably wider distance of the years, he recognized her at once. Of all the unlikely people in all the improbable places. He came out from behind the car and waited till she overtook him. And then, shaking his head slowly from side to side, he said her name. "Caroline."

"Timothy. It's really you."

"None other."

"When I saw you leaving the shop, I knew it was you. I just *knew* it."

That fact established, she wrapped joyous arms around him, and in the instant they clung together he was conscious of the glow of her body and the delicate fragrance of her hair. A swarm of memories buzzed in his head. Simultaneously, they ungripped and stood gaping at each other in that momentary daze that freights any too-sudden breach in the steady flow of time.

"You look . . . wonderful," she said finally, a bit uncertainly.

"You too," he said, only meaning it. The same clear, wide-spaced eyes, cobalt blue with sprinklings of gold. Same abundance of hair rising off the high white brow and splashed over the slender neck and shoulders in a tumbling wash of honey curls. Same cleanly defined bones in a heart-shaped face innocent of makeup but for a touch of coral on the lips. Luster of youth still in the skin. Remarkable. And that's pretty much how he put it: "Like you've been preserved in ice, Caroline."

She rewarded him with a brief, whimsical smile. "I knew there was something absent in my life all these years. How many now?"

"Got to be fifteen."

"Fifteen," she repeated around a rueful sigh, as though the full weight of the number had only just occurred to her.

"Robbie? How's he doing?"

"Robbie? Same as ever. No, that's not right. Better than ever. You know Robbie."

He thought he detected an edge in her voice, the barest trace of irony. Unless he was mistaken. He said, "You two still in Boston?"

"Oh no. Houston. Since 1980."

"Robbie with a firm there?"

"In a manner of speaking. He's got some partners. They're into a lot of things."

"Children. No doubt you have children."

"Boy and a girl, one each. Just slightly under the two-point-two national average for an upscale family like ourselves."

No mistaking the self-mockery in that. He wasn't sure what to say, so he dealt another banality. "And what is it brings you to sunshine heaven?"

"Vacation, I suppose you'd call it. Actually, more of a working vacation, for Robbie anyway. He's become quite the entrepreneur."

"Good for him," Waverly said, watching her. The same Caroline, yes, but taller than he remembered, slimmer, infinitely more elegant somehow. Maybe it was the outfit: candy-striped silk blouse, designer jeans looped by a tooled cowboy belt, carelessly scuffed docksiders. The knockabout wear of the rich. Slung over her shoulder was a soft buckskin handbag with western studs and stitches to match the belt. Around one wrist a gold tennis bracelet laced with tiny glittery diamonds, lady's Rolex on the other. Couple of small stones on the fingers, nothing gaudy. All her easy natural grace, only magnified now by money. That, he decided, was the difference. That, and the peculiar restiveness in her eyes, the odd fluttery motions of emphasis her hands made whenever she spoke.

As now: "What I want to know is what *you're* doing here."

"Getting my hair cut. Same as you, it seems. Styled, I guess, in your case."

"No, *here.*" Her gesture went floating past him to include by implication a wider region.

"Here? This is where I live."

"But I thought—well, we'd heard . . ." She let it trail away. Her face worked through various attitudes, as though not quite certain which one was right. Her eyes searched the ground.

It figured, of course, that she'd know. But it didn't take her long to get to it either. "It's over four years now I've been on the street," he said, a little stiffly. "Paid my debt. Rehabilitated, you might say. More or less."

"I'm sorry, Timothy. About what happened. I wanted to write but I couldn't think of anything to say. I'm truly sorry."

"You shouldn't worry about it."

"I do though. I worried about you."

A silence opened between them. Caroline Vanzoren Crown, sweet Dutch girl grown into this sleek girl-woman, and still worrying about him, or so she said. Robbie Crown, the nearest there had been to a friend in that other life of his, long since vanished, departed to the Ultima Thule of blurred and wistful memory. A lot of past going on here. On impulse he said, "Look, you have time for a drink?" He caught the quick glance at the watch. "You don't, that's all right too."

Now she lifted her eyes and fixed him with a fond gaze. "Nothing I'd rather do, Timothy Waverly."

"Terrific. There's a place right over—"

"But I can't."

Waverly examined his palms. "I understand."

"No you don't. In about two hours there's a cocktail party over on The Island. Command performance, wives *will* be there. I've got to get back to the hotel and arrange my face. In every sense of that awful expression, by the way."

"It's okay, Caroline."

"It's not okay. But we're going to make it so it will be." She fumbled through the handbag, came up with a pen and a scrap of paper, scribbled something, and handed it to him. "That's our room number. We're at the Breakers. Tomorrow it's our turn to host the nightly fest. Seven o'clock. You're instructed to attend."

"We'll see."

"You'll come, Timothy. If you don't I'll have you tracked down and trussed and delivered to the door." Her face clouded suddenly. "Oh, maybe that's not so funny."

He let it go by. "We'll see," he said again.

"That's not good enough. You've *got* to come. Robbie'd do me in if you didn't. Say it."

"Say what?"

"You'll be there."

He thought about it, but not for long. Palm Beach (or The Island, as the locals and other hip insiders liked to call it), the Breakers, the frolicking rich—it was probably safe. And anyway, there were twenty-four solitary hours to reconsider. "I'll be there."

"Good. It's settled, then. Now walk me to my car."

She slipped an arm through his and led the way to a silver Jaguar at the end of the file.

"Nice machine," he said.

"It's a loaner. One of Robbie's partners in intrigue. Guess what I drive at home."

"You're not going to tell me a wagon."

"Bingo."

She disengaged the arm, fitted a key into the lock. And then she turned and faced him, seemed to hesitate. "One question. When I called to you back there, why did you go running behind that car?"

The Jacktown tic, he would have said to almost anyone else. To her he said, "Startled, I suppose. You were among the absolute last people I was expecting to see."

A skeptical look softened slowly into a dreamy smile. "You know, it's curious how things work."

"How's that?"

"The fellow who does my hair whenever we come down here, Perry? He used to work out of the hotel salon. Then he bought this shop over here, about a month ago, he told me just today. Turns out to be the same place you go to. And on the very same day. I'd call that curious, wouldn't you?"

"Well, you remember the old proposition: Set a monkey at a typewriter long enough—"

"And eventually out comes *King Lear*," she finished for him. "I remember. Philosophy 101, the random nature of things. We've come a long way from Calvin College and Grand Rapids, Michigan. All of us."

"That we have."

"It's good to see you again, Timothy. Better than good." She kissed him lightly, quickly. A woman in a hurry. From behind the wheel she said, "Tomorrow night. Seven o'clock." Her fingers wiggled a farewell.

The Jag crossed the lot, darted onto the highway, and vanished in the current of traffic. Waverly watched, wonderstruck. It had all happened so fast it was hard to know if it was real or merely a product of his imagination. Except for the scrap of paper he held in his hand, with a Breakers room number on it and a time and the preemptory injunction *Be there* followed by a line of screamers. That was real.

And then an urgent horn blared behind him, and he turned and saw he was blocking the path of a less than patient female motorist. And as he skipped out of her way another, harsher reality occurred to him: where he was, standing out there in the open, utterly exposed, reckless of caution; and who he was, which was not your average citizen with nothing worse to fear from the glare of daylight than a mild case of sunburn. And that sudden unwelcome nudge of reality was enough to set him scooting for the Seville.

2

At a fitness center located in a shopping plaza less than two miles from where Waverly stood, D'Marco Fontaine, twenty-nine, built, considered fatally handsome by some, himself included, was cranking out his tenth and final set of squats. Fifteen deep ones, all the way down. Two-sixty on the bar. Monitoring his form in the facing mirror. Flawless form: head up, chest high, back flat, butt tight, heels in. Ten reps into it fucking quads felt like they were going to burst through the skin. Last five his breath came in honking gasps. Nevertheless, he ground them out, racked the bar, and sank onto a bench. Blotto.

Today was leg day, real ball-blitzer. Do ten sets of squats, ten sets on the extension and curl machines, half an hour on the Lifecycle—do that and you start to see visions. Paradise City. Course he ought to be working calves, but he was running late, already past five o'clock. Anyway, he didn't want to get himself too whipped, case there was some stutter-stepping to do yet to-night. Man's got to make a living too. Catch the calves tomorrow, after arms.

Once his heart quit clubbing and his wind came back, D'Marco got to his feet, a little wobbly yet, and checked the goods in the mirror. He was not at all displeased with what he saw: wide, square shoulders with a pair of respectable guns dangling from them; lats like a couple vulture wings tapering into the tiny waist and dancer's hips; some nice cuts in the thighs, teardrops coming over the knees; little swell in the glutes, not too much, no donkey ass on him. At six-one, one-ninety-three, a physique of balance, proportion, harmony, nothing too radical, kind that can turn heads without goggling the eyes. Not like your freaks and power hogs, blown up on the gorilla juice. Not for D'Marco Fontaine. It was one thing to keep in shape, take some pride in your body, but you couldn't afford to look too conspicuous either, his line of work.

The spa, known as Stayin Alive, was unfamiliar to him, and he took a wrong turn off one of the exercise rooms and ended up at the front door. He cursed softly, doubled back till he found the men's locker room, got his gym bag, and hit the showers. Thirty minutes later he was ready, but on his way through a mirrored dressing area he paused and stole a moment for another quick self-scrutiny. You were D'Marco Fontaine, it was hard to pass up a mirror.

Look at him there, terminally cool in his summer-weight snap-button sport jacket, dusky blue, 44 long, athletic cut to accommodate the shoulders; his white cotton camp shirt, buttons undone neck to sternum, displaying the line of pec cleavage; his beltless navy trousers cinched around the flat middle; his Etonic running shoes, all that rocketship superstructure on them, cost him a yard and a half. How about that face? Helmet of thick black hair glossy with Vavoom gel, combed straight back off the forehead and over the ears, sheared at the neck; chilly gray eyes hidden behind a pair of Vuarnet blue blocks; shred of a mouth that seldom smiled but when it did displayed a set of perfect, stainless teeth, chiseled cheekbones, and a rock of a jaw. No escaping it: top to bottom, he was the total package. Looked exactly like the Florida player that he was. Except maybe for his skin, talcum-white and, he had to admit it, weird for this part of the world. Fucked if he was going to go along with everybody else in that department, conspicuous or not. Fry yourself in the sun, get all dry and withered, collect your senior discount before you turned thirty, like some of them could easy. Maybe get cancer. Forget that. Some things you don't compromise on.

While D'Marco was admiring himself and his discriminating value system, a pencilneck geek sidled up next to him and pretended to study himself in the mirror. Gave it a moment before he said, supercasual, "Hey, man, I was squintin' you, out on the floor. You lookin' good."

D'Marco acknowledged the praise with a bit of a grunt.

"Trainin' for the Gold Coast next month?"

D'Marco said unh-unh.

"You oughta, man. Ten more quality pounds, you'd place top three, walkover."

"Not into contests," D'Marco said. He didn't believe in wasting words.

Standing side by side, they were talking to each other's reflections. Geek had a punker do, mouse face with some pimples on it, wore a baggy shirt wild with yellow flowers. D'Marco figured whatever he was pitching was coming right up. He figured correct. Geek said, "Y'know, you wanta score some D-ball, put on them ten pounds quick, I could maybe help you out."

"D-ball," D'Marco repeated, drawling it out like it was half a question.

"Yeah, you know, big D, breakfast of champions?"

D'Marco turned slightly, just enough to level his subzero, blueblocks stare. "You peddling juice? That what you're doing here?"

"Offerin' a service, you might say. Realize that fine potential."

"I ask you something?"

"Sure. What's that?"

"How's your skills at making license plates?"

"Huh?"

"You got any idea what my employment is?"

The mouse face tightened. He backed away, shaking his head no.

"Tell you what it is. Palm Beach Sheriff's Department, special task force, narcotics. Steroids, they're a controlled substance. Get you an easy nickel in the bucket."

"C'mon, man, I thought you was a musclehead. Honest mistake, like. Besides, D-ball ain't your serious shit. It's like, say, weed. Everybody on it." He rolled over pleading hands. His voice had risen to a whine.

D'Marco made a small, closed-lip smile. "Tell you something else. On account of I got other business to attend to, today could be your lucky day. Depends on how fast you can move." He glanced at his watch. "What you got, jackoff, is a thirty-second lead. I catch up to you outside, guarantee you won't enjoy it much."

The smile widened as he watched him shoot through the door. Special task force—Jesus, there was a hoot for you. Him with eleven certified pops on his score card (some of them real ingenious too, carried the D'Marco Fontaine trademark) and so many stunts he'd lost count. *Him* sporting a sheriff's shield? Required some imagination, which he had his share of. Same time, he didn't appreciate being hustled everywhere he turned. Take a leak and there's some virus got a deal for you on the pisser. What a world.

Same story out in the lobby. Fluff behind the counter gives him a plaster-of-paris grin, lots of teeth, asks, "You have a good work-out?" Like she gave a shit.

He said it was okay.

"How do you like the club?"

"Nice facility."

"Next month we're putting in a whole new line of machines. State-of-the-art equipment."

"No kidding."

She had on one of those glittery aerobics outfits, metallic gold and black leotard over a white body suit, looked like it was applied with spray paint. Girl from Mars. She leaned over and laid her firm jugs on the counter, let him have a good peek. "We got a special membership offer," she said, flashing the teeth. "First fifty people sign up get an extra year free."

Everybody peddling something. "I'll think about it," D'Marco said.

"Don't think too long. Offer's only good through the end of June."

"Yeah, well, that's—what?—couple weeks? So I got some time yet. Tell you what, though, maybe you can help me out on something else. Anyplace around here serves natural food?"

"Best spot I know is Mother Nature's, out to Singer Island."

"From here, how do you get there?"

She gave him directions and a look that asked, Where you been? "You must be new to North Palm, huh?"

So as not to miss leg day, he'd paid them seven dollars for this one-shot-only workout. That didn't mean he owed them a life history too. "No, I lived here all my life," he said over his shoulder. "It's just I get lost easy."

"You have a good day now," she called after him. "And don't forget the offer."

Yeah, which one's that, he thought sourly, jugs or the free year? Both, probably. Well, bimbette just lost herself a mark. Mark, D'Marco; D'Marco, nobody's mark. He chuckled to himself at the play on words.

A blast of heat greeted him on the other side of the door and he crossed the lot hurriedly, face wrinkling against the sunlight, and slid behind the wheel of his customized Mustang LX. He turned the key in the ignition, the fan kicked on, and inside of thirty seconds the air was chilly as a banker's smile. What a slick little tooler, this vehicle of his, real Sneaky Pete. He'd treated himself to it about three months back, after closing a particularly fat arrangement with a gang of crazy bean dips out of Miami. And next to himself, it was the source of his greatest pride.

With good reason. Under the hood sat a five-liter, multiport fuel-injected V-8, 225 storming horses, take you from a dead stand to sixty in the blink of an eye. Like grabbing hold of a live wire. Break away to an easy 140 on the open road. Had to scare a golden shower out of any poor dumb citizen happened to glance up and catch it in the rearview: Here she comes, color of midnight, sable-tinted windows, extra-wide blackwalls, looking like some goddam demon of darkness swooping down on him—repent, sinner!—day of judgment is at hand!—whoosh!—zap!—way too late!—there she goes! If he had any regret at all, it was he'd never get a chance to see himself piloting it. Talk about your radical visions of cool, that one had to be South Pole.

But for right now he drove like any one of those good citizens, easing carefully into the North Lake traffic, yielding to pedestrians, deferring to the whackadoo lane jumpers. He turned south on Highway 1, kept an eye peeled for Blue Heron Boulevard, the way the girl from Mars had directed. The main arteries he remembered pretty good, but it had been a while since he'd been up on this end of glitter alley, year at least. Lately, all his work had taken him the other direction, and you go where the business says you go.

Blue Heron up ahead. He swung left at the light and passed over the bridge rising in a graceful sweeping arc above the waters of the Intracoastal. Nothing anymore could awe D'Marco Fontaine, but coming over the crest of that bridge there was a diced moment when even he was impressed. The line of towers rooted like bleached tombstones against the sky, the rope of yellow sand, some white specks of sailboat gliding across the greenish surface of the sea, the astonishing brew of color, lavender and gold and deepening violet, at the farthest edge of the horizon—fucking sight to see. Impress a zombie. Someday soon he'd own a condo in one of those towers over there, or someplace like them. Condo, shit, more like a floor, or the whole goddam building, rate he was scooping up the coins. Course a man's got to be practical too, not get careless. It was okay to dream dreams, but you can't go around with your head up your ass either. Still some hoops to jump yet, get from here to there. Like tonight, for instance.

He parked in the lot behind the Ocean Mall and set out for Mother Nature's down at the far end. So-called mall was little more than a string of interconnected snowbird hustle shops broken by an occasional passage leading to the beach. Not many tourists this time of year, but still plenty of diehard sun soakers idly strolling about gawking at the window junk, shamelessly displaying their gross bods. You'd think somebody'd tell them, or they'd take a look in a mirror, recoil in shock and loathing at what they saw. Must be there was no such thing as shame anymore. He averted his eyes, walked faster.

Mother Nature's Pantry—his kind of place. First good sign was the notice posted on the door declaring this a smoke-free zone (nothing worse than the stink of tobacco, spoil a wholesome meal). Inside, the walls were lined with shelves stocking an abundance of exotic health foods, herbal beverages, natural cosmetics, assorted nutritional supplements. One corner was dominated by a large juice and snack bar, behind which stood an eager beach bunny in a ribbon of a halter top and the briefest of shorts. Lots of tanned bare flesh, done-it-all face. Seventeen maybe, going on thirty. She looked him over appraisingly, made a fetching smile.

"Hi. Howya doin'?"

A short affirmative nod served as his reply.

"Whatcha have?"

Way she said it sounded like all her goodies were up for grabs. Didn't surprise him any. Broads get a scope on your D'Marco Fontaine, it knocked 'em horizontal every time. He ignored her, studied the menu a moment. All the exercise had sparked an appetite, but he didn't want to go to work on a full stomach either. That wouldn't do. "Your tuna come water-packed?" he asked her.

"Oh for sure," she said, smartass, perish-the-thought-otherwise tone of voice, like *any*body'd know that.

"Okay, gimme the tuna in a pita, garden salad with some sprouts, no dressing, and a papaya cooler, only hold the banana and throw in some brewer's yeast instead."

"Y'know the sprouts an' yeast, they're extras. Gonna cost you more."

Whole world trying to bust your balls, one way or another. D'Marco laid the menu on the counter and turned on his Lapland glare. "Yeah, well, think maybe I can cover it. Now, you want to get it set up here? I got to be in by midnight."

That got her moving. The smile fell and she huffed away, wiggling her can a little anyway, let him see what he was missing.

All the stools were occupied, so when his order came up he took it out onto the boardwalk and found an empty table with an awning to shield him from the rays of the sun, slanted now but still capable of scorching. He savored the food, chewing each morsel thoroughly. Directly across from where he sat was the

deck of a bar and grill called the Greenhouse, jammed with porkers swilling beer and inhaling relish-drenched burgers and chili
dogs and deep-fried conch fritters. Jesus, the garbage people
stuffed in their swollen bellies—made you sick to watch it. At the
table next to him a couple of sun-puckered geriatrics were earnestly debating how many milligrammed angels of deliverance
danced on the head of a certain multimineral caplet. D'Marco
eavesdropped on them, concluded they didn't know shit about
nutrition. For himself, he took megadoses of vitamins every day.
About your health, you couldn't be too careful.

Now it was 6:45. Time to roll. He drained off the last of the
papaya cooler, got to his feet, and strode to the car. He could feel
the spring coming back into his legs, the old energy surging. Good
feeling, being in shape was. The necessary edge. He drove over
the bridge and up Highway-One, retracing his route. Instructions
were to find a Park Avenue, and when he came on it he hung a
left and followed down some grungy residential blocks till he spotted a row of shops set off from the street by a narrow parking
strip. There it was, lion's-head sign announcing Androcles Hair
Styling, and there were the two pay phones tacked to the wall
out front, just like he'd been told. Jar of Gerber's, so far.

Nevertheless, he did a slow drive-by, checking out the area,
watching for any static signals. The way he saw it, caution was
like money: never enough, business he was in. Everything looked
clean, so he turned in at the far entrance and pulled up a few feet
from the phones. He cut the engine. Down went the window. It
was three minutes before seven. He waited.

Precisely on the hour, one of the phones began jangling.
D'Marco got out of the car, glanced right, left, over his shoulder.
At the agreed-upon fifth ring he lifted the receiver and said sim-
ply, "Yeah."

The voice riding down the line was growly, anxious: "Frog?
That you?"

"Yeah, it's me."

"You have any trouble findin' the place?"

"I'm talking to you, aren't I?"

"Huh?"

D'Marco sighed. "Your directions, they were good."

"Good, good. You set to do some sharkin' tonight?"

"Figured that's what I drove up here for."

"Okay. Here's the skinny."

3

At about the same time D'Marco Fontaine was finishing off his papaya cooler (though by Central Daylight Time an hour earlier on the clock), Sigurd Stumpley was bent to a heaping plate, plowing into his supper. He ate with the controlled intensity of a famine victim, fork moving rhythmically in one hand, thumb of the other busily engaged as pea scoop, sweat beads popping at his temples and eyes bulging in the transfixed gaze of pure internalized pleasure. Sigurd's mom had fixed his favorite summertime meal: a mess of fried smelts, white rice, green peas with pearl onions, slivers of tomato and cuke floating on a sea of vinegar and oil, ice tea to drink, and prune whip for dessert. She hovered over him, watching fondly. Good old Mom. She looked out for her boy.

Except she could get on your nerves too, all that twitchy fluttering. Mouth bubbling like a busted crapper: *More that rice, hon? Get you a lemon for your fish? Eat, eat, you got to eat, Sig.* Jesus, no wonder he weighed what he did, which was thirty pounds the wrong side of two hundred, which at his height was about sixty too many. Comes of being a widow, he supposed, and him an only child. He let her, she'd wipe out his ass for him too, twenty-five years old or not.

She lived in the community of Downers Grove, Illinois, one of the series of faceless suburbs strung out west of Chicago like beads on the chain of the Burlington Railroad. Until he was twenty-one Sigurd had shared her cramped apartment, but after his release from Stateville (where he did a half a nickel on a botched smash-and-grab) he figured he'd better get a place of his own. Wouldn't look right, fast starter his age still living with his mom. Anyway, when the old itch needed scratching—not that it got scratched that often—but when it did he didn't want her on the other side of the wall, all the groaning going on. Man's got to have his privacy too. So what he did was find a spot in Lisle, one burb over, though he always managed to stop by three or four times a week, keep her company. Also to scarf up a decent meal, and to drop off and pick up his laundry, which she insisted on doing for him. Fuck, whatever kept her grinning.

That's what she was crooning about now, laundry, mending socks, some kind of gas like that, he wasn't paying much attention. Finally, three helpings down, he put the fork in the air, stop signal, and said, "Whyn't you just pull up a seat there. Take a load off."

"Oh, that's okay, Sig, I ate already."

"Do it anyway. Too hot to be on your feet today."

Touched by his concern, she sank heavily into a chair opposite him, wheezing. She was a year-round wheezer, Mom was, but even more so, this kind of weather. Ninety-two in the shade out there, air sticky as Super Glue. And not a whole lot better in here. Didn't help any, being on the top floor of a six-story building. Neither did all that heat rising off the stove in the narrow galley kitchen behind them, carrying with it the fragrance of smelt expiring in a spattery puddle of grease. The drapes were drawn at the window of the tiny dining nook, shield against the blaze of setting sun, but he could hear the Burlington rattling down the tracks half a block away. Had to be the 5:55, hauling in the commuters from the city. Least he wasn't one of them, riding a fucking cattle car, scrambling after a couple coins to rub together. So there was always something to be grateful for, when you thought about it, even if it was hotter'n a hooker's twat on New Year's Eve.

Sigurd and his mom lit cigarettes, sagged back in their seats, puffed contentedly. Had a stranger happened on them just then, he would never have mistaken them for anything other than what they were—mother and son. Aside from the gap of thirty-five years and the toll exacted on her by gravity and time, they presented a pair of near-identical faces, absent of planes or edges, shapeless as two hunks of clay. Shocks of ginger hair (hers, discreetly tinted, inclining toward orange) ascended from meager foreheads. Mud-colored, thyroid eyes peered out over pouchy cheeks sprayed with freckles, pickle noses, wide red mouths. In girth they were approximately the same, though Sigurd carried most of his weight forward, in a parabolic arc of belly; and Mom aft, in a broad, high porch of rump. At the hips both of them sported accordion rolls of slack flesh creeping south over chunky thighs (and in Mom's case all the way down, bottoming out at the ankles). There were times when Sigurd wondered, a bit regretfully, why he hadn't had the luck to inherit more of his father's frame and features. Course he'd never actually known the old man, got himself whacked before Sigurd was even out of rompers, but he'd seen plenty of pictures in the family albums. Those photos revealed a standup dude lean as a blade, wolfish face, black hair varnished smooth to the angular skull, black sunken eyes, smile on him a kind of wised-up, hard-guy smirk. Ringer for Uncle Eugene, which, when he considered it, made him feel a little better. In the looks department, Uncle Eugene wasn't exactly mondo-class competition for your Robert Redford.

Mom was chattering away about her day, treating him to a nonstop blow-by-blow. Laundry first thing in the morning, lunch (complete with menu recital) at the Greek's down on Main, grocery shopping out to the Jewel on Ogden, Oprah and her guests in the afternoon. . . . Exhaustive detail. Only thing missing was a description of her daily dump, and if he'd asked she would've supplied that too. They give a black belt in gum flapping, she'd have one for sure. Hire herself out as a human Sominex. Make a bundle.

Along about "People's Court" Sigurd's jaws unhinged in a fly-catcher yawn. She paused, gave him a solicitous look, and said, "You tired, hon? Want to lie down on the sofa, take a nap?"

"Nah, can't do that. Gotta go back to work tonight."

"You shouldn't work so hard, Sig."

Sigurd shrugged, made a weary face that said man's got to do what he's got to do.

"Worries me," his mom said.

"Ain't nothin' to worry about. Fact is, job I'm on now might just roll over into something big." He put a little swagger into his voice, watched for her reaction.

She made no reply. When he was alive, her husband had never ever spoken of business. Neither did her brother-in-law, Eugene, when he dropped by once a month to ask how she was doing and leave a roll of bills—her sole support—on the kitchen counter. Fine with her. Some things ladies weren't supposed to know about.

Her silence only irked Sigurd, and at last he said, "Well, you wanta hear what I been up to?"

"I don't know, Sig. You think you ought to be talking?"

"Won't hurt none, just tellin' you my end of it."

Technically she was right, of course, if you was to put a fine point on it. And ordinarily, scut work they had him on, pigeon boy, couple bills a week and change, there'd be nothing worth spilling anyhow. But getting an invite inside the loop, running with the heavyweights, reporting direct to Uncle Eugene and even meeting Mr. Dietz f'Chrissake—that was shit of your serious variety. That you had to share with *some*body, and if you can't trust your own mom, who you going to?

"Y'see," Sigurd began, "couple days ago, Tuesday it was, Uncle Eugene gives me a call, says meet him out to O'Hare. Seems there's this kike comin' in from Florida and he's pickin' me, Uncle Eugene is, to put the sneak on him."

"You always want to do what Eugene says, Sig. He's a fine man."

"Yeah, yeah, I know that, hey. That ain't the point, purr say." Sigurd had heard Mr. Dietz use that last, that purr say, when he was talking to Uncle Eugene, and even though he didn't know exactly what it meant he liked the ring of it. Sounded like class, so he figured he couldn't go wrong, using it himself.

"Well, don't you forget what he's done for us. After your father passed away. And all."

By that pointed "and all" she meant what they both knew she meant: It was Uncle Eugene got him the high-powered shyster got him thirty months on what could have been a ten-year jolt; and it was Uncle Eugene found him a place in the enterprise once he was back on the sidewalks. Okay, so Uncle Eugene looked out for him. Okay, so he owed him. So what? "Look," he said irritably, "you wanta hear this story or no?"

"I'm listening."

"Okay, we're out to the airport and Uncle Eugene says just hang off in the weeds, keep him in your crosshairs, don't let him make you. Plane comes in and the Jewboy, big sack a lard, gets off and starts happy-handin' Uncle Eugene. They head down the pavement to the Floral Gardens, me on their bumper. At the Gardens they get a booth, throw back a couple pops. Kike's mouth's runnin' like a storm sewer in a rainstorm, arms waggin'. Uncle Eugene, he just sits there eyeballin' his glass, noddin' his head every once in a while. Real cool."

"Speaking of that, glass, you want yours filled up?"

Sigurd took a full breath, glared at her. "I'm tryin' to tell you something heavy here, and you're talkin' ice tea."

"Just thought I'd ask."

"Okay, gimme some more the goddam tea."

She heaved herself up out of the chair and waddled into the

kitchen. Sigurd lit another cigarette while she poured. He waited till she was settled again, then resumed.

"Y'gotta understand all's I got is a balcony seat, so I don't know what it is they're turnin' over. Looks of it, though, it ain't no average chin-'n'-grin. When they get done, Uncle Eugene runs him down Ogden and leaves him off at the Downers Grove Motel up there, which you remember ain't exactly your Palmer House."

"Funny place to be staying," his mom agreed. "Him being a Jew."

"That was my first thought," Sigurd said shrewdly. "Got to tell you something about the weight of his wallet."

"So what did you do then, Sig?"

"What I'm told. Kept a watch on the place all night and into the morning, till Uncle Eugene comes by, says go home and grab some quick Z's, he's gonna need my services next couple days."

"Bet you were all worn out."

"Yeah, I was a little flogged," Sigurd said toughly. "Nothin' I can't handle."

"You got to take care of yourself, son. Good health is precious."

"So's loot, Mom, an' what I'm thinkin' is I'm maybe gonna be slidin' into some. Real soon. See, yesterday afternoon Uncle Eugene calls me again, says meet him at the Hilton up to Arlington Park, one by the track up there. Says wear a suit. Know why, Mom?"

She looked blank.

"Why is because I'm gonna *meet Dietz!* How about that, hey."

Sigurd's mom's mouth fell open. "Dietz? You met Mr. Dietz?"

Sigurd leaned across the dinette table and extended an open hand. "Here—shake the hand that shook the hand of Gunter Dietz."

She pressed his hand between both of hers, drew it to her ample bosom, squeezed. Her eyes went watery. "I'm awful proud of you, hon."

"Told you you'd wanta hear this story." Sigurd reclaimed his hand, pushed on with it. "Now, course I was only with 'em a little while," he said with a becoming modesty, "and then they went into a private huddle, hour or so. But you know, Mom, how I got a habit of keepin' the wax outta my ears? Pick up quick on things? I think I got me a figure on what's shakin' here. Or gonna shake."

Mom was twisting in slow circles around the seat of the chair, like she was trying to polish it with her butt. "It's this part here, Sig, I don't think you should be saying."

Yeah yeah yeah yeah—right again. Trouble was, this was the

part he *wanted* to tell. Good part. "No prol'um," he said, "nothin'
you can't hear." Which was pretty much the truth. Fact of it was,
he was still just peeking through the keyhole, though if he saw
what he thought he saw it was Sugarland for your Sigurd Stumpley, dead ahead.

Still she looked unpersuaded. He said it anyway.

"Line is this kike—or a buddy his, it ain't too clear—nicked
some company product. 'Bout a year back, out in the boonies
someplace, Michigan, thought I heard. Now, we ain't talkin' your
nickel street bag here. Talkin' the big buckaroos. Purr say." He
figured he better skip the part about the troopers went toes in all
the action up there. She'd just worry.

"Mr. Dietz, he naturally ain't too happy about this, so he puts
the buzz in the wind. Takes some time but he gets 'em sniffed,
down to Florida. How you gonna hide from Dietz and company,
hey? So the kike comes up here to see can he squirm out, way
them people always tryin' to do. Knowin' the jacket on Dietz, I'd
say our matzoh ball's couple bricks short of a load, that idea.
Anyway, zipper on it is, I think Uncle Eugene's gonna tag me to—"

Sigurd's mom cut him off with a jabbing finger. Very firmly she
said, "That's enough, Sigurd. I don't want to hear another word."

No way could he stop now. Coming up was the absolute best
part. "It ain't what you're thinkin'," he said, even though it almost
for sure was. "See, after we left the Hilton yesterday, Uncle Eugene puts me back on Jew patrol. Rest of the night and most of
today. I pro'ly ain't slept ten hours, last forty-eight. But that don't
matter. Also, Uncle Eugene, he says get a bag packed, be ready
to roll. Right now they're holdin' a meet out to the Gardens—
Dietz, Uncle Eugene, Israel. An' dependin' on what comes down,
I could be the one trackin' him *all the way to Florida!*"

"Florida?" she said doubtfully. "You?" She had every reason to
be skeptical, for she knew Eugene didn't have the highest opinion
of her son. Back when Sigurd got himself into all that trouble,
Eugene was furious, said Sigurd was so dumb he didn't know if
Christ was crucified or killed in a chariot race. That dumb. And
looking at him now, his chubby face opened in a sunburst grin,
she had to wonder if Eugene wasn't right.

"That's it, hey. You're maybe lookin' at the Florida Kid." Since
he'd never in his whole life been out of Chicago and its immediate
environs (Joliet didn't count), this announcement, even if prema-
ture, was occasion for no little pride.

"I don't like to see you getting mixed up with Jews, Sig. They're
too . . . sneaky. For you."

"Ahh, if this job comes through, be nothin' to it. Room Service." That's what he told her. He knew better. It come through, it was his big chance. Be a shooter at last, real Chicago shooter. Run his own program for a change. It was the giant chimichanga he'd be forking into.

"If," was all she said.

An hour and two helpings of prune whip later, Sigurd reached behind him and picked up the ringing phone. He muttered a few words into it, but mostly he just listened. Eventually he said "Gotcha" and recradled the receiver and lumbered to his feet. He drew himself up to his full height, five-seven, narrowed his eyes, and said, "Time to go back to work."

"You be careful now, Sigurd," his mom lectured him on the way to the door.

4

"**I**'m telling you, Care," Robbie was telling her, voice booming through the open door linking their adjoining rooms. Depending on his mood or audience, he could use that rich baritone any way he wanted, pitch it smooth as butterscotch or corrosive as acid or any gradation between. Sixteen years of marriage had fine-tuned her ear to all its accents and cadences and modulations. What she was hearing now were the brassy resonances of bravado tempered by an undertone, ever so slight, of anxiety.

"The man's indefatigable. Champion arm-twister, working at it all the time. This is a guy who could make a fortune peddling Amway on Worth Avenue. You should have seen him on the course today. Has to be pushing sixty, and he's got the horse-power of a kid."

He was singing the praises of his partner in this current venture (whatever it was, some swampland nirvana for the elderly, Dizzy World of the declining years), one Jack ("Call me Jock") Appelgate. His hero. Jack and his frumpish wife, Avis. Jack and Avis. Sounded like a "Gong Show" dance team, heavy-shoe. First-order boors, to her thinking, added new dimensions of odium to the definition of nouveau riche. But that's not the sort of thing a good helpmeet tells an already jittery spouse, so instead she said, noncommittal, "Must have a good motor."

"What's that?" he called back.

Her words had been drowned in the startup rasp of an electric razor. She didn't bother repeating them. Nobody listening. Neither did she bother getting up out of the cushy chair. No reason to stir. And anyway, the magic red pellets, swallowed half an hour earlier, were gradually seizing hold. An oil slick slow-spreading through torso and limbs. Feathery lightness taking residence in the innermost chambers of her head, casting a soft-focus glaze on the world outside her eyes. Better living through chemistry.

She was dressed and ready: basic black sheath, triumph of understatement; every curl exquisitely in place thanks to the wizardry of Perry (though God knows where those nance-nimble fingers had been before they touched her hair—another thought not to be pursued); face so painstakingly made up it appeared, in the softening light, almost laminated. Robbie had said seven, seven it was. Punctual as always. Dutiful. He was the one late, not she. So there was no good reason to stir from the chair.

From where she sat, feet propped on the floral spread of one of the two king-size beds in the room (talk about conspicuous consumption—two people, four beds), glass of Perrier in hand (time enough for the raw stuff later, plenty of time), she could see twilight descending like a benediction over the Atlantic. Undulating shadows advanced across its calm surface. Pelicans soared. In the theater of her mind, a pair of them performed a stunning pas de deux. Dancers in another element, gliding, floating, tracing easy circles, dipping their wings in a bid for applause, coasting to impossible motionless stalls—look! two birds, pelicans, tacked on a blue-black sky!—and then plunging out of her line of vision in a dramatic, dive-bombing finis. Curtain. Thunderous ovation, bravos. Earthbound, she was flooded with envy, vague longings, nameless regrets.

"These goddam Remingtons just don't do the job anymore."

Oh-oh. Sudden squall on the horizon, rolling in fast. Should have got up, gone in there, put on a *Gee, boss, you're great* face, listened worshipfully. Too late now.

"You may remember I *asked* you to pack my Braun."

Materialized in the doorway, filling it, was a splenetic husband, clad only in his Jockeys, fuming. R. Blake Crown, attorney and counselor-at-law, entrepreneur, deal broker, aspiring tycoon, glowering alternately at her and at the razor clutched in his hand, both equally culpable. "Try a blade?" she asked, probably a little too lightly for the magnitude of the crisis.

"Blade!" he snapped. "You know I can't use blades. Blades chafe my skin, turn it red as a lobster."

The image, even if uninspired, was not totally inaccurate. His face and neck did indeed have a boiled quality, florid mix of sun and bourbon and hypertension; and his arms, up to the sleeve line, were singed the color of weathered brick. The rest of him was cottony white. What we used to call a farmer tan back in

Grand Rapids, Caroline was thinking, suppressing a snicker. "How about powder?" she said. "I've got powder."

"Powder's no help."

"I don't know what else to suggest, Robbie. If you'd told me before, I'd have gone out and bought you the one you want. We've been here two days, you know."

"That's not the point."

"What is?"

"The *point* is," he said, cross-examiner sonorous, "that I rely on you to take care of the packing—i.e., to include all the gear I need. Not all that heavy a burden of responsibility. I assumed— obviously incorrectly—you knew by now which razor I use."

Caroline set the glass on the table beside her. She turned slightly and looked at this two-toned man, so intensely self-absorbed, so firmly dead center at the core of his own universe there were times (such as this one) when she had the uneasy feeling that were he ever to expire, she and all the rest of the world, mere figments of his imagination anyway, would vanish right along with him. Poof. Gone. "Endless apologies," she said. "Tomorrow, first thing, I'll find you a—what is it?—what's the name?"

"Braun. Big fucking help tonight."

"If we're going to argue, Robbie, can't we pick a more inventive topic than electric razors? We're creative people. Or once we were."

No reply. He waited a moment, indulging his sulk. Then he came slouching into the room and made directly for the Servi-Bar in the corner. She pulled her feet off the bed, to let him pass. Watched as he poured whiskey into a water glass, sank onto the farther bed, stared at the pale-green carpet desolately, sighed a sigh of infinite weariness. Transparent moves in the elaborate game of marriage, clearly understood by both parties. Finally he said, "One. Mellow me out."

"Mellow carries the day," she said. "Every time."

He continued his study of the carpet. Sipped at the drink. She recovered her glass, sipped also. Waited. Squall line passing.

"You call the kids?"

"Yes."

"Well?"

"They're fine. They miss us. Everything's under control."

A little more dead air.

"All right," he said, establishing eye contact now, "I'm sorry, Care. But the pressures I'm working under, you wouldn't believe."

Her cue to say, You could try me, so that's what she said. It was sufficient to launch him.

An earnest, fretful monologue on the status of the project, its stuttering progress, enormous hazards. His speech, she noticed, was laced with the synthetic vocabulary of the heady world of moving and shaking. Very cryptic messages encoded in there somewhere. She creased her forehead in a display of concerned attention, but it wasn't long before her eyes were drifting inward. And as she listened to him, or showed the face of listening, it occurred to her, dreamily, how little she knew him, this near-naked fellow on the bed, this hipster of commerce, this stranger. Perhaps she should phone security: Oh, there's a man in my room, in his underwear, speaks a curious alien dialect. Your name, ma'am? She says her name. Room number? She reveals it. Can you describe this intruder? She fashions a description: heavy-shouldered, barrel-chested, wide-waisted, not fat exactly, more meaty, you might say, the way athletic boys grow gracelessly into middle age. Facts only, ma'am—height, weight, build—no editorial embroidery. All right, then, six-three, two-twenty or thereabouts, I don't know, a large, imposing man. Hair? Flaxen, sun-bleached, cunningly arranged over northbound temples and a tiny pink discoid in the back. Eyes? A smeary shade of blue, red-rimmed, faintly sullen. Features? Noble Anglo-Saxon nose, generous mouth, superior dental work, slight sag at the chin, still handsome yet, in a fleshy sort of way. Any distinguishing characteristics? Well, there's that center-of-the-universe thing, and the mercurial mood swings, and the nagging fear of failure and— Ma'am, please, facts.

"Are you listening to *any*thing I'm saying here?"

Coming back, she recognized a familiar chilly gaze fastened on her. The eyes she'd described as smeary (what did that mean, exactly?) to the anonymous disembodied voice in her head were flashing irritation signals. Evidently she'd missed a caesura in the torrent of words. "Of course I am," she said.

"You'd better be, Care, because it's our cookie jar we're talking about, too. Yours and mine. All of it. If this project goes Drano, it's emptied right out, crumbs and all. So if I'm a little edgy, possibly you can understand why. Give some slack."

She considered saying, I give great slack, thought better of it. Much too flippant. Instead, she adjusted her face again: ruminant solicitude, that ought to do.

It did.

"So far we've got close to ten mil subscribed," he chugged on.

"Now everything turns on that raghead. Without him we're toast. And I'm talking the soggy variety."

"He's the Arab gentleman you mentioned once?" She was guessing here, coasting on a dim fragment of memory. "The prince?"

"They're all princes over there," he said impatiently. "Either that or dealers in camel dung."

"But he's not, uh, subscribed yet? This prince?"

"Not yet. When he gets here, we're going to have to give him plenty of face time."

"When is that?"

"Week from tomorrow. Jock's got a bell-and-whistle show planned, but it's going to require some serious chute greasing to get ourselves inside that particular power load."

What a riot of metaphor! He'd wondered—with good reason— if she'd been listening; now she had to wonder if he heard anything at all of the peculiar mangled jargon spilling out of his own mouth. But it was her turn to speak, so she asked if they'd thought of a theme for their development. A little whimsy couldn't hurt. Lighten the air.

"Theme? What do you mean, theme?"

"All parks have themes."

"Yeah, sure," he said in the exasperated tones of a tutor lecturing an impossibly dull charge, "trailer parks, amusement parks. This is not a park, Caroline. We're not targeting the double-wide set. It's an exclusive retirement community, for upscale blueheads with discriminating tastes."

Mortuary Manor, you could name it. Or maybe Shuffleboard Shangri-La. There's a notion. Something alliterative, in any case, slides easily off the tongue. That's what played pratfalls in the vaudeville of her mind; what she said was, "I mean a motif. A sort of subtext." She examined her glass, as though an inspiration might be found lurking in the crystal water. Prudence said leave this one alone, but those Harlequins in her head kept on goading. "How about 'The best is yet to be'?"

She looked up brightly. Squarely into a pair of scowling eyes (that's what smeary meant!—pinched, humorless).

"You mocking me, Care? If you are, I don't appreciate it. Right now I'm like a juggler with one too many balls in the air, and I don't take kindly to your sophomoric jeering." The anger in his voice twined with a trace of injured hurt.

"No, seriously. From that Browning poem, 'Grow old along with me,/ The best is yet to be.' As a theme, or slogan, it seems quite fitting to me."

In the silence that followed the remark, she filched a quick glance his way. He seemed to be peering into some mercantile middle distance. Could it be he was actually entertaining the idea? "Just trying to help," she said, all innocence.

He shot her a look of appraisal. Unamused. Nobody's fool, R. Blake Crown. "You want to help," he said coldly, "then spare the limp witticisms tonight. If that's what they are. They'd be lost, anyway, on this company." He took down the last of the whiskey, rose off the bed, and started for the door. "Speaking of which, I've got to get moving. They're going to wonder where we are."

Where are we? The laws of metaphysics declare without an answer there can be no question. Okay. In this stately fortress overlooking a mild tropical sea—there's an answer. In a pair of elegantly appointed rooms, separate but equal, dominated by beds and couches and walnut desks and tables, Louis XVI fauteuils, custom armoires and headboards, iron lamps on the floors, watercolors on the walls depicting Venetian fountains supported by grinning nymphs. There's another. Too literal, though, both of them. All right, then: caught in the yellowing curd of a soured union—another still. The image pleased her. All riddles yield finally to logic and sweet reason. More of that Philosophy 101. Another image, drifting somewhere on the slushy boundaries of consciousness, returned to her, and to Robbie's retreating back she said, "I ran into Timothy Waverly today."

That brought him up short. He turned in the doorway, eyes widening, head cocked. "Who?"

"Waverly."

"*Our* Tim Waverly?"

"The very same."

"Well, *fuck me!* Where? When? Come on, details."

"At Perry's new salon, over in North Palm. Couple of hours ago."

"Why the hell didn't you mention it before?"

"You'd just got in, you were showering, late. I don't know." It wouldn't do to tell him she'd just now remembered. Nothing served by that kind of disclosure.

The look he gave her was not exactly disgust—too much astonishment in it—but it had the coloring of irritation. "What's he doing here?"

"He says he lives here."

"But I thought . . ."

"So did I. Not so. Apparently he's been out for some time. Four years, I think he told me."

"How's he look?"

"Older. He looks older."

"He say what he's doing? For a job?"

"I didn't get that far. We only spoke a few minutes."

"Tim Waverly," he said, shaking his head, eyes half-closed now. "If that's not a blast from the past for you."

"Fifteen years, by his calculation."

"God, I'd like to see him again. Too bad we're running such a tight schedule here."

Caroline drew in a deep breath. From here on it promised to get sticky. No wonder there'd been that brief memory lapse. "Well," she said, neutral a tone as she could manage, "the thing of it is, Robbie, you probably will. I invited him over tomorrow."

"You did *what?*"

"Invited him to the party, gathering, whatever it is. Tomorrow night."

"Are you yanking my chain again, Care? This another of your sick jokes?"

"It's no joke. I assumed you'd want to see him. You just said you did."

"Jesus, where the fuck's your head," he said, inclining his own head backward and opening his palms at the ceiling. Supplicating the heavens.

"I don't understand the problem."

"You don't understand?"

"No."

"Well let me spell it out for you then. Listen close, now, see if you can follow. First he knocks up some country bimbo, marries her. Bimbo cheats on him, so with that impeccable logic of his he kills her goddam *divorce* attorney. Does hard time in Jackson. You remember hearing about Jackson? One of Michigan's finer academies, sort of like your Moody Bible Institute."

"That's the story we heard," she said quietly. "And I do know what Jackson is, by the way."

"Good. That's very good. So maybe you see my problem. Problem is he's an ex-convict. As in convicted felon. For a capital crime, as in murder. A murderer. Not your guest of choice in polite society generally, and this crew specifically. Is that plain enough for you? Am I getting through to you?"

"He was also a friend."

"Boyhood friend, college friend. All that was a long time ago.

In the game I'm in, friendships are about as valuable as a K-Mart blue-light special. If you weren't shuffling around with your dims on, maybe you'd recognize time passes, circumstances change. Wake up, will you?"

In a voice little more than a whisper, she said, "You're a work in progress, Robbie. You know that?"

"Yeah, well, that may be. You'd better hope it is, one of us showing some progress. Some sense. Now get on the goddam phone and call him and uninvite him. Tell him . . . shit, I don't know . . . make some excuse. You'll think of something. Exercise some of that creative you're telling me about."

"Afraid I can't do that."

"This is not a request here, Care."

"I neglected to get his number."

"Look it up."

"I've already done that. Not listed."

"And you 'neglected' to get it?"

"That's right."

"So there's no way to head him off."

"Not unless he decides against coming. If it's any comfort, he sounded, well, hesitant."

"Hesitant," he said, a voiced sneer. For a moment he stood there, empty of words. Body stiffening in outrage. A frigid light charging the smeary eyes. Then for another moment he seemed to be muttering something under his breath. And then, out loud, a hand chopping the air, he said, "Someday it's going to catch up to you, Caroline. All those dillies you're popping, mother's helpers. All that orbiting in outer space. Going to be a crash landing. Soon. When it comes, don't count on me to pick you up and dust you off again."

And listening to him now, paying attention this time, it came to her, as though in a flash of superior illumination, that the linchpin of marriage, any marriage, is friendship. A marriage can survive major sorrows, lesser hurts, all the thoughtless little day-to-day cruelties; can endure loss of passion, interest, trust—respect, even. As theirs had endured—all those losses, griefs. But destitute of friendship, nothing remains. Disjunction. Vacancy. Void. Her joyless gaze went floating around the room, came finally to rest on him. And looking at him there, this Jockey-shorted man looming over her, inspecting her with a cold contempt, she saw no friend.

5

It was Waverly's contention that the south end of Singer Island had about as many resort apartments as there were clever combinations of the words sun, surf, sand, sea, palms, shores, air, beach, tropic, spray, isle, and maybe a few others he'd overlooked. He believed, moreover, that once those combinations had been exhausted, all construction had necessarily come to a grinding halt. They had, quite simply, run out of ways to spell paradise.

His complex went under the name Tropicaire, four cream-colored, stucco-sided bungalows squared around a tiny, treeless courtyard, two of them fronting Ocean Avenue, two set back from the street. When he first moved in, he'd requested one of the latter. Request denied. "Gonna be doin' some remodelin'," the owner-manager told him, "take a couple weeks. Soon as we're done I'll put you right in one of 'em." That was two months ago. He was still waiting. But at four and a quarter a month, he couldn't be pushy. Or choosy. During the season the same place could command that same amount a week, maybe more. So if there had to be another crunch in his life, better it come out of season. So maybe he should stop the moaning and start tallying up some blessings (the way Bennie was always recommending: "Got to be a good day, boy—it's another one above ground, right?").

All the same, four bills and change didn't buy much anymore. Not on Singer Island, where efficiency meant just what it said and not a stitch more. Look around. Box of a room partitioned by Formica counter into kitchenette fit for a pygmy and what was euphemistically called living space. That space was crammed with Hide-A-Bed sofa cushiony as a concrete slab (blankets and sheets not included, sorry), La-Z-Boy, three wicker counter stools (for dinner guests, presumably), four braided throw rugs, one burn-scarred coffee table, one end table on which sat a squat ceramic Monkey Wards lamp, color TV, on one wall a by-the-numbers painting of a wave-lashed sea, on another a pair of praying hands crafted from tin, on the ceiling a wide-bladed fan. Look over your shoulder, through the door opening onto the closet-sized john: stool, sink—both of them rust-blasted—and shower stall with greenish mold gracing the tiles. And there you have it, one Tropicaire efficiency unit. Paradise. Or the Jugo model thereof.

He was sprawled on the sofa, lord of the manor, surveying his princely domain. He was smoking, leisurely but steadily. The air was thick, blue. The room's sole ashtray, rapidly filling, rested in his lap. Not to worry. On the counter were a pair of gallon milk jugs, their tops sheared off, their insides blackening from the rising accumulation of cigarette ash, two months' supply. His own contribution to the decor. In the weakening light they looked remarkably like a cautionary photo of the autopsied lungs of a cancer victim. Just say no, Mr. Waverly.

He drank a Lite beer, his fourth, or it might have been more, he hadn't kept count. Something he seldom did, solitary drinking. But in the hours following that chance encounter with Caroline Crown, he'd felt a peculiar sense of disorientation, like a man awakening from a deep sleep. And now was no time for disorientation. After the last disastrous Michigan adventure, he'd borrowed from Bennie a formula for the restoration of order. The Benjamin S. Epstein time-tested, fail-safe therapy: willed amnesia, an aggressive lack of interest in the past. A part of him found security in the quantifiable, in the chips and cards and odds and galaxies of numbers whirling in his head. In the tools of his trade, and the focused exercise of that vocation. Another part found a measure of comfort in a serene, numb fatalism. The sky tumbles, let it fall; in the meantime the cells of the body are expiring anyway, silently, millions of them, but one by one. The author of all ruin is imagination, and the only certain means to expunge it is to arrest the contagion of memory.

Sure. Why not? Easy.

Nevertheless, he thought about her (for life wouldn't always accommodate to the pithy epigram). And to think about Caroline Vanzoren Crown was to think equally about Robbie Crown, their mingled childhoods, tangled tricornered friendship. Three institutional brats, raised in the snug shelter of a small private college by determinedly intellectual parents educated almost certainly beyond their capacities, in the way most professorial sorts are.

Grown up together on the same block, Robbie across the street, Caroline three doors down. Drilled from infancy in the undisturbed acceptance of all the old verities. Honor students?—but of course. Scholar-athletes, all three of them, after the Platonic ideal: Robbie a track star, mighty heaver of shot and discus; Caroline a stalwart on the tennis team; he the swimmer. Twenty-two years of earnest camaraderie, from the first frantic tumult of kindergarten through the solemn strains of "Pomp and Circumstance" as rendered by the Calvin College orchestra. All those shared aspirations, easy achievements, dreams, goals, and reflections. All those years. How were you not going to think about them, here in the oppressive lonely silence of a Tropicaire efficiency unit, the past stubbornly unspooling inside your head?

But if you're going to give in to those sunshine memories, what's to keep you from following them further, opening the briefcase of the other side of your life, the darker side, and laying out all its sorry documents for display, a casual scrutiny? Well, nothing, he supposed, and so he did just that, and through the analgesic distancing of time and beer fog that stormy chronicle of mischance, misplaced trust, botched choices, treacheries, wicked luck, explosive, deadly violence, griefs monumental and small, it didn't look quite so bad, maybe after all not so bad. And he, to his thinking, not some cloven-hoofed demon stalking the earth, casting no shadow. Not necessarily.

Look at them, those documents. There's the record of a marriage that could only have been fashioned by a malevolent fate, textbook case of opposites repelling, its only redeeming grace an innocent son, lost to him now forever. And there's the one of his first descent into a kind of furious madness, the cunning, comic payback on his wife's attorney (he could even yet conjure up an image of that grasping, beefy shyster face) backfired, gone suddenly awry, the hapless attorney slumped across an office floor, lifeblood leaking from the gash in his forehead, reddening the beige carpet. An accident? Tragic mistake? Yeah, right. Tell it to His Honor.

You want more, Mr. Waverly? You're rolling now, up to it; and anyway, what have you got better to do? So take a peek at the next one, the jacket compiled through a seven-year holiday in Jacktown (with a brief side trip to Ypsi's Forensic Psychiatry Center, get your head right—don't forget that). But this one's blurrier than the others, your censors charitably blocking a savage jungleland, house of rage, peopled by thuggish brutes on either side of the bars. Out of all those dangerous, desperate years the only memories that surface with anything approaching vividness are of two men, late-arriving mentors, who rescued you from what Conrad once called the "supreme disaster of loneliness and despair," and who taught you how to survive in a world, walled or not, utterly without mercy. One of them was a demented mystic, lifer, visionary, twisted saint, probably dead by now; the other, Bennie Saul Epstein, cellmate and later partner and improbable friend, a man who sees life clearly, untouched by any troubling shades of ambiguity: money is money, enemies are enemies, loyalties run deep. They were both of them, each in his own way, the finest men he'd ever known.

More yet? Maybe you'd like to get literal with those documents, open your shirt and examine the zippers stitched into your torso, permanent record of last year's ill-conceived, ill-starred journey into the past. He didn't undo the buttons on his shirt, but a wash of bitter recollections returned to him out of nowhere all the same, swamped him. Michigan memories, all of them: another faithless woman; a long brutal touchup in the basement of a house in the woods outside Traverse City; the second payback and this one— a corpse incinerating in the back of a Porsche, its head obliterated by a blast of the shotgun held in his own hands—by no reach of the imagination an accident; a brief furious struggle for his life in the dark courtyard of a sleazy Ann Arbor motel. Michigan memories. Not so fond.

Enough.

But if you can't erase the past, how do you suspend it? How? By a conscious effort of will, he catechized himself. By invoking the formula. By focusing on real and present dangers, those private Furies, say, resurrected into what new figurations only God and maybe, by now, Bennie knew for sure. That was how. In his experience, trouble, when it came, usually came quickly and just as often unannounced. So there were other matters to ponder, more urgent even than Caroline and Robbie Crown.

He tried turning his thoughts to those matters, but without much success. He'd eaten nothing since morning (food not being a high priority lately) and, unseasoned drinker, he was fuzzy-headed from the beer. His attention wandered. An indolent breeze stirred the verticals on the open, streetside window. He got up and walked over to it, parted the blinds with his fingers, and peered out.

Not your most breathtaking view. Directly across the road was the sprawling Collonades Beach Hotel, once the jewel of Singer Island, abandoned now, utterly deserted, beginning to crumble. Tropical birds chattered in the cluster of palm trees around the canopied entrance. Twilight shadows lengthened over the decks and windows of the upper floors. Here and there a small light glittered in an empty room or corridor, invitation to a ghostly party. On this side of the road another light, crackling neon, announced the Tropicaire Efficiency Apartments, extending its own kind of runic invitation with the steady yellow glow of a universally acquiescent YES. One pink fender of the Seville was visible in the guest lot around the corner from his unit. The owner's pickup was parked in the tow-away zone out front. A tiny green lizard skittered across the asphalt, minatory dragon in his insect world.

A car appeared at the far end of the street. Waverly released the blinds and drew back from the window. He pulled in a series of quick, shallow breaths. The muscles in his neck and shoulders tightened. He watched the car approach, pass, fade out of sight. The driver was a frail little woman of advancing years, a wheel-clutcher, somebody's grandma. Gradually his breathing decelerated. God, he was weary of jeopardies, hazards, perils. Sick to death of negotiating the demands of caution, vigilance, stealth, strategy, cunning. A world of snares, skirmishes, ambushes, twisted angles of vision. A world crawling with dragons. He felt like a born victim, a man who possesses some dim foreknowledge of his own fate but is powerless to escape it.

His glance fell on the windowsill, littered with the discarded wings of swarmers, or perhaps of the more aptly named death-watch beetles. He touched at them gingerly and they crumbled under his finger, dry as dust. He ran a hand along the sill, discovered a soft grainy powder on its surface. Termite shit. Well, you live in a swamp, you share it with the vermin. Tomorrow, or sometime soon, he'd mention it to the owner. No hurry. With any luck at all he'd be out of here before the walls and ceiling collapsed around him.

He returned to the sofa and stretched out, summoning sleep. For a considerable time it refused to come, though now and again he seemed to doze, and when he did a welter of images romped behind his eyes: playful figures, jesters, clowns, but all of them with faces on which, oddly, there were no smiles. Then the images would flatten, dwindle, vanish altogether, wakening him with a jolt. An hour or more passed in this way. Before he finally sank into a fitful slumber, his last lucid thoughts were of Bennie, where exactly he was that moment, what he was transacting, how he was doing.

6

Not so sensational, is how Bennie would have put it, how he was doing just then. He was sitting in a plush, semicircular booth near the back of the Floral Gardens Lounge, located on Ogden Avenue in the fashionable suburban community of Hinsdale. To his immediate left sat Eugene Stumpley. Facing him was Gunter Dietz. Bennie and Eugene drank Scotch, rocks. Dietz, who had just arrived, was occupied with ordering: martini, up, cocktail mushroom, ice water on the side. "And of course you'll use your Bombay gin," he added, as much polite request as command.

"Of *course*, Mr. Dietz," said the palm-polishing waiter.

Dietz let his glance slide over Bennie. "You ready for another, Mr., uh, Ep-stein, is it?" he asked, laying a faintly derisive stress on the first syllable of Bennie's name.

"Epstein, right. Call me Bennie." Dietz leveled an outland stare on him, called him nothing, so Bennie put a hand on his glass and said, forcedly hearty, "Still workin' on this one. Stumpy and me, we been here awhile, chewin' over the old days."

"Eugene?"

"I'm good too, Mr. Dietz."

Dietz made a signal with his eyes, and the waiter vanished into the jostling crowd. The lounge was packed at this hour, every booth and table and bar stool taken. The mirrored walls swirled with reflected figures, intense-looking men and women—thirtyish, most of them, flawlessly power-dressed. There was no music or TV, only a muted conversational swell broken by an occasional peal of brittle laughter. A giant aquarium teeming with vacant-eyed fish dominated the space between the arms of a horseshoe-shaped bar. Strategically placed crystal chandeliers delivered a subdued yellow light. The carpet and the cushy upholstery of the booths were done in deep turquoise. And faithful to its name, the Floral Gardens accented its decor with an abundance of greenery. Like drinking in the goddam Congo, Bennie thought, fucking plants and trees everywhere you look. What he said though, after the waiter reappeared and set the martini and a tall water glass on the table, was, "Nice place here."

"I've always liked it," Dietz said. "You get a better class of people here. Professional people. Per se." He spoke very deliberately, as though the prolonged pauses helped him edit his thoughts. Coming out of that thin-lipped slit of a mouth the words were chilling, even when he was talking about preferences in bars.

Bennie had never met Dietz before, but over the years he'd heard plenty about him. And from all he remembered of everything he'd heard, he wasn't exactly counting the minutes till this sitdown. "Now they're your best kind," he said, working his baggy face into a shrewd expression, trying the sage man of business on him. Shit, try anything. "Good spenders. Never give you no grief."

"Grief," Dietz said philosophically. "Grief is something we all want to avoid. All of us. When we can."

Bennie decided the best thing to say to that was nothing at all. Grief—least the kind Dietz meant—was a subject better left alone. If you could.

For a long moment a silence hung in the air. Eugene drew his spindly shoulders around him, looked at the ceiling, floor, room at large, settled finally, if briefly, on his lap. Dietz took a decorous sip of martini, followed it with another of ice water. He leaned back, ran a hand through his thick white hair. Adjusted the knot in his silk tie. Stroked his hard jaw. He allowed his wintry gaze to shift slowly between Bennie and Eugene. Even in the confines of the booth, his height and bulk were such that he seemed to tower over both of them. "So," he said at last, "you two boys go back a ways."

"That we do," Bennie affirmed. "All the way back the fifties, when we was a couple young bucks just gettin' our game goin'. I was runnin' my first wire. Five-and-dimer, out of Skokie. And old Stumper here"—he reached over and laid a comradely punch on Eugene's arm—"he was a mule them days, I remember correct. Scootin' for anybody'd take him on."

"It was a long time ago," Eugene said, carefully distancing him-

self from both the chummy punch and the jocular recollection of
their past acquaintance.

"Yeah, thirty years or better," Bennie went right on, adopting
the tones of a wise old codger calling up the foibles of yesteryear.
"You remember them big Caddies we use to drive, Stump? Shark
fins on 'em? 'Bout the size of your basic tank? I tell ya, put a little
green in our wallets, we was King Shit. Them days."

Out of a face full of anxious wiliness, Eugene smuggled a peek
at Dietz, who was nodding thoughtfully, withholding comment,
taking everything in. Eugene was a slight man, delicate-boned,
stringy of physique. His blue polyester pinstripe, best suit in his
wardrobe, had an unfortunate tendency to hang on him loose as
a scarecrow's outfit. Equally unfortunate was a retrograde chin
that gave his head an odd top-heavy appearance, which the sparse
hair slicked over the skull did little to soften. Spidery blood vessels on the hollow cheeks and nose added a dash of color to a
complexion otherwise uniform gray, sooty. His vulture eyes roved
constantly. Right about now he was wishing the gasbag would
stuff a sock in it. The way he remembered, they'd done a little
trafficking, nothing heavy. Yid was making it sound like they'd
been to bed together. Partnered or something.

"Well," Dietz said, addressing Bennie directly, "in any case, it's
a piece of luck you happened to know Eugene. For you, I mean.
The luck."

"Yeah, worked out real good. For everybody."

"Tell me, Mr. Ep-stein, what business are you in now?"

"Now? Oh, I got me a little book. Also run a few players when
there's any action to scare up." He figured he wouldn't mention
the stable of quiff he kept on call. Make that used to keep on call.
Guy like Dietz, sitting there all cool and steady in his white linen
suit, sucking up a martini, Mr. Fortune 500, he'd curl a lip at that
line of work, even though he was probably in it himself. "Sort of
a retirement income, like," he added. Better to undersell, do some
poormouthing.

"That's in Florida?"

"Right, Florida."

"And it's one of those players of yours, brings you up here. I
understand."

Bennie leaned into the table, establishing what he hoped was a
confidential zone. "See, when I heard what went down, Michigan,
I rung up Stumpy here first thing and I—"

Dietz cut him off with a toss of a hand. "Man we're talking
about. Name's Waverly. Is that right too?"

"That's his name."

"And you're here to, ah, represent him?"

"Well, yeah, I s'pose. You might say."

Dietz regarded him with the most remote and glacial of smiles. "Well, either you are or you aren't. Mr. Ep-stein. Can't have it both ways. Which is it?"

Bennie was wearing an open-neck salmon-pink sport shirt, peach-colored trousers, tasseled burgundy loafers. Florida fashion plate. Now he regretted not putting on a jacket, something dark, to hide the sweat drenching his pits, rilling down his chest and the terraced slopes of fat at his midsection, pooling in the band of his shorts. Felt like a fucking rainmaker, or one of them fish in the tank up there. His mouth, in contrast, was dry as chalk. Had to make it work, though, spit out something, so he said, "How it is, Mr. Dietz, this Waverly, he didn't have no idea what he was into. Some ways he's a real intelligent fella. College boy. But he's just got this natural habit for gettin' himself in the glue. Y'see, he put in some time in the bin, puzzle factory, so his head ain't always screwed on tight. What he wants to do, though, is—"

"You forgot the question." Dietz broke in on him again. "What I asked was if you represented him. Or not. That's all."

"Guess I do."

"All right. Good. Glad we got that much clear. So. Let's hear your proposition."

Bennie looked confused. He turned to Eugene. "You didn't tell him?"

Eugene gave a barely perceptible shrug, glanced at Dietz for direction. During his many years of association with Gunter Dietz, he'd learned never to speak till he got a signal. Which he wasn't getting now.

"My understanding," Dietz said, "is that you're prepared to return the monies this, um, associate of yours cost us."

"That's what I come up here for, Mr. Dietz."

"In full?"

"Correct. Half a mil worth of General Georges."

"That's the figure you specified?" Dietz said. He was speaking to Eugene, but his eyes never once left Bennie, and whatever speck of a smile had been on his face was long since gone.

Eugene wriggled in his seat. With his hands he made a series of fluttery, birdlike gestures. "Yeah, right," he said. "That was right, wasn't it? What you said?"

Dietz did some more martini sipping. Watching Bennie over the rim of the glass. Taking his time. Then he set the glass on the table and said, "I'm curious, Mr. Ep-stein, why you're contacting us now. This late date. That Michigan, ah, discord, that was almost a year ago. What took you so long?"

"Well, see, thing of it is, Waverly, he didn't tell me nothin' about it till a couple weeks back. I mean, he told me *some* about it, last fall, but not *who* it was he was steppin' on. Soon as I found out I says to him, 'You gotta straighten this out, boy. Come to the window.' "

"That's what you told him?"

"Them same words."

"And that was how many weeks ago? Two, you say?"

"Something like that. Coulda been a little more."

A flicker of contempt crossed Dietz's gravely composed features. "You know, Mr. Ep-stein, I think maybe you're trying to chump us here. Eugene and me. Play us for fools. What I think is that you heard some friends of ours were making inquiries. Down there in Florida. Picking up the scent, so to speak. And that's when you decided to get in touch. That's why it took you so long."

Jesus Quincy Adams, Bennie was thinking, how you gonna squirrel your sweet Jew ass outta this one, saying, "Hand to God," and elevating one in that general direction, "how it happened was just like I told you. This Waverly boy, what he knows about the life is diddly s. squat. That's how much. All's he knows is cards. He'd of said last year who it was he was dickin' with, I'd of been on your front porch post effin' word haste. Loot in hand."

While he was saying all this, Bennie was conscious of his eyes doing a Eugene, rolling all over the place, like some night fighter caught with a watermelon under his arm. Wasn't helping his case any. Crazy part was, everything he'd said really *was* the truth, but you tell so many lies all that truth guano starts feeling slippery on the tongue. Comes out mushy, way this had.

Dietz squared his hands on the table. "Well," he said tolerantly, "maybe it's not that important. Per se. What matters is you came forward. Which was the right thing to do. Because we'd have found you, you know. Sooner or later. Both of you."

Bennie held in a great sigh, even though he didn't much like the bottomless echo of that *both.* "All's we want to do is square things, Mr. Dietz."

Dietz let a moment go by before responding to that harmonious sentiment. Behind the expressionless face, he seemed to be cal-

culating. Finally he said, "You remember that grief we were talking about? A while ago?"

"Yeah, I remember that," Bennie said cautiously.

"You realize your friend caused us a certain amount of it. Grief.
You do realize that, don't you? Mr. Ep-stein?"

"Know how that goes, that grief."

"Lots of people got hurt, up in Michigan. Good people."

"Yeah, I heard something about that."

"And then there's the, uh, disruption. Of normal business. That's
a kind of grief too, wouldn't you agree?"

Bennie made his head move, to show he agreed. He wasn't
exactly cheered, the way this conversation was squeezing in on
him.

"You see, Mr. Ep-stein, the problem I have with your offer, it
doesn't take into account all our grief and distress. Eugene's and
mine. Some other people too. That's got to be worth something,
don't you think?"

"S'pose it is."

"How much do you think it's worth?" Dietz asked in a quietly
earnest voice that seemed to say he was deeply interested in the
B. Epstein opinion.

"Kinda hard to put a number on it," Bennie said, though the
number fixed in his head was exact, precise, static. Plenty clear.
$561,414. And the handful of coins in his pocket. Sum total of all
they'd been able to pull together, between them, and that was
calling in every marker and shaking every available tree. Fucking
grief and distress top that number and they were dog flop, for
sure.

"Maybe not," Dietz said. "Maybe we can arrive at a number
that's reasonable. Fair." He touched a forefinger to his upper lip,
moved it the length and back again, slowly, considering. "Let me
ask you something, Mr. Ep-stein. You fellows must turn a good
dollar, that business you're in. Am I right?"

"Well, that's the thing right there. More of that Michigan grief
you was sayin'. See, whatever he done up there, Waverly, got the
heat all steamed. Hick town, hick cops, but they do got the long
arm. Reach all the way down to our part of the world. Last couple
months badges been on us fierce, jackin' us around."

"Shame," Dietz said.

"Yeah," Bennie said, warming to the recitation of his woes, "it's
like they opened up a can of whup-butt and sprayed it all over
us."

"So business isn't all that good. Lately."

"More like zippo."

"But there was a time when it was, oh, prosperous. That's what my friends down there tell me. And they're in a position to know these things."

"Well, yeah, we cut up a little plunder, past few years. Not all that much. More just gettin' by."

"But enough to compensate us. For this grief and distress we're discussing. Some number that's, ah—what's the word?—equitable."

"Guess it depends, what that number's gonna be."

"Let's think about it," Dietz said, massaging the lip again, seeming to do just that, eyes icy with inner reckonings. "You invest half a million dollars these days, you'll likely return ten percent. That's fifty thousand right there. The grief and distress factor, another, oh, say, quarter mil ought to cover that. That sound fair?"

"Jesus, Mr. Dietz, three hundred K, that's a pretty heavy vigorish."

Dietz favored Eugene with an inquiring glance. "What do you say, Eugene?"

"Sounds right to me. Real generous."

Dietz turned his gaze back on Bennie. "Think of it as a small surcharge," he said, adding with a twitch of a smile, "the postage and handling of our business."

Bennie's face went pale and very still, but he couldn't slow the calculator flashing numbers in his head, going at it quick-time, simple arithmetic, all of it subtraction, whittling down to zero. "The interest we can maybe do," he said carefully. "But I got to tell you, the two-fifty we just ain't got."

"You strike me as a resourceful man, Mr. Ep-stein. I'm betting you'll find a way to raise it."

Bennie was boxed in, and he knew it. All the shuck-and-dodge moves he was making, trying to make, didn't mean dick. Not with this fucker, never quit coming at you. Best he could do now was buy time, and so that's how he put it. "Might be we could. Take some time, though."

"Two weeks is what you've got."

"Two weeks!" Bennie yelped. "Holy Habakkuk! Two-five-oh in big ballons in two weeks, that ain't possible."

"When you've got your priorities right," Dietz said mildly, "anything's possible."

Sure. Easy for him to say. Mr. Norman Fucking Vincent Fucking Peale. "Look, Mr. Dietz," Bennie said, startled at the rising quaver in his voice, trying to subdue it, "you know we want your good will. Waverly and me. Otherwise why'd I be here, first place? But we got to have more'n two weeks."

"And you're not listening. Mr. Ep-stein. This isn't up for negotiation. No appeals boards here."

Now Bennie's face wore the stunned look of a man in mourning. Or someone who's just been poleaxed. "See what we can do," he mumbled.

"Do that. Go on back to your motel now. Have some dinner. Get some rest. Tomorrow, I understand, you're going to deliver the first installment to Eugene. That'll include the ten percent, of course. Show of good faith, you might say, show us those priorities are in order. After that what I think you should do is catch an early plane south. When you get home, sit down with that player friend of yours. Put your heads together. Do some brainstorming. Concentrate. You'll find there's always a solution."

No mistaking the dismissal in that. And in the no-prisoners world of Gunter Dietz, there was no more room for pleading. Without a word, Bennie slid out of the booth and took a lurching step toward the door. Dietz snapped a finger, not so much in afterthought as in the curt summons of a miscreant hound.

"Oh, one other thing," he said evenly and without a hint of rancor, though his eyes were filled with a cold menacing light. "You remember what that boxer, Joe Louis it was, said? About some opponent, I forget which one. 'He can run but he can't hide,' is what he said. No fool, Joe. Anyway, you might want to think about that. Lot of truth in it. Per se."

As soon as Bennie was gone, Dietz turned his attention to Eugene. "You got somebody on him?"

"Round the clock. No problem there, Mr. Dietz."

"Who?"

"Young fella was with me yesterday. You remember him, Sigurd? Nephew mine. My brother's boy."

Dietz's forehead creased in a frown. "This nephew of yours, Eugene, he didn't look like any deep thinker. To me."

"Well, he's maybe a little low on the candlepower," Eugene said through a twittery approximation of a smile. "Comes to the glue work, though, he's real good. Y'know the kind, all instinct, no imagination."

"Better be. We're not going to have any replays of Michigan.

Stiffed by a cardsmith and a Jew—not this time. You understand that, Eugene?"

Eugene nodded vigorously. His fingers drummed the tabletop, rhythm to his thoughts, which at that moment swung between a concrete image of his lumpish nephew and the abstract notion of his own rash decision to trust him with this assignment, and which were not, consequently, without misgivings. His toothpick legs crossed and uncrossed, crossed again. Anxiety scrawled its signature on his sunken face. In the past, most of his commerce with Mr. Dietz had been transacted by phone, and so in the actual presence of someone of that much weight all his gestures and mannerisms and expressions were naturally magnified.

"Good," Dietz said. "Now, more to the point, what do we have arranged in Florida?"

"I made some calls last night. Like you said. Got a line on a shooter with a triple-A jacket on him, dude name of—"

"No names, Eugene."

"Oh, yeah, sure. Forgot. Anyway, this boy's a freelancer, done all kinds good work down there. At paper-layin', everybody I talk to say he's an artist. Mediterraneans used him, your various wetback outfits, even that Jamaican bunch, Posse, I heard."

"Umm," Dietz ummed. "Good credentials."

For a moment he was silent. Eugene watched him out of the corner of an eye. Features were immobile, shoulders drooped—looked like he was half-dozing. Eugene kept quiet.

The silence lengthened. Eugene looked at his empty glass, wished he'd ordered another when he'd had the chance. Wished he could light a cigarette, except he knew Mr. Dietz didn't like smoking. Wished he'd say something, f'Chrissake.

Eventually he did.

"Call him tonight, Eugene. Engage his services. Pay top dollar if you have to. But I want you to tell him to wait out the two weeks. Stay with them, report in regularly, but do nothing till we say."

Eugene looked puzzled. "You don't want 'em snipped right off?"

"No, let's give it the two weeks. See how good they are at scrambling."

"You think they can hustle up that kind of loot, couple weeks?" Eugene said skeptically.

Dietz's lips parted in a vague smile, not a bit of mirth in it, and intended for no one but himself. "You see how that hebe was sweating? You notice that, Eugene?"

"Yeah, I saw."

"That's just openers. For both of them. After you make that collection tomorrow, anything else is frosting. Loose change. Like a, oh, gratuity, you could say. That's fine. Doesn't matter. This isn't about money, Eugene. Not anymore."

7

Powderman, torchman, wheel-
man, stuntman, sandman—in profession as in person, he was the
total package, D'Marco was. Full-service enterprise in himself. To
his clients he was known as Frog, a kind of code name. He didn't
mind the tag. Quite the opposite, he was proud of his Gallic an-
cestry. After all, how many authentic Frenchmen (albeit third-
generation and with a suspected Swiss strain, his mother's side)
you going to find down here in mongrel land, home of the greas-
ers and sheenies and rednecks and spades? Answer to that was
self-evident: not many. If any. So he figured it was his birthright
to be special, close to unique; and from an early age he'd operated
on that assumption, built himself this armorplate physique, mastered the intricacies of his chosen vocation, cultivated an aloof
and regal air befitting the natural distinction equated with natural
superiority. And he'd done it all on his own, from scratch, no
ethnic juice like the dagos had, no extended-family tradition to
draw on (his father was a timid optician back in Memphis, where
D'Marco had grown up), no youth gang apprenticeships (a model
boy, he had once attained the rank of Life Scout). No, he was the
invention of his own imagination, end product of a self-generated
capacity for myth brewing. But it wasn't always easy, being an
original, and you had to work at it, and sometimes, among the
proles, it invited a certain snickery disrespect.

Take tonight, for instance. Even though tonight was only a
stunt, a quick-and-dirty, and even though there were a couple of
hours to tick off before the proceedings could commence, no way
was he going to indulge in drink (which he very, very rarely did
anyway). Cloud the head, dull the reflexes—not for D'Marco Fontaine. Short money job or not, he had a reputation to maintain.

So when he first came in and found a seat at the end of the oval bar with a panoramic view of the long rectangular dimly lit room, the cluster of tables approaching and encircling a puddle of dance floor overlooked by a musicians' platform, the entrance to the right and the corridor leading to a dining room somewhere off in back—when he did that, sat down and ordered a Bloody Mary only hold the vodka, it elicited from the runt of a bartender a wise-fuck smirk. And as the time wore slowly on and he waited, sipping the tomato juice and nibbling at the celery stalk, studying the layout, the gathering crowd, the rising action with a keen professional eye, the runt grew bolder and on the refill order announced loudly, grinning, " 'Nother kiddie cocktail, comin' right up." So when the glass was set in front of him, D'Marco did what he always did with wise fucks, backed him off with a stone-cold hangman's glare, and the grin collapsed and the runt went scurrying down to the other end of the bar and joined his fellow booze-blenders in another of their periodic snappy, spontaneous bursts of off-key song: "Andy ain't mad at no-body, no-o-o bah-dee a'tall."

Andy's Old Fashion Chophouse and Fun Time Saloon. Italian cuisine our specialty. Live entertainment nightly. An easy drive north on Highway One, just past Juno Beach. Your host: Andrew J. "Andy" Scalisi. Real happy place here, had its own anthem even, which was being belted out again, encore chorus, many of the patrons, D'Marco not among them, joining in. One of the lead singers, the runt, struck a gong, and a zigzag pattern of lights began flashing above the bar. Cheers, shouts, glasses lifted and thumped on tables. Yeah, real good-time crib, Andy's. Except if Andy ain't mad at nobody, somebody sure as shit had a hard-on against him.

For what, that wasn't any of his business, though the phone voice had—unnecessarily and unprofessionally, to D'Marco's thinking—supplied some of the details. Hashing the liquor, skimming the register, shaking down the suppliers—these were just a few of Andy's lesser, forgivable sins. But when your wife was the daughter of a major player and you were where you were (which was nowhere anyway, running a ground-level loot laundry) only by his sufferance, then it was dumber than imbecile to be boffing the female vocalist, sleek blonde slinking her way toward the platform right now, and for bad measure making sandwiches out of the cocktail waitresses in your spare time. Especially when you've been warned. Slow study, Andy. Requires some serious private tutoring. Professor Fontaine to the rescue.

Five minutes to nine, and the live entertainment began the showy ritual of setting up. Three cadaverous young men with electrified hair and pale, gaunt faces joined the blonde on the platform, did some ostentatious tinkering with their bewildering array of equipment. Background extras, they wore identical black jumpsuits. She had on a shimmering silvery outfit, looked like a sequined wraparound towel, cut an inch or so above her plump powdered jugs and a micrometer below her crotch. Handsome display of creamy flesh. Some remarks were traded *sotto voce*, some sleepy knowing smiles exchanged. One of the jumpsuits, ax dangling rakishly, came out from behind one of the several speakers flanking the platform like upright coffins and adjusted a microphone, tapped it twice, sending a hollow echo resonating through the room, and intoned, "Testing one three six nine—" He hesitated, did a double-take, said, "Six, nine—that's sixty-nine. Anybody out there havin' fun tonight?"

Comedian. It got a generous laugh.

"Good evening, lady and gentleman—both of you, one each—and the rest of you too, and welcome to Andy's Fun Time Saloon." His voice was slurred, whispery, somewhat hoarse. The second guitar and drummer strummed and brushed a slow, muted riff. At an adjacent mike the blonde stood motionless under a nimbus of light. "We're the Winds of Change, featuring Miss Lala—oh, sorry, that's Lola—Rivers, and we're here to entertain you with your favorite jiggle jazz and maybe a few huggy-bear sounds in between." The riff was meanwhile building in an urgent driving beat. "So if everybody's ready—let's start bobbin' and diddlin' and shakin' our cans—le-e-e-e-t's *party!*" He hoisted his ax, brandished it, and the music broke on a flooding roar, and a mob of dancers charged the floor, and the blonde, eyes tightly squeezed, as though in carnal shock, seized her mike with both hands and howled:

"That was yesterday.
Things're changin' now,
Visions of the past
Never gon-na last;
Winds're risin' fast,
Measureless and vast.
Nothin' never last."

D'Marco looked on in disgust. He despised all that pounding jungle music and all the wiggling and writhing that went with it. Personally, he liked Barry Manilow or Neil Diamond. Some of the

old Sinatra songs were good too. Winds of Change—sounded to
him more like fucking broken wind, inflated elephant wind. And
he had ninety minutes of it yet to endure. Every job you took you
earned your money, but some—like this one—a whole lot more
than others.

Along about 9:30 a portly fellow in a beryl blue suit appeared
in the entrance, and the caterwauling din broke off midnumber,
and the blonde uncoiled an arm in his direction, and the drummer
did a roll, and every head in the place swiveled, D'Marco's even,
while the entertainers and bartenders joined in still another rous-
ing chorus of the Andy anthem. The object of all this unmelodic
celebration acknowledged it with a hand in the air, fingers
splayed, and an elaborate bow. Then he signaled a resumption of
the revel, and on command the music swelled, the frame-frozen
dancers reanimated. Prince Andy swaggered into the room and
circulated through the crowd, palm-slapping, rump-patting, bicep-
clutching, smiling widely, now and again fabricating a stagy laugh.
Sharing the largesse of his attention and substantial person. His
head was uncommonly large, shaggy with a thick brush of iron-
gray hair, and anchored to his shoulders by a fat-ridged neck.
Piglet eyes bulged from a swarthy, jowly face ruined by assorted
excesses, framed by Dumbo ears, and propped by secondary, ter-
tiary, and a dwindling succession of nether chins. He seemed to
move with a kind of ponderous deliberation, as though he were
towed along behind the beam of that headlights smile. Eventually
it led him to a table near the platform, where a place was hurriedly made. He eased his bulk into the chair, a drink was produced and thrust into his hand, and he tilted his head back and
bubbled it down. D'Marco watched him with a mix of pity and
contempt. About an hour of smiling left.

Shortly after ten a woman came weaving up to the bar, made
straight for D'Marco, and invited him to dance. Not a bad-looking
head, if you liked the flashy, slutty, pavement princess type. Which
he didn't. Zoned-out witch like that probably call it a dry hump
and present you with a bill the minute the music stopped. And a
case of AIDS six weeks later. Dose of clap at the very least.

"I don't dance," he said, staring her down coldly.

"Well, *par*-don me, your fuckin' highness," she siren-shrilled,
staring right back, hands planted on hips, swaying a little. Her
bleary eyes settled on the pecs bulging under his shirt. "Thought
maybe you musclemen had something swingin' between your legs.
Guess I was wrong."

D'Marco could feel himself reddening. Feel the amused eyes of everyone at the bar skimming over him. Ordinarily and in a different place under different circumstances he'd've decked her, cold-cocked her. Showed her what wrong really meant. But he couldn't afford any messy tangles just then. "Why don't you go try your luck with somebody else," he said.

"It's you I'm talkin' to, Mr. Muscleman."

"Yeah, well, you're talking to yourself," he muttered, turning away.

" 'Smatter, you don't like girls?"

None of this was in his plan. Last thing he needed. He came to his feet and big-shouldered his way around her and through the knots of people, heading for the door and the asylum of the parking lot. "Muscleman don't like girls," he could hear her calling after him, "gonna find a boy to hit on." Braying barroom laughter trailed him to the door. He didn't look back.

And now, standing at the rear of his LX in the deserted lot, all he could feel was a mounting fury. Focus it, he instructed himself, channel it, direct it. You know who you are. Where you're going. Fewer than fifteen minutes left to wait anyway (so the luminous dial on his watch told him); better to spend it out here, in the clean air and silence, under a brilliant night sky swarming with stars. Right? Right.

These internal dialogues had a way of soothing him, settling him down. He inserted a key and lifted the trunk. Inside was the canvas bag that held all his stunt gear. Earlier he had narrowed his choices down to two: blowtorch or pick. Fire or ice. He'd been given carte blanche on this assignment. ("You're the expert, Frog," the phone voice had said. "Do what you want, long as it stings.") So the decision was his to make. Flame was always good, but the conditions here didn't favor it. Go for the cold tonight. He rummaged through the bag till he found the icepick and a roll of adhesive tape. These went into one of the pockets of his jacket. Into the other he fitted the .32 he habitually carried along on stunting, throw-down piece, case the subject got frisky. Insurance.

He closed the trunk and took just a moment to scan the terrain. Andy's Fun House was located out in what was left of the country north of Juno Beach and south of Jupiter, set well back from the highway, parking lot in front and along one side, stand of fishtail palms on the other. Its nearest neighbor, a competitor saloon, was a quarter of a mile down the road. The LX was parked at the far end of the outer file of cars, with direct and easy access to the highway. Arrangement couldn't be more ideal if he'd laid it out himself. But then he knew that already, since he'd taken pains to scout it when he first arrived.

At a leisurely pace, he walked through the front lot and past the entrance and around the corner and down the side of the building, trees side, keeping to the shadows. In the back was a single door with a small light above it; and a few feet beyond, next to the wall, a dumpster; and beyond that, in a space reserved for Mr. Scalisi by a prominent sign, a white Lincoln Town Car. Otherwise there was nothing at all back here, just a ribbon of asphalt bordered by an empty field of scraggle grass reaching off into the distance. More of that ideal.

D'Marco slipped behind the dumpster and squeezed himself between it and the wall. His position was such that he could cover both the car and the door. He'd been assured Andy held to pattern, came through the door five minutes after the first set ended, climbed in the back seat of the Lincoln and waited for the blonde to follow, ten minutes after that, like they had everyone fooled, and kneel on the floor of the car and transport him into rapture-land. That's what he'd been told, but he didn't like surprises. As it was, he was working inside a narrow window of time. And his line of work, even stunting, allowed for no witnesses.

And so he stood there, bathed in moonlight, flattened against the dumpster, rhythmically filling his lungs with the pure night air (tainted a bit by the sour stink of various unidentifiable table leavings sifting through the crack beneath the lowered lid), listening to the insistent screech of bug buzz rising from the field and the muffled throb of music from the other side of the wall. Steadying himself. Waiting.

There were no surprises. At 10:30 the music suddenly ceased. At 10:33 Andy came marching purposefully through the door, humming some spirited, unrecognizable tune. Early tonight, must be in serious heat. D'Marco stepped out from behind the dumpster and stationed himself between Lincoln and hurrying wop and said in the sunny, hayseed voice he liked to affect at the onset of a stunt, "Hi there, Mr. Andy. Come out to take the air?"

Andy stopped. The humming stopped. The distance between them was maybe ten feet, no more, and Andy squinted through it with the intense prying gaze of the man who sizes you up rapidly and classifies you according to a simple test: Can I use him? Can he hurt me? Fall anywhere outside those elemental categories and you were a cipher in the eyes of Andrew J. Scalisi, invisible. From the wary look on his face and the belligerent, wide-legged stance, he didn't seem certain yet which pigeonhole this figure blocking his path fitted, though he wasn't taking any chances either. "Fuck're you?" he growled.

"Friend of some friends of yours," D'Marco said good-humoredly. This was the part he always liked best, the prelims. "They asked me to have a word with you."

"Yeah, 'bout what?"

"Oh, nothing special. They just said drop by, get acquainted."

"Get acquainted, huh? Which friends mine is it, told you that?"

"Forget their names. You got so many."

"You forget," Andy sneered after a pause, as if he'd used the instant to consider D'Marco's answer carefully, assess him, and consign him to his proper rank, which was somewhere below worm level. "Okay. That's cool. Tell you what, them names come back to you, you come see me. Make an appointment. Right now I got business."

He took a step forward. D'Marco stretched out an arresting hand, rolled it over to show it was empty, harmless, and said in a wheedling tone, "I was hoping maybe we could talk tonight. Only take a minute of your time."

Andy braked again, only now he squared his fleshy shoulders and poked out his oversize head, and his fists began balling, and in a voice dipped low and snarly and filled with cruising menace he said, "Listen, ratfart, I don't know you, don't wanta know you, and don't got no friends who'd know a dickdribble rube like you. So what I'm recommendin' here is you do a Casper. Before you end up bruised."

D'Marco put both hands in the air and backed away slowly. "C'mon, Mr. Andy," he said, still in his whiny gear, "I just come by to have a friendly chat with you. Way they sing it inside, you're not supposed to be mad at nobody."

Preceded by the aromatic trumpet of his musky aftershave, Andy advanced on the retreating D'Marco, saying, "You got turds in your ears, boy? Watch the lips. They're tellin' you get lost. Vanish. While you still can."

Now D'Marco felt the door of the Lincoln pressed against his spine. He reached inside the pocket of his jacket and removed the .32 and leveled it and brought the stalking Andy to another sudden halt. A slow, dangerous smile spread across D'Marco's face. "Funny how you put that," he said casually, though no longer whining. "Like a coincidence. Y'see, that's what your friends said was your problem too. Hearing, I mean. Said you were getting to be a regular deafie, comes to paying attention."

Andy's eyes wavered. All his expression changed. "Hey, don't go ballistic on me," he said, indicating the gun.

"Oh, you don't want to worry about that any. I always had a real steady piece hand." D'Marco extended it, as though in evidence, and then he came around behind Andy and laid the muzzle against his trembling neck. He did a quick patdown, found nothing.

"Look," Andy said with a kind of beggarly desperation, "you wanta talk, we'll talk. Whatever they're payin' you I can beat easy. Doubles. Trips."

"Honest, Andy, that the goods? You'd give me that kind of money?"

"Name the figure and you got it."

D'Marco went silent a moment, like he was actually seriously considering. Give the greaseball a sliver of hope. Before the roof caved in. Finally he said, "Well, that's awful tempting. Got to think that one over. While I do, I'd be obliged if you'd just lay down on the ground there."

"Ground?"

"That's right. On your tummy, arms behind your back. Think you can do that for me?"

"Listen, I'm talkin' the large dollar here—" Andy started to say, but D'Marco jabbed the gun into one of the sausage rolls at the neck and Andy expelled a long despairing sigh and got down on hands and knees and then, as directed, stretched himself out across the asphalt and crossed his arms over the small of his back. D'Marco dropped onto him, straddling him and pinning the arms with the full weight of his body, and in a series of nimble moves he slipped the gun in one jacket pocket and got the tape and icepick out of the other. He grabbed a hank of Andy's hair and yanked his head back and rolled a wide swatch of tape over his mouth. Still grasping the hair, which felt slick and oily in his hand, he wrenched the head sideways and held the icepick in front of the eyes and traced lazy rolling circles in the air. Leaning in close, he said, "That's a real handsome offer you're making me, Mr. Andy. Triple money. Afraid I got to decline, though. Man's got to protect his good name. You can understand that."

Their faces were only inches apart. A coil of veins pulsed in Andy's temple. From under the tape came gagging noises, as if he were having difficulty catching his breath. His naturally bulging eyes were steep with terror, full of pleading, dread. But in all the twenty-nine years of his life, D'Marco had yet to perform his first act of mercy, and tonight would be no exception to that impeccable record. "You know what they say," he said solemnly, "buy the ticket, take the ride. That's just how it is, man."

He forced one side of Andy's face flat against the ground and spiked the icepick into the exposed ear. Then he rotated the head and punctured the other ear. He bounded to his feet as the tidal wave of pain rolled south through the twitching body, washed up on its farthest extremities, reversed itself and surged back again, stringing a trail of convulsive shudders in its wake. Andy's hands, abruptly freed, clawed at his ears as though to stop off some immense thunderous roar audible only to himself, for in fact the only distinct sound was the whistling screech of the army of insects in the field behind him. D'Marco stood there a moment, how long he couldn't say, not long, observing the results of his efforts with a clinical dispassion. And then, because time was closing in on him, he got out of there fast.

By driving at a sensible speed, well within the limit, D'Marco was able to make it home shortly before midnight. Home was a spacious, expensively furnished, immaculately clean apartment in a small complex just off Glades Road in Boca Raton. Nice quiet location, respectable neighbors, elderly folks mostly, a few studious-looking Florida Atlantic graduate students, a widow or two. For the time being a good place to live, handy to all the routine facets of his orderly life.

The first thing he noticed on coming through the door was the flashing red light of the answering machine. He was radically beat, what with the late hour (on nights he wasn't professionally engaged he was ordinarily in bed by ten), the drive, workout, stunt, inhaling all that smoke in the rackety bedlam of a bar— been a long day. But since his number was of course unlisted, the winking light could only signal more potential business, so he figured he'd better at least listen to the message. He set the canvas bag on the floor and pushed the button to Play and the tape rewound and a voice unfamiliar to him said, "Frog? Callin' on a referral from some associates of yours, Miami, said you might be interested in takin' on an assignment for us. You are, you wanna call this number, tonight if you can, tomorrow morning latest? Ask for Eugene."

D'Marco printed the number on the ruled notepad labeled "Things to Do Today" that he kept beside the phone. He didn't recognize the area code, so he opened the directory and checked the listings. Northeastern Illinois—had to be Chicago, for certain. Nothing else up that way.

In spite of his weariness, D'Marco felt a flutter of excitement. He'd never gotten any business out of the Midwest, didn't know anyone up there. Though in the past couple of years he'd done a little here-and-there work for some people in New Jersey, essentially his bread-and-butter trade was local. So he took this as a piece of encouraging news. Maybe the beginning of the making of a nationwide rep. His impulse was to place the call right then, but he made it a practice never to act on impulse and after careful deliberation rejected that notion. Tomorrow would do just fine. The quintessence of cool was never to have to reach.

He went into the kitchen and shook a handful of vitamins from his pill container and swallowed them with water. In the bedroom he got out of his clothes and hung trousers and jacket on pants and coat hangers respectively, noting with some irritation the stain on the jacket's back. Goddam dumpster. Stain better come out. If it didn't, he'd factor the replacement cost into his expenses fee, along with mileage and dinner. That was only fair, pricey jacket like that. In the bathroom he washed his face and brushed his teeth and scrubbed his hands and shot a couple of quick flexing poses at the mirror. And in bed he fell immediately into a sound and dreamless sleep.

PART
TWO

8

Friday, June 19—a day for phone conversations.

At 8:30 A.M. (an hour later by Eastern time) Bennie placed a person-to-person call to an officer of the Palm Beach Gardens branch of the Barnett Bank. Over the years he and this gentleman had done a considerable amount of business, much of it by phone and not all of it strictly banking, and so Bennie's request—to wire fifty thousand dollars immediately to a small bank in Downers Grove, Illinois—came as no great surprise to the officer, though he did indicate it would require the better part of the day for the transaction to be effected, and he observed, in passing and with bankerly solemnity, the Key Line Services, Inc. account balance was dipping perilously low. Bennie said Yeah yeah yeah, just get it up here, okay? And the officer said Certainly; and they rang off.

Next he phoned Eugene. "Stump," he said, "I got the principal for you, but that fifty K vigorish, that's gonna take a little while."

"You heard what Dietz said last night, about negotiatin'."

"I'm talkin' a few hours here, Stump."

"How few?" Eugene demanded, and in his voice there was none of the warmth of friendship renewed after the lapse of these many years.

"Be here by three, four this afternoon," Bennie said, putting some good-news music in it, thinking all the while how he'd never really liked the sneaky little schmuck anyway, much as he remembered of him. He waited through a protracted silence. Finally he said, "So how you wanta handle the pass? Do it all at once or—"

"Pick you up in an hour. Take delivery on that principal right now, rest of it this afternoon."

"Hey, overload, Stumper!" Bennie said heartily. "We can maybe jack around some while we're—" But there was no point in completing the truckling thought, for he was talking to the hum of the dial tone.

The third and last call Bennie made that morning was to a travel agency selected at random out of the yellow pages and from which lengthy dialogue he learned, astonishingly and to his thoroughgoing disgust, there were no seats available on any flights to Palm Beach International until the next morning, all his pleading notwithstanding. So he secured a place on one of them, and to the agent's cheery parting instruction to have a nice day he replied with an obscenity and a pronounced slam of the receiver.

He thought about phoning Waverly, but a glance at his watch told him time was running short. The calls had been made from the bed, where he sat propped against the headboard, a sheet drawn over his nakedness, puffing a cigar. Now he got up heavily and showered and shaved and strained at the stool (for travel and anxiety always bound his bowels) and dressed. From inside a balled-up pair of dirty shorts he removed and pocketed the key to a safe deposit box rented at the Downers Grove bank. The box was empty but for another key to a locker at O'Hare, which contained a satchel filled with bills of various denominations totaling five hundred thousand dollars. He kept the safe deposit key where he did simply because no better hiding place occurred to him. He was out of touch with this corner of the life, all these slippery stratagems. Too old for this kind of poop.

While waiting for Eugene, he peeked around the drape through the window and discovered, as expected, the Olds Cutlass parked across the lot. About as subtle as a boot square in the ass. The driver, same moon-faced prowler who'd been trailing him, inexpertly, since he first arrived, appeared to be dozing. Bennie had to wonder where they got their hired help these days—fucking classifieds?—and for a moment he found himself entertaining the notion of a fast trip down the wind, if this was the best they could do. But only for a moment, till Dietz's farewell admonition returned to him, and he realized they had no need for subtlety, for without a doubt there was indeed nowhere to hide.

D'Marco purposely delayed till 10:00 A.M. before pecking out the number on his Touch Tone. To the curt Yeah greeting he said, "Calling for Eugene."

"This is him."

"Frog," D'Marco said, just as cryptically.

"Frog, hey, glad you called back."

To this D'Marco made no reply, so Eugene said, "Got your name from some people—"

"Who?" D'Marco interrupted him.

Eugene named some reliable names.

"Okay," D'Marco said, "those people are cool. What do you got in mind?"

Eugene explained the proposition. D'Marco listened carefully, taking some notes on his "Things to Do" pad, saying nothing. "So what do you think?" Eugene concluded. "You be interested?"

"See if I got this right. Sounds like a two-week tagalong and then a maybe snuffing."

"No maybe on the snuffin'. Only maybe is when. That you get from us."

"And there's two of them?"

"Correct."

D'Marco thought it a minute. "I could do it for you," he said. "But it'll cost you some."

"How much we talkin'?"

D'Marco specified a figure. A low whistle came down the line. "That your best quote?" Eugene said.

"That's the fare. Plus expenses for the two weeks. Up front."

"Ain't what you'd call exactly cheap."

"You can get it done bargain basement or you can get it done right. With me it's right. Money-back guarantee. Ask those people you talked to, you want."

Even for Eugene, who dealt with these matters routinely, the figure seemed outrageous, a real stickup, but remembering Dietz's instructions and the ice in his voice and his eyes, he said, "Okay, you got a deal."

D'Marco said good.

With that verbal equivalent of a handshake across the miles, Eugene got down to particulars. "Yid's name is Bennie Epstein. He'll be flyin' into West Palm tonight or tomorrow—I'll get back to you on that soon's I find out for sure. We'll have a boy on the plane, make 'im for you."

"How you want to do the matchup, your boy and me?"

"We'll work out a signal, I'll let you know," Eugene said, a trifle impatiently. Too many goddam details to juggle. "So anyway, yid'll lead you to the other one, dude name of Waverly, Timothy

Waverly. That's the one's badass, done us a lot of damage up here. You're gonna want to watch him."

"I'll do that," D'Marco said. He was printing the names on the pad. Under Waverly's he drew a line, framed it with doodles.

"For now all's you got to do is stay with 'em, like I said. Don't crowd 'em or nothin'. Call in every night, let us know what's shakin'."

"*Every* night? For two weeks?"

"Well, yeah," Eugene said, sort of half-apologetic. And then, because now was as good a time as any, hoping to grease it in gently, no pain, he added, "You're tied up or something, you can have the boy do it."

D'Marco stopped doodling. "Which boy is that?"

"One from the plane. See, I want him to stay down there, hang out with you them two weeks. Pick up some pointers maybe, good habits. Okay?"

"Negative," D'Marco said coldly. "Not okay. If you talked to the people you said you talked to, you know I work strictly solo."

"Yeah, I heard that. But I was thinkin' maybe you'd make an exception this one time. This boy won't get in your way. He just needs some experience is all. Learn from a real pro." Even to him the fawning sounded bogus, labored.

"No exceptions. I'm not in the schoolhousing business."

Eugene sucked in his breath, hesitated, and then produced those words that, so rarely spoken, cost him intense distress and all but choked him on utterance. "How 'bout I sweeten the arrangement. Kick in a little bonus my own. Ten long, say." It was unbelievable what you had to bring yourself to do, watching out for family.

D'Marco did some fast calculating, strategies in his head, numbers on the notepad, and though the two were in serious conflict, it was the numbers prevailed. "For a flat ten long—independent of the fee, also up front—I'll do it."

"Deal. Guarantee you he won't be no problem."

With the understanding that D'Marco would stay by the phone and Eugene would get back to him sometime before the day was out, they both hung up. Eugene, on his end, experienced a momentary relief, thinking how the ten long would be money well spent if he could get his fuckup nephew initiated and disciplined and trained in some gainful facet of their profession, and how maybe, with any luck, just maybe he might even get some of the costly burden of family off his back. And D'Marco, on his end, felt a sudden jubilant rush at the remarkable figure he'd negotiated, largest in his career to date, though his elation was tempered by some misgivings over the babysitting concession he'd agreed to, as well as a certain irritation over the breach in his daily exercise regimen. Arm day shot to shit, and probably all the rest of his workouts too, next couple of weeks.

Waverly's call that day was not made until close to 3:00 P.M. and then only uncertainly and after wrestling with the idea of it, turning it over, weighing it, rejecting it, resolutely dispatching it from his head only to discover it stubbornly insinuating itself into his thoughts again, will of its own. It was there when he woke, roused by an urgent bladder, and stumbled into the john and relieved himself and, a little groggy yet from the beer, stretched and yawned and splashed his face with cold water. It was still there when he went back into the living room, so he dropped to the floor and did pushups, a hundred of them, and with his ankles wedged under the sofa, situps, five hundred of those, and after this salutary drill it was gone. Step one in the Zen of solitary, a survival skill once mastered, now only dimly remembered. But coming back to him, coming back.

After a shower and liquid breakfast, juice and instant coffee, he deliberately brought it out again and spent perhaps an hour analyzing the options open to him, which were really only two. We'll see, he had told her, yet in the rectangular bars of harsh morning light filtering through the verticals what he saw clearly was nothing at all. After a while he was struck with a powerful sense of absurdity, that an offhand invitation, impulsively offered in a euphoric daze of nostalgia and almost certainly regretted moments after the fact, should be giving him all this vexation. The murderer (twice over now, if the full truth were ever known) at the party, diverting the guests with dark and hilarious tales of Jacktown? Of course he wouldn't go; stupid even to play with the notion, lower than lunatic. To say nothing of risky. When you go to ground that's what you do: flatten out and stay down.

That decision made, he considered what to do with the remainder of the day. Nothing occurred to him till he happened to glance at the window, and remembering its sill full of bug droppings he went outside and strolled down the interior walk and rapped on the door of the apartment occupied by the Tropicaire's owner, one Ignatius O'Boyle. Oh Boy O'Boyle, as he liked to refer to himself in his jollier moods, which were seldom. The door opened slightly and a seamed, ruddy face appeared in the crack and gazed through it, mildly annoyed. Waverly alerted him to the potential termite hazard, downplaying it in the hope Oh Boy would ask him in, as he sometimes did, for coffee and a chat that invariably issued as monologue, racy yarns of youth, flight from snow country (Massachusetts, Waverly thought he heard, his attention was rarely focused), Florida fun, many marriages, many more conquests, the tribulations and triumphs and fantasies of an old man. Disjointed, self-aggrandizing chronicle of a life. Tedious, repetitious, dull, but a voice apart from the one in his head (still nagging, by the way), audible words. It was a way to pass some of the long hours, now and again. But not this morning. Waverly could hear a faint stirring behind the door, and Oh Boy winked lewdly and said right now he was busy, he'd pop in and take a look tomorrow or first thing Monday. Covering his disappointment, Waverly said Sure, no rush, and returned to his own apartment.

For the next several hours he battled Level 6 of Chess Challenger, the game of chess reduced to a contest between himself and shrewd coils of germanium fed by electric blood. He had taken black and looked on as the strategies unfolded and the white pieces advanced relentlessly, marching to a tempo of electronic whines and beeps and dots of red numbers flashing like vengeful neon on the beige surface of the board. Occasionally he was distracted by a passing image of Caroline Crown, but he couldn't blame his foundering play on that. Level 6 was a formidable adversary. Yesterday he had beaten it but yesterday he was white. Today he lost.

In the early afternoon he slept. When he woke he got himself off the sofa and went to the window again and stood there staring blankly at an abandoned hotel and a street that seemed to burn in the midday light. He looked up at a scattering of puffy clouds hung in a sky white with heat. High above them a jet moved in slow motion, unreeling a track to slit the heavens in half. Eventually it vanished beyond the window jamb, its trail dissolving like crystals of powdered milk in pale water, but not before he had time to speculate on the people up there, unfettered, free to fly to exotic places, Zambia, say, or Smolensk. They could doze or linger over drinks, read *Business Week*, strike up conversations with strangers, if they liked, spin a flirtation, arrange a rendezvous. Now and perhaps forever, these elementary pleasures were denied him.

He turned away and looked through the shabby silent room. His eyes moved between the phone fastened to the kitchenette wall and the chessboard set up and plugged in and waiting on the counter. The rules of chess, so rigid and orderly. Stiff universe of causes and predictable effects. Why is it no one would share the rules of life with him? And at the steady prompting of memories and longings no longer understood or controlled, he crossed the room and picked up the phone and dialed the number Caroline had given him; and when she answered he made some lame stabs at wit and asked, casually, about the nature of the party; and she explained it was informal, a few of Robbie's associates and their wives, certainly no black-tie affair, nothing like that, insisting again and then again she was counting on him to attend. Beneath the supple rush of words there was in her voice a rippled trace of tremor, slight but unmistakable. It was his business to listen for such things. But with all the reckless surety of the man convinced he leads a charmed life, he said what he'd said the day before: "I'll be there."

Around 5:30 Eugene phoned Dietz, who took the call on the private line in his study at home.

"Mr. Dietz? Eugene. Got some news think you're gonna like to hear."

"I'm always interested in good news, Eugene."

"Just collected on that first installment."

"All of it?"

"Full bundle. Five-five-oh."

"Very promising."

"That was my thought. There's more, too."

"Tell me."

"The Florida connection? It's all wired. Lock and load."

"And this individual understands the, ah, agenda?"

"Got it all worked out, Mr. Dietz."

"What about our Hebrew friend?"

"Found out he's headin' south in the morning. I got one boy on 'im tonight, another one goin' to ride along on the plane an' then when—"

"That's enough detail, Eugene."

"Right, yeah. So. Anything else I can tell you, Mr. Dietz?"

"That seems to cover it. For now."

"Okay. Be back in touch soon's I hear something."

"Oh, there is one more thing, Eugene. That I want to be sure you understand. That everyone involved understands."

"What's that?" Eugene said, even though he had a pretty good idea what that one more thing was going to be.

There was a pause and then, in a studiedly neutral tone bracketed by businesslike authority on the one side, philosophical rumination on the other, Dietz said, "We must never lose sight of how the world works, Eugene. They shined on us once. They're going to try and do it again. But we're not going to let that happen, are we? This time."

"No sir, Mr. Dietz. This time is nailin' time."

"Good. I was hoping you'd say that. Now I'll be expecting regular progress reports from you. I want to stay on top of this. Who knows? I might even make a trip down there myself. For the, uh, closing."

As soon as he was finished with Dietz, Eugene called his nephew, who had been instructed to wait at his apartment in Lisle. He told Sigurd he was going to Florida, pack enough clothes for a two-week stay. He gave him the name of the airline and the flight number and departure time, and directed him to come by first thing in the morning to pick up his ticket, expense money, and an envelope full of cash to be delivered to the contract man. He prescribed his travel wardrobe: salmon-colored sport jacket with a Chicago Bears T-shirt under it, blue twill trousers, high-top Reeboks. In meticulous detail he explained his duties and responsibilities. Finally, he concluded with advice and a warning: "This dude you be runnin' with, he's a starter. First-string varsity. You pay attention, watch him, listen, you maybe learn something. But he ain't gonna tolerate no dickin' around. You hearin' what I'm sayin'?"

"I'm hearin' you, hey," Sigurd said.

Eugene was not much cheered by all the cocky sass in the voice. "Listen, kid, I ain't frontin' here. This is heavy action. Heaviest kind. It's Dietz you're workin' for now. Dietz direct. Anything go wrong, you know who's gonna take the weight. Am I gettin' through?"

"You got 'er, Uncle Eugene. Zip in the sweat department, hey."

No sooner had they put their respective phones down than they were back on the line again, Sigurd to his mom with the spectacular news (which was greeted by another cautionary sermon, less than delighted), and Eugene to D'Marco with all the pertinent information and instructions (which, for the most part, were received either with silence or surly monosyllabic grunts). After their calls were completed, Sigurd popped a can of Coors, switched on the TV, and kicked back and relaxed, visions of an opulent future romping through his head, while his uncle got himself quietly, worriedly, reclusively wasted.

* * *

And while Sigurd and Eugene were thus engaged, a seriously agitated Bennie was trying to reach Waverly. Without success. Four times between 5:30 and 7:00 he dialed the Tropicaire number and four times he slammed the phone in disgust and filled the otherwise silent room with a litany of curses. Keep the fug down, was what he'd told him. Some down. Here he was, busting ass, taking the deep detour just to help out. And getting his own nuts laid out on the chopping block for his trouble. Anybody listen to your B. Epstein anymore?

It occurred to him he hadn't eaten anything substantial since morning, driving around with that toothpick Stumpley all day, so he picked up the phone again and ordered a pizza, large, pepperoni, sausage, anchovies, onions, and chop-chop, okay? While he waited he poured himself a short slackener from the bottle of Johnnie Walker Red on the dresser. Forty-five minutes later a delivery boy pounded on the door. Bennie opened up, and as he was paying he noticed a different car parked across the lot, different guy slouched behind the wheel. This one wasn't sleeping. He bolted the door and took the pizza inside and tucked it away, right down to the last cooling crust. Least the old appetite hadn't flagged, which got to mean you ain't dead yet. He poured another drink, tall one. Been a long, wire-strung day. Sonbitch on the nerves.

Soon the food and fatigue and booze and rhythmic *hsk hsk* of the Friday night traffic swooshing down Ogden lulled him to sleep. At ten he woke with something of a start. All his bones ached and his belly burned. He shuffled into the john, took a leak, burped and farted, both explosively, and came back and tried phoning Waverly again. No answer. Now he was wide awake and with not a goddam thing to do. From ten till a little after midnight he finished off the Johnnie Walker and gaped at the television until the screen began to blur. By then he was truly hammered, knocked out. Nevertheless, he made one last Waverly call, and this time he got him.

9

Because it was a Seville he was driving, and a gaudy pink one at that, Waverly searched out the most remote and least conspicuous spot in the Breakers lot, which proved to be behind a pea-green Dodge, another tacky intruder in this principality of wealth. He cut the engine and checked his appearance in the rearview, ran a comb through his hair. His hands were not steady. In spite of the chill air flooding the car, he perspired. He looked at his watch: thirty minutes ahead of the appointed hour. He felt like a bumbling adolescent on his way to the junior prom. Something of a fool.

It wasn't Palm Beach or the Breakers that intimidated him. Not in the slightest. In his four years in Florida he'd been over here many times, though always in a professional capacity, rather like a skilled artisan, a master plumber or technician, come to service the rich. Been some memorable, hard-fought games played in that hotel, for the plutocrats of this world, he'd discovered, took their cards as seriously as they took themselves and were not graceful losers. Or winners either, for that matter. No, it wasn't the setting made him uneasy so much as the peculiar sense of stepping backward, squeezing through the neck of the bottle of time and emerging in the haunted, shimmering province of the past. The naked feel of a persona vacated. Of course you could always take this carny wagon out of the lot and down the drive and back up Cocoanut Row and back across Flagler Bridge and back into that familiar country of the life and the character you've invented for yourself (so a mocking voice in his head reminded him). Not too late, you could do that. But you won't.

A rush of dank sultry air met him outside the car. He did what he could to smooth the wrinkles out of the jacket and trousers of his summer-weight suit, and then he threaded through the files of sleek vehicles. Columns of spray in the Florentine fountain at the entrance made miniature rainbows in the gradually receding light. He came through the lobby and walked all the way down the south loggia to the Alcazar Lounge. It was too early for much of a crowd: a scattering of couples here and there, a few men at the bar, substantial-looking sorts, all of them, gravely conscious of where they were. He took a table by one of the windows over-looking the ocean. A waitress hurried over. Brandy and water, he told her, and in a finger snap it was set before him. He drank slowly, watching a mass of gold-fringed clouds hurtling across a pale sky ornamented by a slender shaving of moon. To the north the clouds were black, heavy with rain, moving in fast. He smoked some cigarettes, ordered another drink. Settled into the velvet-covered, cane-backed chair. Close to an hour passed. At 7:30 he called for the check, laid some bills on the table, and got to his feet. He went back to the lobby and rode the elevator to the appropriate floor and walked down a corridor and around a cor-ner and down another till he arrived at the designated room. From the other side of the door came urgent party noises: high-velocity voices, clinking glasses, ripples of unsustained laughter. He hesitated. But not long. Come this far, no more stalling. Any-way, what else you going to do?

He knocked and nothing happened. Knocked again and the door swung open and a tall woman with a long horsey face stood in it and said a simple, uninflected, "Yes."

"Ah, this is the Crowns' room?"

"Yes."

"I was invited."

Her eyes ran over him, head to foot, before she said, "Expect you'd better come in, then. Since you're invited."

She moved aside just enough to allow him to enter, pushed the door shut behind her. She clutched a glass in a veiny hand equipped with bejeweled fingers and nails painted like red talons. "I'm Avis Appelgate," she said. The tone implied it ought to mean something to him.

"Timothy Waverly."

"You an investor?"

"No."

"Not an investor. What, then?"

This woman with the improbable name Avis Appelgate wore a floor-length caftan of so violent a green it appeared to be electri-cally charged. Silvery balls dangled from her ears and jiggled when she spoke, and when she did her voice had a squeaky elfish quality incongruous in a woman so large-boned and rangy. She looked to be late forties, older maybe, with Florida women it was difficult to tell, and for all the pronounced elongated features maybe even partly pretty once, a couple of cosmetic surgeries ago. "Just a friend," Waverly said.

"Friend. Well, this is the place, friend." With a toss of her head and a roll of her eyes she indicated the room. "The funhouse."

It was shrouded in smoke, the funhouse, and swarming with guests, elegantly coutured ladies and impeccably tailored males. Middle-aged and up, most of them. Faces locked in relentless professional smiles. Jostling for position. Lots of emphatic gesturing going on, some hand pumping, a certain amount of smacky-face. Bottles, glasses, buckets of ice, and trays of hors d'oeuvre dominated the table and desk and nightstands and bureau and the top of the Servi-Bar. A door led to another room that appeared to be similarly engaged.

"Better help yourself to the sauce," Avis Appelgate advised him. "Your hosts are mingling, I would imagine."

"Thanks, I'll do that," Waverly said, but before he could, Caroline materialized out of the strident commerce of the party, and at the sight of him all her presence seemed infused with a sudden joy.

"Timothy! I was afraid you weren't going to come."

And stepping into her scented embrace, he said, "Would I fail you?"

She laughed, but with a little more merriment than the remark justified. She released her grip and moved back and gazed at him. And he at her. Under the strata of makeup the delicate bone geometry of her face still asserted itself, but in her eyes there was a kind of feverish glitter. For a moment she seemed unaware of Avis Appelgate standing there, taking it all in, and then, remembering the amenities, she said, or started to say, "Avis, this is—"

"I know. A friend. We met."

"We grew up together," Caroline said, by way of explanation.

Avis arched a brow. Her wide mouth opened in a wicked smirk. "Isn't that nice," she said.

Caroline ignored it and turned to Waverly and said, "We've got to find Robbie. I know he's dying to see you."

Avis murmured something that sounded like I'm sure. Out loud, and out of a face pinched with malice, she said, "Just look for my husband. That's where you'll certainly find him."

"Excuse us, Avis."

Caroline took Waverly's arm and guided him through the crush of people. She leaned in close, and with an over-the-shoulder nod whispered, "A perfectly awful woman. How long did you have to endure her?"

"Not long."

"Same old Waverly. Stoic as ever."

Her breath carried a sweetish aroma of gin, and when she spoke her hands fluttered in the way he had noticed the day before. There was about all her gestures and expressions a tense, exaggerated, almost theatric quality. "Stoics are sentimental people," he said, "under it all. Why else would I be here?"

She created a curious distant smile and drew away slightly and beckoned him through the door to the adjoining room. She paused, glanced around. "There he is," she said, pointing. "Score another one for sweet Avis."

Between the weaving knots of bodies Waverly caught a glimpse of a couch set along the opposite wall. It was occupied by a round, sturdy fellow in a cream-colored suit who looked nothing at all like Robbie. Much too old. However, facing the couch, straddling a chair, his back to the crowd, was another man, this one wearing a suit of pastel blue. He appeared to be speaking with considerable intensity, for his head bobbed vigorously and both his hands polished the air. That now, that would be Robbie.

"Come along," Caroline said, and they made their way across the room.

The man on the couch saw them coming and raised a flagging arm. The chair-straddler swiveled his head, following the gesture. A quicksilver frown crossed his face and quickly recast itself into a nurtured grin, and he rose and turned toward them.

"Someone here I thought you might want to see," Caroline said to him, yesterday's irony skirting the bright edges of her voice.

"Waverly. Son of a bitch. Tim Waverly."

Under the thickened flesh of the accumulating years was the outline of the Robbie Crown features, blurred, ill-defined, but quite unmistakable. "How're you doing, Rob?" Waverly said, extending a hand.

Robbie pushed it aside, bear-hugged him instead. "Great to see you, Tim," he said. "Just great." Then he stepped back and fixed him with a long, charitable stare. "Look at you. Look how trim you are. Like you just climbed out of the Calvin College pool. How the hell you do it?" As a show of contrast he patted his own ample midsection.

There was in that benevolent scrutinizing stare, as in his very stance and bearing, something faintly patronizing, something that seemed to say You're trimmer maybe but I'm taller, wider, stronger, and in all the ways that matter in this world just a tad smarter than you. It was the Robbie Crown he remembered. "It's clean living does it," Waverly said. "Nasty thoughts, but clean habits."

From the hoarse, booming Rotarian laugh and the eyes, inflamed with drink, that went darting worriedly over his shoulder, Waverly recognized instantly he was not welcome here. Robbie turned around and, indicating the man on the couch, said, "You want to meet a really nasty thinker, press palms with this fella here. Nastiest player on the Gold Coast. Jack Appelgate, Tim Waverly."

"Call me Jock," said this nasty player, and though he didn't move from the couch he did thrust out a hand, and Waverly came forward and got to shake with someone after all.

"Tim and I went to school together," Robbie elaborated. "Christ, we ran amok from kindergarten right on up through college."

It seemed an odd way to describe their tranquil, disciplined youth. "More of a contained amok-running," Waverly amended.

"Not another one of you Michigan boys," Jock Appelgate said, mainly to Robbie. "You Yankees going to bury us poor crackers yet."

Both of them, Waverly noticed, had baked red faces, golf-course-and-bourbon faces. Both had harsh, immediate voices. Authority voices, accustomed to deference. He wondered what he was doing here.

"Where's your drink?" Robbie said. He turned on his wife. "Care, where's Tim's drink?"

The slightly mordant smile she had worn through all this jovial introductory banter suddenly faded, displaced by a helpless expression, near to dazed. "I don't know. I must have forgot."

" 'I forgot,' " Robbie mimicked, more or less good-humoredly, though with a trace of a sneer in it.

"Hey, you lighten up on that lovely lady, y'hear," Jock said, also good-humored, leering at her.

"What're you drinking, Tim?"

"You have some brandy?"

Jock answered for him. "You name it, he's got it here somewheres. That's right, Robber?"

Robbie affirmed that it was right.

"I call him Robber on account of he's a lawyer," Jock explained for Waverly's benefit, chortling at his excellent joke. Like his wife, he had a prominent mouth framed by purplish, night-crawler lips. He held out his glass to Caroline and said, "While you're at it, little lady, you want to put a head on this. Out of that Wild Turkey jug your worser half keeps locked in the safe."

Jock and Robbie hooted in unison at this sally of wit.

"What about you, husband dear?" Caroline asked.

Robbie said he was okay yet, and she took Jock's glass and disappeared into the churning crowd.

"Why don't you boys squat before you stumble," Jock suggested.

Robbie restraddled the chair, and at Jock's further direction Waverly took the other end of the couch.

A moment of stiff silence.

Plainly to put something into it, Robbie said, "Pretty weird, you and Care running into each other like that."

"It was a surprise, all right. After all these years. Pleasant one, of course."

To bring Jock into it Robbie said, addressing him, "Fifteen years we haven't seen or heard from this clown, and then yesterday Care comes out of her ugly shop over in North Palm and walks right into him."

Jock clucked his tongue, clearly not much interested in this token illustration of the vagaries of chance. "So," he said, "all three you from the same hometown up north there?"

Waverly said they were, and Robbie, somewhat repetitiously, expanded on it, filling an awkward juncture with words. "Grew up on the same street, went to the same schools. When it came time to go to college all we had to do was walk a couple blocks down and there it was."

"Calvin College," Waverly said. "The hotbed of student rest, in those days."

Robbie's laugh was loud and surprisingly genuine, as if the remark and the recollection it inspired truly amused him. Because Jock looked puzzled, he said, "It was during the Vietnam thing. Those campus demonstrations. At Calvin we missed all that. It's an arm of the Christian Reformed Church, exists strictly for the glory of God."

"Thought you told me you were a Harvard grad-u-ate."

"That came after, Jock. To pick up my union card."

Jock snorted, not without some contempt. "Make you a legal hustler, huh? Live up to your name. How 'bout you?" he demanded of Waverly. "You one of them Ivy League eggheads too?"

"No," Waverly said, and with a glance at Robbie he said also, "I attended some other institutions."

"Tim went on to the University of Michigan," Robbie put in quickly. "Graduate school."

"So I gather neither you boys suited up, your arm' forces."

"We missed that one, too," Waverly said.

"Well, tell you what I think," Jock said, settling back in the couch like a round, wise, not-so-benign Buddha. "I think we should of kicked gook ass, that war. Little smartass ass here at home, too. Course, what do I know?" he added rhetorically and in that tone that implies the answer is manifestly everything at all worth knowing. "I never had the good fortune to go to college, like you two. Just an old dirt farmer and nail-pounder, worked with these hands all my life." He held them up for display, two extraordinarily large, knob-knuckled, work- and weather-coarsened hands, the fingers adorned by blinding gold wedding band and diamond pinkie rings, the nails perfectly manicured.

"You've heard of Appelgate Developers?" Robbie asked Waverly.

"Afraid not."

"Well, it's that kind of hard work got this old nail-pounder title to half of Palm Beach County," Robbie declared, finest bootlicking, tail-wagging delivery.

Waverly widened his eyes, to show he was impressed, and Jock's wormy lips parted in a slow smile with a mean twist in it. His shrewd eyes fairly twinkled. He seemed not at all displeased to be exactly who he was—Jock Appelgate. "Now all's we want's the other half," he said to Waverly, "me and the Robber here. Right, Robber?"

Before the Robber could reply, Caroline appeared bearing two glasses, saying, "Drinks are served, gentlemen." One glass she handed to Waverly, her glance lingering on him. He met her gaze, and her glittery eyes seemed to soften and fill with a warm light. The other glass to Jock, who said, "Why thank you, sweet lady," folding slightly at the belly in a small effort at a courtly, seated bow.

"Decidedly all my pleasure, excellency, sir."

Robbie's already flushed face went crimson. He gripped her elbow and pulled her toward him and hissed something in her ear. Her eyebrows lifted in a motion of surprise and to no one in particular she said, "Oh, yes, of course, man talk." And then to Waverly directly, "Perhaps we'll get a chance to talk later, Tim.

Old times and all that. I've been instructed to circulate." She did a mock curtsy at Appelgate and was gone.

Over the cheery clamor of the party a rumble of thunder echoed in the distance. Robbie tried covering an obvious discomfort by remarking on it. "Supposed to be a heavy rainstorm moving in tonight."

"That's a sassy little woman you've got there," Jock said, evidently uninterested in the weather. He was still smiling, but his mouth had a grim set to it. "Real pistol."

Or loadie, Waverly was thinking, for she was certainly on something and he suspected it was something more than just the booze. Robbie asked him how long he'd been in Florida. "About four years now," he said. The whole conversation seemed to be advancing at strange cross-purposes.

"Maybe your friend here'd like a little piece of this action we're contemplating," Jock said.

"Oh, I doubt that," Robbie said hastily and through the sickliest of grins. "Tim was never much into business. He's more the literary type. Am I right, Tim?"

"I expect that's accurate. Or it used to be."

"Well," Jock said, straight at Robbie, " 'less you get that sand-nigger in line, won't matter anyway. Won't be any action to split. Minus him, all's we're holding's a handful of dog shit."

Behind the jolly old boy inflections and the ungenerous smile there was in his words and expression a clear cold threat, and Robbie chewed his underlip and squirmed in his seat. His masterly bulk seemed diminished, actually to shrink somehow, and he said lightly, weakly, "Jocko, old buddy, have I ever let you down? So the camel jockey's an ass burn. I'll find the springs that turn his clock."

"I'm sure hoping that's how it turns out, Robber. Bottom line, he's the one's driving the problem."

Waverly felt acutely uncomfortable, rather like an eavesdropper on a murky dialogue he was never intended to hear. More than ever did he wonder what he was doing sitting on this couch in these rooms in this hotel. Here. It was time to escape. Past time. He was about to make his move when Appelgate called their collective attention to someone across the room. "Hey, there's Bulldog."

Robbie turned. "Where?"

"Over there," Appelgate said, pointing at a man standing by himself near the door, sucking a pipe with a moronic gravity.

"Old Bulldog," Robbie said. "He's looking lost. I'd better go point him to the bar. Be back in a minute."

He shot out of the chair and got out of there fast. Another fugitive, Waverly thought, more nimble than I. And now it's just me and Jock, one on one. Seriously cornered.

"Heavy investor in this little venture of ours," Appelgate said in identification of the pipe-sucker. "Name's Norman Drummond. We call him Bulldog."

Early on, Waverly had decided there was nothing to like about this man, this squat Buddha with the round, red, well-fed face and the squinty eyes full of malice and cunning. No redeeming qualities whatsoever. And he had nothing at stake here. In a few moments he'd be long gone. "That's clever," he said.

Now the Appelgate lips compressed in a grimace. "We think so."

Waverly lit a cigarette. Something in his hand. He said nothing.

"Thought I heard Robber say you was literary. Some such. What's that mean exactly? You a schoolteacher?"

Schoolteacher, rendered as synonymous with waiter or valet or florist or male hairdresser, some servitor, something sissy, something beneath notice. "No," Waverly said.

Appelgate lifted his glass and took a long, satisfying swallow. Here it comes.

"What business you in, Mr. Waverly?"

"I'm a gambler," Waverly said, watching the eyes narrow on him skeptically.

"Gambler. You don't say. I'd of never figured you for a gambler. You play the ponies? Dogs?"

"No, I've never understood animals."

"What, then?"

"Cards. I play cards."

"Well, now, that's real interesting. Y'see, I like to rustle a deck some myself. Little vice of mine."

"Everybody's entitled to one. Vice, that is."

"It's when you got a dozen of 'em or better gets you in the soup."

"My thought exactly."

Now the Appelgate gaze was steady. Measuring, appraising. "Poker's mine. Stud, draw, low ball, hi-lo, hold-'em, you name it, I play 'em all. Even some of them crazy, wild card games."

"Really. How's your luck?"

"Good. Mostly good. Course I don't work at it like you probably got to do. If that's your living."

"When it's your living, you work at it."

"Bet you do. Y'know, Mr. Waverly, it's a real coincidence, you being a card-playing professional. See, next week we're having a little game for some of the boys here. Keep 'em entertained, you might say, while we're waiting to seal this arrangement. Could be you'd like to sit in?"

"Thanks, but I don't think so."

"Don't play with amateurs?"

"All the time. Amateur or pro, it still all turns finally on the fall of the cards."

"We got a few sharp players," Appelgate said, gun-slinger challenge underlining the glycerin in his voice. "Take Drummond, for a for instance. He's a doctor by trade, owns a whole string of nursing homes, but he's about as close to a professional, like yourself, as you're likely to meet. And I hear that A-rab fella, be in later in the week, he's among the best there is, comes to cards. Say he's a money player, too. Could be some real action around here, next few days. Sure I can't twist your arm?"

"Appreciate the invitation, Mr. Appelgate—"

"Jock."

"Jock. Appreciate it, but I'm going to have to pass on this one. I expect to be gone by then. Out of town."

"Shame. Well, you change your mind, you let us know. Talk to Robber."

Waverly glanced at the tail of ash dangling from his cigarette. No ashtray in reach. An escape hatch. He cupped a hand under it and stood and said, "Better find a place to butt this. Excuse me." He went around the couch and through the partially opened slider and onto the deck and flipped the cigarette into the darkened void below him. Thick and sodden as the air was out here, it was still a welcome relief from the claustrophobic room. Off on the horizon the jeweled lights of a steamer starred the black ocean. A streak of lightning laid a flash print on the black sky. A shock wave of thunder followed, and in a moment there was rain in his face.

He came back inside and, skirting the couch, took sanctuary in the crowd. No one had anything to say to him. Over by the door Robbie was talking earnestly to the man they called Bulldog, who had a severe overbite that set his mouth in the appearance of a perpetual vacant grin. Waverly avoided the door. A cluster of people stood gaping at a television on a portable cart along a wall. He joined them. The feature playing was, in effect, a Breakers commercial, a long and loving paen to itself. A molasses overvoice invited the viewers' attention to the fountain out front, the Italian Renaissance architecture of the interior, the lobby's vaulted, frescoed ceiling, the fifteenth-century Flemish tapestries, the enormous chandeliers. Then it went statistical: 140 acres of grounds, 528 rooms, staff of 1200 fluent in 28 languages, 5 restaurants, 17,000 wines on stock, other numbers, many more. The unctuous voice rhapsodized in the toplofty argot of opulence: magnificent, majestic, massive, lush, tranquil, intimate, ultimate—modifiers like that. He thought he heard a grandeur in there too. Background music swelled. Voice and images elicited some approving commentary from this audience, an occasional appreciative gasp. Another voice in his ear, sardonic, murmured, "Are you properly awed?"

He turned and discovered Caroline beside him. Nodding at the screen, he said, "It's almost like being there, isn't it."

"Waverly, Waverly, you never change, do you?" she said, and she graced him with a smile so wistful, so wounded, it singed his heart.

"Never change? Would that it were so."

"You see? That's what I mean. Who else would put it that way?"

"Some other sententious dinosaur. There's still a few of us around, I hear."

"Not in these rooms."

"No, you're right. Not here."

"Let's go stand in the hall. You want to?"

"Best idea I've heard all night."

"You go ahead. I'll get my purse."

On his way to the door he passed Avis Appelgate. She asked him if he was having a good time, her malign eyes drifting over him slowly. Nice match, the Appelgates. Smashing, he told her.

In the corridor he lit another cigarette. Soon Caroline was there. She noticed the cigarette and fumbled through the purse for one of her own. Waverly held out a light while she fitted it in a small plastic cylinder. Her hands trembled. "An Aquafilter," she explained. "Makes smoking positively healthy."

"Whatever works."

"I don't remember you addicted to this evil habit. When we were young."

"See now, there's one of those many changes you missed. I do it because it insulates you."

"Against what?"

"Oh, that quaint set of assumptions we like to call reality, maybe."

They were talking about smoking? He wondered what was going on. He had no idea. She asked him how he liked the party. "Nice party," he said.

"What do you think of our guests?"

"Good moneyed folk."

"And Jock? What about him?"

"You want my opinion of Jock?"

"That's what I'm curious to hear."

"Jock Appelgate. Soul of a dentist, imagination of a dermatologist. Which is doubtless why he's as successful as he obviously is."

Caroline threw back her head and laughed. Shrill-pitched, near-hysteria laugh, filling the empty hall. She seemed to sway a little. To steady herself, she laid a hand against the wall.

"It really wasn't that funny," Waverly said.

"Tell me," she said, once the hilarity was under control. "What do you think of my outfit? Be honest."

The white cocktail dress clung to the elegant lines of her slender figure. "I like it," he said.

"It's from Saks."

"Now I like it even more."

"My earrings?"

Two long pendants sparkled beneath her ears. "They're good too," he said.

"Diamonds and rubies."

"Very impressive."

"What do you do, Tim?"

"Pardon me?" He was having serious problems with all these corkscrew conversations tonight. Verbal mirror houses.

"Do. What do you do here? In Florida."

"Get by," he said. "On that heroic wit of mine. Keep people in stitches."

"All right, then. Where do you live?"

"On Singer Island. At the moment."

"Ask me over. I want to see where you live."

"I don't think you do. It's nothing like this." With a sweep of an arm he included the rooms and corridor and entire hotel.

"Nevertheless, I want to see it. I want to talk to you again. Before we leave."

"I'm not so sure that's a good idea. There's only so much past you can chase down." As we're discovering right now, he might have added, though he didn't.

"I'll be the judge of that. Write it down for me."

"Write what?"

"Your phone."

He rolled over empty palms. "Nothing to scribble on."

"I'll find something." She started searching her purse when the door opened and Robbie poked his scowly face through it and in a snappish voice said, "Care, where the hell—" Seeing Waverly, he broke off and came into the hall, forcing a smile. He seemed less unhappy to find him out here rather than inside. "Tim," he said, voice gone suddenly mellow, "you enjoying yourself?"

Everyone auditing his pleasure quotient tonight. Waverly said he was having an excellent time.

"Terrific. That's terrific." To Caroline he said, "We've got guests in there, luv."

"Feeling neglected, are they?"

Robbie managed the difficult feat of glaring at his wife while still retaining a smile for his old friend. Quite adroitly, at that. "The point is," he said to her, "we're getting ready to leave. Jock wants us all to go over to his compound."

"For compound, read house," she said to Waverly, and then to her husband, "I thought you'd made reservations at Jo's."

"It's raining too hard. Anyway, he doesn't like that French food. Avis is going to whip up some omelets."

"How domestic. The little woman toiling at the stove. Maybe they'll serve a side of grits."

Now the smile evaporated utterly. Only the glare left, and it was baleful. "Goddam it, Caroline, will you lay off the nut-cracking. Give it a rest, for Christ's sake."

Caroline put a hand behind an ear, made a comic alert face. "Her master's voice," she said.

Waverly cleared his throat. This was nothing he wanted to be witness to. "Ah, I've got to be going. Thanks for everything. It was good seeing you both again." Routine departure noises.

Robbie looked at him as if he'd forgotten who he was. Very cautiously he said, "Oh, well, Jock did say be sure and tell you to come along. He seems to have the idea you're a gambler or something. Why'd you tell him that, Tim?"

"I suppose because it's the truth."

"No shit. That's what you're up to these days, gambling?"

"No shit."

"Jock's quite a poker player himself."

"So he said. Give him my apologies. I really do have to leave now."

"Hey, sorry you can't make it," Robbie said, smile recovering, looking not at all distressed. "Listen, we're going to be here another couple weeks. Let's get together, pop back some quiet ones." He offered a hand and this time they shook, warmly. "Call me."

"I'll be sure and do that."

Robbie turned to the door and Waverly started down the hall. Caroline stepped into his path, hugged him, bussed his cheek. "Tell me the number," she whispered. "I'll remember."

And in that shaved instant of choice, it occurred to him a bogus number or even a simple transposition of digits could resolve this awkward circumstance for good and all, restore his life to as much of order and what he had come to accept as normalcy as it would ever be capable of sustaining. But he did neither. He told her the number, and she rewarded him with a very secret, radiant smile, quite different from Robbie's.

He lay on the sofa of his Tropicaire room, staring into the dark, listening to the sounds of the rain lashing the roof the way a child, snug in his bed, listens to the sounds of a storm. A great oppressive loneliness overtook him. Sleep was elusive. In prison he had developed a method for courting it that had served him often and well. Breezed him right through a three-week hole holiday once, this method had. He tried it again now, squeezed his eyes shut and ran a reel of his own imagination behind them.

He created a submarine, a marvel of flawless mechanics and technology. He peopled it with crew, gave them names, faces, traits, identities. He stocked it with provisions, established a mission, destination. Put himself at the helm. Commander Waverly. Stalwart, resourceful, steely-eyed, fearless. He had a loose story line. In this scenario the world was savaged by nuclear war, and it was their charge to search for signs of life. Something like that movie *On the Beach* he had seen as a child. They set out from some Arctic port unaccountably spared destruction, in Greenland, say, or northern Labrador. Down the eastern seaboard they came, slowing for periscope views of devastated cities and landscapes swept by firestorms and thick rolling poisoned clouds. No survivors were discovered; they were alone in the world, but safe beneath the sea. Manfully, heroically, he guided their voyage, possessed of all that arcane, mysterious knowledge sub skippers possessed, instead of what he really had, which was nothing more than the low lore of odds and percentages and strategies and angles, and a stealthy grasp of giveaway expressions and gestures and mannerisms and vocal intonations, and—oh yes—a fading memory of the lives and works of some dead poets and the vocabulary and syntax of a few dead languages. And so they sailed on, down the coast, past the dangling topographic member that was Florida, through the Caribbean, along the humpback of Brazil, and into the South Atlantic, and as his vessel rounded Cape Horn sleep came to him at last.

Though not, it seemed, for long. It seemed he had no more pointed his ship north, following the long mountainous spine of Chile, than a piercing jangle shook him into semiconsciousness. He sat up on the sofa, grinding at his eye sockets with the heels of his hands. His mouth felt as if it were varnished with a coat of nicotine and brandy. His stomach felt hollow. Gradually he recognized where he was and what was happening: back in the Tropicaire, the phone rattling. Insistently. He switched on the Monkey Wards lamp and shambled into the kitchenette and lifted the receiver and mumbled a hello.

"Timothy? That you?"

"Yes. Speaking."

"Bennie."

"Bennie. Where are you? What time is it?"

"Late. Like in later than you think. Where you been? I been tryin' to get you all night."

"Uh, oh, out. I was out. For a while."

"What'd I tell you about stayin' down?"

"Yeah, well, I was out. But nobody whacked me. Least I don't think. I'm talking to you."

A pause. A whistle. Protracted and in the key of exasperation. "You in the bag? Juiced?"

"No. Couple drinks, is all."

"Puts you one up on me."

"Where are you?"

"Downers Grove. It's in Illinois. One of your finer suburb communities."

"So how did it go? Are we straight?"

"How'd it go? You're askin' me how'd it go?"

Waverly was coming awake now, and what he heard in his friend and partner's somewhat slurred voice was not reassuring, not at all what he'd hoped to hear. "It's a natural question, Bennie."

"Answer is not good. How'd it go?—not good. Feels like they turned me over and didn't use no grease."

"Are you okay? They didn't—"

"Nah, nothin' like that. Not yet, anyhow."

"What happened?"

"Now ain't the time to get into it. Tomorrow is. Tomorrow we'll get it out and look at it, when we're both thinkin' right. Speakin' of which, reminds me why I called. Want you to pick me up tomorrow at PBI. You got some writin' materials there?"

Waverly found a pencil and a scrap of paper. "Go ahead," he said.

Bennie gave him the details of his flight. "You got all that now?"

"I've got it."

"Okay, I'll be lookin' for you. An' listen, meantime what I want you to do—make that tellin' you to do—is keep the fuck down. We're wadin' in some serious shit, Timothy. Life you save may be mine."

10

Thirty thousand feet up, winging east and south at what had to be an easy thousand miles an hour, sitting stuffed and shell-backed in a window seat of this airborne cattle car, barred from lighting up a steadying smoke for the next four hours, Sigurd Stumpley occupied himself with thoughtful reflections on mortality. Mortality generally, his own in particular. This fragile scrap of aluminum could drop like a rock falling from the sky; down there a truck or a bus or even just another car could skid into your lane and flatten you; go strutting down a street whistling, dreaming about your next ham-slamming, you could slip on a banana peel, open your skull; accidentally stick a knife in a toaster and electricity'd fry you; take a swim in the lake or a snooze in the tub and water'd drown you; poisoned air could choke you, tainted food poison you; get a headache and pop an aspirn and some weirdo's laced it with cyanide; business he was in, turn your back and—whap!—somebody blindside you. Dangerous fucking world to try and make your way through.

Still, for all these morbid musings, he felt a whole lot better than when he first boarded and the plane taxied onto the field, hesitated, engines revving and fuselage shuddering, and then went blazing down the runway and almost imperceptibly lifted into the air, banking at a steep angle, tilting the earth crazily beneath him. First time in an airplane, it shook the very shit loose in him: heart two-fisting, eyes goggling, ears popping. But now, getting the hang of it, he was starting to feel good again. His old self again. Cocked, locked, and ready to rock. Florida-bound.

Maybe just a little tight yet over the prospect of the two weeks ahead, teaming up with this prime-time contractor, running with him, watching him work, maybe even getting a piece of the final zotzing. Helluvan opportunity. Also, of course, soaking up some rays and for sure getting balled by some of that bowl-a-honey Florida quiff. Florida everybody got laid. Thinking about it made him feel almost warm toward Uncle Eugene, even if the old unc had chewed on him this morning: Stay out of the way, keep your eyes and ears open, see how it's done, take notes, learn, it ain't no vacation you're on, you're there to learn. Same shit as last night. Sound like he had the fucking rag on, like he was talking to some mutt just come up out of the street gang ranks. Well, he'd show him Sigurd Stumpley had a pretty sly head on his shoulders, wasn't nobody you'd want to try and fuck over. Show 'em all.

Speaking of heads, if he craned his neck a little he could see the back of the bald one on the kike, aisle seat three rows up. Chrometop with a couple greased strands, looked like paint streaks, laid across it. Probably going through it right now was the figure to make a dash once they touched down. Forget that, Jewbaby; this boy stuck to your ass like a month-old dingleberry, you ain't going noplace at all. Couple times since they'd been in the air Jew'd gotten up and lurched toward the can in the back. Both times it looked like he'd cut a glance Sigurd's way, or least it seemed like it looked like he had. Hard to tell for sure. Imagination, most likely. Nothing to get twisted about. Just stay cool, do your number.

Also speaking of head, slightly different slant, it was hard not to notice the spook stewardess prancing up and down the aisle flashing them gleaming teeth out of that black face with the bones in it high and sharp and clean as a white girl's, regular nose, no baboon look to it, normal-size lips glossed in silver, pile of crimped black hair, sweet round firm rump on her, way that suntan cooze gets put together sometimes, legs about nine foot long, kind can wrap around you twice. Hard not to notice all that. She was coming toward his row now, dragging a drinks cart. Sigurd's eyes were tacked on her, and when she bent over to serve some dipshit across the aisle what he was thinking was how he'd eat the crotch right out of her panties just to get at her black ass. Black or not, he'd be first in line. Come to laying tube, he wasn't prejudice.

When she asked him if he'd care for anything to drink he said, "Why sure, honey. Whiskey and water go down real nice." Getting a *go down* in there for her to hear, give her something to think about. Seemed like she winced a little, though he might have imagined that too, but just in case he hadn't he handed her a tenner and before she could make change said, "That's okay, sweetcakes, you keep it for yourself, hey." Nothing like the old green to crack open a smile, especially with your coloreds. She gushed a gratitude and, noticing the logo on the T-shirt under his jacket, declared she was a super Bears fan too. See, right off they had something in common, but before he could establish that bond she gave the cart a tug and was gone. Maybe with a little luck he'd get another shot at it, get up and take a leak, say, and run into her, or catch her on the way out after they landed, talk a little street smack at her, make a connection, get a number. Little luck, he might even be doing the dirty dark hula this very night.

Sigurd was discovering there was something about travel—the manic bustle of airports, the squeeze on the balls in the cramped seats, the gentle rocking motion of the plane, the pillars of clouds rising against a blue sky on the other side of the window—made you extra horny. Made you ready to wet your wanger in the nearest knothole. Course you got to be practical. Can't lose track of what you're here for, which is the serious business of tagging Mr. Bagel and company and which business, Dietz business, could put the serious snag in your love life. Lot of it going to turn on his soon-to-be partner, kind of dude he'd be, if he'd be the kind liked some yucks, liked to go bouncing after hours. And thinking about him now, trying to picture how he'd look, how they'd get on, Sigurd felt a surge of anticipation tinged with a little doubt, but not much. Just be yourself, he told himself, reinforcing what Mom always told him: People are people. You want to get along, this world, don't ever try and be nothing but who you are. Old Mom—right again.

D'Marco Fontaine, at that moment, was doing much the same thing as Sigurd; that is, speculating on the personality and character of the young man he was going to be stuck with for the next two weeks. None too happily. From the physical description ("This boy's kinda short, little on the heavy side—well, got quite a gut on him, actual'—sorta reddish in the hair, freckles . . .") he sounded like no one D'Marco would, under ordinary circumstances, be at all interested in knowing. Who'd want to know anybody looked like that? Also the name, which when he first heard it he thought was intended as some kind of joke. Sigurd Stumpley? Jesus. Outside of the comics pages and the Saturday morning kiddie cartoons, who was named Sigurd? And from the particulars of the identifying outfit, D'Marco could make the educated guess this wasn't somebody heavy into fashion.

Unlike himself, for D'Marco was wearing a tan silk sport jacket, cream cotton polo shirt, tan linen slacks set off by a brandy leather belt, and hand-sewn pebble-grain road mocs with wraparound soles. Whole ensemble looked like something created by one of those exclusive, lighter-than-air wop designers, even though everything he had on was in fact purchased off the rack at Burdine's. Never mind, his time was coming.

He sat in the cafeteria–coffee shop located on the main concourse of Palm Beach International, no smoking naturally, though that was its own kind of bad joke, what with the cigarette fumes drifting in from the adjacent suicide section and settling over his table and his clothes and his carefully spritzed hair like some noxious cloud of mustard gas. To say nothing of the heavy fried odors elevating off the sizzling grill behind the counter. Not exactly your venue of choice for D'Marco Fontaine, but there wasn't a lot he could do about it, since the terminal was mobbed with weekend travelers and every chair out on the floor was taken. Somewhere he'd heard or read they were supposed to be building a new airport, and they damn well ought to get to it, get it done, was his thought. This place was a fucking disgrace. Had the greasy feel of a we-never-close diner to it, offensive to the sensibilities of anyone who cared anything about the quality of the air he breathed and a sanitary environment and general tranquillity. Which he did.

But remembering the guiding principle of his professional life— you go where the business says you go—D'Marco sat there anyway, sipping an orange juice (which was certainly not fresh-squeezed and was probably sugared, judging by the taste) and waiting. It was one o'clock, less than an hour remaining. He was beginning to experience some of the gathering rush that comes with the onset of a new assignment, particularly one like this that promised to be lucrative. He was ready. Out in the lot the LX was gassed and serviced. In it were three bags, four if you counted the gym bag. Two contained clothes and other necessaries for an extended stay, the third his working gear, just about all of it, for he had received no specific instructions yet on how this double pop was to be handled and, like any good craftsman, he liked to be prepared for any eventuality. Some people wanted a quick clean clip, a no-muss-no-fuss; others preferred a stinging. It was the hallmark of his work that he always gave the client what he asked for, and often as not with the singular D'Marco Fontaine stamp, like with Andy the other night. The gym bag he brought along in case an opportunity to sneak in a workout presented

itself, as it very well might. Two weeks of tracking, there was
bound to be some down time. The one advantage to the nurse-
maiding side job, only one he could see outside the ten long, was
he could maybe put this Chicago mule onto covering the marks
and now and then get some of that slack time to himself, not fall
too far behind training-wise. That of course would depend totally
on the level of smarts evidenced, and with somebody named Sigurd Stumpley you didn't want to get your hopes too high. Well,
nothing to be done about it now. Another hour tell the tale on
that one.

Shoehorned into a seat custom-designed for a dwarf, swollen
head, pouchy eyes, dumpster mouth, hippo breath, sour stomach,
calcified bowels—for B. Epstein it was not shaping up one of your
better days. Make that years. Been a slum of a year, when he
thought about it, which he was trying not to do, trying instead to
follow the philosophy of his own advice, so freely dispensed to
his partner, which advice, reduced to its essence, resembled the
Henry Ford, Sr., judgment on history, which in Epstein para-
phrase was to declare that one's personal past is, equally, bunk.
What went down, went down; can't bring it up again (he sermon-
ized himself, though given the bilious condition of his viscera,
even he recognized the image was infelicitous). What matters is
now or, more pointedly, two weeks from now. Got to look ahead,
focus on them fourteen days, turn up a solution. You don't, you
got a engraved invite to the Dietz garden party—main course:
worms.
   Yet in spite of his best efforts at concentration, no solutions
occurred to him, and his thoughts perversely remained rutted in
the past. This time twelve months ago everything was running
slick as dog spit: dozen broads working regular; three or four
steady players, Waverly easily the best of the lot, producing some
nice change; book churning loot; little juice pacifying the local
heat. Key Line Services, Ink, which was to say himself, doing just
fine, thank you. Better'n fine—sensational. Shit, his old man, who
he hadn't thought about in years, decades maybe, and who he
was thinking about now, God knows why, be real proud, he could
see how far this Jewboy had come.
   But that was twelve months ago. Take a good scope on him
now and what do you see? Key Line Services gone toes, eleven
small left in the till, every well tapped dry and every note and
favor called in. Look at the numbers. A big two-and-a-half balloons in the red. And an even bigger fourteen days—thirteen now,

you counted yesterday, and for sure Dietz was—looming bigger the more it shrunk. And a Prussian collector waiting on delivery, sooner turn you into a lampshade than give you the steam off his shit. Fuck, who wants to look down the road, that view?

Bitch of it was, none of it was any of his doing. What had he done? Teamed with Waverly, who was about as standup a goy as you're gonna find. Couldn't deny that. Two years celling and scamming in Jacktown City and four more minting money in Florida testified to that. And goy or not, he had to admit he'd always sort of liked Waverly, even if he couldn't pack in the cards without getting himself in the glue. That liking part, that was probably his biggest mistake, probably where he went wrong. Year ago, this time, they were wiping their butts with fifty-dollar bills (another unfortunate image, his burdened bowels reminded him), and then he has to go up to Michigan and tangle with some cornmeal talent turns out to be on the Dietz payroll. Sets off an atom bomb up there and brings the fallout home with him. Trouble is, as he'd discovered in Illinois, that fallout ain't confined to Timothy Waverly. Nosir, it's catching.

So you follow it back far enough and that's all he'd done—been a goddamned good Samaritan, way your Bible says to do. That's what he'd done, sum total. Look where it got him: ass-deep in the quicksand pit in the Dietz jungle and nobody on the bank throwing him a rope or an oar or a branch or whatever it was they threw in the fucking jungle, and he wasn't hearing no Tarzan rescue call coming through the bush either. Where's old Tarzan when you need him? Ripping one off with Jane, his luck, or buggering Cheetah.

Twice during these morose meditations a distant stirring in his lower regions, heralded by a muffled gust of flatus, extended the taunting promise of relief, and he got out of his seat and swayed down the aisle, making for the john. False alarms, both times. Both trips, though, he got a good look at the Chicago tag player hunched against a window and pretending not to notice. Wasn't gonna win no academy awards, that performance. Which came as no surprise, since it was the same weenie who'd been on him most of the week and who sure as shit (which he was beginning to believe offered no guarantees itself anymore, like everything else in his upended life) couldn't be no shooter. Not a burned-out bulb like that, carrying all that tonnage. Didn't make him feel any better, though; Florida wasn't exactly short on shooters.

Later the chocolate drop came by and he ordered a Bloody Mary, see if it would settle him down some, get his head right. In

normal times he'd of jived her a little, got her to grinning, flashing
them eyeballs and teeth. Nice piece dark meat like that, normal
times he'd give her his card, maybe line her up for some part-
time employment. He'd had stews on the Key Line roster before,
and some of 'em worked out real good. Layover work, haw haw.

But times wasn't normal no more. Best he could do for right
now was get himself home, get his system blasted out, get some
space to think things through. You want to talk space, how you
gonna think on a goddam airplane? Can't even smoke, f'Chrissake. He wished he could fire up a cigar, go with the Mary. Since
he couldn't, he nursed it along, and before it was finished a voice
came crackling over the intercom, alerting them to their immi-
nent arrival.

Assuming an hour would be more than enough time to get to
the airport, and remembering last night's injunction to keep down,
Waverly didn't leave the Tropicaire apartment until one o'clock
that afternoon. His assumption was wrong. The narrow streets
behind the Ocean Mall were congested, and it took what seemed
like five minutes just to make a left onto Blue Heron Boulevard.
It didn't get any better across the bridge. I-95 of course moved
faster, the traffic hurling furiously into the midday heat, but then
an accident north of the Okeechobee exchange, a jackknifed semi,
slowed everything first to a crawl, then a dead halt. He sat there
tapping the wheel impatiently. Time ticked by. The Seville's windows were not tinted ("I want 'em all to see it's Captain B. Epstein
pilotin' this sucker," went the Bennie rationale), and a dazzle of
sun glinted off the pink hood. From what he remembered of their
middle-of-the-night conversation, its ominous tones, he had to
wonder if Bennie wouldn't regret that decision, among several
others, now.

Eventually the line of cars began to creep forward, funneled
into a single lane. Soon they were accelerated, barreling again,
and he pulled into the PBI lot with twenty minutes to spare. Ten
of them, however, were consumed searching for a spot. A bag-
lugging citizen finally appeared and surrendered one, and Waverly parked and took off sprinting for the terminal.

So it was a breathless and somewhat sweaty Timothy Waverly
who stood at the designated gate on the upper level of the concourse, three minutes before the scheduled arrival time. A crowd
was gathering near the entrance, seniors mostly, the men in gaudy
sport shirts, their ladies in filmy blouses, both sexes often as not
in shorts that exposed mushy thighs and vein-latticed calves bet-

ter left concealed. Unmistakable Florida sorts, so machine-stamped they were hardly worthy of a second glance.

The sole exception was a rather smartly dressed young man who stood apart from everyone else, his back to the guard rail overlooking the main floor. Waverly took special notice of him. The cut of the clothes suggested that underneath was a body bursting with health, a kind of brute vigor. He had the treacherous good looks of a born-to-the-business thug, the slicked black hair, honed features, the remote, carefully cultivated absence of expression, giving away nothing. The Outlaw Look. Waverly had seen it before, in the Jacktown yard and elsewhere, many a time. Predictably, the eyes were shrouded by opaque lenses, but Waverly would have given odds those eyes were all but vacant of light. Dead eyes. Or eyes that bespoke death.

Waverly moved to a spot along the facing wall, where he could watch him. There had been many coincidences in his life, but he suspected this was not going to be one of them. He could be wrong of course, but he was not ready to bet on it.

The seat belt sign came on and the plane began its long, slow descent. Sigurd's ears were doing strange things, none of them pleasant. His forehead was pressed against the window. Tufted clouds sailed on by, airy and unsubstantial as dreams. Down below, the earth was laid out in moss-green rectangles. They passed over an enormous blue lake. Small settlements appeared, more moss, then larger ones, shrinking pockets of moss, and then suddenly that was all he could see, settlement, city, mile after mile of it, block after block, sprawling south to the rim of the horizon. Not a trace of the gray, poisoned haze that blurred Chicago. They dipped lower. Everything came into sharper focus. Vehicles moved like tokens on a giant Monopoly board. The round blue eyes of backyard pools gazed up at him, winked as they caught the sunlight. The coastline appeared. A strand of beach teemed with figures, matchsticks scattered randomly across the yellow sand. White triangles flecked a sapphire sea. Florida. Living fucking color. Ears dinging or not, he was here at last.

The plane did a steep curve over the ocean and went into a long glide, and in a moment they were on the ground. Mindful of his charge, Sigurd broke the line of passengers spilling into the aisle and kept a keen eye trained on Epstein, four bodies ahead of him. His own body felt tight and stiff, like he'd been wedged into a packing crate. He desperately needed a smoke. For a while nothing happened, no movement. Then slowly they started inching forward. He saw the coon princess up by the exit, dispensing farewells through a set smile. When it came his turn Sigurd said, "You wanna come along, hey, do some more flyin' tonight?" figuring why not, don't cost nothing to ask. The answer was a nerd-squashing look and a clipped goodbye, smartass heavy on the *bye* half. Fucking uppity niggers. He had his way, they'd bring back slavery.

No time to brood on it, though. For a sack of shit like that, Jewbaby scooted along real fast. Sigurd caught up to him near the end of the ramp and hung in close as they came through the entrance to the gate. The people up ahead were fanning out, some of them falling into shrieking welcoming embraces, others heading purposefully for the corridor, a few, like Epstein and like himself, just standing there looking orphaned. This was the crunch part. Part Uncle Eugene had warned him about. What he had to do was make the connection and at the same time not lose the kike. Two things at once.

He shook loose a cigarette, lit it, parked it toughly in a corner of his mouth, and stood with his hands in his pockets, nervously rearranging his nuts. The crowd swirled around him. He felt a faint stirring of panic, and then he felt a light touch on his arm and he turned and looked into a face hard-jawed and handsome enough to be up on a movie screen.

"You'd be Sigurd."

"Yeah, right, correct. Frog?"

"Name's D'Marco. Call me that." Voice was curt, soldierly. No nonsense allowed. Not your best sign.

"Sure, man," Sigurd said. "Call you anything you want."

"That the mark?" the movie star said with a short nod past Sigurd's shoulder.

Sigurd turned again and through the gradually thinning crowd he saw the Jewboy with some guy over by the check-in counter. "That's the one," he confirmed. "How'd you tell?"

"Educated guess."

"His name's Bennie Epstein. Don't know who the other dude is."

"I already got his name," D'Marco said ungraciously. "Other one's probably the badass player."

"Him? Don't look like much."

Behind the blue blocks, D'Marco was staring at them steadily. Assessing. "Yeah, well," he drawled, "they never do. Come on, they're leaving."

D'Marco in the lead, they set out following the pair. Sigurd was obliged to step smartly just to keep up. In the corridor he caught a glimpse of the black stewardess strutting along arm-in-arm with a tall blond beach boy, another movie star, snuggling up to him. Jesus, it was fucking disgusting, colored and white together like that, right out in plain view, like they was proud of it or something. With an effort, he pushed it out of his mind. Back to business.

On the stairs leading to the baggage claim he said, for something to say, for his new partner didn't seem to be exactly what you'd call a lip-flapper, "You have any problem makin' me?"

Without looking at him D'Marco replied, "No, your T-shirt, it shows up good."

"Been a real hoot if everybody on the airplane turn out to be a Bears fan," Sigurd said. "All of 'em come off wearin' these shirts. Like in them comedies you see." He grinned hugely at the thought.

Now D'Marco gave him a sidelong glance. But no responsive grin. "Think maybe I'd've spotted you anyway," he said, matter-of-fact and more contempt than mirth in it.

"Yeah? How's that?"

"Instinct."

A flock of anxious travelers milled around a U-shaped baggage belt. Epstein and friend among them. At the moment, the belt was motionless. D'Marco asked Sigurd how many bags he had.

"One is all. Crammed full. Florida fun and sun, hey."

From under a curling lip D'Marco said, "Okay. Get in there and get set to pick it up when they come through. Stand over on the other side from those two. I'm going to lay back here, cover them."

"You got it."

D'Marco watched him thread through the crowd, moving with a rocking, cheeks-jiggling, side-to-side waddle, the way some fatties, too stupid to know enough to be ashamed, move. Watched him take a wide-legged stance and stand there with thumbs hooked in a belt overhung by blubber. Watched as he removed one of the hands and brought it to the side of his bowling ball head and dug a finger in an ear, withdrew it, and examined the find as carefully as if he'd extracted a precious stone. Thinking dismally of the upcoming two weeks in the company of this major hick, looming ahead like two light-years, and thinking also how hard it was to turn a decent dollar these days.

And the ear-gouging Sigurd, for his part, was thinking how this Florida whacker he'd been hearing so much about didn't look nothing like he'd expected, for sure nothing like the heavy hitters he'd seen in Chicago or in Stateville. Whereas them boys all looked exactly like what they was, which was street scrappers, veterans, sported a zipper or two to prove it, this one looked like he could as easy be a dick merchant serviced rich old ladies for a living, or a sissy actor playing at Mr. Mean. Hard-on talker, okay, but talk's your basic El Cuffo, don't show nothing. Just being from Florida and being a mint in the looks and build department don't make you bad. Don't make you no Gunter Dietz. You wanted bad, there was bad. So Sigurd figured what he'd do was wait and see, take direction, sure, because he was off his turf and because that's what Uncle Eugene said to do, but he wasn't gonna squat down and produce tailor-made turds on order either. He'd been around the corner couple times himself, wasn't nobody's chump. Was who he was, Sigurd Stumpley, no more, no less, what you see is what you get, take it or go diddle yourself.

Bennie chewed at the torpedo of a cigar projecting from his mouth. The sausage fingers of his hands coiled and uncoiled, fisting air. At the startup lurch of the belt he stiffened like a rabbit caught in the headlights of an onrushing car. In all their years of association Waverly had never seen him like this: tight, jagged-edged, skittish, uncharacteristically silent. In the past his eternal yea-sayer friend had always managed somehow to extract a nugget of cheer (or at the very least some twisted dark humor) from the abundant dross of life's insults and reversals. Not now. Silent Bennie. Which was like saying anorexic Nigerian, or thieves' honor, or legal ethics. Classic oxymoron.

Bags came winding around the loop, vanished behind a portal in the wall, reappeared through another. Across from them and on either side travelers seized theirs and departed, wearing those complacent smiles immensely relieved people will often wear. No B. Epstein bag.

"All's I need, top off this sensational holiday, is for 'em to lose it," Bennie growled.

"Relax," Waverly said. "It'll be here."

"Relax. Easy for you to say."

They continued to stare at the belt, its hypnotic snaking motion and its dwindling cargo. Moment by moment, bag by bag, the crowd shrank around them. "It ain't comin'," Bennie said heavily, miserably.

"Give it one more turn."

They did, and the bag appeared. Bennie yanked it off the belt and without a word, though with considerable wheezing, stalked toward the nearest exit. Waverly offered a hand, got a snapped rejection: "Nah, nah, I got it. Let's just get the fuck outta here."

With the errant bag safely in the trunk of the Seville, they headed north on I-95, Waverly behind the wheel. He drove slowly, cautiously, keeping to the right lane. Traffic whizzed past them. Waves of heat rose from the highway, shimmered in the blaze of afternoon light. Occasionally he stole a glance at Bennie sitting there hump-shouldered, gazing stonily ahead, filling the car's interior with blue cigar vapor but not his usual torrent of words. Best to go along with it, Waverly decided, let it come when it would. And of course eventually it did.

"You make 'em, back there?" Bennie said as they were approaching the Blue Heron exit.

"I think so. One with the glasses, shoulders on him?"

"That's gotta be him. Also the fireplug got off the plane with me, looks like a turnip seed. You catch him?"

"I did. Matter of fact, they're right behind us now. Black Mustang. I wouldn't look."

"Nobody's lookin'," Bennie said grimly.

"Want me to try and lose them?"

"Nah, you ain't no wheel man, you couldn't shake 'em. Wouldn't mean shit anyhow. Can't drive away from this one."

"You going to tell me what's going on?"

"When we get to your place."

"My place?"

Since he had unloaded his own condo a few weeks back (taking a serious wash on the selling price too, as he'd been quick to let Waverly know), Bennie had been staying at the Singer Island Hilton, and Waverly naturally assumed that's where he'd want to go now. Another mistaken assumption.

"Right, your place. Here on out it's su casa mi casa, amigo. We ain't got the scratch for nothin' else no more."

At the Tropicaire apartment Bennie heaved his bag onto the sofa and made straight for the john, patting his lardy rump and declaring, "I got a charge a TNT in here about to blow." Actually, the rude sounds emanating from the other side of the door were more on the order of volcanic eruptions, Krakatoa magnitude. Waverly retreated to the window. He parted the verticals and saw the black Mustang parked across the street, a memento mori idling in the empty drive of the empty hotel. Impossible to make out anything behind the murky glass. He moved away from the window. Krakatoa—or was it Vesuvius now, or Mt. St. Helens?— proceeded to rumble and blast.

About a quarter of an hour later Bennie came out mopping his sweat-beaded brow and bald pate with a damp towel. "Whew!" he exclaimed. "Jesus! Listen, do yourself a service, stay outta there awhile. Think I shit a rat."

"I heard," Waverly said.

"I swear my asshole got a built-in radar, gets north a Jupiter it knows automatic, corks up like a cell-block door slammed shut on it."

"South of Jupiter it seems to function pretty well."

"Thank the Big Warden upstairs, small favors. Whaddya got to eat here?"

Waverly gestured toward the kitchenette. "Whatever you can turn up. Help yourself."

Bennie went around the counter, flipped the towel into the sink, and ransacked the cupboards and refrigerator. Waverly watched him, thinking there was going to be a whole lot of togetherness in this abbreviated space. And wondering how long it was going to last.

"Think I'll sink a beer," Bennie called from behind the open refrigerator door. "You?"

"None for me."

He came back toting a box of Wheat Thins, a slab of cheese, and a can of Coors. "Your Publix Market this place ain't, food-wise," he said, kicking off his shoes and settling into the La-Z-Boy.

Waverly put the bag on the floor and sat on the sofa, facing him. Waiting for the somber travelogue to unroll.

"Sure you won't join me in a cold one?"

"I don't want any beer, Bennie. What I want is to hear where we stand."

"Might go down easier with a beer."

Waverly threw up his hands. "You going to talk or be coy?"

"Okay," he said through a mouthful of cheese. "Now we talk."

"Y'know," Sigurd ventured, "we ain't exactly under the heavy wraps here."

No response.

He gave it a moment and tried again, more explicit this time. "What I'm sayin' is all they got to do is peek out that front window there and we're smoked." The way he saw it, they were violating every sound principle of tracking he'd ever heard of, and he felt an obligation to speak up. After all, part of this action belonged to him too.

In a flat, toneless, and utterly indifferent voice D'Marco said, "One of them's doing that right now."

Sigurd leaned into the dash and cupped a hand over his eyes and squinted through the windshield at the boxy bungalow across the street. "No shit. Where? I don't see nobody." Tinted glass or not, he was having trouble adjusting to the brilliant, eyeball-piercing light down here. Fucking sun like a clenched fist of it in the white glare of sky. Never been a sun like that in Chicago.

"Too late. You missed him."

"See, what'd I say? Knew that was gonna happen, way you was ridin' their ass on the road back there. Sittin' out here so plain Stevie Wonder could see us. Might as well send 'em over our jackets and mug shots."

"You think this Epstein hasn't got you made already?"

"Yeah. I mean no, I think—know—he ain't."

D'Marco expelled a scornful puff of air. "Dick is what you know."

"Dick?" Sigurd said indignantly. "Yeah, well, I know they get spooked, wasn't me done it, hey."

Another sneery exhalation. "You got a lot to learn, Chubbo. Spooked is how you want them, long-term job like this one. Spark a little fear. Case they get any vanishing ideas."

"Okay, say you're right, which I ain't sayin', but say you are. Now we got 'em for sure spooked, now what we gonna do?"

For Sigurd, sitting cramped and stiff in the thimble-sized seat, the question was more than academic, for in spite of the air going in the car he was still hot and sticky and his limbs ached and his boxers were creeping into his asshole and his bladder was backed all the way up to his Adam's apple. Add beat to that. Travel, he was discovering, made you horny but it knocked you out too. Shower and a little snooze be good right about now.

"Do?" D'Marco said. "Tell you what we're going to do. I'm going to stroll over there and have a word with the manager, find out what kind of arrangement they got. What you're going to do is stay right here. Keep your eyes open. Don't move. See what other good ideas you can come up with. Think you can manage that?"

He didn't wait for an answer. He cut the engine, pocketed the keys, got out, and sauntered across the road in the direction of the bungalow with the Manager sign in the window. Sigurd's glower followed him. Look at him, moving in that fluid easy roll, like he didn't know the sun was blitzing him, or didn't care. Like he had air condition built right into his clothes. Immediately the car flooded with suffocating heat. Cockfucker done it on purpose, Sigurd thought bitterly. Could've left it running. Chubbo, was he, didn't know dick? Florida wiseass. Now the wiseass was knocking on the manager's door. Now he was inside.

For perhaps five minutes, maybe fewer, Sigurd sat there as instructed, sweltering, frying, his breath coming in progressively heavier gasps. And then he said to himself Fuck it, life's too fuckin' short; and in open defiance of those instructions he stepped out of the car and into the full ferocity of the Florida heat. About twenty yards from the car was the canopy above the main entrance to the Collonades. Some small relief. He walked hurriedly that way, sweat streaking down his chest, eyes stinging from the intensity of the sudden fiery light. It was a little better there in the shade, not a whole lot. Least his vision was coming back, even if slowly. Be here two weeks, he was going to for sure have to get himself a pair of them Hollywood goggles, kind Mr. Wiseass wore. Either that or go home leashed to one of them seeing-eye dogs.

He stood lounging against one of the square white pillars, smoking his first cigarette since the airport, since he'd been told, coldly and firmly, smoking wasn't allowed in the car. Top of everything else, Wiseass was a little old lady too. There was absolutely nothing happening across the road, either bungalow, but out of the corner of one eye he thought he detected a slight movement. He stuck his head around the paint-bubbled edge of the pillar and found himself face to face, eyeball to tiny eyeball, with a fearsome green lizard, no more than three inches separating them, and it so startled him he let out a terrified squawk and sprang away gasping, but now not for breath. Jesus holy fuck, what kinda place is this anyways, crawling with peewee dragons? He was aware suddenly of the immense looming presence of the deserted hotel, the sheer size of it, its graveyard silence. He backed up to the door, turned cautiously, and peered through the dusty glass. He could make out a lobby and a desk and what seemed to be an entrance to a bar. A long corridor led to an enormous glassed-in dining room. White tablecloths still covered the tables and some of them, near as he could tell, appeared even to have place settings, as if a ghostly banquet were about to begin or maybe in progress right now. Phantoms feasting. Place was so fucking creepy he half-expected to see cups and forks and knives floating in air, see linen napkins dabbing daintily at unseen lips, hear phantom voices rising through the empty gloom.

But it was a real voice that shook him back into the world he understood as palpable, material, real, a harsh and insolent voice, saying, "You looking to book a room?" He spun around and there stood Wiseass, materialized out of nowhere, staring at him (or at least looking like he was staring at him, them blackout shields, how you gonna tell?), a dangerous wicked smirk on his face.

"Marks're over there," D'Marco said, wagging a thumb over his shoulder. "Remember?"

"Yeah, sure. Course I remember."

"That's real promising, you remember that. How is it, then, you don't remember what I told you to do, which was to stay in the car, watch them?"

"I did," Sigurd said defensively. "Got too goddam hot in there."

"Too hot. Okay. See we got to lay out some ground rules here. First one's easy: You don't follow directions, you're going to find out what real heat is. And you're not going to like it. You got my money-back guarantee on that. You with me so far?"

Sigurd nodded yes.

"Good," D'Marco said, turning away and starting for the car. "Come on."

Sigurd fell in behind him. "Where we headed?"

"You'll see."

"This Dietz," Bennie began, "he ain't long on your basic patience and charity virtues."

"You met him?"

"Oh yeah."

"How did you arrange that?"

"Through my contact up there. And lemme tell you, Timothy, goin' a couple rounds with him about cured my dumpin' problem right on the spot."

"How do you read him?"

"With Dietz it's read 'im and weep. See, what you got to picture in your mind here is a world-class storm trooper, kinda guy you say Hello, he says Sieg Heil. Wears his jackboots to bed. All the time we was talkin', he was eyein' me like I was a bar your Dial soap. I got a suspicion he ain't strong on affection for us chosen people."

"So what does he want?"

"Wants what's his."

Waverly turned over empty palms, a gesture of impossibility. "I can't give him what's gone, Bennie. I explained that. You knew that going in."

"Yeah, I know it and you know it. Trick is gettin' *him* to know it. Make that buy it. That was five hundred balloons worth of snow you torched, Timothy, Michigan."

"And we agreed to pay for it, right? Full damages."

"More'n agreed. He's already got it."

"But it's not enough," Waverly said flatly, no question implied. "Not near enough."

"Then why don't you cut to the chase, Bennie, tell me what is enough. Make it plain."

"You want plain? Try a three hundred K gratuity, fifty which I hadda give him up front. Meanin' we're runnin' on eleven thin and whatever we're carryin' on our hips. Meanin' empty. That plain?"

When this conversation first began, Bennie's voice had been reasonably calm, considering the message. Waverly attributed that encouraging signal partly to the steadying influence of the food and beer, partly to the salutary effect of the recently evacuated bowels, and partly also to what he assumed was the gradual surfacing of his friend's unflagging optimism, the natural buoyancy of the man who persists in seeing life through the optical illusion of hope. Now, however, the voice was risen to an agitated skirl, a piping tremor riding through it. "Two hundred fifty thousand," Waverly said. "How much time?"

"Try on two weeks, see how it fits."

"Two weeks!" Waverly said, stunned. He could feel the tremor invading his own voice. "Two?"

"Count 'em."

Waverly shook his head slowly. "Can't be done. Not off an eleven thou stake."

"Even if it could, we're outta business here, you remember, thanks to that steam you generated up north. Badges ain't exactly fast on renewin' our license, not last I heard."

"What if we were to make a lunge for the exit?"

"C'mon, you know better'n that. You seen that shooter out to the airport."

"All right. Out of the action, no place to run—what do you suggest?"

"Got no suggestin' to do. You been to college, I was hopin' maybe you'd have some thoughts."

"Fresh out," Waverly said, though in fact a desperate notion was stirring in what he had believed was a permanently sealed crypt in his head.

"Look, this Dietz, he ain't sellin' no wolf tickets. Right now we're still on the friendly side a disaster. Two weeks' insulation.

But when it comes time to own up, you own up. Either that or turn up mort. That's just how it is, Timothy, so you better get to like it."

Waverly said nothing. He was slumped back on the couch, gazing numbly at a palmetto bug in leisurely residence on the counter, thinking about Caroline and Robbie and Jock Appelgate, and remembering the taunting challenge issued last night and the offhand mention of a card-slinging Arab, possibly an even bigger fish, and thinking of all the risks and hazards and pitfalls ahead of him, and thinking also of the curious shifts and turns in human fortune generally, his own particularly, and how all life—his, anyway—was finally nothing more than one long false start.

"You listenin' to what I'm tellin' you here?"

"What?"

"Two weeks, man. I'm askin' for some ideas."

Waverly lifted his face from the bug and fixed in on the face of his friend, and what he saw was a droopy face scored by worry, fatigue, strain, dread. "You know, Bennie," he said quietly, "you were the innocent bystander in all this. Mushroom caught in a driveby crossfire. For that, I'm sorry. For what it's worth, I apologize."

Bennie brushed at air with a meaty hand. "Aah, that don't matter. Coulda been the other way around. You and me, we got a history. But we gotta scare up something, as in pronto Tonto, or this time it's all wrote."

"I think there may be a way. Very long odds."

"Long's better'n zip."

11

Directly to the north of the once resplendent Collonades Hotel was a considerably more modest establishment known as the Sea Spray Inn. The sign above its entrance (yellow on black and topped by a gold crown reminiscent of the trademark of a certain margarine) announced its affiliation with the Best Western chain, and unlike its derelict neighbor, the Sea Spray remained a thriving hostelry. It offered such amenities as a heated pool, a communal sun deck dominated by a canopied refreshment station, access to the "widest and cleanest beach you'll ever see" (so its brochure claimed, not so modestly), a rooftop lounge and dining room, appropriately if none too imaginatively named Top O' Spray, with a "magnificent view overlooking the beach and ocean" (another brochure assertion), and of course three floors of guest rooms. Each room came with two extra-length double beds, color TV, Touch Tone phone, a pair of sturdy upholstered chairs, an octagonal table adorned with a basket of artificial flowers, a large dresser, a small bath, and on the exterior wall a brace of windows and a glass slider opening onto a private deck. In the second-floor room situated on the extreme southwest corner of the building, a figure stood at a window overlooking neither sand nor sea but rather a scraggly palm tree, a wing of the untenanted Collonades that even in the harsh morning light appeared eerie, and diagonally across the sun-blistered road, the Tropicaire Apartments. The figure was male. He was scowling. Clearly not happy. He was D'Marco Fontaine.

D'Marco's sour temper arose not from what he saw through the window. That was pretty much what he expected: the pimp-wagon Caddie still parked in the same spot, no sign of unusual activity in or around the bungalow. Pretty routine. Pretty dull. By now the marks had the message, understood he was out here some-where, on watch, wasn't going to go away. Their personal cancer. Terminal variety. His instructions were to give them a little slack, not too much, and that's what he was doing. From everything he'd got out of Chicago and from his own seasoned judgment, D'Marco had them sized up as savvy enough players not to try and run any games on him. Not yet anyway; that would come later, at showdown time, and by then it would be far too late. For a little added insurance he had the manager wired in, hot line, in case they had some cute sudden moves in mind. Last night he'd phoned Chicago and reported what there was to report, which wasn't much: snag-free connection and identification, so far an easy tracking. Also he'd collected his expense and babysitting monies, so that piece of critical business was accounted for. So for the moment all the bases were covered and everything was under control, jobwise. So that wasn't the reason for the intense displeasure he was feeling just then.

No. The reason was obvious and easy to pinpoint, for it was right in this very room, right behind him, right *here*. The reason was this . . . this . . . what the fuck could you call him would do justice to so odious a presence? Champion jagoff, heavyweight class? Gross and disgusting whale? Superrube? Certainly not part-ner, for D'Marco Fontaine had no partners and never would, needed no one, wanted no one, was sufficient to himself. Call him what, then? The answer came from a buried childhood memory returned to him out of nowhere, an image of his mother, pinched, dolorous, long-suffering, Bible-cuffing (for she was too routed by life ever to be a thumper) woman who explained away life's man-ifold miseries and burdens and defeats with a simple all-purpose dictum: cross to bear. And now, years later, he understood at last what she meant. Sigurd Stumpley—his own unique cross to bear in the interminable days ahead. Reason enough for a dismay shad-ing over near to despair.

He turned away from the window and surveyed a room that, for all his heroic efforts to preserve at least a semblance of order, appeared to have been swept by a whirlwind. The floor was strewn with indifferently stepped-out-of clothes, a sock here, T-shirt there, even a pair of dirty shorts (boxers!—nobody wore boxers!). Remnants of a late-night, ordered-in snack—fish sticks, fries, puddle of slaw—littered the table. Beer cans graced the nightstand and dresser top. Ashtrays spilled over. A room reduced overnight to chaos, ruin.

The author of it all, the cross, sat thrown back in a chair, bare feet propped on a crumpled heap of covers on an unmade bed, bulgy eyes fastened in transfixed gaze on a blaring television, mouth a gaping chute into which was periodically, unconsciously, thrust a rapidly shrinking Hostess Nutty HoHo followed immediately by a wash of Royal Crown Cola. This morning he was outfitted in orange Bermudas so radiant they looked to be waxed, and a fresh T-shirt that bore the oafish legend: *liquor up front, poker in the rear.* The shirt had crept up, exposing a buttery roll of belly peaked by a jewel of a navel wreathed in tufts of wiry red hair.

Overcome by a sick revulsion at everything he saw, D'Marco said, "Jesus, how can you stand to live in this hog wallow? Jesus!"

As if in mocking echo, the television gave him back a chanted *Jee-zus Jee-zus.* On the screen a swaying, eyeball-rolling, God-intoxicated black preacher petitioned his Maker with quivery uplifted arms, and behind him an undulating choir belted out an exultant raucous anthem.

"I'm tellin' ya," Sigurd said, ignoring the question, "anybody say them darkies ain't got natural rhythm, I say he got his head up his ass. Lookit 'em do the Jesus boogaloo there, hey."

D'Marco sank into the other chair. He stared at the screen full of wildly writhing black bodies, thinking if you took away the choir robes and put them in jockstraps or G-strings or whatever it was those natives in Africa wore you could as easy be looking at a tribe of Zulus doing a war dance. However, he had no intention of giving away anything to this lardball beside him, so he said, "Ahh, that's what you call a myth. They got no more rhythm than you or me or anybody else."

"Listen, that's a true fact. It's in science. I read it someplace. Anyway, I been around enough of 'em to know."

"Yeah, where's that?" D'Marco didn't really give a fuck, but it was a way to pass some of the down time, which on the best of jobs always made him restless, edgy.

"Joint."

"You were in the joint?" D'Marco said skeptically.

"Yeah, small-change stretch. How 'bout you? You ever done time?"

"No."

"Well, I ain't recommendin' it," Sigurd said, voice husky with the resonances of an experience rueful and vast. "Particularly guy like you, all them fine muscles you got. Them blackjacks have you drawn, spread, and reamed before you could say Martin Luther Coon."

"Huh, that'd be the day," D'Marco snorted, remembering how his very first pop, years ago, had been on a spade, some rollover, probably had it coming anyway. But apart from that episode, which was purely business, he had nothing against your coloreds, never thought about them one way or the other.

"You think it be the day. Inside, they outnumber you ten to one. Just like they gettin' to do out here, free world. Up my way, you do down the Loop you're lucky to see a white face anymore. Go down the South Side, it's Tanganfuckinyika, big time."

D'Marco had nothing to say to that. Racial issues, or for that matter anything unrelated to himself, held no interest for him whatsoever. Live and let live was his policy, except of course when it comes to business. There you had to be color-blind, equal-opportunity hitter. Anyway, he was getting sick of the subject.

Not so Sigurd, who said ruminantly, "Y'know, gotta be a lot a money be made off them people, you think about it. I ain't talkin' your regular street scams now. Everybody into that. Talkin' legit loot." For a moment his face creased under the burdensome weight of thought, and then a sudden inspiration seemed to come to him. "What a guy oughta do is make a movie for 'em."

"What country you from, dickbrain? They already done that. Made a hundred of them."

"Yeah, yeah, I know that, but what I'm thinkin' of here is a western. They ain't never made a western for 'em."

"Western? For spades?"

"Right, all black western," Sigurd said, and warmed by the creative fires his scenario unfolded spontaneously. "See, your movie starts with just this black screen, not a thing on it, black as a spook's ass. No music neither. Everything real quiet. Then you see a little line a light right across the bottom, like it's maybe a sun comin' up, an' you hear some music, real soft at first but what you can hear of it sounds like that hiphop music they play. Sorta like on the TV here. Okay. Then what you see is this little black dot, like, way the fuck off, can't make out what it is but it's comin' at you, slow-like but gettin' bigger all the time. Music gettin' little louder, not too much yet. Pretty soon you can tell it's a guy ridin' a horse, but it's still too fuckin' dark to see who he is. Music gettin' louder now too, an' the horse and the guy startin' to fill up the screen, light comin' up behind 'em. Finally you can see what it is—black horse, big black buck in the saddle, baddest nigger you ever want to see. An' just exactly when you can tell that for sure, when they cover the whole goddam screen, music goes nuts and on comes the title: *Ride, Muthafucka, Ride.*"

In the exhilarating rush of invention Sigurd's hands had been sweeping the air grandly. Now he leaned forward in the chair and laced them under his swell of stomach, as if to forestall its precipitate slide to the floor. He looked at D'Marco expectantly. "So whaddya think?"

"You're asking me what I think?" D'Marco said in a voice taken over by a harsh argumentative tone.

"Yeah. Honest opinion."

"Honest opinion. Okay. I think your movie sucks bad wind. Same as you do."

Now Sigurd looked surprised, even a little hurt. "Well, needs some work maybe. Gotta have your wagon trains, redskins, gun fights, all that good stuff." An image of the stewardess on the plane yesterday appeared to him. "Dance hall girl, black one course, you gotta have that too, a western. Like a, y'know, story."

"Spare me your fucking story."

"Hey, I'm tellin' ya, jiggers'd eat it up. It'd play."

"Play in a twitch factory," D'Marco sneered, wondering what he was doing, sitting here in the midst of this radical mess, actually listening to some goddam retard, brains of a smackhead, yammering about some goddam make-believe movie like it was real, like he was a goddam Hollywood producer or something. Talk about your twitch factories. Jesus, he was living in one. Worse, he was buying into it.

He got up out of the chair and returned to his post at the window. Some reality therapy. Except the scene across the road was unchanged. Absolutely no action, nothing going on. He rubbed a hand over his eyes. There seemed to be deep circles under them, which came as no surprise, badly as he'd slept last night. How do you sleep to a lullaby of honking, spluttering snores? Under his tight polo shirt he spread batwing lats, tensed a high shelf of pecs. They felt deflated. Three days without a workout, he was surely shrinking. A cigarette lighter snapped behind him. His nostrils twitched against the rising coils of smoke. "You got to do that in here?" he said, glancing distastefully over a shoulder that appeared also to be diminishing in size and width.

"I'm payin' half, I smoke in half."

"How is it your half is wherever I am?"

"Carry it with me, is how. Go take a leak, that's my half. Sit in front of the TV or out on the deck there, that's my half too. My half's where I'm at at the time. That's only fair."

D'Marco looked bullets at him. It was a measure of the control he'd lost over the past twenty-four hours that he had no ready argument for that irresistible logic. Another, surer measure was the room, slovenly enough to rattle a procession of saints. The scowl, which had never really left his face, deepened. "Look at this place," he said. "It's eleven o'clock. Where's the goddam maid?"

"C'mon, be cool. Sunday morning, she's pro'ly administerin' little church service to the guests. Church of the Open Twat, hey, haw haw. Ain't that how it's done, Florida?"

D'Marco was unwilling to dignify that with a reply. He turned back to the window, and just in time, too, for at that moment the fat one, Epstein, came out of the bungalow, got in the Caddie, and drove north on Ocean Avenue.

"Turn off the fucking TV," D'Marco barked.

Sigurd recognized instantly the back-to-work inflection in the gruff command. Too bad. He was just getting settled in and was still mentally plotting his epic western. He switched off the set and padded over to the window. "Something goin' on out there?"

"Yeah something going on. One of them just left."

"Which one?"

"Jew. Get away from me with that cigarette. Your half's not right next to me. And get your shoes on. I got a feeling we're going to be stepping quick-time here."

He was right. Inside of two minutes the other one came through the door, glanced to the right and left, and then set out up the street, moving at an unhurried pace. Sunday morning stroll. Sure. It was that quick glance gave him away.

"There he goes," D'Marco muttered mainly to himself. "Let's see what he's up to."

He wheeled around, feeling better at once, on firm familiar ground again: action, movement, pursuit. Business. Control. Till he saw his cross standing at the table, vanishing another HoHo and swilling the last of the soda. Standing there in his Superrube outfit, asinine T-shirt tucked in and a tube of fat spilling over the neon shorts. Superrube? Make that Superlout. His spirits suddenly sagged. "You going to wear that shirt?" he said.

"Yeah, it always gets the big yucks."

"Bet. Come on."

When they came out the Sea Spray entrance the mark was about a block up the street, heading, it appeared, for the Ocean Mall. They fell in behind, keeping a distance but keeping him in clear sight too. Already Sigurd was puffing from the exertion, heat. But still in lively humor. "Y'know," he said, "I was polishin' off that Royal Crown, I got to thinkin' another idea."

"Yeah, what's that?" D'Marco assumed he was talking about the task immediately at hand. He was wrong.

"What a fella oughta do is make this special pop just for your spookaroos, call it Nat King Cola. Pure watermelon juice. You didn't like the movie idea, whaddya think a that one?"

D'Marco stopped abruptly. He glared at Sigurd, who was grinning hugely, like a clown with a hard streak of malice in him. Behind his blue blocks D'Marco's eyes were cold as a winter sky. Voice the same temperature, he said, "Back there"—nodding in the direction of the Sea Spray—"you can play at being the asshole comedian all you want. Out here, business, you do what I say you do. Which is to scrub the comedy. You got that?"

Sigurd gave a compliant shrug. "You got 'er, chief."

From his table near the back of the Greenhouse, Waverly had an unobstructed view of the tranquil ocean and the feverish beach-rat parade. By contrast with the blaze of sunlight flooding the deck just beyond the glass wall, it was relatively dark back here and, relatively speaking, cool. The deck tables were beginning to fill, but except for himself and a few Sunday morning juicers at the bar, the interior of the place was empty. He had a ginger ale in front of him, pulled deeply on a cigarette. Breakfast. Cinched belt notwithstanding, his slacks, once a nice fit, were loose around the middle and his sport shirt felt baggy at the chest and shoulders. The Florida Gambling Man's Diet: how to lose weight through worry.

And worried he was. An hour earlier he had phoned the Breakers, fully expecting to get Robbie. Ten o'clock on a Sunday morning, it seemed a reasonable notion. Wrong again. Instead it was Caroline answered with the irritable, sleep-dazed intelligence that No, Robbie wasn't there, was golfing or something, she didn't know, what time was it, anyway? God! Who's calling? There was nothing to do but tell her, and instantly all the irritation vanished and an animation came into her voice. She was free for lunch, insisted they meet: You name the place, I'll be there. Bennie had some business to attend to, needed the car, so he named the Greenhouse. It was the only place nearby that came to mind. She'd never heard of it but she listened to his directions and said she'd find it, give her an hour, maybe a little more.

And so he sat there waiting, full of approach-avoidance misgivings. If he were to be entirely honest with himself (and that would be a switch), then he'd have to admit he wanted to see her again. But then that same elusive honesty would also impel him to the inescapable conclusion that the last thing needed in a life already in deep hazard and sorry disarray was yet another complication. Still and all, this was an innocent enough meeting—lunch, some nostalgia-tripping, nothing more. And it had a useful purpose too, when you thought about it, for he had to get to Robbie to get to Appelgate to get to the action that might, with any kind of luck, deliver him and a blameless partner from this perilous tangle he'd singlehandedly gotten them into. Or might not. So much for honesty, another familiar partner whispered in a cobwebbed room in a remote corner of his head.

It was close to noon when Caroline arrived, and by then he was on his third ginger ale and the Greenhouse was infested with people. All of the bar stools and most of the tables, inside and out, were occupied. Waitresses scurried about. Smoke thickened the air. Music throbbed. She stood in the entrance, looking a little hesitant, a little confused, as if she was having difficulty adjusting to the clamor and the sudden dim light. After a moment her eyes picked out his beckoning arm and she wound her way expertly through the crowded room and dropped into the chair opposite him, saying, somewhat breathlessly, "Sorry I'm late."

"It's all right. You have trouble finding this place?"

"None at all. It's the morning Lazarus syndrome. You know how that goes."

"I know."

"Sorry also for snapping when you called. Same syndrome."

Waverly raised an apology-arresting hand, and she gave him back a radiant smile, just a trace of fatigue in it. She wore ice-washed jeans and a man's denim shirt with the sleeves rolled up to the elbows. Tousled, honey-colored curls framed the fine planes of her face. Except for the peculiar lucent sheen in the eyes and the hands that made twittery flights in the air, it could have been the Caroline Vanzoren—not yet Crown—from twenty years ago sitting across from him now, a girl of extraordinary flair, remarkable elements, and many unexpected parts. No denying it, he was glad she was here.

A waitress appeared, hovered over them, tapped an impatient foot.

"What would you like?" he asked Caroline.

"Oh, anything. What do you have there?"

"It's a ginger ale."

She made a face. "No, not that. Better make it a Rusty Nail."

One of his eyebrows floated upward, and after the waitress was gone she said, lightly but with an edge of challenge, "You don't approve, morning drinking?"

"Didn't say a word."

"But you don't do it yourself."

"Not often. For me it's like watching morning TV. That's for me, you understand. I pass no judgment on anyone else."

"Well," she said, and her smile went meager, almost desolate, "it does get the engine cranked."

"That sounds like a Robbie turn of phrase," Waverly said and immediately wondered why he'd said it.

"I believe you're right," she said dreamily. "I believe that's where I heard it first."

At the party the other night they had discussed smoking. Today it was drinking. Deliberations on the vices. To turn the conversation in another, more expedient, direction, he said, "Speaking of Robbie, when do you expect him?"

"I really haven't any idea. Later this afternoon. Tonight. Why?"

"I need to talk to him. Today, if possible."

"It's only fair to tell you, Tim, Robbie's not heavy into old friendships anymore, old times. He's a deal maker now, man of business, substance. Maybe you noticed."

"I noticed, and I understand what you're saying. But this *is* business. Of a sort."

"Don't tell me you want to be one of his investors?"

"No, more like one of his entertainers."

"What does that mean?"

"Do you remember mention of a card game?"

"Only dimly. You'll have to fill me in."

"They're having a game this week, hosted, I gather, by Jock Appelgate. He invited me to play. I said no. Now I've changed my mind."

"What changed it for you?"

Before he could answer, the waitress was there with the drink. "You guys wanna order?" she asked.

"Caroline?"

"God, no. No food for me."

"You're sure about that?"

"I'm sure. But go ahead if you like."

He shook his head, and the waitress shrugged and hurried away.

"I thought we were having lunch," he said.

"Ah, lunch, that's an all-purpose term. Covers a multitude of things."

Careful choice of words there, *things* for the anticipated *sins*.

Waverly looked at her narrowly, trying to take a compass reading from an expression that gave away nothing other than a tightly contained melancholy behind the preternaturally bright, restive eyes.

"You really should eat something, Timothy. You're awfully skinny, you know."

She seemed to have forgotten her last question, which was just as well. "I choose to think of it as trim," he said.

"Face it, it's skinny."

"Yeah, well, okay. I'll embark on a serious training regimen, first thing tomorrow."

That got a short laugh. She pointed at her drink and said, "Do you want to say grace? It is Sunday."

"Why not just consider it said."

She brought the glass to her lips and took a sip, dainty but long. "Do you remember how our parents used to do that? Say grace, I mean."

"I remember it well."

"We always believed their world was so much wiser than ours. So much better."

"We were young."

"How's your father, Tim?"

"My father?" He was momentarily rattled by this sudden conversational fork. "My father's dead. Many years now."

"I'm sorry."

"Don't be. It wasn't your fault."

"Nevertheless, I am. I always admired your father."

"He was a decent man," Waverly said, thinking about him now, trying to picture him. "Very devout, very earnest. There are times, you know, when I'll pass a mirror and see what I'm sure is his face, looking out at me through my own. It can be startling."

"Isn't it strange how bits and pieces of your childhood come back to visit you? Your father, the reciting of a grace—like whispers on the wind. You forget how much you miss them." A moist disturbance came into her eyes. "Isn't that strange, Timothy?"

"What's wrong, Caroline?"

"Wrong? Nothing. Everything."

"It's you and Robbie."

"You noticed that too."

"Pretty hard to miss."

"I expect it must be."

Waverly had a sure sense of treading a dangerous path here,

but not a single graceful detour occurred to him, so he said, reluctantly, "Why do you stay?"

"Oldest excuse of them all: the kids. Did I tell you I have two lovely children?"

"I think you did."

"Would you like to see a picture? That's what you're supposed to do, isn't it, trade photos?"

"I understand that's the usual drill."

She reached into her purse, removed a wallet, flipped it open, and handed it to him. Under the clear plastic the photo revealed a stiff-looking boy in blue blazer and correct tie, mini-man, and an angel-faced girl in a frilly white dress. Both of them had fair hair and wide-margained Crown features. It was one of those rigid studio poses, and both of their smiles were counterfeit, induced.

"Handsome children," Waverly said. "Do I get vital statistics?"

"Jennifer's seven. She's her father's darling. Mine too."

"And the boy? What's his name?"

"Robbie Blake, of course. What else? He's ten. He's the troubled one."

"How's that?"

"At ten you pick up signals. He knows something's going on. He's a very unhappy child."

Waverly didn't know what to say to that so he said nothing. The photo ritual done, she returned the wallet to her purse. Took another long sip of the drink. Lit a cigarette. Brushed a hand across her eyes. He waited it out.

"You see," she said in a voice contemplative and even, voice of stoic reason, "it's my contention that most of us adults get just about what we've got coming. Pretty much what we deserve. If it were just the two of us, Robbie and me, I could walk away from this wreckage of a marriage without a look back. I could do that, I think." She paused, and a puff of carefully exhaled smoke trailed after her words like an editorial notation written on the air. "I know it's not fashionable to talk about sin anymore, but if there is such a thing, then it has to be the infliction of pain on innocent children. That's sin. Or all we have left of it. Can you understand that, Tim?"

"Better than many," Waverly said.

"Well, that's the long-winded answer to your question. That's why I stay. And that's your Calvinist sermon for this Sunday morning."

"I guess it's my turn to be sorry."

"No, it's your turn to tell a sorry tale. I want to hear what happened to you. What went wrong."

"What's to tell? I was married, I had a son, I was divorced. I behaved badly. It cost me seven years."

"But you're out of your prison now. I'm still in mine."

"Believe me when I tell you there's a difference."

"Your son. Where is he?"

"With his mother and her husband. In Michigan."

"Do you miss him?"

What do you say to that? These questions weren't about him. What she was looking for was a means of remapping the geography of the heart. For answers he didn't have. "He's better off where he is," Waverly said. "Sometimes I wish there were a way to, well, make it up to him. Everything I did. But there isn't. It's rather like a friend of mine says: 'That's just the way it is, man, so you better get to like it.' And that's *your* lesson for the day."

Caroline shook her head sadly. "What a pair we are, Timothy. Aren't you glad I asked you to lunch?"

"It was still a good idea."

"I think I need another drink."

Waverly looked around the room, searching for a waitress. None in evidence. Instead his roving glance fell on a wide-shouldered figure standing at the bar, watching them from behind the concealment of opaque sunglasses, wearing a twist of a smile venomous and thin. At the instant of eye contact, or what Waverly assumed was contact, no way to be sure, the man lifted a forefinger and touched the rim of his glasses lightly. Gesture of greeting. Ominous salute. In a world of desperate cruelty, certain payback, to expect anything less is certainly to be disappointed. Knowing that hard truth, accepting it, Waverly was shaken all the same. For a moment there he had almost forgotten. "Come on," he said, "we're leaving now."

Caroline looked baffled. "Leaving? We just sat down."

Waverly got out of his chair and laid some bills on the table. "Trust me," he said, "it's time to go."

When they first arrived at the Greenhouse, Sigurd and D'Marco took a table at the corner of the deck. D'Marco chose it deliberately because it had an awning and because its position allowed him to cover the entrances and, through the glass wall, most of the interior, including the table where Waverly sat. He was beginning to think of both the luckless marks by name now, which is what he liked to do whenever he could and especially on an extended assignment like this one. Helped him get into the job, personalize it, give it his own distinctive touch. Epstein and Waverly. An oinker and a badass. World going to be short one oinker and one badass by the time D'Marco Fontaine was finished. Small loss.

A waitress breezed over. "What'll it be?"

Sigurd, deferring to his mentor, asked, "We gonna get a chance to eat, you think?"

D'Marco could see Waverly had some kind of drink in front of him. He looked anchored to his chair, didn't seem to be in any hurry. Looked more like he was in a goddam trance or something. Probably scared out of his mind, as well he ought to be. Whether or not he'd spotted them yet, D'Marco couldn't tell for sure. "Do what you want," he said.

"Little chow sounds right." Sigurd turned to the waitress. "So what's your house special here, honey?"

"Everybody likes the conch fritters." Her eyes were drifting away from his face. Her lips moved as she read the legend on his shirt.

"Never had none a them before. Better gimme some. When in Rome, hey?"

"Love your T-shirt," she said, smiling at him, apparently meaning it. "That's real cute, what it says. Naughty, but cute."

Sigurd burst into a sunshine grin. "Yours ain't so bad either." No question about his sincerity, for her shirt, a loose-fitting black one inscribed with small white block letters located directly under a heavy sag of jugs, announced: *It should be easy for me to make it hard for you.* The message was belied by her thin frizzy hair, color of dried paste, an uncommonly homely face that several layers of paint did little to enhance or conceal, and a dumpy broad-beamed figure; but the contradiction seemed lost on Sigurd, who said, "What's your name, sugarbuns?"

The homely face opened in a smile wide enough to match his own. "Maylene. What's yours?"

"Burt."

"Well, Burt," she said, wisecracking street-smart voice, "think you're gonna enjoy our fritters."

"You damn sure straight I am," Sigurd declared.

D'Marco had been watching this coy exchange with a disgust bordering on the monumental. An image of the two of them locked in a sweaty bucking embrace came to him, unbidden and unwelcome. Couple of rhinos mating. Talk about your obscene.

Rather indifferently, the female rhino said to him, "How 'bout for you?"

"You got any fruit juices here? I mean real juice, not that canned stuff."

"Just what they use up at the bar. You want any of those weirdo drinks, you got to go next door, Mother Nature's."

Unamused, D'Marco said curtly, "Make it a tomato juice then."

"Better gimme a beer," Sigurd said, "Bud Light." Thumping at his belly, he added, "Gotta watch them calories, hey."

They traded leers, and she strutted away.

As soon as she was out of earshot Sigurd punched the air triumphantly. "Awright! You see that? Practically beggin' me to slide on into home plate."

"Yeah, I saw. Burt."

Sigurd looked a little sheepish but not very much. "Oh, that. See, what I always do is I give 'em a hard-guy name. All your squiff like them kinda names. Gets 'em thinkin' along the right lines."

"So you call yourself Burt, huh?"

"Sometimes Burt. Jake's good too, or Vic, or Al. It's like a, y'know, strategy. Works every time."

"Can see what it works on," D'Marco said, nodding significantly after the departing waitress, whose jumbo buttocks swelled her jeans and rolled loosely side to side.

"What, Maylene there? Well, yeah, she ain't too long in the looks department. But I'm tellin' ya, man, don't never pay to be fussy, tailwise."

"Looks like that's one problem you don't have to worry about."

"Damn right I don't. Tell you why. I knew this dude in the joint, Skeeter we called him, was a four-star Johnson pounder. Always goin' after it, like to beat that poor little fella to death, rub him raw. Pretty soon he—"

"I don't want to hear any your jailhouse stories," D'Marco broke in on him. "We got business to do here."

"What business? Our man ain't goin' no place." Sigurd indicated Waverly sitting impassively at the table beyond the glass wall. Indisputable evidence. D'Marco was unable to produce a rebuttal, so he scowled instead and said nothing. Sigurd interpreted the silence as sanction to resume his story, and he did.

"Anyway," he said earnestly, "there's a real important point to this one. A lesson, like. See, Skeeter was doin' a serious jolt, fifteen to twenty, forget what for, don't matter none, and after about five of 'em was down he gets to thinkin' this just ain't gonna do the job for him. The whackin' at it, I mean."

"I know what you mean, suckwad."

"Okay, okay. So it's like a inspiration comes to him and what he does is he juices a hack and gets him to smuggle in one of them sex dolls, kind you blow up, got all the right holes on 'em. Kind they make special for the guy ain't got no imagination at all." Sigurd thought about that a minute, amended it. "Or maybe too much. You know the kind I'm talkin' about here?"

"Just hurry up the goddam story," D'Marco said sourly.

"This doll, he names her Brandy, keeps her flattened out and stashed under the mattress on his bunk when she ain't in use, which is about every night. Skeeter's doin' just fine now, doin' his own time, got his Brandy, he's in love. Look to everybody like he's gonna make his stretch easy, headstand. Guess you can figure what's comin' up next, hey. Ain't no happy ending here. One day our block pulls a full shakedown and they turn up Brandy. Earns Skeeter some kennels time and Brandy, she's history, pro'ly some guard captain bangin' her now. Couple weeks after, old Skeeter, he's so snakebelly low, misses his Brandy so bad, he just does a flyer off the top tier. All the way down. You shoulda seen it. Looked like a bug gone splat on your windshield."

Upturned palms and somewhat bemused expression signaled the end of the tale.

D'Marco's fingers drummed the table. "So what is it?" he demanded.

"What's what?"

"Seems to me I heard you say there's a point to this stupid fucking story."

"You don't get it?"

"No."

Sigurd was seriously perplexed. How the fuck do you explain the obvious? Like trying to explain the punchline on a joke. And this boy was supposed to be famous for his smarts? Made you wonder. Happily for him a means presented itself in the person of the waitress coming toward them just then, balancing a tray on a fleshy arm, hefty ass jiggling. "Gets back to Maylene there," he said in a patient, if slightly superior, tone. "So she ain't exactly Hollywood material. What I'm tryin' to tell ya is a squirrel in the hand—even if she got to be a blowup doll, like Brandy—beats spankin' the monkey any day. Now you get it?"

"*That's* your point?"

"That's it."

D'Marco's eyes did a hopeless spin.

People were beginning to stream into the place now, and Maylene's homely face wore a stressed look as she got their order off the tray and laid out on the table. Nevertheless, she stole an instant to favor Sigurd with a broad wink and the smirky injunction "Enjoy," and then she was gone.

Sigurd grinned at D'Marco. "What'd I say? Home plate."

D'Marco ignored him. He wasn't interested in any more lessons from the academy of dumb. He sipped the tomato juice sullenly. Tasted like lukewarm piss. What can you do? Job was a job. Still nothing going on inside. Waverly still sitting there looking for answers in his glass. Forget it, boy, no answers there. Anywhere.

So what you do is wait. Wait and, because there was no way to avoid it, watch a moron stuffing his face with fritters and slugging beer direct from the can. Lots of lip-smacking, slurping noises. Made the gorge rise just looking at it, hearing it. Enough to turn you on to fasting. When he could contain himself no longer, D'Marco said, "You got any idea what you're doing to your body?"

Sigurd, jaws grinding methodically, glanced up from the fritter basket. "Whaddya mean?"

"Mean that garbage you're inhaling."

Sigurd paused midchew. His mouth hung open. Fritter fragments slivered his teeth. "What're you talkin' about, man? Them're good. You want one?"

"Them? You're offering me one of them?"

"Yeah, help yourself. Plenty left."

D'Marco's tightening lips registered only a fraction of his scorn. "I'd sooner take a dose of strychnine," he said. "Be no worse than that shit."

"Hey, food's food."

"Yeah, *food* food. Real food. What you eat is pure poison. Already today you had a soda and a fucking Twinkie—"

"That was a HoHo."

"—and now you're topping it off with beer and deep-fried dog turds. Tell you something. What you're doing there is committing suicide. By mouth."

Sigurd looked genuinely puzzled. "What, you're sayin' these eats here's killin' me?"

"Right. Exactly. That's what I'm saying."

"Aah, that's bughouse."

"You'll think bughouse when some quack opens you up, finds you full of cancer."

"Cancer! From beer and fritters?"

"That and everything else you're shoveling into that garbage-pit gut yours."

Sigurd shook his head slowly. "Jesus, fuck, man, you do got a problem. You oughta get yourself some professional help." With a toss of a hand he dismissed the Fontaine nutritional advice and theory and returned to his dwindling supply of fritters.

D'Marco turned away, visibly annoyed. What the fuck was he doing anyway, wasting good breath on this imbecile? Let the dungbucket eat what he wants, eat himself right into maggot food, worm banquet. Nothing to him. Sigurd caught the attention of the harried Maylene and, as if in defiance of D'Marco's warning, ordered a crabcake sandwich and, as he put it, "another brewskie." Silence fell over the table, or as much of silence as could be hoped for given the rude lapping sounds of gulped food and swigged beer. Thirty minutes went by. Not a word passed between them.

At about noon D'Marco noticed an attractive woman standing in the entrance opposite the bar. She was slender, quite tall, casually dressed in jeans and denim shirt. Kind of woman you call striking. She peered into the crowded room. She seemed confused. He looked past her and saw Waverly's arm in the air. She saw it too and joined him.

Okay, something coming down. Finally. "You see that?" he said to Sigurd.

"See what?"

"In there."

Sigurd leaned over the arm of his chair for a better look. "Hey," he said, mouth full of crabcake, "our boy got himself a slim."

D'Marco's view of the table was slanted, and with the woman there he could only barely keep Waverly in sight. Not good. He slid his chair out to the right. This angle was a little better but not all that much, and now the awning no longer shielded him from the fiery sun.

"Who you s'pose she is?" Sigurd wondered aloud.

D'Marco didn't respond. He watched them. For ten, maybe fifteen minutes he watched. Nothing. Talk, a drink, that was it. Could go on all day like this. And he could be sitting here all day, frying the delicate skin on his face and neck and arms. Already it felt prickly. He grew restless. So did Sigurd, who said finally, "Whoever she is, he better get his porkin' done quick. He ain't got time for foreplay."

"You know what I think?" D'Marco said.

"What's that?"

"For a change you got something right." D'Marco came to his feet. "You wait here. But be ready to move."

"Where you goin'?"

"Going to apply a little steam. See what happens."

D'Marco went through the entrance and stood at the end of the bar. It took a minute for his vision to adjust to the dim light. Blue blocks didn't help. He kept them on anyway. The air was thick with smoke in here and the music grating, loud. Least there was no more sun. And his view of the table was good now. He could see them both, both their faces. Heavy conversation going on. Very intense. Looked like even a little waterworks, the broad. Waverly probably giving her the bad news: It's a dead man you're talking to, honey.

After maybe three, four minutes, not long, Waverly's eyes began to roam about the room, clearly seeking out a waitress. But eventually they fell on him. Their gazes met, locked. D'Marco shaped his lips in a practiced, dangerous smile, put a finger to the rim of his blue blocks. Hello, Mr. Dead Meat.

That got his attention. He hustled the broad out of her chair and guided her toward the door. To get there they had to approach and pass the very spot where D'Marco stood. He stared at them all the way. The smile was gone from his face. The broad looked surprised, flustered, didn't seem to notice him. But Waverly did, and that was all that mattered. The object of this little exercise. They kept going.

D'Marco came out onto the deck. He motioned to Sigurd, and they followed the pair through the narrow passage leading to the parking lot. Near the end of the passage D'Marco stopped abruptly.

"What's up?" Sigurd said.

"Watch and see."

They watched them cross the lot and get into a silver Jaguar, broad behind the wheel, and edge into the line of traffic moving slowly down the one-way street in back of the mall.

"Holy shit," Sigurd exclaimed. "This time you really spooked 'em."

D'Marco said nothing.

"Why'd you wanta do that?"

"What I want is for you to shut the fuck up a minute. I said watch."

The Jaguar turned left at the corner. Without a word of warning, D'Marco suddenly took off sprinting. He could hear the moron calling something after him. He ignored it. The street broke on the beach, so now the Jag could only go one of two ways: left again, back in the direction of Blue Heron Boulevard, or right, onto Ocean Avenue. He got to the corner in time to see it swing right. Just like he figured. He slowed to an easy walk. A panting, wheezing Sigurd caught up to him at the intersection.

"F'Chrisfuckinsake, man, how about givin' little notice when you gonna do the rabbit number."

"Why? You run any faster if I did?"

Sigurd had no ready reply for that, so he said, still gasping some, "S'pose you lost 'em for good now."

"Look down there," D'Marco said, pointing at the Jaguar pulled up in front of the Tropicaire Apartments, less than two blocks away. "See anything familiar?"

In spite of himself, Sigurd was impressed. "How'd you know they'd be headed there?"

"First thing you got to learn, this business, is listen to your instinct." D'Marco cast a short glance Sigurd's way, and in that glance there was an even blend of complacence, pity, and an infinite withering contempt. "Course first you got to have the instinct."

"What was that all about, back there?"

"Better you don't ask."

"You're in some kind of trouble?"

"You might say."

"Why don't you, then? Say. You listened to mine."

"It's an altogether different kind of trouble, Caroline. From an altogether different world than you understand."

"Maybe I could help."

"You want to help, make certain Robbie calls me tonight. That'll be help enough."

"End of discussion, huh?"

"Right."

"All right. Let me try another tack. Why are we stopped here?"

They were parked facing the cream-colored box of a bungalow he was obliged to call home. She had left the Jaguar's engine running, and a blast of chill air filled the car. Waverly could see the tail of the Seville in the lot around the corner. He glanced over his shoulder and saw the two trackers coming down the street behind them, taking their time. Couple of sightseers out for a stroll. One of them, fat one in shorts and T-shirt, waddler, looked like somebody's idea of a bad joke. The other one, with his coolly empty thousand-yard stare, was no joke. They turned in at the Sea Spray and stood under the canopy at the entrance. Watching.

"Tim?"

"Uh, yes. Could you repeat the question?"

"I asked what we're doing here."

"Here is where I live."

"Here? You live here?"

She was trying her best to smother the astonishment in her voice but without much success. Nice try anyway. " 'Fraid so," he said. "I warned you it wasn't The Breakers."

"Will you invite me in?"

"That's not a good idea, Caroline."

"Why isn't it?"

"For one thing, I've got a roommate."

"Roommate," she said skeptically. "A woman?"

"No. A partner. Business partner. He's in there now."

"You could introduce me. A lost friend, returned from your past."

"You wouldn't know what to make of him. He's from that world I just mentioned."

"Is there a woman, Timothy? Since your divorce, I mean, and . . . all the rest of it."

Even though he could see it coming, the question caught Waverly off balance. He thought about it a minute, about another woman he had known and trusted, in Michigan, in another time of trouble, not all that long ago. It was a thought he didn't care to follow too far. Finally he said, "There was one. Once. Not anymore."

"What happened? Tell me."

"Nothing to tell. It was an encounter, an episode. Call it a touching, the way those things can sometimes be. Nothing more than a memory now."

"A memory," she echoed, and her curiously luminous eyes went far, far away. "We have memories too, Tim, you and I."

"Almost twenty years' worth."

"Here's one for you. Our high school senior prom. Four of us, there were, Robbie, me, you and your date, someone, I can't recall her name."

"Jane. It was Jane something."

"Robbie got himself badly wasted and we only had one car so we dropped her off first, whoever she was, this Jane, and you were driving and I was in the front seat with you, and Robbie was laid out in the back, unconscious." The memory seemed to return to her in a tumbling procession of words. Her hands fluttered the air. "You took me home and we sat awhile in the drive.

Talking, like this, like now. I was blubbering because Robbie had ruined the evening, or so I thought. You were trying to comfort me. The way a friend would. And then you took my hand and led me to the door, and because there was no one to kiss me goodnight you did that too. Do you remember that, Tim?"

"No," he said, remembering it well, all of it, and more vividly than she, remembering the unseasonably warm May night and the cloudless Michigan sky spattered with stars and the fragrance of peonies rising from the flower bed by the Vanzoren front porch and the perfume of her hair and the cool chaste touch of her lips and the moment of tender melancholy clinging and the hopeless romantic dreams buzzing in his head while a swarm of insects assaulted the light above the door.

"None of it?" she said with all a child's hurt.

"Maybe a little, now that you remind me."

"You know how you can look back in your life and discover crossings? Turning points you missed?"

"That I understand."

"Well, that was one of those turning points, Tim, that night." She looked at him steadily, and in her eyes there was a radiance, an unmistakable promise. "This could be another."

"I don't think so."

"Why not? Tell me why."

"Because that was a season in our lives, Caroline. Yours and mine, Robbie's. It's over now. And for whatever's happened in the years between, for each of us, you are married to him and he was a friend."

"That's a quaint sense of honor your have, Timothy. Peculiar, for this age."

"Maybe it's just the last faint tug of conscience."

"Live long enough and there's an exhaustion of conscience inevitably sets in."

Her voice had taken on a kind of studied irony, oddly inconsistent with the stricken smile. She brushed the feathery curls off her high, intelligent brow. There was another memory, that gesture. Caroline brushing the abundant hair back from her forehead in a motion of intense tunneling focus on a knotty chemistry formula, or a convoluted equation in math, or some desiccated exegesis of a murky literary text. Caroline the brightest of the three of them, most gifted, easily the most diligent. Caroline the achiever. What had gone wrong for her, for all of them?

"What a shame we can't grow young again," she said, soft as a voiced reverie, like a fragile word-filled balloon drifting above her head.

"The thing of it is, it would all doubtless come to the same." Another quick glance over his shoulder confirmed this cheerless judgment. The two figures—one comic, one sinister, like the two halves of the dark joke of his life, prologue and punchline—still remained in the Sea Spray entrance. Still watched. "I have to go now. I'm hoping you'll think to ask your husband to call. I'd be in your debt."

"Oh, I'll certainly think about it," she said, suddenly brightening. She leaned over and laid a lingering kiss on his lips. "Meanwhile, that's for you to think about."

12

The phone lines were busy that night, Sunday, June 21.

Around eleven, after observing no further movement in or out of the Tropicaire apartment and after it appeared as though the two marks were safely tucked away for the night, D'Marco figured it was time to check in with Chicago. He didn't feel like talking—day in the company of Captain Numbnuts, that was talk enough—so he instructed Sigurd to make the call. Nothing really to report, was the way Sigurd saw it, but he didn't argue. He phoned Uncle Eugene and filled him on everything gone down since he and the Jewboy got off the plane yesterday afternoon, which of course was nothing much at all. He told him about this morning's brief bit of action. Make that inaction, since it led nowhere, led to them hanging out in this room rest of the whole fucking day, nice way to see Florida—that's what he thought, but he didn't say it. He used a lot of *we*'s, making it sound like he and D'Marco were co-partners in this enterprise, equals. He looked up from the phone once and saw D'Marco at the window, staring across the street, same as he'd been doing most of the day. Fucker got to be made out of a block of Greenland ice. Iceman.

Uncle Eugene listened to his elaborate, occasionally embroidered chronicle without comment, that is, until Sigurd was finished, and then all he asked him was if he'd been paying attention, keeping out of the way. Tone of voice like you'd use on a squirrely kid, got his eye on the jam jar. Like a warning. Somewhat indignantly, Sigurd told him Yeah yeah yeah, he was doin' all that good stuff. He heard Uncle Eugene's heavy sigh and then he heard a snappish, "Lemme have Frog."

Sigurd put a hand over the speaker and said to D'Marco's back, "He wants to talk to you."

D'Marco didn't turn. "What about? You covered it all. All 'we' been doing."

"Beats shit outta me. He didn't say."

D'Marco came across the room and snatched the phone. He said, "Yeah?"

"Frog?"

"Yeah. Speaking."

"How about you rewind it for me, huh?"

"It's pretty much like he said."

"They're stickin' *that* close to where they holed up?"

"Correct."

"You hangin' tight to 'em?"

"Tight enough they know I'm here," D'Marco said. His use of the singular was deliberate.

"But you ain't crowdin' too close?" Voice was anxious, jittery, driven by doubt.

"Look, I'm doing it by the numbers. Your numbers. Way you said.."

"And they ain't made no moves yet?"

"I just told you. What kind of moves we talking?"

"Loot-gathering moves." Now the voice was exasperated, irked. "Layin' bets, hustlin' cards, movin' goods—fuck, I dunno. *Some-thing.* They owe money up here."

"None of that going on. Unless the Jew made some bets while he was out this morning, or unless they're phoning a wire. Otherwise only way they could be raising money is printing it over there."

"How about that cunt Sigurd said? How you read her?"

"No way to tell. Probably just that, some cunt your badass running with."

"Overall, like, how's it look to you? You think they might be up to something? Lookin' to break? Ride the wind?"

D'Marco was thinking what the fuck does this nutless shithead want—crystal ball reading? Wondering what kind of players come out of there anyway, Chicago. Losing all respect for that town if these two, radical hick here in the room and the whiny voice on the other end of the line, were any measure. He said, flatly, that which was incontestably true. "Who ever knows? You give them two weeks' slack time, let them know you're out here, sure, they could get some vanishing ideas. But that's how you said you wanted it played. I'm going by your rules."

"Can't let that happen, Frog. That wind-ridin', I'm sayin'. Too much turnin' on this. For everybody."

To D'Marco that sounded very near the edge of a threat. He didn't like threats. "So what are you trying to tell me?" he said, putting some dead of winter into his own voice.

"Nothin'. Not tryin' to tell you nothin'. Just sayin' keep on top of it, willya?"

"You hire me for a job, it gets done. Think I already told you that before. You got to hear it again?"

"Okay, okay. Don't get all twisted. Just lettin' you know this is a serious piece a work here, okay?"

"What else?"

"Huh?"

"What else you got to let me know?"

"Uh, guess that's about it. You stay in touch, okay?"

For reassurance and farewell, D'Marco gave him a dial tone. No sooner had he replaced the phone on the nightstand than Sigurd, slumped across a bed, reached for it. D'Marco stood there glowering at him.

"Who you calling?"

"Nobody particular."

"That 'nobody' better not be your Greenhouse queen. Not having any fluff in here. You got that?"

"Ain't callin' Maylene," Sigurd grouched right back at him. Jesus, sizzle your nerves, celling with a fucking monk like this one. "Callin' my old lady up home, you got to know."

Sigurd was careful to use the ambiguous "old lady" instead of mom in the slender hope he could keep the call private, though Christ only knew how you'd do that, room this size, especially with the Iceman monk sitting over on the other bed, couple feet away, like he was now, watching him, listening. Do a highwire, this conversation. Keep it short was the ticket. If you could.

After the tenth ring he was about to let it go when a croaky voice announced: "Stumpley residence. Yeallo."

"Sigurd, hey. How's she goin'?"

His mom expressed delight at the call, and then she proceeded to answer his how's she goin' question. In awesome detail. Daily play-by-play. Right down to the windup—what she ate for Sunday supper. Nytol Mom. Not going to be any trouble zonking off tonight, only trouble was keeping his eyelids boosted, all that wheeze rolling down the line. Maybe just as well though, took the weight off his end except for a now and again "That right?"

or a "No kiddin' " or other assorted monosyllables, just enough
to keep her tooling along.

Till she ran out of snooze gas and started asking what was he
doing? Job going all right? Was he okay? Was he eating good?
Taking care of himself? Sigurd danced around it best he could,
never once used the word *Mom*, mostly just said Yeah, sure, doin'
real fine, can't talk about it, phone. Smoke like that. But he could
see D'Marco was taking it all in, not so much glowering anymore
as smirking, wiseass smirk.

Sigurd said he had to hang up now, but before he could his
mom told him to stay out of trouble and do his best that's all
anybody could ask, and then she said, in parting: Remember, Sig,
yard by yard, life is hard; inch by inch, it's a cinch. Whatever that
meant. Another fucking warning, he supposed. Gut full of warn-
ings today, he'd had.

Finally, mercifully, he was able to put up the phone. On the
table there was one can left out of a sixer he'd ordered in, so he
got off the bed and went over and popped it. He could feel
D'Marco's eyes on him. He avoided them.

"That's real sweet," D'Marco said, "you calling your mother."

"Makes you think it's my mom?"

"Wild guess."

"Yeah, well, so what if it is. She's old, she worries."

"She tell you take a bath? Wash behind your ears? Be sure and
change your underwear? Don't do naughty things with naughty
ladies?"

"Hey, you wanna lighten up, hey?"

"Boy always want to listen to what his mother tells him. She's
his best friend, isn't that what they say?"

"Aah, fug off," Sigurd growled, thinking next time he called
Mom it would sure be from a phone booth.

D'Marco had one more call to make, but this one he didn't mind
so much since he wouldn't have to do any talking. Even ragging
on the sagass, giving him back a little of the grief he'd been enduring all day, even that got old quick. He picked up the phone,
tapped out the number of his apartment in Boca, listened to his
own chilly recorded greeting, and then hit his three-digit code.
The message on the tape was cryptic, cautionary, and nothing he
expected to hear: "Frog? About that Andy action, other night?—
nice piece work, by the way, our people real happy with it—
anyway, somebody must of made you out there, his place. Buzz
comin' in is the deafie's laid paper on you. Thought you better
know. So watch your back, man, hear?"

D'Marco ran the tape again. He listened thoughtfully, a distant alarm sounding in his head. This was something new to him, trackee instead of a tracker, and he wasn't sure he liked it. Whole new ball game, with a whole new set of rules. Felt strange. When he looked up, Sigurd was watching him, wearing a shit-gargle smile of his own now.

"What's matter? *Your* mom not home?"

D'Marco recradled the phone. "See that chair?"

"Yeah, I see it."

"Drag it over by the window. Facing out."

Sigurd did as he was told.

"Now sit in it."

Sigurd sat. "Okay, now what?"

"You like to make up movies, right? Pretend this is a war one. I'm the officer, you get to be the grunt. It's guard duty, those prisoners across the road. And you just pulled first watch."

"So when's it over?"

D'Marco stretched out on the bed and propped a pillow under his head. "When I say."

Eugene had to think about it awhile before he dialed Dietz's number. He wasn't too fast on calling him at home this late hour, a Sunday night. He could wait till morning, but he figured that wasn't a good idea either. Not with them goddam progress reports he was supposed to be making. Some fucking progress. By now you'd think the two marks be out scrambling instead of holing up with the covers pulled over their head, like if they say their prayers hard enough it maybe all go away. That's what you'd think. Sure as fuck make for a better report. Dietz, he wasn't gonna be happy. Be no happier in the morning though, maybe less. So finally Eugene decided the best thing to do was just get it over with.

Voice on the other end, sounded like a Jap, said, "Who calling, please?"

"Tell 'im Eugene."

He heard footsteps receding, returning. "One moment, please."

A moment passed. The next voice identified itself as Gunter Dietz.

"Eugene, Mr. Dietz. Sorry to be callin' this late."

"Perfectly all right, Eugene. I was just catching up on my reading."

Pin a gold fucking star on you, Eugene thought, but he said,

"Yeah, well, just got off the horn, down south. Figured you'd want an update."

"Absolutely. So. What do you hear?"

Eugene told him everything he'd heard. He waited out the silence that followed his account.

"No movement of any sort," Dietz said finally, not a question, more like thinking out loud. He didn't sound too hacked, which was a relief.

"Just what I said. Course they could be layin' off bets by phone," Eugene added, appropriating the Frog theory.

"Very doubtful. They couldn't raise that kind of money with some sideline wagers."

"Maybe they lookin' to push some product."

"That's even less likely, Eugene. Not from everything our sources tell us. These are five-and-dimers, pimp and a card scuffler. No. Only one way they could hope to put together the, uh, obligation package. They have to scare up some action, and my assessment is that's exactly what they're trying to do right now."

"Thing bothers me, Mr. Dietz, is they might be gettin' some bail-out ideas."

There was another silence, a little longer this time. When he spoke, Dietz's voice was still mild, even, but Eugene could feel a fire smoldering under it.

"That's always a possibility, of course, but I'm assuming our people down there can, well, discourage any such notions. You engaged them, Eugene. You should know. This is a fair assumption, I, uh, trust. Am I right?"

"Oh yeah," Eugene said quickly, not forgetting how one of them people he'd engaged was his single-cylinder nephew and wishing now he hadn't and hoping the fuck this Frog lived up to his jacket. "But what I was thinkin' was, they don't start makin' some right moves maybe we oughta just call in the pop. If this ain't about the cash, like you said, I don't see no percentage waitin'."

It sounded good to Eugene, what he just said. Like reasonable. And it was what he really wanted to do: take them out, get it done now, before somebody—and he had a pretty solid idea who that somebody might be—jammed it up and he got squeezed in the middle. His suggestion was met with silence. Longer yet.

At last, in a tone clement and even a bit charitable about invariably being right, Dietz said, "One of your basic principles of business, Eugene, is what you see is what you see. Just that. Nothing more. Now, what you *get*, that can be something entirely different. Consider this present situation. Our Jew got back only yesterday. And today's only Sunday. You're absolutely right about the money; it's not at issue anymore. Per se. Still, they could surprise us yet, make an honest effort and come up with part of the debt. Or even all. Who knows? In business, Eugene, it never pays to act too hasty. Panic."

There goes the suggestion. Deep-sixed. Dietz-wise, Eugene was too screwed into the go-along to raise any protest. He said, "If that's how you want it, Mr. Dietz."

"That's how. For now we'll proceed as planned. Give them a little more squirm time. For now. But I'm hearing you, Eugene. If we don't get any, uh, positive movement by, oh, say, Wednesday, then I think we'll have to reassess."

Earlier that evening, about ten o'clock, the call Waverly had been anticipating with neither patience nor confidence finally came through. He sprang off the La-Z-Boy and got to the phone on the second ring. Bennie, sprawled on the couch, made a flapping, slow-down gesture. Which was right, of course, wouldn't do to appear too eager. On the fourth ring he picked up the receiver and said hello.

"Tim? Robbie. How you doing, boy?"

"Doing fine, Robbie. You?"

"Super. Well, okay, maybe just a little knocked back. Swinging clubs all day. That part's not so bad, it's that nineteenth hole catches up with you. Believe it."

Waverly could believe it. The voice he was hearing was fueled by drink but its fraudulent heartiness seemed particularly forced, running on empty. He made a feeble joke about the hazards of drunken golfing. The preliminary dance.

Robbie's dutiful chortle expired quickly. "So. What's up? Care said you called."

Near as he could tell from the sound of it, that's all she'd told him. Left out the midday rendezvous. Shrewd girl. With a nonchalance as labored as the heartiness, Waverly said, "You remember that game your friend Appelgate mentioned? At the party?"

"Sure do. It's on for tomorrow night. Why?"

Very flat *why.* On the temperature gauge of hearty, the reading was in steep plunge. "I think I'd like to play after all. If the invitation's still open, that is."

There was just enough of a pause to let him know the welcome mat was seriously frayed at the edges.

"Changed your mind, huh?"

"That's right," Waverly said stiffly. He needed this action, but he wasn't quite ready to abase himself for it either. "Seems to me Appelgate wanted what he likes to call a pro at the table."

"Hey, don't get me wrong. Jock'll be delighted."

That makes one of you, Waverly thought. He said, "Pleased to hear that. I'm looking forward to the game."

"Be warned, though. It's like I told you, Jock's a pretty sly player. And it won't be any dime-ante table. I've seen him walk away with thirty, forty thou. And up."

"Appreciate the alert."

"Just so you know. At poker these good old boys are strictly out to punish. I mean, they go for the jugular."

"What about you? Same instincts?"

"Oh, I don't play. Only gambling I'll do is on a sure thing."

"But you'll be there?"

"Listen, you couldn't keep me away. It's just the cards I don't play." The voice slid into confidential gear. Man to man wink in it. "Other games, that's another story."

"I see," Waverly said, remembering his conversation with Caroline this morning and seeing only too well and more of the disastrous Crown union than he wanted or was entitled to see. To wind things down he asked for the game's time and venue, and the information was delivered with all the enthusiasm of an advanced narcoleptic. "Tomorrow night, then," he said.

"Ah, Tim, one thing. Can you maybe go light on your, y'know, past history? These fellows, they're businessmen. They wouldn't understand."

"But you do."

"Well, sure. You and me, it's different."

"Set your fears to rest," Waverly said coldly. "I promise to leave my manacles and striped shirt at home. Not a word about hacks or fish or hard time. If food is served, I'll even eat with a fork. I won't humiliate you."

"C'mon, Tim. You know what I'm saying. Look at it from my angle. This is a premium package I'm trying to hold together here. Very fragile. And for me it's a swing deal. Boom or bomb. I get porched on this one and I'm twisting in the wind. That's all I'm trying to tell you."

"I hear you."

"It's nothing personal. You know better than that."

"See you tomorrow, Robbie."

He hung up the phone and came around the counter and sank into the chair. His hands were trembling. From what—anger? anxiety? shame? general dismay?—he couldn't tell. No parsing the baffling syntax of his emotions anymore. Bennie was sitting up on the couch now, chewing a nervous unlit cigar, watching him. Waiting for a summation of the call, for assurances. He had to give him something. He owed him that much.

"You heard all that?" Waverly said.

"Yeah. It's nailed down?"

"Looks that way. I'm going to need the stake. Can you get it tomorrow?"

"Get you what there is of it. You remember we're talkin' ten long, little more, and that's it. Runs us dry. So you better keep your eye on them aces, huh?"

"Do what I can."

"What kinda rollers these guys? You get any idea?"

"Sound high enough. I think I heard a forty K figure in there somewhere."

"That'd be a start. An' this A-rab comin' in, you say he's major-league?"

Waverly was desperately weary of it all, all the analyzing, scheming, pinching, and prodding after some wispy hope. The endless torrent of words. In the past twenty-four hours they'd been over it, many times. Nothing left to extract. He said, "All I know is what I've told you, Bennie."

"He's a date-picker, he gotta be packin' a fat wallet. An' for sure got an open credit line, your Mecca First National." For a moment he gazed off into some far, numerative distance. Sums, tallies, reckonings, totals seemed to dance behind his eyes. "So if you can clean house tomorrow," he said, resuming the thought, "or next day, however long it takes, we maybe got a run at the red zone yet."

"If the cards fall right tomorrow," Waverly said. "And if the line on the Arab is true."

"Couple serious ifs in there, Timothy."

"I know. I heard them. But that's as much as we've got."

Bennie struck a match and fired his cigar. He puffed vigorously. The ceiling fan lifted the smoke into a halo standing above his head. The tarnished angel of chance. "Let me ask you something else here," he said.

"What's that?"

"This chum yours, this Crown. You boys were real tight?"

"We were pretty close friends. Once. But that was a long time ago."

"Close. Okay, how about you an' his old lady?"

Waverly could see where this was leading and he was not much taken with the direction. "We were friends too. The three of us were friends."

Bennie's lips did a slow curl around the tube of cigar. He cocked his head slightly. His doughy features settled into an expression canny, measuring. "Friendship, yeah. I seen what kinda friendship you got goin' there, you two was pulled up out front today."

"What, you were watching?"

"Hey, dish a doodoo we're in, you watch out for everything."

"All right, you want to find out how it is, let me spare you the fishing. Here's how. I needed her to get to her husband to get to the game to get to the Arab to raise the cash to cut—try to cut— a deal for our lives." Waverly could feel the indignation rising through his voice. His hands were still trembling. He paused, steadied himself. "And that's how it is. That make any sense to you?"

"So you give her a big smooch for all her trouble, huh?"

"Jesus, what am I talking to you for?"

"C'mon, Timothy, this is your Uncle Bennie here. You know there ain't no such thing as friendship, guy and a cooze. One of 'em's always got their mind on their crotch."

"I appreciate the locker room wisdom. I'll take it under advisement."

"You maybe remember some other advice I give you once, women?"

"You've advised me on a lot of subjects, Bennie. Women was probably among them."

"Bet your ass it was. Said women was poison to you. Look back, you don't believe me. We playin' a double-down hand here, Timothy. One card left to deal. Dietz, he ain't lookin' at pardon petitions no more. So what I'm hopin' is you ain't gonna do another Michigan on me, this broad."

"If I tell you there's nothing to worry about—at least along those lines—will you accept that? Let it rest?"

"Yeah, I can buy that, you mean it."

"I mean it," Waverly said with as much conviction as he could muster. "But let me tell you one thing more. About that hand we're holding. You know who we're playing against. They're not going to let us off with just the money. Assuming we're lucky enough to come up with it. You know that and I know it and we both know *they* know it."

Bennie looked puzzled. "Well yeah, sure, course. What'd you expect? You been in Jacktown. That's just how things are. But if we got the gelt we're holdin' the big bargain chip. This Dietz is mean but he's greedier'n he is mean. You bring me that quarter mil and I'll negotiate a trade. That's what I do."

Waverly had neither the energy nor the desire to turn it over anymore. The topic was exhausted, and so was he. He got out of the chair and went to the coat closet, saying, "Look, I'm really whipped. Going to call it a night."

"Good idea. You got a long day tomorrow."

On the floor of the closet was an air mattress generously supplied by Oh Boy O'Boyle. Waverly took it into the john and inflated it with Bennie's hair dryer. Half a dozen lank and isolate strands threaded over his glistening dome and he owned a hair dryer. Well, why not? No more contradictory or preposterous than anything else in his life. In *their* lives.

He carried the mattress back into the living room and laid it on the floor by the counter. Stretched himself out. Surprisingly, it was rather comfortable. Better than the couch anyway, of the two. Bennie had moved over to the La-Z-Boy. He held a beer in one hand, a hunk of cheese in the other. The television was going.

"This gonna bother you?" Bennie said.

"No. Fine. Go ahead and watch."

"Nothin' better to do."

"Right."

"You get some rest, boy. You gonna need it. I'd say don't let the fuckin' bedbugs bite but that maybe ain't so funny, this ant farm."

"Good night, Bennie."

Waverly put an arm over his eyes. With a conscious effort he closed out the racketing sounds of the television. He felt the first faint signals of a toxic headache brewing at the base of his skull. A vagrant cramp stitched across his lower abdomen and then was suddenly gone. An ulcer?—appendix about to rupture?—something worse? He tried not to think about life's manifold catastrophic possibilities. It wasn't easy. Once, when he was very young, he saw a newsreel feature on a balloon disaster. Two men—tiny, dark stick figures—tugged at the mooring ropes of the swollen bag of air hovering above them, drenching them in shadow. And then some capricious god summoned a violent gust of wind, and before his astonished eyes the balloon was darting across the sky, hundreds of feet in the air, and the two stick figures still clung to the trailing ropes. Why hadn't they let go? Hang on, hang on! In a fraction of an instant the first came tumbling to earth. The second held on longer, but not much, and when he did finally give it up his arms and legs flailed the air all the way down.

With another effort Waverly pushed the unwelcome memory out of his head, and the last thing he heard before surrendering to sleep was the whisper of the fan on the ceiling.

PART
THREE

13

"**D**uck for Bulldog, finley, hey!—nother big spoiler for the big guy, nice lady for our *professional*, skin no help, and dealer here catches a little maggie no help neither."

Jock's nonstop commentary proceeded from a mouth set in a relentless facsimile of a smile. It was delivered in that jolly malevolent singsong peculiar to carnival barkers and intended, evidently, to exhibit his mastery of the lingo. Or to rattle his opponents. Or some combination of the two. His merry, prowling eyes scanned the display of cards on the table. Five out in a hand of seven-card stud, everybody still hanging in. So far. He said, "Your aces doin' the driving, B.B."

Buel Bogardus, sometimes addressed as B.B., other times as "big guy" in joshing reference to his almost drawfish proportions, took a moment to peek at his hole cards. Satisfied they were unchanged, he cleared his throat and pushed a blue chip into the pot. "Aces say five," he said, ever so slight chirp in his voice.

"Whoa!" Jock bellowed. "Mr. B.B. gonna rough it up on us."

Waverly was sitting on two pair, queens over sixes. Not a mighty hand, as it stood, but on the basis of everything showing, the odds of catching his full house were good. Good enough anyway to pay to see the sixth card. He called the bet.

The player to his left muttered a grumbly "Drop" and flipped over his cards. He was a corpulent man, filled a chair. Banker by profession, Rodney Merritt by name. But since his middle initial was an unfortunate D. for Douglas, he was known in this festive company as Demerit. His features were heavy, porcine, sulky in defeat, which was frequent, rapturous in triumph, which was exceedingly rare. An eminently readable face.

"Demerit gonna dog, huh?" Jock said, fingering one of the mounting pillars of chips in front of him. Now it was his turn. He studied his up cards. His head bobbed reflectively. He looked first at Buel, then at Waverly. "Sure give a nickel to know what you boys got lurkin' down there in the darkness." Neither of them could help him on that. He hesitated some more. Funnels of doubt creased his brow. Finally, a man submitting to a cruel fate, he removed a blue chip and slid it gingerly toward the pot. "Well," he said, "somebody got to keep you two honest."

Waverly watched him carefully. Nice moves, all of them. Particularly coming off a hand that appeared to be dead in the water: eight, seven, and the puny three he'd just dealt himself. Except the eight and three were diamonds, and with thirty cards out only three other diamonds had surfaced. Waverly figured him for two more in the hole. Chasing after a flush. Or possibly an open-end straight. Either one, possibly.

Bulldog Drummond was next. He scrutinized his cards thoughtfully. Unlike the give-away faces of Demerit and Buel, Bulldog's was utterly unreadable, due in no small measure to his indelible overbit grin. Nature's compensation: the perfect poker face. Win or lose (and more often than not it was the former; early on, Waverly had marked him for an artful player, second only to Jock as competition at this table), those protuberant teeth remained fixed in what appeared to be a silent jeer. It could get disconcerting. He was showing a pair of nines and the lonely deuce. He rolled them over. "Nope, not this time," he said. Anyone looking at him would think he'd just announced a piece of extraordinary good news, except for the eyes, which shone like sun-polished ice.

The last man up went under the improbable name Orton Gillingham. Another banker, though in contrast to Demerit he was painfully thin, all hollows and steep angles everywhere, hollow chest, hollow temples, hollow cheeks, morose sunken eyes set deep under a bony ridge of forehead, pinched mouth nested in tiny vertical wrinkles. When they were first introduced, Waverly wondered if he was suffering from some terminal illness. Later he overheard Orton remarking pridefully on his jogging distance for the morning, a respectable seven miles. Which settled that concern. His athletic prowess and endurance did not, however, extend to the game of stud poker. In close to four hours of play he had taken one pot, shortcake at that, and the loser's glazed, listless expression was seeping into his cadaverous face. The quintessential cypher, born to carry a spear. He sniffed at his cards peevishly. Turned them down. "I'm out," he declared bleakly.

"C'mon, Orton," Jock said, voice full of mock pleading, "you goin' to abandon me to them two evil shooters?"

"Too rich for me."

About that, anyway, Orton was right. Waverly calculated the pot at somewhere near thirty-five hundred and rising. A nice touch to score and he was long overdue, was in fact not all that far behind the hapless Orton in the loser track. Eight consecutive hands without a hit. Of his original five-K buy-in, under a thousand remained. If the full boat came, he'd have to dig for cash to stay in, but it would at least be a stutter step on the road to recovery. If it came.

Jock resumed the deal. Just the three of them left, he went at it slow motion, lots of vocal annotation, milking the suspense. Another nice ploy. "Oh, my Lord!" he exclaimed at the sight of Buel's third ace. "Be no stoppin' the big fella now." Buel tried to hold in a jubilant giggle, unsuccessfully. The fingers of his delicate hands drummed the table.

Jock delivered Waverly's card. A worthless five. "Don't look like much from here," he observed for the edification of the table at large, "but you just don't never know, your professionals." Waverly felt a sudden rush of dismay. Nevertheless, he didn't blink. All evening he had been absorbing the "professional" taunt without a word. He said nothing now.

Jock dealt himself a card. It was a queen, Waverly's queen. Diamond queen. "Wouldya lookit that," Jock said, looking squarely at Waverly, eyes twinkly with malice. "Seems I picked up your lady. Ain't fortune unkind sometimes?" When Waverly made no reply he turned his gaze, just as mean but with a hint of amusement in it now, on Buel. "You still drivin', B.B."

"Five more," said little Buel manfully. His first mistake.

"Mr. Waverly?"

His rightful queen one hand to the left, ace trips to the right— no p.c. chasing that kind of power. Waverly said "Fold" and put up his cards.

Jock was scratching his scalp, a show of indecision. A shower of dandruff fell around his ears, powdering the shoulders of his black polo shirt. His wormy lips tightened, loosened, puckered again. "Well," he allowed, "got a feeling all I'm doin' here is makin' a charity contribution to the Bogardus Foundation, but you come this far you got to have a peek at that last down-and-dirty." He pushed a blue chip into the pot, grinned at Buel. Buel grinned back bravely, weakly.

Waverly watched the play carefully. Hand by hand he was beginning to know them, all of them. For certain Jock had caught his flush. And the pathetic little big guy was riding the trips, nothing more, hoping with the hunch player's desperate hope to fill in a pair on the final card.

Jock dealt it. Buel examined his and then took another revealing look at the other two hole cards. His second mistake. He tried hard to resuscitate what was left of his grin.

Jock barely glanced at his own card. "So what's the punishment, big fella? How many lashes you gonna lay on?"

Buel dropped a blue and three red chips into the pot. "Eight hundred," he said, squeaky tough.

Incredibly, he was going to steer a bluff. His third mistake, fatal. Poor Buel. In the face of Jock's obvious grasp of the arithmetic of the game and, behind that hayseed persona, his shrewd understanding of its psychology, little Buel was sadly outclassed. A mini-massacre in the making.

"Eight bills!" Jock bawled. "Holy hallelujah, Mr. B., you tryin' to run me straight to the poorhouse?" Only by a visible effort could he restrain his glee. He peered across the table at Buel's neat stacks of chips. "How much you got in your pile there?"

Buel did a quick tally. "Fourteen-four," he said. His natural tenor was elevating perilously near to soprano range.

Methodically, savoring the moment, Jock counted out a similar sum, added the eight hundred and pushed the chips to the center of the table. "Gonna have to call your eight," he said, and then he paused, wringing it for full dramatic effect, and then he said gravely, "and bump you the rest, see if you got that full barge for a fact."

Buel's face went white as chalk dust. He swallowed. "Your raise is fourteen-four?"

"Table stakes, boy. That's the rules. Prosper by the rules or perish by 'em."

Let it go, Waverly urged him with all the telepathic currents at his disposal, Your manhood's not on the line, let it go. The unheard advice was lost in the smoky ether of the room. Buel shoved his pile of chips into the pot. "I don't think you've got anything there, Jocker. I think you're bluffing."

Jock displayed his flush. "Well, I got these five red sparklers. Course if you're squirreling a pair down below you gonna take home the big banana."

There was, of course, no pair. Buel turned over his cards, mumbled, "It's yours." He looked to be in serious need of a blood transfusion. Under the table his tiny feet did an agitated brush step on the carpet.

Jock raked in the pot. "Warned you, B.B.," he said, salting the open wound. "I'm out to scorch the earth tonight, thousand miles around, every direction." He looked meaningfully at Waverly. His jowly face fairly beamed.

Demerit said to Buel, "When he picked up that queen and called your bet, it was obvious he'd filled a flush. You should have seen it coming." A results player, Demerit liked to share his matchless rearview vision.

Buel ignored him. He wasn't listening to any advice tonight, audible or otherwise. He got a fat wad out of his pocket and began peeling off bills. "Another five thou," he said defiantly.

Jock glanced at his watch. "Ten to midnight. Guess we can squeeze in another hand. Just play off your cash, B.B. Bank'll be open after the break." He surveyed the stacks of chips around the table. Again his eyes came to rest on Waverly. "Might be some of these other boys want to replenish their pantries."

Again Waverly gave no response.

Jock gathered up the cards, squared the deck, and handed it to Drummond. "Better make it five-card, Bulldog. That's all we got time for."

"Five-card it is," said the malleable Bulldog.

Jock's place, his rules, his bank, his program. Wherever he sat was the head of the table. Over a dandruff-flecked shoulder he called, "Robber, you make them arrangements up at the hotel?"

Robbie was huddled with two other men in a far corner of the spacious room. "All taken care of, Jock," he called back.

"Better be, or you'll be back to ambulance chasin'."

It got a general laugh all around, even from Robbie.

Drummond shuffled the deck and the last hand before Jock's designated break came out. Waverly caught nothing. Another ante forfeited. Got to stop thinking that way, he lectured himself: it's units out there, not money, and four hours of bad beat can't put you on tilt. Still, he had to wonder how long this storm could last. Certainly he'd ridden through longer ones, but that was in days when time and a dangerously thin stake were not an issue. The cards were unforgiving, yes, but they were also amnesiac. They had to turn. One of the game's immutable laws. But with his five K and some decimal points left (units! units!) against all the basic money power at this table, they had to turn soon. That was another firm ordinance of the game.

He lit a cigarette and settled back and studied the play. The exercise helped steady him. Jock and Drummond wisely folded on the third card, leaving the three rabbits to battle it out. Demerit dropped on card four, and Orton and Buel went at it head to head. Clash of the titans. At showdown time it was Orton by a couple of low pair over Buel's jacks. Orton scooped in the pot joyously, his second stroke of the evening. A win of maybe nine hundred, outside. Jock looked on with ill-concealed scorn, Bulldog grinned his static vacant grin, and Demerit explained Buel's blunders to him.

"Okay," Jock announced, "we gonna hang it up for an hour. Game resumes at one, sharp." He turned to Robbie and demanded, "Robber, where's that entertainment you supposed to be in charge of?"

Robbie came scurrying to the table. "Should be here any minute, Jock. Want me to call?"

"Damn right I do. You tell Zack to shag ass. Us old-timers got to have our R-and-R too. Only take thirty seconds to get the job done anymore, but it's that thirty minutes gettin' 'er aloft cuts into your break time."

To Waverly it sounded suspiciously like a set piece, but from this dutiful audience it got a nice howl. Robbie hurried out of the room, and Jock hauled himself stiffly out of his chair, signal for everyone else to rise, and they all did, all but Waverly.

"Bar's set up in the kitchen," Jock said. "You boys help yourselves. Food and other indulgences on its way."

The room cleared. Waverly remained seated and the host regarded his guest critically, quizzically, a bug under glass.

"You not gonna stretch your legs, Mr. Waverly?"

"This is fine, thanks."

"Care to join me in a little sip?"

Wanted some gloating time, no doubt. He wasn't going to let it alone, so Waverly said sure and started to get to his feet.

Jock motioned him back. "No, no, you stay where you are, I'll bring it in. What're you drinkin'?"

"Ginger ale if you have it. If not, any kind of soda."

Jock's purplish lips retracted slightly. "Gonna lay in the weeds, huh, ambush us poor drunks?"

Waverly shrugged. "I play better on a clear head."

"Me, it's just the other way around. Get a little sozzled and it's like I'm blessed, cards just won't quit on me. Funny how that works."

Remarkably crude psych job. Waverly was surprised; he would have expected something less transparent. Unless it was another tightly convoluted ploy, more innocent hayseed business: Oh, lucky old me, what do I know? Waverly agreed it was strange, and Jock directed him to wait there, be right back.

And in a moment he was, bearing two glasses and the burden of his simulated smile. He thrust a glass at Waverly and said, "Let's flop in something cushy, give the buns a rest."

They took facing chairs by a wide glass slider overlooking the road and the golf course just beyond it. In the distance the lights of the Sheraton glittered against the night sky.

"What do you think of my little hideout here?" Jock asked.

The hideout was a luxury condo situated on the grounds of the PGA National Golf Course. Apart from this one room, to which he had been ushered directly on arrival, Waverly had seen very little of it and in his intense focus on the game taken notice of even less. Now he glanced around the room, what Jock had earlier described as the "cash flow" room. The card table, casino quality, was set squarely in the middle, and plush chairs and sofas, carefully arranged in conversation groupings, ringed the perimeter. A trophy case filled with gold-plated statuettes, club-swingers, replicas presumably of the redoubtable Jock, dominated one wall. Above it was a display of plaques and framed photos of Jock with assorted luminaries, and above that an enormous mounted fish of some species unknown to Waverly, no sportsman himself. "Very elegant," he said. "Makes a statement."

Jock chuckled complacently. Impervious, it seemed, to irony. "Also makes for a good spot to hunker down. Man's got to escape the castle dragon and the kids now and then."

"You have children?" Waverly said for something to say to his genial host.

Jock held up one splayed hand and lifted the forefinger of the other. "Six," he said, and then his face suddenly clouded and the forefinger curled over his glass. "Well, five actually. Youngest boy got himself killed."

"Sorry to hear that."

"It was a while back. Motorcycle smashup." His eyes misted over, the corners of his mouth dropped. He allowed himself a moment of silence, as though in grieving memory of the departed son, and then he reached for a cigar from a vertical stack in a lead crystal container on the coffee table between them. "You like one of these?" he offered.

"No thanks."

"You oughta try one. Macanudos. About the finest tobacco you can find."

"Maybe later."

Jock put a flame to the cigar. Smoke filled his rapidly recovering face. The smile resurfaced. "Tell me, Mr. Waverly, you enjoyin' yourself tonight? Reason I ask is you don't seem too lively up there at the table."

"It's a game of few words. Doesn't require a wide vocabulary."

"How about the company? What do you think of these boys?"

"Seem like pleasant fellows."

"I mean as players."

"Drummond's very good. So are you."

The compliment was acknowledged with a hint of a smirk. "And the rest of 'em?"

"The other three, well, they're pretty soft. Way off their level."

"Let me ask you something else, speakin' of the game of poker. You're a pro, how much of it you think's luck?"

"Hard to say. I've heard some very skilled players rate it as low as five percent. Personally, I think it's higher than that."

"About how high a percent," Jock persisted, "your opinion?"

"Twenty maybe. Assuming we're talking about real poker now, not the garbage games."

"How'd you split up that other eighty?"

"Thirty of it simple arithmetic, the rest instinct. What some people like to call psychology."

Jock took a long pull on his fine cigar. He made his mobile features thoughtful, heavy with skepticism.

"You don't agree?" Waverly said.

" 'Fraid not. Y'see, my thought is game of poker's a lot like life: once you got the numbers down, rest of it's pure dumbass luck. That psychology, that's just another way of sayin' human nature, which is another way of sayin' luck. Some fellas luck's a born gimme, others couldn't catch it if you give 'em a Concorde jet airplane." His tone left little doubt which category pertained to the fortune-flooded Jock Appelgate, and his enunciation of *human nature* implied there was considerably more in it to despise than ever to admire.

"Well, I can't dispute your theory," Waverly said, nodding toward the table. "You've got an Alps of chips up there in evidence."

"Yeah," Jock drawled, his best impression of humility, "cards been fallin' right for me so far." He knuckle-drilled his forehead, fastened Waverly with an innocent mocking stare. "Haven't been doin' so good by you though, have they."

"Game's just getting under way."

"That it is. But you know, that garbage poker you was mentionin'? After the next break we gonna have to open it up to them kind of games, keep Orton and B.B. happy."

"I understand."

"Then all your numbers, psychology, they go right down the Chinese toilet. You're playin' off fool luck then. Bets gonna be flyin'."

Waverly met the steady probing gaze. "I came to play," he said.

"Guess you did at that."

A sudden jarring whoop rose from the next room.

"Sounds like our social chairman finally delivered the goods," Jock said. He got out of the chair and started for the door. Again Waverly didn't budge. "You're not gonna come have a look at the meat show?"

"I'll pass this time."

"Players get first pick. That's another house rule."

"You can have mine. Think of it as a gift."

"Gift, huh? No booze, no pussy, you're what they call a disciplined man, Mr. Waverly." The *disciplined* was pronounced with about the same accent and intonation as *human nature* had been.

"I'm working, remember?" Waverly said from behind his own wisp of a smile. Two could play at these head games.

Jock squinted at him like a man taking aim, drawing a deadly bead. "So you are," he said, and for a flicker of an instant the hayseed mask was off. "I'm going to keep that in mind when we sit back down at the table here. Catch you later."

14

"**L**ook, if I stick my head out the window none of the smoke'll get in here. There sure as fuck ain't no breeze."

"No."

"No. Okay. How about I just step outside then, go stand at the back of the car."

"Said no, brain-dead."

"C'mon, man, we could be here all night. I need a weed."

"What you're going to get is a five-finger sandwich, you don't stuff a rag in it."

Sigurd muttered something under his breath and lapsed into a sullen silence. He had probably been more uncomfortable in his life, but he couldn't remember when. Couldn't smoke, couldn't eat, couldn't move, couldn't talk—Jesus, might as well be doing a turn in the Stateville hole.

They were parked about thirty yards up the street from the Appelgate hideout, the LX concealed in a band of shadow cast by moonlight slanting across the cluster of condos. For well over three hours they had been sitting there, ever since the Jewboy dropped off his partner, and despite the fact both windows were wide open, the air in the car was muggy and close, sticky as flypaper. Middle of the night not a whole lot better than high noon down here, thought Sigurd bitterly; still felt like a goddam steam bath. Grab a handful of that soggy air you likely squeeze out a puddle of Mother Nature's finer piss. Fucking Florida, you could keep it.

What he'd really like to be doing right about now is kicking back in the chilly room at the Spray, feet up on the bed, TV on, cold beer in one hand, Maylene or somebody like her riding the prong finger on the other, lubing herself up for him to climb aboard and bang the holy shit out of her. What he said though, tentatively and after a decent pouty interval, was "What do you figure's goin' on in there?"

D'Marco didn't answer, which was not surprising, since apart from the scanty words required to deny the periodic requests for a desperately needed cigarette he'd said next to nothing in all the time they'd been there.

"You think he's with that twat from yesterday, Greenhouse? Do a little wick-dippin'?" Sigurd's conjecture was somewhat inspired by the image of a lust-maddened Maylene, or somebody like her, still spinning behind his eyes.

D'Marco sighed. "How many cars you count?"

"Look like seven."

"Seven cars. You had something between your ears besides dog shit it might come to you he's not there for any romance."

"Could be a party goin' on," Sigurd said defensively.

"Try again."

Sigurd thought a minute. "Maybe he turned up a game. You think it's a game?"

D'Marco snapped a finger. "Now, how'd you ever hit on that? Here you got a dude with a jacket for a card mechanic, got a ring in his nose for going lame on your people, and got two weeks to bring up the loot. And out of those little clues you hit dead on your genius conclusion. You know what you ought to do?"

Sigurd figured it was going to be more wiseass but he said anyway, "Yeah, what's that?"

"You ought to sign up for the detective squad. Hear they're looking for a few good men. They might even make you chief, that kind of deduction."

Sigurd clutched his genitalia. "Deduct this."

"Word on the street is it's already been deducted, flea fucker. Now shut the fuck up and pay attention to what we're doing here. I'm not going to tell you again."

Thirty wordless minutes passed. Shortly after midnight a van came down the road from the hotel and pulled up in front of the condo. The driver got out, opened the side panel, and led a crew of tight-skirted women to the door. He hit the bell and a light flashed on above their head and the door swung open and a man appeared in it, throwing up his arms in boisterous welcome. The women did some on-cue squealing as he ushered them in.

"Look like they ordered out," said Sigurd, whose mind remained fixed on basic appetites. "Box lunches, hey."

D'Marco poked his head out the window for a better look, but cautiously, first glancing behind the car and up and down the dark street.

After all the women were inside, the driver went back to the van and then returned carrying trays, which he handed to the man in the doorway. Several such trips were made. At the last one the man clapped the driver on the shoulder and pressed some bills into his open palm. The driver gave a snappy little salute, the door closed in his face, and the light went out. He walked to the van, whistling tunelessly, and drove off toward the hotel.

D'Marco turned the key in the ignition and eased the LX into the street.

Sigurd looked at him puzzledly. "What are we doin' here?"

"You ever heard of following? They do any of that in Chicago?"

"Can see that. What I'm askin' is why? Just some pimp up there, right?"

"Pimps got good thoughts too."

The van pulled into the guest lot and parked at the far end of a long file of cars. D'Marco found a spot between it and the hotel.

"Okay," he said, "what we're going to do now is have a word with him. Only it's going to be *my* word, me doing the talking. You keep it clamped shut unless I say something at you. You got that?"

"Yeah yeah, I got it."

The driver came sauntering through the lot, still whistling, until two figures stepped out of the shadows behind a car and planted themselves squarely in his path. Then the whistling suddenly stopped. So did he.

"You," D'Marco said, beckoning him with a finger. "Over here."

The driver approached warily. He was a young man, early twenties, correctly dressed in jacket and tie, built like a surfer: tall, angular, trim. Under the shock of sun-bleached hair his face was lean, sun-darkened, blankly innocent, except for the eyes. Crafty, dealer's eyes, which were just then shifting about the lot and discovering no one else in sight. He stuck a greeter smile on the innocent face and said, "What can I do for you fellas?"

"You employed by the hotel?"

"No, but I know my way around inside. Help you out with something?"

"That's peculiar. You not working for them, I mean. Could of sworn I saw you making a delivery up the road."

"Well, I don't exactly work *for* it. The hotel. More like out of it. Sort of."

"That right? What is it you sort of exactly do?"

"Catering. I'm a caterer." The smile was beginning to come unstuck.

"Huh," Sigurd said, unable to restrain himself, "cunt caterer." He liked the alliterative melody of it.

D'Marco gave him a sidelong scowl. To the driver he said, "He got that right, what he just said?"

"What I do is my business. Who are you guys, anyway?"

D'Marco watched him. The smile was dismantled entirely now. Chummy didn't work, try tough instead. An enterprising kid but way out of his league. "Vice maybe got an interest in your kind of business," he said.

"Vice," the driver sneered. "You two, Vice? You and the Pillsbury Doughboy there? Sure."

Sigurd stiffened. He started to say something but D'Marco cut him off with a silencing gesture, so he stood there, balling impotent fists, jaws clenching furiously. All the shit he'd been eating lately, it wasn't easy taking a cheap zinger off a pimp, punk one at that.

"What's your name, boy?" D'Marco said.

"Zack."

"Zack. Okay, Zack, so far we been real polite, way we're supposed to be with you citizens. But you keep insulting my partner and I can't be responsible, what happens. So I'm going to ask you again, still polite, what kind of catering business you got?"

"If you guys are Vice, let's see some shields. Otherwise you can go fuck yourselves."

"That's one idea," D'Marco said, nodding thoughtfully, as though he were seriously entertaining the Zack recommendation. "Here's another." He stepped up and punched him once, hard, well below the level of the belt line. Zack gave an astonished grunt and doubled over, hugging his midsection, and D'Marco grabbed a handful of the yellow hair and, steadying the trembling head, brought a fist down across the back of the neck. It felt good, releasing four, almost five days' worth of bottled-up bile, energy. Zack slumped to his knees. D'Marco stooped down and grasped him by the lapels of his jacket and yanked him to his feet and shoved him against the side of a car, not his own but the one next to it, wasn't going to run the risk of scratching or in any way damaging the LX even though it looked like all the cuffing needed to get some attention was done.

That's what D'Marco confirmed first: "We got your attention now, Zack?"

Zack groaned something that sounded affirmative.

"Good. Got that part sorted out, we can go back to what we were discussing. Namely, the nature of your business."

"What is it you guys after?" Zack said in a voice reedy, feeble. "Slice of the action?"

D'Marco filled his face with shock. "Hear that, Burt?" he said without looking at Sigurd. "Sounds like he's trying to bribe us."

But to Sigurd that sounded more like a clear invitation to join in. "Bribin', that's a mighty heavy offense. Get you a long time in the can, no parole. And I'm tellin' ya, boy, them fudge-packin' niggers in there just love to make a sweet Oreo cookie outta—" He broke off abruptly under D'Marco's baleful glare. Too bad. He was just getting the feel of it too, the rhythm.

"You don't want money," said Zack, growing rapidly desperate now, "what then?"

D'Marco leveled the glare on him. "Want to know who it was you made delivery to tonight. Who all's in there, what's going on inside. Easy questions like that."

"It's Mr. Appelgate's place. I don't know any of the other people."

"Who's he, this Appelgate?"

"I don't know, some fast-buck builder, something. Lives over on The Island. That's his playhouse down there."

"What else you deliver? Besides the night ladies, I mean. You supply them with blow, that kind of commodity?"

"Nah, man, these guys aren't into that. Strictly broads and booze. They're old. Freeze-dried."

"How about cards? Wouldn't be an illegal gambling game going on in there?"

"Well, yeah, sure, they're playing some cards. It's a party."

"Card party, huh? Tell me something, Zack, what kind of money they play for? These friendly games or they chasing the large dollar?"

"Shit, I got no way of knowing that."

"But you got to hear things. Being in the catering business like you are."

"Hearing things, that's not my strong point."

D'Marco shook his head sadly and then he seized Zack by the throat, both hands, and drove him down across the hood of the car. "How about breathing? That one of your strong points?"

"Good-size games," Zack sputtered between gagging noises. "Serious money."

"How long they go on, these parties?"

"All night . . . at least . . . sometimes longer. . . ." His face was purpling under the tightening grip.

D'Marco suddenly released him and turned to Sigurd. "What do you think, Burt? Think we should book him?"

Sigurd, caught off guard, hesitated. Seemed like a real question, kind he was supposed to answer, so he ventured an opinion: "Think he needs another touchup. Pussy hustler, he got it comin'." He was doing his best to extemporize, but excluded for so long, he'd lost the beat.

"Well, that's a good thought too, that touchup," D'Marco said, measuring out the words carefully, like he was deliberating on it. Then he turned again and faced Zack, whose eyes, no longer quite so crafty, swam with fear, and he said, "What you're catering goes against the laws of Palm Beach County, state of Florida. Now, it happens we got a particular interest in what's going on in that condo, got nothing to do with your illegal business, so this is maybe your lucky day. Maybe. Depends on your conduct, we decide to let you off. For instance, you get it in your head to call your client down there, pass along what we been discussing, well, that's the wrong kind of conduct. Ungrateful kind. Makes us awful unhappy."

"Listen, I won't—"

"No, you listen up a minute, Zack. I'm not finished. When we get unhappy we get awful mean, especially my partner here. You know what a sapper is?"

Zack shook his head yes.

"Sergeant Burt, he packs one. See, what he likes to do, he's bringing in a felon, is use it for that touchup you heard him mention. Calls it resisting arrest. It's sort of like a hobby with him."

"Make my own cranberry jelly that way," Sigurd volunteered, underscoring the message, hoping for another shot at center stage.

Hoping in vain, for D'Marco disregarded his contribution and said to Zack, "So we're going to let you go now, long as we got an understanding. We do got an understanding, don't we?"

Another motioned yes.

D'Marco stepped aside. Zack looked at him uncertainly, still petrified, unable to believe in the miracle of deliverance. D'Marco swept an arm in the direction of the hotel and Zack edged around him and set out, moving slowly at first, stealing furtive over-the-shoulder glances, then picking up speed as the distance between them widened, finally breaking into a stiff, hobbling sprint.

"Lookit him scoot," Sigurd brayed. "Guess we scared the livin' peepee right outta him."

"Didn't we though. Sergeant."

"That was good, hey, you callin' me sergeant. Poor dumb fuck, he actual' believed we was steam."

"Yeah, that part was good. The not-so-good part was you not doing what I told you to do."

"Hey, what're you sayin'? I didn't talk any 'less you asked something. Except once maybe." Sigurd was genuinely hurt. That word *partner*, he'd heard that in there, couple times, figured it maybe counted for something, signaled some sort of breakthrough in their chilly alliance. For as sour-assed as this Florida flash was, Sigurd had to admit he knew his stuff. That was a real downtown vamping number he done on the pussy pusher, real nice job of work. Uncle Eugene was right: things to pick up from this boy.

"Once is once too many. So what you're going to do now is head on back to the Sea Spray."

"Huh?"

"You got the same hearing problem as the kid? Said you're out of here."

"I heard what you said. Wanta know how come." Sigurd was of two minds about the curt directive. On the one hand it opened up a dazzle of possibilities: night still young, hey, got to be a lot of sweet meat still on the prowl. On the other hand it had the ring of finality, dismissal, and he was not about to be dismissed. Nosirfuckinree. Any dismissing got done, it come direct from Dietz, or Uncle Eugene anyway, not Captain Pinchnuts here.

"How come," D'Marco repeated. "You want to know how come. Okay." He held up a hand and began enumerating on the fingers. "Because I'm telling you to, that's one. Because when you get back there you're going to check in with Chicago, let them know what's shaking down here tonight, if you can get any of it straight. That's two. And three is because you're going to stay in that room and keep a scope on the Jew across the street. Not going to move till you hear different from me. That enough how comes for you?"

It was enough. More than Sigurd wanted to hear, especially that number three, which put the permanent squash on any of those good after-hours ideas of his. "So how'm I suppose to get back?" he said peevishly. "You got the wheels."

"Beats me," D'Marco said, moving toward the LX. "You could catch a cab up at the hotel. Or you could hoof it. Can't be much more than, oh, ten miles. Little stroll in the night air do you good, trim off some of that lard."

"That's real cute, hey. You're a real clown. You oughta try out for the circus."

"Oh yeah, almost forgot," D'Marco said from behind the wheel, his voice thorned and ugly with spite, "number four on those how-come reasons is I can't stand listening to any more of that shit dribbling out of that bunghole in the middle of your face," and he hit the accelerator and roared away.

He was once again parked in the shadows up the street from the condo. Nothing changed down there: lights on all over the place, drapes drawn, seven cars still out front. Nothing to do but wait. And so he waited, but uneasily and with a vague disgruntled restiveness and with the utter absence of the dash and zest he normally found in his work.

The reason for D'Marco's surlier-than-normal temper was that nothing *felt* normal anymore, not since he heard that disturbing message on his answering machine. The whole notion of someone else stalking *him*, D'Marco Fontaine, was so foreign, so far outside the range of his experience, it wound him tight as piano wire. Now, in addition to working through this present arrangement, which seemed to be dragging on forever even though he was actually only three days into it, he had to cover his own back as well. Didn't help any, having the mouth-breather along, whining about nicotine and all the other poisons he was sucking and stuffing into that corrupted system of his. Neither did it help being way off the lockstep regimen that was his normal life: the regular bomb-and-blitz workouts, the painstaking attention to nutrition, the proper rest (somewhere he'd read that after ninety-six hours muscles unexercised and unattended began to atrophy, and for him those hours were used up).

It was unsettling, all of it, threw him off stride. He didn't believe in luck—man made his own luck, same as he sculpted his own body and created his own character, destiny—but he was beginning to feel something very near to superstition about this job. And if he could have identified it, he might have admitted to another curious emotion equally alien to him, and if he could have named it it would have to go under no other name than dread.

15

The smoke formations—fueled by Drummond's pipe, Jock's Macanudos, and Waverly's chain of cigarettes—seemed to hang motionless in the air above the table, like some miraculously levitated fixture of the room. Over on a couch a nonplayer guest listlessly stroked the heroic bosoms of a woman whose tar-black hair and harlot red lipstick presented a stark contrast to the abundance of creamy flesh. Another couch was ornamented by a nubile nymphet, a natural blonde, looked about fifteen. Her shimmery satin teddy, direct mail, Fredrick's of Hollywood, lay in a heap on the floor beside a kneeling man whose bald head was buried in her crotch. Both of them appeared to be sleeping. Some giggling, washed-out and faint, could be heard from the kitchen; otherwise all was silence but for the occasional nuanceless utterances of the game. A party rapidly running down.

"Seven-stud, nothing wild," Waverly said. Dealer's choice, he chose what he always did when it rolled around his turn. A breath of sanity in the loony medley of games gone progressively more bizarre. Games of suicidal risk, in which the elements of skill and patience and numeration and cunning were all but canceled out and which, in a sinister inversion of the rightful order, seemed designed to punish the worthy and reward the undeserving. Follow the Bitch, Stalingrad, Woolworth, Dr Pepper, Baseball and its baroque offspring No Peekee Midnight Baseball, Pass the Trash—name your aberration and someone at this table, in a stupor of fatigue and drink and other intemperances, was bound to call it.

The cards came out. Waverly played with a cool serenity, soothed by the reassuring machinery of a rational game and the peculiar suspension of time that comes with taking in life through a filter of numbers. By sixth street he sat on the power: two exposed aces, another in the cellar. Everyone had folded but Demerit, who showed three consecutive cards supporting a blind faith in a straight the count dictated as next to impossible to come by. Nothing in that hand but dreams. Waverly bet an unthreatening eight hundred, as though he were seriously entertaining the fiction of the straight. And Demerit, readable as ever, raised five bills. Waverly called. He knew him. After the last card was down Waverly pushed four blue chips to the center of the table. "Two long," he said. Demerit hesitated. His waxy features registered profound struggle. In his mind he wanted desperately to ride the bluff, but in his heart there was an acute poverty of nerve. He turned over his cards, muttering an ill-natured, "Go on, take it."

Waverly gathered in the chips. Twenty-three hours of play—four on, one off, following Jock's mandated formula—and he was up fifteen K or thereabouts, somewhere in that neighborhood. Ordinarily a tidy take for a day's work, but measured against that remote and towering quarter mil it was chump change. Like chipping away at an iceberg with a penknife. What he really needed was to score one of those monster pots the garbage games occasionally generated, at least walk out of here with something more than cab fare. But this was the final session—another Appelgate mandate—and with less than an hour remaining the prospects of such a happy stroke were not encouraging.

Over forty minutes passed before he hit again, and then it was a short-money hand, nothing consequential. As he was collecting the meager pile of chips, Robbie came lurching into the room sporting a girl on either arm, one black, one oriental. Trophies. They wore matching outfits: nylon spandex cutout dresses, flame red, easy access zippers, second skin fit—the latest in sidewalk hostess fashion. Also the practiced carnal smirks that come with the territory. Robbie's clothes were rumpled and stained. The buttons on his shirt were undone, neck to navel, revealing an overhang of paunch. He was barefoot. His face was flushed, eyes puffy, pink-veined. Nevertheless, he was grinning, wide tell-all grin. A jolly threesome.

"Lookit old Robber there," Jock said, leering wickedly. "Got himself a pair a bookends. Plankin' 'em two at a time now, are you, counselor?"

Robbie disengaged both arms and cupped a hand over the black girl's firm swell of buttocks. "Pursey Sue here, she just came along to cover the end zone." His voice was hoarse, whispery, slushy on the sibilants.

"Yeah, whose end?"

"Don't ask."

Robbie gave each of the girls a playful spank and shooed them away. He pulled a chair up alongside Waverly and sank into it, straddling it the way he liked to sit. "How you doin', old buddy? Makin' any money?"

"Holding my own, Robbie," Waverly said in the forbearant sing-song one reserves for drunks and children.

Robbie's bleary eyes made a slow circuit of the table, came to rest on Jock's substantial hoard of chips. "Looks like Mr. Jocko's the big hitter." He elbow-nudged Waverly. "I warned you about these boys. Did I warn you?"

"You warned me."

The deal had passed to Jock. He was shuffling. "Tell me something, Robber," he demanded. "That black stuff rub off?"

Robbie did a mock inspection of his arms and torso and feet. "Not so's you can tell. Check the rest of the gear tomorrow."

"Better not wait. Be hell to pay, you come home with soot on your dick."

This quip evoked some obedient tepid laughter. Haw haw haw. Unwilling to leave it alone, Jock delivered a few more thrusts of wit: once you gone black, you never go back; you ain't a man till you split dark oak; old Robber likes his women same as he does his coffee—hot and black. That kind of knee-slapper. A share of his jeering ebullience remained, but not all that much, and what was left seemed forced, sluggish. His eyes were squinty, ringed with weariness. His jowls sagged. Sated himself, he was clearly ready to call it a night.

Which is what he did. "Okay, this goin' to be the last hand," he announced, squaring the deck. "We're playin' Stalingrad. Separate the men from the boys. Or maybe," he amended, "that oughta be the amateurs from the pros. What do you say, Mr. Waverly?"

Waverly met the squinty, malicious gaze. "Roll the cards and we'll find out," he said.

"Comin' right at you."

The game known at this table as Stalingrad was simply a variant of high-low split. In Stalingrad a perfect low was 5 1/2, perfect high 21 1/2. Half points were made with face cards, aces counted one or eleven (or, rarely, both), and everything else was worth its numbered value. On the first round two cards were dealt, one up, one down. A player could either hit or decline and hit on subsequent rounds if he so elected. Each round was followed with a bet. As long as at least one player took a hit, the game and the betting continued; when everyone stood pat, the final bet was placed and high or low declarations made. And then came showdown time. With the right combination of cards it was remotely possible to go both ways, take it all. Possible, but very unlikely and very very risky. It was a bluffer's game, which was one of the reasons Jock liked it, for naturally he fancied himself an inscrutable player. It was also the sort of game could build a mammoth pot, though once that pot was halved it didn't always look quite so gargantuan.

Round one. Drummond showed a deuce, Orton a six, Buel an eight, Demerit a three, and Jock a big ten. Waverly caught an up four and a face card in the hole. Four and a half. Promising, but a long way off any cinch hand. Particularly against three other potential lows.

Jock turned to Drummond. "What's the quote, Bulldog?"

Drummond engaged in a moment of thoughtful pipe-sucking. Dragons of smoke escaped from behind his overbit teeth, crawled up his vacant face. Since in this game there was no power, as such, the player to the dealer's left sat under the gun: first to bet, first to hit or pass on a card. The dealer, of course, went last, both counts. Prime position. Another reason Jock favored Stalingrad when the deck passed to him.

Finally Drummond pushed two blue chips into the pot. "Thousand."

"Thousand!" Jock exclaimed. "Whooee! Gonna call you pit bull after this hand."

There was some grousing from Orton and Demerit, heavy losers both, but nobody folded.

Round two. Jock said, "Okay, who's takin' slaps? Bull?"

Drummond made a negative gesture. Waverly figured him for a concealed three or four, half a point off home plate. Over the course of the night he'd determined that when Drummond had them, he bet them.

Orton also declined, but the disconsolate look on his gaunt face revealed the sorry story of his gaming life. He was just along for the ride.

Little Buel signaled for a card. "Oh-oh," Jock said, "look like me and the big boy in a foot race for high man," and he dealt him a nine. Buel's mouth twisted. He looked as if he were about to weep. Probably wishing they were playing 31 1/2 high.

"Mr. *Pro*fessional?" Jock said around a nasty beaming smile. Fatigue seemed to bring out his natural meanness, and as jeer leader he was getting his second, or final, wind. Waverly shook his head. Wait it out a round or so, see who's going where.

Demerit said no, but without any force or conviction. Despite his bulk he looked shrunken, sallow, wasted. Already his few remaining chips were arranged in orderly stacks. A man prepared to cash out and slink on home.

Jock took a hit. Another ten. He allowed himself just a hint of a trace of a smile. "Lookit that, wouldya? Paired 'em. I called the wrong game." Lots of theatric dismay. Twenty showing, if he was light down below he could be near to perfect. Or he could have gone right through the roof. The bet would tell. Jock's taint was greed, and it was his wagering gave him away.

Drummond laid out another thousand in chips. When it came around to Jock, he said innocently, "Gonna have to bump you two more. Nourish the pot." That dropped Demerit. Waverly made a mental note never to do business with the Demerit First National. Not if he banked the way he played.

On the third round Drummond stood pat. Orton asked for a card. Spooked for low, he was apparently making a desperate run after high. Madness. Suicide. He got a king, and a whistling sigh issued from his pinched lips.

"Be a long slow climb, that rate," Jock observed. "But that's okay, Orton. You got the money, we got the time."

Buel was next. He neither spoke nor gestured. A paralysis seemed to have set in on him, except for the tic beating under an eye, regular as a metronome. Jock regarded him inquiringly. "That mean no, B.B.?"

"Yes. No."

"Well, which one is it?"

"No."

"You and Orton gonna keep me on the straight and narrow topside, huh?" He turned to Waverly. "Sir?"

"No."

"No for the pro, Demerit already boot the wiener, and dealer doin' just fine where he is. So what do you say, Bull Boy?"

Drummond said two thousand. Which meant for sure he held either a five or a six hand. And which was enough to ax Orton and Buel. For Waverly it was nothing but bad news. They had him boxed in, Drummond and Jock, and he had too much on the line to cut and run now. He slid in the chips. Jock raised another two. With high locked in, he was going to make good on his earth-scorching pledge. He and Drummond exchanged quick glances, and then Drummond raised him right back. The squeeze was on.

"Okay," Jock said, "just the three of us treadin' water here. Pot right?"

The pot was right.

"Bulldog, you care for a tap?"

Drummond's reply was a flat "Nope."

"Mr. Waverly?"

"I'll take a card," Waverly said. He was looking for a facer to rescue him, salvage half of a half of the swollen pot. Miraculously, he caught an ace. Five and a half, dead on the money.

"A spoiler!" Jock boomed. "Now there's a man lives right. Look to me like this game ain't quite over. I'm still sittin' pretty-pretty. Bull, you steerin'."

The sight of the ace had tightened Drummond's clench on the pipe, and for a moment it appeared as if he might bite through the stem, snap it right off. He looked at Waverly's cards, then directly at Waverly, first eye contact in twenty-four hours, and then for the first time in that same span he voiced a judgment: "I don't think you got it. Bet is four thousand."

Waverly's supply of chips was dangerously low, and there was no longer any Bankroll Bennie waiting *deus ex machina* in the wings. All he could do was call the bet. Not the best way to play poker.

"Let's put four on top of that," said the predictable Jock, grinning devilishly. "Got to feed my share of the pot."

Drummond, not so confident anymore, merely called. Waverly did the same. Jock announced last call for hits. Drummond's head went no. Waverly made a negative motion.

Jock's turn. He paused dramatically. "Well, you two battlin' it out for low, seem to me I got a really heavy decision to make here. I don't take a card and we got just this one more bet and then we're hangin' it up for the night. But if I was to lay a nice easy love pat on my tens, we could take us another stroll around the block, pad that pot a little. What do you boys think?"

Waverly shrugged. Drummond said nothing, but the stem of his pipe looked to be still in serious jeopardy.

"You ain't no help," Jock grumbled with counterfeit petulance, taunting them. He was loving every minute of it, wouldn't be happy till he'd swept the felt clean, sent them home in barrels. And he needed an audience. The dropouts, restless and sulky, had quickly lost interest in the game, so he turned to Robbie. "Robber, you're in the advice-givin' business. What do you say?"

Robbie had been watching the hand unfold, but without much attention or comprehension. His eyes were glazing over and his shoulders drooped. He worked up an enervated grin, said, "You got me, Jocker. You're the card shark."

"Huh, no help no place. Guess a man's all alone in this world." To prolong the moment Jock did some meditative chin-stroking. Creased his forehead. At last he said, "Well, expect we better run it by one more time." He peeled off a card. It was a six. For a flicker of an instant uncertainty clouded his face. Just a flicker. Just enough. He reassembled his fallen smile, but it was slightly off-center, slightly crooked. He glanced at Drummond. "Bulldog, what's the punishment?"

Drummond checked the bet.

"Up to you, Mr. Waverly."

Now Waverly took his time. Considered. He held a cinch low. But he also held a 15 1/2 high hand, six long points off perfect. The rules of Stanlingrad were Draconian: go both ways and you'd better take both; lose one and you lost it all. Jock was showing twenty-six. If he had an ace or a face card down in the dark, either one, Waverly was drowned. If. But Waverly had seen that flicker. It hadn't escaped him. He tallied his remaining chips: 14 blues, a couple of reds, a lonely white. "I've got seven K and some loose change here," he said. "That's my wager."

"Well well well well," Jock crooned. "Pro finally takin' the gloves off. What was you thinkin' to do if me or Bull slapped a raise on your seven K and change? Your money store looks all tapped out."

"Have to go light, I suppose. Or maybe float a loan from Robbie here."

Robbie fired both arms overhead, polished the blue air. "Oh no, you don't. Leave me out of this brawl."

"Just making a little joke," Waverly said to him. And then to Jock he said, "I could give you a marker. Would that do?"

"No need for that, Mr. Waverly. This is a friendly table. I'll just see your wager. Don't pay to get too greedy."

He counted out the chips and pushed them into the pot. Drummond did nothing. He appeared to be brooding on some intense inner vision. A seance with himself. Plumes of smoke rose from the bowl of his pipe. He turned over his cards. He said, "Fold."

Jock waggled his eyebrows. His mouth widened in triumph, but here was some relief in it too. "Looks like we got ourselves a nice little bird to carve up, Mr. Waverly."

"I believe we declare first," Waverly said mildly. He was feeling good now, very centered and controlled.

"What's to declare? You got the low boat, right?"

"I declare low *and* high."

"Both?"

"That's right, Mr. Appelgate. Both. I'm guessing you took one hit too many. Purely a guess, you understand."

"Okay, that's how you want to play it," Jock said, all bluster and insolence. "What do you call for high?"

Waverly displayed his hole card. "Fifteen and a half. You?"

Jock looked stunned. The triumphant smirk soured. He turned up a two. "You're a good guesser. " 'Fraid my scud here's just a whisker off. Shoulda tucked it in when I had it locked."

Waverly raked in the sprawl of chips. "You remember what Savonarola says: 'Cleanse us of our vanities.' Wise words."

"Who's that, Savona-whatever?"

"Ask Robbie. He'd know."

Robbie was dozing, head lolled over the back of the chair. The sound of his name revived him. His eyes goggled at the sight of the enormous pot resting in front of Waverly. "Hey, what happened, Jocker? Thought you had that one all wrapped."

Jock didn't respond. His stony gaze was fastened on Waverly. They watched each other. A hostile silence unrolled between them. Suddenly Jock burst into a harsh, honking laugh, utterly empty of mirth. "I like you, Waverly. You're a real street mugger. Down and dirty. My kind a man."

"Thanks. I'm flattered."

"That's a handsome pile a change you collected tonight."

"Pays the rent."

"You're goin' to need it, that A-rab ambush we're plannin' next week. What I hear, he only plays no-limit."

"If that's an invitation, I'll be there."

"Oh, it's an invite, all right. Formal. Way I see it, I got a rematch comin'. Bulldog and the rest of the boys too."

Waverly seemed to smile. "I'll be there," he said again.

Jock stuck a Macanudo in his mouth. The hand that held the lighter trembled a little. "Robber," he said through a gust of smoke, hail-fellow hearty now, "whyn't you get that piece a chocolate cake over here. Help your old school chum celebrate his earnings."

"Now *that's* a slick idea," Robbie sad. "What do you think, Tim?"

"I think I'll pass."

Jock snorted contemptuously. "This man ain't human. Don't drink, don't eat, don't screw. For friends, you two sure ain't a whole lot alike. The Robber here's horny as a double-peckered goat."

Robbie's face cracked open in a wide lewd grin. Evidently he'd been complimented. "You sure, Tim? Pursey Sue's a world-class paste swallower. Roll and a half."

Waverly looked at his onetime friend, thinking how the past is always something other than you imagine it to be, and smaller. "Maybe I'll find another way to celebrate," he said.

Bennie occupied the La-Z-Boy with about as much composure as a man in a dentist's chair awaiting the grinding rasp of a drill. His face was a map of the coterminous countries of hope and fear. "So," he said, "we drawin' breath or suckin' worms?"

Waverly laid several thick wads of bills on the counter. "You be the judge."

Bennie got to his feet and hurried over and began to count. His expert fingers flicked the bills rhythmically; his mobile lips kept silent time to the tally. Finished, he turned to Waverly, and now his face was flooded with relief. "Seventy-eight dimes here. And some pitchin' pennies to boot. Timothy, you are down with the program. Mr. Wizard."

"Oh yeah, that's me all right. The wizard of chance."

"Don't knock it. You got us a third of the way home, practically. I'm gonna crack you a beer, boy. Tonight you got it comin'."

"None for me. I'm wiped out."

"One you can do. Bring you down easy."

He went around to the refrigerator and got out two Löwenbräus. Waverly dropped onto a counter stool. Too weary to argue. His body was a stiff bundled package of ache. Some of the depression he always felt following an extended stretch at the table was gradually overtaking him. The too sudden unraveling of that tight little island universe, with its exhilarating properties of risk balanced against the serene administration of the iron ordinances of the numbers. Game's over, sorry, time to go home. Time to return to that other world: drab, gray, prosy, but slippery too, infinitely more tangled, and cluttered with all of life's lesser and greater cataclysms. It was too abrupt. Too dispiriting.

Bennie took a stool opposite him. He lifted his Löwenbräu in a toast. "Here's to you and me and the big buckaroos gonna bring us home free. Little victory poem for ya."

"Lyrical," Waverly said.

They clinked bottles.

Bennie took a long gurgly chug. Swiped at his mouth with the back of a hand. Harnessed a rising burp. "So fill me in. How'd it go? How was the competition?"

"It wasn't any waltz. A couple of them were good. Really good."

"Not in your league though, huh?"

"I'm not so sure about that."

"But you got the booty to prove it."

"Mostly we were playing scut poker. That money represents pure dumb luck."

Bennie indicated the stacks of bills. "Call that a nice piece of dumb luck."

"Next inning we're going to need more than luck, dumb or otherwise."

"Yeah, how's that? You get a line on Arabia?"

"Only that he likes to play no-limit. Which means that seventy-eight thousand's an awfully slim cushion. The cards turn on me, I hit a run of bad hands, and we're toes up."

Bennie tilted his bottle, took down another wash of beer. For a moment he was silent, pensive, his fleshy features furrowed with doubt. "So what you're sayin' here is don't go buyin' any green bananas."

"Not just yet, I wouldn't."

"Tell you something, Timothy. Game of poker there's levels and then there's levels. One you're at is ass-peeling level. I got faith in you."

"Wish I could be so sanguine."

"How about talkin' American. That's what I understand."

"Optimistic. Positive. Confident. Like you seem to be, God knows why."

"Why is because comes to cards you're the best I ever seen. And that's sixty years lookin' in all the right places. Also you got a good history. Step in the poop bucket and come out smellin' like a rose."

"In that case we've got nothing to worry about. Evidence like that."

Bennie looked at him steadily. Steady, probing gaze. "It ain't the cards worries me," he said carefully. "It's when you're not playin' I get the damp sweats. Wonder how long that history gonna hold up."

"Maybe you want to tell me what that means."

"Means you got a phone call while you was out. Lady."

Waverly waited. Nothing more forthcoming. Finally he said, "That's it? Any name? Message?"

"Name's Caroline. Said to call back. Said you'd know the number."

Waverly swallowed some beer. Bitter, it tasted bitter. He pushed the bottle across the counter. "You finish mine," he said. "I've got to crash."

He went to the closet, got the mattress, got it inflated, got himself stretched out. He lay there staring at the fissured ceiling, conscious of Bennie's eyes on him. Their conversation wasn't over yet. Not yet.

"Before you nod off there," Bennie said, "you care to let me in on your thinkin', this matter?"

"Which matter is that?"

Bennie sighed heavily. "Phone call matter. Lady matter. One givin' me all them wet sweats. That one. C'mon, Timothy, we partnered too long. Way I figure it, you owe me."

About that he was surely right. Indisputably right. "I don't know," Waverly said truthfully. As near as he was able to distinguish truth anymore, that was the truth. "Sleep on it."

16

The next night he sat at a table along a glass wall overlooking a narrow channel of the Intracoastal. On the opposite bank the landmark Jupiter Lighthouse towered above a cluster of trees swaying under a small breeze. He was frowning into a twilight that moment by moment blackened lighthouse and trees against a deepening sky. But he was saying something about the lighthouse, its Civil War origins, historical significance, something pedantic, rambling, bland. Spilling out words. Professor Waverly, at your service. Professor of windy wheeze.

An urgent dining room buzz rose up from behind him. And across from him, smiling a wise, secret smile at him, Caroline Crown listened patiently. Her eyes were at once intensely on him, as though he delivered wisdom of the highest and most fascinating order, and far far away. When finally he was run down, she said gently, "Are you nervous, Tim?"

"Nervous? No, I don't think I'm nervous. Well, maybe a little."

"You needn't be, you know. I've covered my tracks pretty well."

"You mind my asking how?"

"Shopping. Shopping's like lunch. Above suspicion."

To Waverly that sounded suspiciously like experience speaking, but he didn't remark on it. Instead he said, "And your husband? Where's he tonight?"

"His name's Robbie, remember? You can still use his name."

"Where's Robbie, then?"

"Oh, off with Jock somewhere. Tending to business, I suppose. I don't know." She underlined the nebulous answer with a quick fluttery motion through the air. Gesture of dismissal. She glanced around the crowded dining room. "What is this place called again?"

"Harpoon Louie's."

"It's very Florida. All the glass and tropical greenery, the water, your lighthouse over there. Do you come here often?"

"Now and again. Not often."

"Why tonight?"

"So I could dazzle you with my lighthouse lecture. Also because you're not likely to run into any of your Palm Beach friends up here. It's out of their orbit."

"I guess finally I'm not all that worried about it anymore. Actually, if you want the truth, I was more worried you wouldn't call. *Your* friend didn't sound too enthusiastic."

"He doesn't approve."

"That much I gathered. That was plain."

"You have to understand, he's got worries of his own. Principally me."

"Tell me, Tim, why *did* you call?"

He thought about that a minute. No good answer occurred to him, but the question triggered a cluster of blurry memories. One of them, a curious echo of this very moment, separated itself from the rest and came into sharp focus behind his eyes. A spring day, their last year in college, Robbie off somewhere—a track meet, debate trip, somewhere out of the picture—and she called him and they spent the day together: tennis (her game, she trounced him), a fast-food dinner, some beers. And talk. He remembered lots of talk. She and Robbie were to be married that summer, and the inevitable second thoughts were setting in. And as he listened, trusted friend but less than comfortable, he thought he sensed an undertone to all that talk, something a little more than the shared confidences of friends, something more on the order of an invitation, or maybe even an appeal. Skirting the edge of an unspoken alternative, she seemed to be pleading: Say the right words now and everything can be different, for both of us, but you have to say them now.

What he'd said then were all the tired commonplace bromides of reassurance, and what he said now, a decade and a half later, was just as uninspired. "Who knows. Better to leave it unexamined. It defies all reason. We're here, maybe that's enough."

Her intense gaze faltered. The smile wilted. "So we are," she said.

There they were, all right, stirring their drinks silently, almost wistfully. There they were, conscious, both of them, of tampering with an unalterable past. And looking at her there, her spare elegant body, her hair a corona of golden light, her sad lovely private face with its distressed smile and its eyes full of the dark troubles of the heart—seeing her that way, Waverly felt a portentous sense of time hovering like a phantom above their heads, and all the promise and resilience of their shared youth dried up and gone.

As if to scatter the melancholy that had settled over the table, she said brightly, "Maybe it will cheer you to know that Robbie says Jock says you're the best card player he's gone up against in years."

"That's very gratifying. I'll try to keep my ego in check."

"You must have impressed them. Which is quite a feat. You've probably noticed neither of them is easily impressed."

"I was lucky."

"From the way Robbie tells it, it was more than luck."

"You don't want to believe everything you hear. As I remember, Robbie was always given to hyperbole."

"Wasn't he, though. Still is." A short bitter laugh seemed to die on her lips. "He says you're going to play next week, when the long-awaited gentleman from Arabia arrives."

"That's my intention."

"And you intend to win again?"

"You always go in intending to win. But who can ever predict? Cards are unreliable. Did you know the Puritans called them the devil's picture books?"

Caroline laughed again, only this time mirthfully and without a trace of bitterness. And with only a touch of irony she said, "Lighthouses, card lore—it's very instructive talking with you, Timothy. Very edifying."

"Just one nugget of intelligence after another."

"Well, here's one for you to consider," she said, her voice flat, earnest, gone back to serious. "Jock may be impressed by you, but he doesn't like you. In Robbie's phrase, he's gunning for you, lining you up in his crosshairs."

"Appreciate the caution," Waverly said, trying with his own inflections to restore some of the lightness.

Without success. "I wouldn't underestimate him," she said, somewhat impatiently. "This is a mean-spirited man. The kind who defines low animal cunning. He's capable of anything."

"That sounds ominous. You're not suggesting cheating here? Nobody cheats at this level of play."

"I'm telling you what I heard. I don't know what I'm suggesting.

But I do know Jock Appelgate. And he passionately hates to lose. At anything."

"Don't we all."

Caroline shook her head and sighed. Long, helpless sigh. "I thought you ought to know. I can't pretend to understand what it is you do, Tim. Or why you're doing it."

Waverly turned over empty palms, a show of concession, disclosure. "Nothing to understand," he said. "I'm grateful for your concern, but it's how I make my living these days. It has its risks." The direction of this talk made him acutely uncomfortable. He didn't want to take it too far.

He didn't have to. She said, "Time for a new topic, correct?" Way out in front of him, as she'd always been.

"I've exhausted lighthouses. Maybe if we have another drink something will come to me."

"That sounds right."

He glanced over his shoulder. Approaching them, drinks in hand, was their waitress. "You read minds," he said to her as she set the two glasses on the table.

For a moment she looked puzzled. Then, waitressly beamish, she said, "Oh no, sir. These are compliments of the gentleman over there."

Waverly suddenly stiffened. "Which gentleman is that?"

"The fellow with the shades," she said, nodding toward the bar, "one with the nice build on him. He said to tell you enjoy, so you do that now, y'hear?"

She bustled away.

"Friend of yours?" Caroline asked.

Waverly shifted in his chair for a better look. The generous fellow with the shades and the nice build on him sat by himself at the end of the bar. Under a mint green, form-hugging sport shirt his torso was kite-shaped from the wedge of latissimus muscles and the steep slope of trapezius. His slicked black hair was glossy as a coat of fresh enamel. He appeared to be staring at them. A thin, carefully selected smile creased his chiseled face. He lifted a hand, fashioned a pistol out of thumb and forefinger, aimed it at them and slowly, very slowly, depressed the thumb trigger.

"In a manner of speaking," Waverly said. "Excuse me a minute. I'll be right back."

He got out of the chair and started across the room. The blank, opaque stare seemed to follow him. The smile widened a little, not much. Waverly came around the bar and came up alongside him. "Thanks for the drink," he said.

D'Marco turned slightly and arched a quizzical brow. "You didn't have to take the trouble, come all the way over here just to thank me."

"It was no trouble."

"Anyway, it's your friends in Chicago you want to thank. They said be sure and buy the man a drink."

"Very thoughtful of them."

"Oh, they're thinking a lot about you, Mr., uh, Waverly is it?"

"That's right."

"For instance, they're hoping the cards were good to you last night."

"Tolerable, tell them."

"Tolerable," D'Marco repeated doubtfully. "Guess that'll make them happy, hear that."

"Anything else bothering them?"

D'Marco leaned back in the barstool and crossed bulgy arms under a pectoral shelf. Seemed to deliberate. He had the iron slinger's nervous habit of flicking his muscles, making them dance, as if to certify their substance and presence. "Well," he said finally, "come to think of it, they did say remind you to keep an eye on the calendar. Said time's running down. About a week left, if I got it right."

"You got it right. Now, is that it? Anything else you have to say to me?"

"That pretty much covers it."

"Then I have a message for you. Back off. Stay out of my face. Keep a distance. When the week's up we'll talk again, you and I will."

D'Marco produced a scrimp of a laugh. "Sounds like a threat. You threatening me, Mr. Waverly?"

"Think of it as a commitment."

D'Marco cocked his head. He inspected him, this scarecrow in the floppy jacket, looked about three sizes too big, and the shirt and tie loose around a scrawny neck, standing there ballsy and badass, facing *him* down. Inspected him in the amused tolerant way one inspects a feisty toy terrier straining at a leash, growling menacingly, innocent of its powerlessness. "This commitment," he drawled, "how you planning to make good on it?"

"I'll think of something," Waverly said, speaking slowly and in a voice clear and considered, every word measured. "Trust me."

He could feel the first gusts of a storm of fury gathering in his chest, rising through his throat. He spun on his heels and walked away. And trailing after him came the sneered maledictory: "I'll be looking forward to our little chat next week."

They were parked in one of the spaces reserved for guests of the Tropicaire Efficiency Apartments. A shattering rain, come up out of nowhere, thumped the Jaguar's roof. Through the streaked windshield a dim light was visible in a window of Waverly's unit, though Bennie's Cadillac was gone. Where and for how long was anybody's guess. Behind them the Tropicaire sign, shimmery in the rain, winked its persistent assentive YES. Across the street the abandoned Collonades Beach Hotel loomed like a wall of shadow on the depthless sky.

Waverly had said nothing on the drive back, letting the impotent fury subside, letting it go. He said nothing now.

"Why is it," Caroline said quietly, breaking the silence, "whenever I'm with you we always seem to be ducking?"

Waverly stared morosely at the dash. He took in a deep breath. "That's one of those things you really don't want to know."

"Oh, but I do."

He shrugged. "You say do, I say don't."

"It's that trouble you're in, right?"

"Yes."

"And that man at the bar, he's part of it?"

"He's one part. There's considerably more."

"Is this how it always is for you, Tim—dodging, ducking, running?"

"Not always. Just lately."

"I wish there were a way I could help you," she said in a small, mournful voice, as though some of his gloom had infected her.

"Being here, that's help enough."

She reached over and covered his hand with hers. There was another silence.

After a while she murmured, "Do you remember what you said when I asked why you'd called?"

"I said I didn't know why. Something like that."

"You said it defied reason."

"And so it does. Neither of us should be here."

"The other day you said the past was a season in our lives. Remember that?"

"I remember."

She squeezed out from behind the steering wheel and leaned over and put an arm around his neck. She stroked his cheek gently, kissed him tenderly on the forehead. "There's a line from a Cummings poem that goes, 'Love is a deeper season than reason,' " she said, and then, almost violently, she kissed him on the mouth. A cascade of her perfumed hair fell across his face.

"Do you want to go inside?" he said. "My partner's gone, it ought to be—"

She laid a finger on her lips, a silencing gesture. "No more words. I want to finish what we should have finished in another car, twenty years ago."

Waverly surrendered himself to her touch, and in the awkward threshing and the dizzying accelerating spiral the scroll of time seemed momentarily, miraculously, to roll backward; and after a long violent surge, violent as her kiss, a peace seemed to settle over and between them, while the rain beat a steady tattoo on the roof of the car.

17

Mr. Badass. Trying to do a Bogart on D'Marco Fontaine. What a hoot.

D'Marco watched him march back to the table, hustle the fluff out of her chair, and steer her to the door. He let them go. No reason not. It wasn't like there was anyplace they could get to where he couldn't find them. Anyway, the lines were drawn now and the clock was running and he meant it, every word, when he said he was looking forward to next week. This one, better than most, he was going to enjoy.

In the meantime, though, there were a couple of other nagging problems to ponder. Not that there was a whole lot he could do about either of them. That waste case he'd left back at the hotel, couldn't tolerate another evening of whiny questions and bitching and general mush-brain talk—what could he do about him? Answer was not a dog-fucking thing; until this arrangement was wrapped, Sigurd Suckwad Stumpley wasn't going to go away. And then there was the more urgent—more alarming, when you thought about it—matter of the message on the answering machine. And thinking about it now, he scanned the faces around the bar, searching for a shooter's empty expression or a chilly eye sliding over him. Takes a pro to mark a pro. But he saw nothing other than a collection of jolly, noisy, juicers, out-of-season-tourist types mostly, whooping it up in Florida on the cheap. No, when that one came it was going to come fierce and sudden and blindside, the way he'd do it himself. Cover your back, boy.

D'Marco finished the last of his vodka-free Bloody Mary and sauntered out to the parking lot. He glanced about warily, side to side and over his shoulder. All clear. He got behind the wheel of the LX and took it out onto the street and over to Highway One. Pointed it south, driving at good-citizen speed. Cars zipped past him. Periodically he checked the rearview. Nothing out of order back there. Around Juno Beach the sky opened up. The highway blurred in the furious downpour. He drove on, slower and more cautious than ever.

And so it was easily half an hour or better after he left Harpoon Louie's before he came through the door of the Sea Spray Room. And when he did, the sight that greeted him was so stunning, so utterly unnerving, so invincibly repellent that for an instant all his studied cool deserted him and his jaws unhinged and his stomach churned under a sudden rush of nausea.

He saw: two swollen blimps, locked and coiled in a classic goatish sixty-nine, jiggly white flesh writhing twitching squirming, shameless in the glare of the harsh overhead light.

He heard: a symphony of grunts, delirious groans, rude slavering noises.

He inhaled: a monkey stink of sweat, assorted body fluids, some cheap vile perfume, a musky aftershave, and other nameless aromas rising from the bed and filling the room like a pestilent gas.

He felt: apart from the nausea, cold rage.

You want to talk about your mountain peaks of disgust, this was Everest.

Sigurd lifted his head and twisted it enough to take in D'Marco. A half-moon grin lit the simpleton face. "Hey, champ, you remember Maylene? Greenhouse?"

D'Marco didn't answer. His mouth had recompressed, the skin drawn tight at the corners.

Sigurd, speaking now down the length of the grotesque coupling, said, "Maybelle, honey? Sugarlips? Say hello to my partner." By way of explanation he added, "We're cellin' together here."

Introductions going around.

Maylene disengaged her head and peered out from under a chunky Stumpley thigh. Damp tendrils of paste-colored hair fell across her eyes. She swiped at them irritably and glowered at D'Marco. Her cheeks glowed like live coals. Her droop-jugged chest heaved up and down, whether from the lingering aftermath of arrested heat or from animus at its untimely breach—certainly not from shame—was impossible to tell. "Nice timin' he's got," she mumbled crossly, thickly.

In a voice icy with control, layer on layer of control, D'Marco, addressing Sigurd directly, said, "Speaking of timing, you got exactly three minutes to get this whale out of here."

"Who you callin' a whale?" Maylene sputtered.

"I'm payin' half on this room," Sigurd protested. "I got rights too."

"Three. And counting."

Sigurd heard the low rumbling menace in the voice. And no mistaking the storm clouds in those eyes. His indignation faltered and he scrambled off the bed and began pawing feverishly through the heaps of discarded clothing on the floor.

D'Marco wheeled around and went back into the hall, banging the door behind him. He stood there ticking off the seconds on his watch, listening to the muffled voices, one low-toned, placating, the words unintelligible, and the other a ranting repetitive squawk—"Where's he get off callin' me a whale?"—punctuated by a coda of curses.

In just under the appointed three minutes the door swung open and Maylene, disheveled but more or less dressed in baggy blouse and circus-tent jeans and spike heels that impelled her into a top-heavy crouch, came stomping through it. Sigurd, wearing only his boxer shorts and a grin gone slack, peeked around the corner and called after her, "Don't be a stranger, hey." Without looking back she elevated a hand, bird finger extended, and kept on flouncing down the hall.

"Look like she got a case of the serious red ass," Sigurd allowed.

D'Marco pushed past him. Sigurd waited in the entrance, watching the frigid eyes sweep the war zone room, the hard jaw tighten, the head nod slowly, wondrously. He guessed maybe the best thing to do or say was nothing at all. Not just yet. Let the ice thaw a little first. Eventually, of course, the eyes fell on him. He gave a helpless shrug.

"Shut the door," D'Marco ordered.

Sigurd shut the door.

"Lock it."

He locked it.

"Now get your fucking clothes on before I lose my lunch."

Sigurd got into his clothes hastily.

Once he was fully dressed, D'Marco said, "This your idea how a job gets done?"

Sigurd lifted an arm like a man taking an oath. "Hey, listen, the Jewboy scooted outta there in his Caddie right after you left. Was nothin' I could do."

"So you figured you'd take a little time out, huh? Do some hippo squiffing?"

"Figured it couldn't hurt none. You was gone. All I knew, you wouldn't be back till morning."

"What'd I tell you about cunts in here?"

Sigurd moved the oath-taking arm through the air. "Okay okay okay," he chanted. "Don't see why it's fryin' your ass any. We been at it—what?—week now, almost. Man's entitl' to some knob-polishin'." It sounded eminently reasonable to him. "Most guys," he added meaningfully, "be ready for it by now."

A shadow crossed D'Marco's face. He went over and flopped on his bed, the single unsullied spot remaining in the room. For a moment he was silent, gazing at the ceiling, deliberating. Then he turned the dark gaze on Sigurd. "You come down here to learn big-time stalking, right?"

Sigurd said Yeah. He didn't like that gaze at all, not one little bit.

"Okay, here's a lesson for you." D'Marco pointed to the deck and said, "Get out there and watch everything going on across the street."

A violent rain slapped against the glass slider, splashed the deck. Sigurd looked out at it, looked back at D'Marco. Got to be a joke. He grinned weakly. "C'mon, man, it's *rainin'.*"

The steady gaze shaded over into something cold, murderous. No joke. "Jesus fuck," Sigurd muttered bitterly, but he opened the slider anyway and stepped onto the deck.

"Leave it open," D'Marco said. "Air out this monkey pit."

Sigurd, instantaneously drenched and miserable, called in a warning: "Gonna rain all over the rug."

"Fuck the rug."

About 2:00 A.M. D'Marco came bolting out of a sleep riddled by terrifying dreams, the substance of which eluded him, though a few vagrant images—disaster images, every one of them: run-away trains, crumbling towers, flaming zeppelins falling out of the sky—still shimmered in his head; and the unaccountable dread he'd felt the other night, alone in the car, overtook him once again. He got out of bed and slipped over to the open slider. The carpet squished softly under his bare feet. The rain had passed, the air was dank and thick. Sigurd was slumped in a deck chair, dozing, head thrown back, mouth a gaping cavern, soggy clothes clinging to him, hair plastered flat to his skull. D'Marco studied him with a curious mixture of contempt and, yes, envy. Imbecile like that, probably sleeps the innocent dreamless sleep of a child. Nothing was fair. He poked him on the shoulder and said gruffly, "Anything happening over there?"

Sigurd snorted a bit before coming back to life. "Huh?"

"Said anything happening?"

"Nah, nothin' goin' on. Couldn't see shit anyway till the rain quit. Kikemobile come in around midnight. Lights went out and there ain't been nothin' since."

"How would you know."

"Look for yourself."

The Cadillac sat in a yellow shaft of neon falling from the Tropicaire sign. The bungalow was dark, enveloped in shadow. "Okay," D'Marco said, "you can go inside."

Too wretched and weary even to give voice to his grievances, Sigurd merely mumbled, "Yeah, thanks a whole bunch," and lumbered out of the chair, shuffled into the room, and collapsed across the tangle of snarled sheets on his bed. In a moment his rhythmic snores, each consisting of a croaky yawp followed immediately by a long wheezing whistle, drifted out onto the deck.

D'Marco stood at the rail. For a switch, the moron was right: nothing to see across the street and, at this hour, not a fucking thing to do. What he needed was rest. After a while he went inside and climbed into bed. He lay on his back wide awake and staring into the dark, listening to the honking lullaby resonating off the walls and ceiling. And astonishingly, in time it stroked him into slumber, fitful and dream-tossed, but a kind of sleep all the same, and better than nothing.

Along with a child's capacity for untroubled sleep, Sigurd was doubly blessed with an infantile gift for annulling the distresses of the near and distant past, dismissing the anxieties and hopes of a murky future, and telescoping the time horizons of his life into the sentient hours of each given, certified day. And so it was that by early the following afternoon he was parked in front of the TV; hoeing contentedly into a brunch of two chili dogs, large fries, side of slaw and, as a nod to his weight problem, a two-liter jug of Diet Pepsi; and quite amnesiac of his misery and aborted passion of the night before. For everything that appeared on the screen, commercials and all, he had an opinion or a comment. He jeered at the magic of Zamfir: "Yeah, sure, master of the fuckin' skin flute." Aqua Ban's guarantee to get rid of the bloat inspired a resolve to "try out some a that shit" tomorrow or as soon as he got back to Chicago. Advanced Dream Away's remarkable pledge to melt off the pounds while you sleep prompted a skeptical hoot. But it was the sight of a grinning fitness guru positioned suggestively behind a shapely leotarded blonde right-angled at the hips, arms windmilling, that evoked his most wildly enthusiastic response: "Oh Jesus, Jake's goin' after the bunghole again!" He sprang spontaneously to his feet and, in imitation of the televised mentor, ground his pelvis at the imagined backside of a wholly imagined nymph, and exhorted her to "Fly like a birdie, honey, squawk like a chicken."

D'Marco, sitting over by a window with a view of the Tropicaire Apartments, laid his forehead in the palm of a hand. One more week. There was nothing to do but endure.

"I tell ya, man," Sigurd told him, "old Jake's got the key to snatch city." He dropped back into his chair, swigged some Pepsi, and looked at D'Marco appraisingly, as though an excellent thought had just come to him. "Y'know, you oughta think about breakin' into that racket yourself, all them boss muscles you're sportin'."

"I got a profession," D'Marco said dourly, thinking about the relentless shrinkage of his unexercised physique.

"Might be you wanta go legit someday. That line a work you'd be a regular ass bandit. More tail'n you could shake your schwantz at."

"Like the kind you had in here last night? Pass on that."

"Yeah, well, Maylene's little on the blubbery side, no gettin' around it. Tell ya, though, it's your porkers sometimes make the best bangin'. What I always look for is them little round fat pockets on the back of the legs, up by the ass. Cell-u-light, think they call it."

"Leet," D'Marco corrected him. "You say it cell-u-leet."

"Light, leet, don't matter, you know what I'm talkin' about."

"I know what cellulite is. Don't know what the fuck you're talkin' about."

"Well, I got a theory about your cooze who carry it."

"Couldn't be you're going to let me in on that genius theory?"

"Sure, you wanna hear it?"

D'Marco neither objected nor consented, and so with the born storyteller's sure sense of pacing, Sigurd dispatched the last bite of chili dog, polished off the fries, washed it all down on a Niagara of Pepsi, thumped his belly contentedly, and blew a burp. "Y'see," he began, "some quiff got it, some don't. That cell-u-light, I mean. Mostly it's on the jumbos, but that ain't always the case. You'll find it on some of your skinny ones too. Either way, question's got to be how they come by it."

"Let me guess. You got the answer."

Sigurd nodded his head wisely. "Think maybe I do. Way I figure how they come by it is by puttin' in some heavy-duty back time. See, all that spike drivin' got to flatten 'em out in the hips and can and thighs. Do it long enough and hard enough and you get your cell-u-light. It's like a badge they're wearin'. Dead giveaway you got a fireball pussy up top."

"So you go after the whales."

"Go after the cell-u-light, anyplace you find it, whale or toothpick. I'm tellin' ya, it never fails. Take Maylene. Back of her legs look like bowl of day-old oatmeal, but she's got a quicksand cunt on her, and she can suck a basketball through forty foot a hose."

"Which proves your theory, huh?"

Sigurd's face opened in a fond recollective leer. He turned over evincive palms. "Checked out perfect on her. You coulda tested it yourself, you hadn't been so sizzle-assed last night."

D'Marco winced. The thought, its very mention, the ugly, ugly image it evoked, made him vaguely sick. He couldn't believe he was doing this, sitting still for it, listening to this bubblebrain, responding to him, actually joining in on this bughouse conversation. It was a measure of the monotony of the day, the wearisome inaction across the street. It was dismaying. And it wore you down. "Do me a favor," he said.

"Yeah, what's that?"

"Go find something to do. Take the afternoon off."

Sigurd squinted at him narrowly. "Hey, you mean that?"

"Said it, didn't I? Say it, I mean it."

Sigurd leaped out of his chair and began stripping off his clothes, leaving a trail of them in his wake. "Aw*right!*" he cheered. "Gonna head on down to the pool, get me a Florida suntan, do some pussy prowlin'."

"Yeah, you do that, go test your Einstein theory," D'Marco said scornfully and mostly to himself.

Sigurd wasn't listening anyway. In a moment he stood there in trunks electric blue and skimpy as posing briefs, terraced pink flesh ascending and descending from them in billowy folds, a towel draped around his stub of a neck, his eyes hidden behind a pair of blue blocks identical to D'Marco's. Stood there like he was modeling the latest fashion in beachwear, delighted, excited, and utterly unashamed. D'Marco turned away. Too much for an already queasy stomach.

"Sure you don't want me to spell you, hey?" Sigurd asked without the slightest enthusiasm.

"Just get out of here, will you? And turn off that goddam babble box on your way."

"You got 'er, champ."

"Quit calling me champ."

"Okay. How about chief?"

D'Marco swatted blindly at air. "Get-the-fuck-*out!*"

"You got 'er, chief."

The door swung shut and he was gone. D'Marco glanced around the mercifully silent room, cleaned and squared away only this morning (he'd supervised the maid himself: vacuum over here, dust back in there, empty this, scrub that) and now lapsed into the familiar clutter and disarray. He felt helpless in the face of a power elemental and elusive as wind, scattering his finest efforts at order and pattern and direction and control. Mark challenging you, turnip-seed buffoon tormenting you, shooter stalking you— it was like the whole world was abruptly upended, nobody in his designated space anymore. Can't let it spook you, he lectured himself; nobody spooks D'Marco Fontaine. Seven more days. Endure, endure.

For three hours he sat motionless as an owl, watching the Tropicaire bungalow shimmer under a blistering sun, watching a scene of ongoing and absolute inaction, enduring. A little after four the phone jangled. He went over and picked it up. A twangy Midwestern voice, identified cryptically as Chicago, demanded to know what was happening. D'Marco summarized the nonevents of the past thirty-six hours, omitting the verbal encounter with Mr. Badass. The voice wanted to know if that was it? No more loot scramblin'? No cute moves? D'Marco told him that was it. The voice whined about their not calling in regular. D'Marco said he was leaving that up to the toejam they'd sent down here, he had enough on his mind, there was something worth reporting he'd punch in. The voice pleaded for some parting reassurances. D'Marco had none to offer. Be in touch, he said coldly, and recradled the receiver and resumed his post at the window.

Inside of ten minutes the phone rang again. D'Marco, cursing, got to his feet again and picked it up again and said, "Yeah?"

Silence.

He said Yeah again, louder, snappish.

More silence.

"Who's calling?"

There was no reply.

D'Marco suddenly understood. "I'll be waiting for you," he said in a voice pitched low and even and freighted with his best menace. But this time he slammed the receiver and threatened the air with curses, though when finally they ran down he discovered to his intense surprise his heart clubbing hysterically in his chest and his tongue stalled on the last feeble invective and glued to the roof of his mouth.

An hour later D'Marco's wandering reflections were ruptured by a pounding on the chain-locked door and an impatient voice yammering, "Hey, man, it's me, Sigurd, open up." D'Marco had backed his chair against the wall, positioned it so he could cover both window and door. He was by now recovered, icily calm, more or less himself again. He got out of the chair and approached the door. His hand was on the butt of a .38-caliber revolver holstered under his shoulder and concealed by a loose-fitting sport jacket, a precaution he had taken immediately following the second call. "You alone?" he said.

"Course I'm alone. C'mon, lemme in."

D'Marco unhooked the chain and Sigurd came bursting into the room. His un-Aqua Banned bloat was streaked with suntan oil and sweat, the skin fried the color of red clay, but he was nonetheless grinning—wide, spill-it-all grin. And innocent of preliminaries, a rush of words poured breathlessly from that jubilant gap in the singed pudge of face: "Wait'll you hear what I turned up, poolside. This one you're gonna like. Guaran-fuckin'-tee-ya, nothing but good news comin' down this line."

"About time for some good news," D'Marco said, locking and chaining the door and edging around him and getting back to his chair. "So what's yours?"

Sigurd was planted squarely in the middle of the room. He had removed the blue blocks, exposing eyes white-fringed and glittery with excitement. "Okay, I'm out there soakin' up some rays and a brew or two, scopin' the twat parade—some fair stuff but nothin' special—till along comes this awesome blonde, better'n that one Jake was corn huskin' on the TV even, that good."

For a moment he seemed to lose his train of thought. It returned and he pushed on.

"So anyway, here she comes struttin' across the deck, got on this suit ain't nothin' more'n a couple pasties on the headlights— Jesus, what a pair!—and a string goes over the gash, crawls down under and creeps right up the crack a the ass. You ain't never seen nothin' like it."

His hands shaped delicious curves in the air, visual aids to the rhapsodic description. There was more.

"Bitch looks like a fuckin' ice cream soda, hair's the Cool Whip on top and mouth's the cherry—and you better believe that's the only thing left cherry on this one. We're talkin' super squeeze here, man, and I'm tellin' ya, it's like instant airborne, every schwantz out there. Christ, I damn near fired a wad on the spot, just watchin' her wiggle."

He paused, and the glittery eyes went dreamy at the memory. D'Marco scowled at him. *"That's* your news?"

"Whole helluva lot more to it'n that. And all of it aces up for you."

"Me, huh?"

"Yeah, right, you. Wait'll you hear the next part."

"Make it quick."

"Okay, she wiggles her way around the pool and plunks that sweet ass in a chair right by where I'm layin'. You think the old pronger didn't stand up and salute? It stood up. But I'm figurin', Forget it, Sig boy, gotta be some lucky dude got his brand on her, sugar pop pro'ly, gonna show up any minute. I give it five, ten clicks. No dude. So now I'm figurin' what the fuck, hey, what's to lose? So we gets to talkin'—ain't it hot today? where you from? shit like that, stuff you say—and she tells me she's on vacation, stayin' here at the hotel, all by herself—"

"Said quick, asshole."

"Awright awright. You want quick, here it comes. Turns out she's—you ready for this?—last year's Miss Rhode Fuckin' Island!"

D'Marco started to say something but Sigurd forestalled it with a waggly finger.

"Hold on, it gets better. She starts tellin' me how she's lonesome, can't meet nobody, all the men act like they're scared of her. Read between the lines and the message is Rhode Island's top slash ain't gettin' any ham slammin' lately. Well, old Dr. Sigurd got the quick fix for that little problem. Meanin' you. See, I know her and me ain't on the same planet, ballin'-wise. Least not till I get the gelt, buy anything I want. Meantime, man's gotta be practical, know his limitations. So I tells her, hey, you're in luck, I got this friend you gotta meet, looks like a movie star, muscles comin' out his shit, cooler'n outer space, sensational personality on him—had to fudge it on that last one—and she lights right up, says, 'Why I'd be just de-*light*-ed. When?' That's what she said. Well, I got to back off 'cause I can't say for sure when, but I get her room number and before she leaves she says, 'Be sure and have your friend call me, don't forget, now.' So I'm thinkin' we get a little break here, tonight, tomorrow maybe, it's high times and home plate for you, chief, dead ahead."

High times. Home plate. Miss Rhode Island. D'Marco shook his head slowly, defeatedly. He regarded him—this leering lump of slicked boiled flesh, this cross to bear—with a profound and wordless disgust. "You finished?" he said.

"That's it," Sigurd said with no small measure of pride. "Your latest poolside bulletin. Good news or what?"

"Okay, I got a bulletin for you. Get that greased ass yours in the goddam shower. Get dressed. See if you can get that peanut brain off your dick and back on business. Do it now."

A battery of expressions worked their way across Sigurd's face: disappointment, resentment (some guys so natural sour-tempered they wouldn't be happy you hand 'em a one way to heaven, which is what he just done), puzzlement, expectancy. "What, something shakin' down?" he asked, nodding at the window. "We goin' someplace?"

"Just do what I tell you."

Sigurd shrugged and started for the john. In the doorway he paused, said uncertainly, "Uh, you want her number yet?"

"Now!" D'Marco barked.

Thirty minutes later Sigurd, reeking of Noxzema and Old Spice, stood once again in the center of the room and announced, "Okay, chief, like your homeboys say it, I'm ready go hangin', bangin', and slangin'."

D'Marco sat stiffly erect, shoulders tight and squared, looking pained at what he saw: a study in greens—apple-green polyester sport coat with needle-peaked lapels, shamrock green shirt with jewel patterns running through it, pleated pea-green slacks—set off by the beaming dumpling face burned brick red. Looked like a goddam Christmas tree, teeth and eyes for lights. It was dispiriting. It was all he had. "You come down here packing?" he said.

"Well, matter a fact, no. My uncle said I needed a piece, you'd provide."

D'Marco got up and went to the dresser and removed his gear bag from the bottom drawer. He set the bag on the bed and began searching through it. Sigurd watched, mouth agape, eyes goggled. "Jesus G. Gawd, you got enough hardware there blow away whole state of Florida." D'Marco ignored him. He was debating between two pistols, a .25-caliber and a 9-mm., both of them semiauts. It was a dice roll; shithead probably aim at a wall and hit the ceiling, but when the crunch came even a few popped caps might help out, create a diversion, draw some fire off himself.

D'Marco settled finally on the 9-mm. He handed it and a shoulder holster to Sigurd and said, "Here on out I want you to keep this on you. Wherever we go, wherever I'm standing or sitting or moving, you take my back. Keep your eyes open and do what you can to keep your mouth shut. You follow what I'm saying to you?"

"What's goin' on, man?"

"Just do it."

Obediently Sigurd took off the jacket, strapped on the holster, and fitted the pistol inside it. With the jacket back on it made only a slight bulge under the old pit. Felt good up there, heavy and solid, real downtown shooter's piece. He was tingly with excitement, but he tried not to let it show. "Where we headed now?" he said toughly.

"You're headed back out on the deck," D'Marco said, shifting his chair to face the door. "You see any action over there, sing out."

Sigurd looked seriously crestfallen. " 'Thought we was goin' sharkin'."

"Looks like you thought wrong."

For over an hour they sat that way, one covering the street and the Tropicaire Apartments, the other the door. Shortly after seven Sigurd called through the open slider, "One of 'em's cuttin' out."

"Which one?"

"Card shuffler."

"Wheels or feet?"

"He's walkin'."

"All right, let's roll. *Move* it."

18

In the bungalow across the road there were stories being told through the better part of that long, lethargic Thursday afternoon, snippets of the varied and colorful life and times of Bennie Saul Epstein. He was eased back in the La-Z-Boy, sipping Scotch, grown uncharacteristically reflective. "He use to say to me—" he was saying to Waverly, seated on the couch opposite him, watching him curiously, surprised and puzzled by these revelations—" 'Benjamin' ('Benjamin,' that's what he always called me, Pop did), 'what you gotta remember is we're the only Jews in Iowa, so we gotta hang together, watch out for each other.' "

"I didn't know you were from Iowa," Waverly said. Which was true. In all the years they'd teamed, Bennie, vision confidently locked on the day after tomorrow, had seldom spoken of his past, and never in any detail.

"Waterloo, Iowa. Born and raised. Your original Hawkeye Hebe."

"What did he do out there, your father?"

"Ran a pool hall. Idle Hour and Gentleman's Billiard Academy, that's what he called it. He always had class. Wasn't a billiard table in the joint, just your straight pool and snooker, but them dillweeds loved it just the same. Saturday night at the Academy—they thought they was livin' in premium cow flop. Also he took some side action. He was a shrewd guy, Pop, nobody's chump. Academy was the closest thing to a book in Waterloo, them days."

"That's where you learned the business?"

"Came later, actual'. I was, oh, fourteen, fifteen when my old lady up and run off with some squarehead. Swede, f'Chrissake, lutefisk eater, sold ladies' foundations door to door. Must a got right down to her foundation though, 'cause she cleaned out all Pop's loot and flew the coop. Never did see her again, so I guess maybe he did get chumped at least once in his life."

Bennie's voice had taken on a throaty, husky quality. In a long swallow he drained the glass, leaned over, and poured another from the bottle on the floor by the chair. The day's heat filled the room, and in the small silence the only sounds to be heard were the hum of the ceiling fan and the steady, ineffective chug of a window air conditioner.

"Well, don't do no good thinkin' about them things," he went on. "Anyway, answer your question, wasn't till after that I started learnin' the profession. Pop had to sell the Academy, and he pulled me outta school and we went on the road. He got a job as a fertilizer salesman. You picture that? Here's a Jewboy name a Saul Epstein peddlin' manure in Iowa. Talk about your alien corn, or whatever it says in your good book there. Didn't bother Pop none. He'd say, 'Benjamin, boy, our future is in shit.' "

He closed his eyes and seemed to smile at the memory shining behind them. Then on he went.

"Course the job was just a cover for the wagerin' we was doin' all over that fine state. Pop had the fever all right, rather bet than screw. Sometimes it was Fat City—Fat Acres, guess you'd say, out there—sometimes we was deadass busted, but all the time we was one hop ahead a the heat. It was some education, I can tell ya. Taught me a lot, Pop did. Well."

"How long were you at it?" Waverly asked.

"Couple years, is all. We're over in this little bug drop of a town, never forget the name—Ida Grove. Stayin' at a dump called the Biggs Hotel—won't forget that one neither. Citizens like to say Biggs Hotel ain't got no ballroom, haw haw, little cornmeal humor. About that, though, they was right. Rooms about the size a your basic closet, damp sheets on the bed, make what we got here look like the Breakers.

"So anyway, Pop services his account and then he goes lookin' for some action. Tells me to wait in the room, he's gonna scare up some hay shakers, roll a few numbers. Couple hours later this plowboy shows up at the door, looks at me funny, and says, 'You an Epstein?' Like I'm some kinda special breed a cow. I tell him Yeah and he goes, 'You better come see to your daddy.' Takes me down to the Biggs cellar and there's Pop flat out on the stone floor, stone cold himself. 'Must a had a stroke,' says the seed, 'but least he made his point before he croaked.' That's what he said, croaked.

"Not that there's any plunder left, y'understand. Rubes long gone and all the loose change with 'em. So I take all the cash I got left and find an undertaker, give Pop a decent plantin', do it up right. Figure he's got it comin'. Day a the funeral we pull outta the stiff house in this hearse, long black mother, me ridin' up front, and we turns onto Main and—wait'll you hear this part— gets caught square in the middle of a goddam *circus* parade. Elephants out ahead of us, clowns alongside, band blastin' in back, citizens on the sidewalk wavin' at us, figure we're just another part a the entertainment. Y'know, Timothy, first I busted out bawlin'—I'm seventeen, remember—and then I got to thinkin' about it and next thing I'm laughin' out loud, wavin' right back, thinkin' if Pop could only see it he'd be hootin' himself, his kind a joke. Yeah, he was some old man, Pop was. Wish I'd've told him that."

A bewildered melancholy, the look that spoke of things lost and gone, settled over his paunchy face. He balanced the glass in his lap and rubbed whiskey-saddened eyes with the palms of his hands.

Waverly sat silently, looking at his own hands, thinking how little he knew this man, this partner of his. And it occurred to him how much less even, for all his fine formal learning, he understood the measureless ranges and ragged landscapes of the human heart. Finally he prompted, "After that, then, what happened?"

"After that?" Bennie repeated absently, coming back from wherever it was the memory had taken him. "Well, after I got Pop settled, Ida Grove Eternal Rest—Saul Epstein in there with all them goys, that's another one he'd've liked—after that I'm dippin' on empty, lootwise; and now I'm the *only* Jew left in Iowa I figure I better start thinkin' the way he would've. So I go back into town and get on with the circus. Circus got a lot a scam games and I'm lucky enough to hook up with a grifter, taught me how to run a basic flat store. Next three, four years I'm all over your corn belt, makin' good money gaffin' the wide-eyes. Time I'm twenty-one I think I know it all, ready for the majors, so I head west, Vegas."

"When was all this?" Waverly asked him. He had the orderly man's urgent need for facts, statistics, chronologies.

"Oh, after the war sometime," Bennie said vaguely. "Back then Vegas wasn't nothin' like it is now. Meds had a headlock on it, was a risky town to be runnin' a scuffle, I can tell you that. But I'm twenty-one, king shit flatty, what do I know?

"Got a job dealin' craps in a sawdust joint downtown, and after a while this crossroader buttonholes me, such a deal he's got for young B. Epstein. Way it's suppose to work is I wear a sub—you know what a sub is?"

"No."

"Sub is a piece material sewn inside your pants, like a big sock, catch the chips you nick on each payoff. Soon as there's heavy action around the table the crossroader shows up, plays noisy, like he's sauced or something, keepin' the boxman occupied, makin' shade. Meantime I'm slidin' house chips in my sub, slow and steady, few at a time. Breaks I go back to the can, pass 'em to a cleanup man. Eight-hour shift we'd easy clear five bills minimum, sometimes up to a couple long. Nice night's take.

"Them days security wasn't so scientific. Payback was, though, once they nailed you, and they did. Me, that is, got the nailin'. My partners Caspered, left me holdin' the sub."

"What did they do to you?"

Bennie smiled ruefully. "Dinged my chimes good. One thing you gotta give your wops, comes to touchups they got imagination. Broke my right arm and right hand, money hand, and my left leg. You got any idea how that slows you down, Timothy? It slows you down."

The glass was empty again. He filled it, held up the bottle in an offering gesture. Before Waverly could decline, there was a sharp rap on the door. They looked at each other, startled.

"You expectin' company?" Bennie said pointedly.

Waverly shook his head and went to the window, opened the verticals, and peered out. A stork-shouldered elderly man stood in the walk, frowning and tapping an impatient foot. Oh Boy O'Boyle. "It's the manager," Waverly said.

"Oh yeah, forgot to tell you, he was in here that day you was workin'. Checkin' out the termite damage, he said. Windy old fart but he's okay, harmless. Go on, let him in."

Waverly got the door, stood in it, and the manager's frown instantly shifted to a bogus landlordish good-news grin. And that's what he said. "Got good news for you fellas, that bug problem. Gonna get 'er cleaned right up for you."

Waverly didn't invite him in; he wasn't up to any Oh Boy fantasy yarns today. "Really," he said. "How are you going to do that?"

"Tenting," Oh Boy said, tilting a little in an unsubtle effort to peek into the room. "Tent the whole unit. Ass-fix-e-ate them termites for good. Exterminators lined up for next week. Wednesday."

Bennie, rooted to the chair, hadn't bothered to move, but now he lifted a languid hailing arm and called over his shoulder, "Howya doin', old-timer? Keepin' 'er wet?"

"Soppin' wet, Mr. Goldstein." Oh Boy's eyes lit and his purplish lips widened, turning the grin rakish and revealing stained teeth notched and jagged as a saw.

"That's Epstein," Bennie corrected.

"Doin' super, Mr. Epstein. You?"

"Hangin' loose," Bennie said sluggishly. "Just hangin' loose."

"She hot enough for ya?"

"Hot one," Bennie confirmed.

Waverly was not of a humor to encourage this vacuous exchange, so he said, "What do you have in mind for us while the tenting's going on?"

"Got that all worked out," Oh Boy said briskly, back to business. "Folks in unit three movin' out, so I can put you fellas over there while it airs out in here. Probably be couple days, that gas they use kill anything can draw breath."

"All right," Waverly said, dismissive tone, "We'll plan on it, then. Wednesday."

Before he could get the door shut Oh Boy snapped a finger, as if in afterthought. "Wednesday. That's right, Wednesday's the first. Rent day. You *are* stayin' on?"

Waverly didn't have an answer to that question. For all the tangle and peril of their present circumstance and for all his careful count of the days rapidly whittling away, he had lost track of the numbers of the calendar altogether. He said, "Bennie?"

And Bennie, addressing the opposite wall, said listlessly, a sigh coming through it, "Yeah, sure we'll engage the place 'nother month. Why not?"

Oh Boy seemed satisfied with that. "I'll come by Tuesday night and we'll get you set up over in three. Nice talkin' to you fellas." He gave a snappy little salute and departed down the walk in an arthritic strut, relieved and happy at the promise of another month's rent.

Waverly locked the door and returned to the couch. "I don't think you should let him in here," he said. "They could have got to him by now."

Bennie brushed the caution away with a flip of a hand. "Aah, can't hurt even if they did. What's gonna happen, gonna happen. Anyway, the old wind-passer got some good stories. Hear him tell it, he's your high-octane Singer Island swordsman. Doin' a nasty with a different slash every night a the week. Twice on Sundays."

"His imagination's overheated."

"Yeah, well, least it's all in the head, his case."

Waverly looked at him steadily. "What does that mean?"

"You think I don't know what's goin' on, Timothy, you and your friend? Lady one, I'm referrin' to. One married to your other friend, who also just happens to be the one we're countin' on get us to the game to get us maybe—heavy on that maybe—oiled outta this worm can we're in. You think I don't know about that? I know."

"It was never a secret," Waverly said evenly, but without much conviction. "And it's nothing you have to concern yourself with. I'll be at that game. I've got things under control."

"Control!" The word was dispatched on a sputtery film of spittle, repeated. "Control. Your history with the snatch, and you're talkin' control. Jesus. Lemme tell you something, Timothy," he told him from behind a jabbing finger. "You're doin' a highwire in your army boots, this one, and I'm right up there in the ozone with you. Gonna do us both in yet. Broads is your blindside. Face it."

Waverly didn't want to argue this. Nothing to debate. Everything he was hearing was right, and he knew it. He lit a cigarette. A slender thread of smoke, thin and pale as breath, rose to the ceiling on the tow of the fan. Bennie took down the rest of his drink and with exaggerated deliberateness poured another. The bottle was emptying fast. There was silence for a time. Long, uneasy silence.

After a while Bennie said, "Speakin' a blind, you wanna hear my best thought on women?" His speech was slurred, sloshy. His eyelids fluttered. All the flesh in his face—cheeks, jowls, chins—sagged precipitously, as though gravity exerted a tug so magnified and focused that if his forehead could have carried loose fat, it would be drooping too.

"What would that be?"

"What a man oughta do is get himself a blind girl," he said, letting it dangle in the air like some grand Delphic pronouncement.

"That's it? That's your best thought?"

"Think about it. Blind ones, you take 'em out, eats, drinks, they can't be always checkin' out the goods in the room, lookin' to improve themselves, move up in the world. So they gonna be loyal, starters. Also can't be nosin' around in your business, seein' how they can't see. There's another plus. And for certain they got to be nut-busters between the sheets, go at it nonstop, touch bein' all they got. What else they gonna do, entertainment-wise?

Pro'ly real grateful too—most of 'em, anyway. So how you gonna top that combination, huh? Go on, tell me, how you beat it?"

The summary question was direct, insistent, demanding of a reply. "Very astute thought," Waverly said, "very insightful. Penetrates right to the heart of the matter."

"Bet your ass, penetrate. Nothin' but penetration, your lady cane-tappers. So you pay attention now, your old Uncle Bennie here, find yourself a nice blind girl, Timothy, keep you straight, outta the glue. . . ."

The voice trailed away, a diminuendo of inebriate advice. The eyes fell shut, the mouth slackened. He farted once, softly, this sodden Nestor, and then he slept.

Waverly got up and gently removed the glass from his hand. He set it on the counter and went to the front window. Nothing to see but waves of heat rising off the street like kerosene fumes. He went to the back window. Nothing there either but for a lawn sprinkler fanning the tiny patch of yellowed grass in the courtyard and a sun pulsing in the white sky. Back to the couch. He felt restless, fidgety. It seemed as if something should be happening; what, he wasn't quite sure. The afternoon wore on. He waited.

Evening came, and the day began to burn itself out in damp heat. A little before seven the phone rattled. He sprinted across the room and caught it on the second ring. Caroline's whispery voice came down the line, message chopped, urgent: Tim? . . . need to see you . . . tonight . . . now . . . good news, I think . . . only get away a few minutes . . . somewhere discreet . . . where? Other sounds filled the background: chattery voices, tinsel laughter, party noises.

Waverly had to think a minute. Discreet, yes, but safe too. Thursday, he remembered, was something they called Key West Night at a marina on the west shore of the island, an outdoor arts-and-crafts show, music, lights, throngs of people milling about. Some small safety in numbers. Walking distance for him, an easy drive for her. He gave her directions, and she said, "Ten minutes," and rang off quickly.

Waverly put up the phone and glanced over at his partner, who slept on, undisturbed. He tiptoed to the door, opened it, noiseless as he could, and closed and locked it behind him. He searched up and down Ocean Avenue. No one in sight. He checked across the street. Here and there a pale light flickered in a room or down a black corridor of the deserted Collonades. Otherwise nothing. He set out walking.

* * *

Half an hour later Caroline came threading through the crowd on the cobblestone walk of the Sailfish Marina and hurrying down the yacht-lined dock extending into the waters of Lake Worth. Waverly waited at the dock's end, their designated meeting place. As soon as she spotted him she stepped faster, stepped right up to him and took him by the arm, and looked into his face tenderly.

"So, Inspector Crown," he said in a tone of mock, low menace, "we meet again."

"So we do," she said, picking up on it, "but this time your evil will not go unpunished. This time you shall pay dearly."

"We shall see who pays. We shall see."

She wrestled unsuccessfully against a smile that broke on a quivery, excited laugh. Long cables of amber-colored hair flowed around the fine, firm planes of her face. She was casually outfitted in denim skirt and filmy blouse, powder blue, to bring out the depth of her eyes, which seemed almost to glisten with an unnatural light, as though they had been polished to a high glossy sheen. She squeezed his arm and laid a soft brushing kiss on his mouth.

"If that's the cruel punishment you exact," Waverly said, "then I must endure."

"Don't think you'll get off that easily. There's worse in store for you, much worse. Which is what I'm here to reveal."

" 'Worse?' he cried. His hand clutched a withered heart, his world began to topple."

Caroline made a mildly impatient face. "Serious now, Tim. You know I can only stay a minute."

"That is serious. Now it collapses in shuddering fall. That world of mine, I mean."

"Come on, smartass."

He put up surrender palms. "Okay, serious."

She released his arm and cast a darting glance down the length of the dock. "Sorry I'm late," she said. "It was tricky, getting away." Her speech was clipped, telegraphic. All her gestures and motions had a twittery, birdlike quality.

"Another soiree?"

"A barbecue, for God's sake. If you can imagine that. At the Appelgate manse. Jock presiding over the grill, in an apron with something precious printed on it, can't remember what. Mercifully."

"So how did you manage it, the escape?"

"With vast ingenuity. Said I'd forgotten my ration back at the hotel, absolutely had to have it. Even sweet Avis could appreciate that."

Waverly looked blank. "Ration?"

And she looked back at him curiously. "Yes, you know, poppers, uppers. Of course I had them in my purse all along. White Cross—don't leave home without it."

Waverly said nothing. They watched each other, seemed to contemplate each other. Her expression turned annoyed, then defensive.

"Remember how they drilled us in Christian forbearance, Timothy, when we were kids? Be charitable, now. You need a ration and a half to get through a night like this one."

"I'm in no position to judge anyone. I told you that the other day. But I can still be sorry. Generally, for the way things fall out."

A kind of melancholy resignation softened the sheen in her eyes. "Too late for sorry," she said wistfully.

"Maybe not," Waverly said, but with no more conviction than he'd displayed earlier, with Bennie.

For a moment they stood side by side, staring at the calm surface of the lake, clear and smooth as green glass. The settling sun pinked the western sky. The silence lengthened. To break it, Caroline fluttered a hand in front of his face.

"I came with news, Tim, not to examine my character flaws. You want to hear it?"

"Tell me."

"It's good," she said, forcing a brightness back into her voice. "For us, anyway. The prince of Arabia is coming in tomorrow night. Miami, his own jet, naturally. Robbie and Jock are going to meet him, and they've already announced they'll be late. Which means—ta da!—I'll be free a good share of the night." Almost timidly, she added, "If you're available, that is."

"My social calendar's pretty empty these days. I'm available."

She clapped her hands delightedly. "Terrific. I've got a marvelous surprise for you."

Waverly shook his head slowly. "Everything about you is a surprise, Caroline."

Her smile was fragile, wispy, its own reward. "I'll pick you up tomorrow afternoon. Around five."

Remembering Bennie, Waverly said, "Maybe it would be better if I met you somewhere."

"Why? Is there a problem?"

"No problem. It would just be easier that way."

She gave a little shrug. "Where, then?"

"How about the corner of Highway One and Blue Heron? You remember, it's the intersection where you turned to get the bridge over here."

"Whatever you say." Her eyes moved to her watch. "I'm going to have to get back now."

"Before you go, one question. Did Robbie or Jock mention anything about a game?"

"Game?"

"Poker game. With the Arab."

"No. I heard them say they're going to take him on a tour of the development site, either Saturday or Sunday. Nothing about a game, though."

Waverly's forehead creased in a worried frown.

"What is it, Tim?"

"Look, you could help me by finding out anything you can about that game. Particularly when they're planning to play."

"You want me to ask?"

"More like listen, see what you hear."

"I can do that," she said, glancing again at the watch. "But I really do have to leave now. I'm stretching my credibility as it is."

"I know."

"Walk me to the car?"

"Sure."

She slipped her hand inside his, and they started down the dock. On the shore they turned in the direction of the parking lot. Waverly scanned the faces in the jostling crowd. So far nothing, or nothing he could see. Behind them the strains of a Calypso trio twanged the muggy air. They passed the display booths of jewelry, hand-painted ceramics, driftwood sculpture, assorted trinkets and gewgaws, all of it gaudy and all of it up for sale. Farther down was the artwork, seascapes and tropical scenes, mostly, though vessels seemed to be big too: yachts, schooners, tall-masted sailing ships, even an anachronous trireme.

"Pretty garish, aren't they," Caroline said.

"What's that?"

"The paintings."

"Oh, yeah, well, it's amateur night," Waverly said. "So you want to remember that charity."

"Look," Caroline said, stopping abruptly. "Look at that."

She pointed toward a booth just ahead. In among all those uniformly predictable scenes was an incongruous watercolor depict-

ing a snug cottage cloaked in a froth of wind-whipped blue snow.
Behind it a dark woods rose in stark and unsubtle contrast, and
above it a coil of chimney smoke led the eye to an intense violet
sky.

"Reminds you of Michigan, doesn't it?" she said.

"Maybe a little."

"More than a little, I think. It's very strange."

"A Proustian moment?"

"Something like that. Like a flicker of a dream of our childhoods. Yours and mine."

"Or the cartoon representation of that dream. The way it never
was."

"But should have been."

"Yes, you're right. Should have been."

For a moment they stared at it silently, both of them, sifting
through separate visions of a lost childhood, its vanished innocence. On impulse, Waverly said, "You like it? I'll buy it for you."

"That's very sweet, Tim, but I'd better not. I could never explain how I came by it."

"I understand." The spell broken, he glanced down the walk
beyond the booth. Suddenly he stiffened.

"What is it?"

Standing there was a figure in every way unremarkable: a man
of indeterminate years, maybe thirty, maybe forty, square-built
and stocky, a bit on the short side, mouse-colored hair, swarthy
Mediterranean face with dented cheeks and a wide, full-lipped
mouth, unsmiling. Unremarkable in every way but one—the eyes,
cold black marble eyes, blank, uncomplicated by any emotion or
expression other than the borderline madness of the born-to-the-
art shooter. They were tacked on something, those unmistakable
shooter eyes, but it wasn't him. Waverly followed them across the
cobblestone walk, through the flocks of people, and discovered
the muscled young man from last night and his comic opera sidekick, the waddler, both of them watching him, craning their necks
to keep him in sight, apparently unaware they were watched
themselves. He looked back at the other one, mystifying new
dimension in this perilous game. A deadly triangulation of vision.

"Tim, what's the matter?"

"Uh, nothing, it's nothing."

"I've *got* to get started."

"I know. You go on now. I'm going to stay here awhile."

"What's wrong? The car's right over there."

"Please, just do it the way I say."

She looked baffled, hurt, a trifle vexed.

"Please," he said again.

"All right. I'll see you tomorrow, then?"

"Five o'clock."

She set out for the parking lot, weaving through the booths, moving at a nervous, quickened pace. Waverly watched till she arrived at the Jaguar, slipped inside, and sped away. And gazing after her that way, he was for an instant swamped by a peculiar alien sensation. For though he had the meticulous memory of the man who's done hard time, this elegant departing woman seemed remote and strange somehow, as if she belonged to a moment in his life he could scarcely remember, fragment of an all-but-forgotten dream, while his waking life, real life, waited patiently behind him, also watching, and being watched.

19

Sigurd was getting worried. They were parked, engine idling, behind the entry building, Port of Palm Beach. On the other side of the high wire fence a queue of jolly tourists snaked back from the gangplank of the cruise ship towering above the dock. Among them were the hard case and his squeeze. Sigurd glanced at D'Marco, who watched impassively, his expression dour and blank. Finally Sigurd said, "Whaddya s'pose he's up to, hey?"

The question was, of course, ignored.

He tried again. "Think he's lookin' to get a game over on us?" Also unanswered.

"Tellya what I think," Sigurd said, agitation elevating his voice, "think he's got it in his head to make a run. Think we oughta be doin' something besides just sittin' on our can, wavin' him bye-bye, have a nice trip. Before suddenly, too."

D'Marco gave him a slow, sidelong glance full of withering scorn. "That's what you think, huh?"

"Right, correct. I don't wanta be the one gets the rap, him duckin' out. You wouldn't either, you knew the man contractin' us. Lemme tellya, that dude carries weight."

"Sort of like yourself, does he? All the wrong places?"

"Yeah, you'll think wrong places, we lose this mark. Like a spear in the ass, one of them places."

"All of a sudden you're taking a real heavy interest in this assignment. Feeling some panic? Shake City?"

"What I'm feelin' is what I just said. Lookit over there. He's almost on board. And we ain't doin' basic diddly."

"Where do you figure he's going to run to, that boat?"

"Shit, I dunno. Wherever it's headed."

"Think it's headed for Cancun? Rio? South Pole? Some exotic spot like that?"

"Said I dunno. You're the Florida flash, got all the answers, not me."

"Well let me tell you something, dickbrain," D'Marco said acidly. "This is what they call an evening cruise. You ever heard of that? Where you been, I suppose not. What they do is sail out three, four miles, drop anchor, let the snowbirds and the chumps do some five-and-dime gambling, swill booze, stuff their faces, and then they come on in. He's not going anywhere."

"It's comin' back tonight? Back here?"

"You do pick up on things quick, don't you?"

"Still couldn't hurt to stick with 'em," Sigurd grumbled, unwilling to concede the point too easily. Besides, he'd never been on a ship before, and from the description of what went on—booze, bets, eats—it sounded like his kind of night. Probably had hookers too, pork 'em on the aft deck, pump 'em on the bridge, or whatever it was they called them places, ships. "Maybe we should go along, hey," he said, floating the notion, testing it.

"You don't listen good at all. You want to go someplace, that it?"

From the looks of the dark scowl playing across D'Marco's face and the nasty wintry edge in the voice, Sigurd figured maybe he'd better drop the cruise idea. "Just wanta do the job right, is all," he said.

"Okay, you want to take some of that radical Chicago action, do something useful, go on in that building there and find out what time the boat comes in tonight. Do it now."

Sigurd didn't argue.

D'Marco watched him stepping smartly through the lot, watched how he moved, fascinated in spite of himself, the way you'd be fascinated by the discovery of an unexpected puddle of puke at your feet, or a mound of dog stool, something disagreeable anyway, disgusting. Miserable dink, had to be the only man alive could combine slouch, waddle, and strut in the same walk. D'Marco shifted his gaze back onto the dock. Across some fifty yards he could make out the badass and his fluff inching toward the foot of the gangplank, where a photographer bottlenecked the line by posing the happy travelers for souvenir snaps, coaxing beamy faces out of them. D'Marco's fingers drummed the wheel impatiently. Give it a few days, about five more now, see who'd be doing the beaming.

Speaking of that, beaming, in a moment the weenie was back,

announcing excitedly, "Be two o'clock in the A.M. before they pull in. How 'bout that! Look like you and me got ourselves eight big free ones."

D'Marco sighed. Another whole night to kill, and in this company. Eight big free ones—didn't he know it.

"So whaddya say, chief? Wanna go bouncin' while we wait?"

What D'Marco said was nothing at all. He cut the engine on the LX, settled back in his seat.

Sigurd looked puzzled and more than a little disappointed. "We just gonna hang out here all eight hours?" he whined.

"What we're going to do, numbnuts, is wait till the boat clears the harbor, be sure he's not thinking some cute bootleg turn. Then you're going to get on the horn, Chicago, fill them in on what's shaking down."

"Which is what?"

"I don't know," D'Marco said flatly. And he didn't, either. None of it seemed to compute. Jewboy keeping down out at the Tropicaire, badass on the boat, carrying on his fine romance. Time ticking by and neither of them doing a goddam thing about that heavy debt they supposed to be working on. Like they were hiding their heads in the sand, hoping it would all go away. Players like that, they'd know better. Nothing goes away. So it didn't compute and he didn't like it, not one bit.

"Okay," Sigurd persisted, "after that, what?"

"After that I'll let you know."

"Smile, Tim."

"I am smiling."

He was, too, or at least trying his best, though it felt more like a stiff grimace stuck on his face. The cruise was one thing, but about this picture taking he wasn't so sure. Seemed to him a needless risk, but she'd insisted: a token of the night, a remembrance.

The photographer joined right in. "C'mon, sir, it's a cruise you're going on, not a wake."

Waverly tightened the corners of his mouth dutifully.

"That's better," the photographer said, with the *sotto voce* qualifier, "a little." He snapped the shutter and waved them on.

The gangplank opened onto an interior deck, and they wound through a gunmetal gray corridor, directionless, pressed along by the lively crowd. They emerged on an open-air lounge at the rear of the ship. Waverly spotted an empty table by the rail overlooking the dock and guided her that way. They sank into facing chairs, and immediately a waiter materialized, a diminutive brown-skinned fellow sporting white jacket, harassed look, and prominent set of bared teeth. Another forced smiler.

"Champagne," Caroline said. "You too, Tim. Tonight we drink only champagne."

Waverly nodded and the waiter hurried away.

"So," she said, opening her arms expansively, taking in the entire ship, "what do you think?"

"It's a lovely surprise, Caroline."

"I hoped you'd like it. And this isn't all. There's more yet to come."

"What more?"

"You'll see," she said over a feverish, ripply laugh. "First I need to wind down. All day I've been tight as a coiled spring."

That he could believe. Her face was flushed, makeup streaking ever so slightly under the lingering heat of the day. Her eyes were luminous, delighted as a child's. Whether she owed the color and electric radiance to excitement or anxiety or chemistry or some combination of the three was impossible to tell, an open question, one he was no more disposed to pursue than the mystery of what was coming next. Not tonight. Her surprise, let her orchestrate it as she would.

The lounge filled rapidly, every table occupied. At the far end a trio of black musicians entertained, calypso of course, setting the mood with lyrics properly risqué:

> "Lulu had a boyfriend,
> Drove a garbage truck,
> Never collect no garbage,
> All he did was—
> Bang bang, Lulu,
> Lulu gone away,
> Lulu gone a'bangin',
> When Lulu gone away."

Howls of riotous laughter. Applause. An audience eager to be pleased.

Soon the champagne arrived. Caroline lifted her glass. "Here's to us, Tim. You and me. And a beautiful evening."

"Who deserves it more?"

"Who indeed."

They clinked glasses.

"I gather you didn't have any trouble getting away," Waverly said.

"Why? Because I was on time for a change?"

"Partly that. Also the very fact you're here."

"There was no problem. Oh, Avis and some other wives were planning to meet for drinks and dinner, but I begged off. Told them I needed a time-out."

"Robbie?"

"He and Jock left just before I did. Don't wait up, were my instructions." She took a sip of champagne, set the glass down, reached across the table, and laid a hand on his arm. "Let's not think about them, Tim. Any of them. We've got tonight. That's enough."

"Carpe diem?"

A fragile, recollective smile crossed her face. "Remember that Marvell line, 'Tear our pleasures with rough strife, / Through the iron gates of life'?"

"I remember, but only barely. In my line of work there tends to be a steady depletion of intellectual capital."

"Well, who's going to argue with a metaphysical poet?"

Now Waverly raised his glass, touched it to hers. "Certainly not I," he said, and this time his own smile was genuine, uninduced. "You're on."

A little after seven the vessel shuddered slightly beneath them and, almost imperceptibly, began to slip away from the dock. "Let's watch," Caroline said, and so they stood leaning into the rail, gazing silently at the harbor gradually receding behind them, the knot of frantically waving figures shrinking in the widening distance between ship and shore, and beyond the port the line of urgent traffic whooshing down Highway One, and beyond that the flat orange disk of sun tacked on the fringe of the sky. And for a moment Waverly was overtaken by that peculiar wordless sense of wonder that overtakes the outward-bound voyager, the curious sense of gazing into one's own past. Till his eyes fell on a black Mustang parked along the fence behind the entry building, and he understood suddenly and in a way he had not before, the hounds of the past were relentless in their chase, remorseless, and utterly empty of forgiveness.

The ship, led by a tiny pilot boat, rounded Peanut Island and passed through the Lake Worth Inlet and out to sea, cleaving the placid water and trailing a cleft of tumbling, billowy suds in its wake. Caroline turned to him and said, "I booked us a cabin, Tim. Royale class. Top of the line. And that's the last surprise."

Jock had a little surprise to spring too, but he was sitting on it just then, saving it for later. For right now he was content just settled back in the stretch limo streaking south on I-95, working on his second Wild Turkey, watching the trail of smoke from his Macanudo coil through the air, and listening noncommittally to his partner—let's make that employee, keep our ranks straight— blowing far less substantial smoke. Nonstop, breathless. Sounded like some twitchy third-stringer trying to psych himself up. Smack talk. Smoke.

Patient as a spider, Jock waited for it to run down. Somewhere around Lantana it did, and in a tone dry, skeptical, he said, "So all's we got to do is reel him in, huh? Pan-fried raghead?"

"Absolutely," Robbie said with a firm, chopping gesture. "We do some fancy gang-bangin'—i.e., walk him over the site, show him the blueprints, let him get a peek at the numbers, projections, keep him entertained—we do all that, it ought to be a lay-down sell. Should be nailed by Tuesday, Wednesday on the outside."

"That quick? Here I'd've figured he'd be maybe havin' some cash-flow problems, price of oil bein' where it is."

Robbie's face cracked open in a slick smile. "Not this one. He just pumps overtime. I'm told he's famous for scamming on the quotas."

"Yeah, who told you that?"

"Some traders I met in London. When I was over there greasing him."

"When was that, again?"

"Last February."

"February," Jock repeated. "Four months, goin' on five, things can change. Your A-rab magic carpets, they ain't flyin' so high these days."

Robbie produced some automatic chuckling noises, but no reply. His glance strayed to the glass in his hand, fastened on it.

"Well, sure do hope you're right," Jock said with a kind of easy congeniality, but drawling it out a little longer than necessary and squinting at him, eyes full of twinkly malice. " 'Bout that sellin' job you said. 'Cause if you're not, then somebody gonna be left holdin' a nasty steamin' turd here." And the way he pitched that made it plain the *somebody* was not going to be Jock Appelgate.

"Listen, our man's a baller, authentic prince, I've had him checked, got more money than camel apples, wells good for another half century, I'm on top of it." The words came firing out, rat-a-tat, but tremulous too, defensive, and much too agitated. Robbie seemed suddenly to recognize it, slowed himself down. "We've got nothing to sweat. It's as good as sealed."

"Real glad to hear that," Jock said amiably. "I do dislike sweat-in'. Too old for it anymore. Comes easier to you young bucks."

Robbie had nothing to say to that. He tossed down his drink, poured another and held out the bottle to Jock, whose head shook no. They rode awhile in a silence exaggerated by the smooth, sound-proof glide of the limo. Exits whisked on by: Delray, Boca, Deerfield. A little south of Pompano, Jock started things up again.

"That entertainment you was speakin' of, what all you got lined up?"

"For starters, a whole stable of blue-eyed blondes. Florida girls. Buzz is that's the way he likes them."

Jock snorted. "Figures," he said with some disgust. "Scratch a A-rab, you gonna find a closet coon underneath every time. Can't get enough a that white meat."

"Maybe that's why they call them sand niggers."

"Huh, worse'n niggers, comes to pussy."

Robbie made a short laugh. "Also there's the game, of course. I mentioned it when I called Wednesday."

"So what's he think about that?"

"He's looking forward to it. Impatiently, is what he said."

"Tell him about your pro-fessional friend?" Jock asked, trace of a sneer on the *friend*.

Robbie winced a little but he said quickly, "Oh yes. That notion really seized him. You know how good he thinks he is."

"Yeah, I heard. Well, we'll for sure find out, won't we? Oughta be a real mean shootout."

Robbie seemed relieved at the direction the conversation had taken. Firmer ground. Encouraged, he went on talking, mostly about agendas, strategies, numbers. Things like that. More of the smoke.

Jock showed a listening face, but there was distance in it too, and he pretty much tuned him out. Biding his time, collecting his thoughts and his words. In business, where allegiances were liquid as sweat, timing was all. So he waited till they turned onto the Airport Expressway; and then at a break in the rushing mono-logue he cocked his head slightly, like a man with a problem to settle in his mind, and unloaded his surprise.

"Y'know, Robber, other night I was layin' some numbers of my own on the calculator machine. Come up with a mighty hefty figure you're into me for. I'm speakin' of that up-front money I advanced you a while back, keep you floatin'. Looks of 'em, them numbers I'm referrin' to, you ain't been pullin' your weight, this venture."

Robbie looked stunned. "Well—yeah—that may be—but—" His voice was stuttery, ascending toward the higher registers. He started over. "That was the arrangement, Jock, for the time being, anyway. It's only short-term. You know I'm good for it. And I like to think I've been making it up in dogwork lately, keeping this whole package glued together." It came out lower now, steadier. Filled with sweet reason.

"That's what you like to think, is it? Lemme tell you something, counselor. That dogwork worth about two shakes of a rat's ass. Don't mean jack shit. Everybody else in, takin' all the risk. I'm done carryin' you, boy. Come up with your share or I'm cuttin' you loose. Simple as that."

"But it's *not* that simple," Robbie said, straining to hold onto the reasonable tone. "You know how hard it is to float a loan right now, my part of the world. Houston's a ghost town, everything up for auction. It could take a while."

"Well, I can understand," Jock said clemently. "Maybe we can work something out. Half might do, show you was in earnest."

"Half! That's still large money. What kind of time are we talking?"

Jock set his glass on the tray. He pursed his lips, laid a thoughtful finger along the side of his nose. "Oh, next week be just fine. Before you head on home, say."

Robbie's boiled face blanched. "Jesus," he said, squirmy in his seat, voice on the rise again. "That's not possible. How am I going to do that, raise the money and juggle everything here at the same time?"

Jock snickered a little, fixed him with a relentless squinty smile, allowed, "I got faith in you, Robber. Always did. You're the kind a fella you throw in the pigpen, you just naturally come out CEO of the hogs."

At about eight o'clock that evening, by Central Time, Gunter Dietz was summoned to the phone. He apologized to his dinner guests, avoided his wife's black glare, and retreated to the privacy of his study to take the call. With the door securely shut behind him, he cleared his throat, lifted the receiver, and in his best business voice—calm, steady, firm—said his name.

"Me, Mr. Dietz. Eugene. Sorry to be callin' you at the house again."

"Quite all right, Eugene. I rather expected it would be you." Among their guests that night was a titled Englishman, and Dietz, who was always looking to improve himself, had picked up some of that gentleman's inflections and speech patterns. But since it was Eugene he was speaking to now, he slipped in and out of a more natural vernacular. "So. What do you hear?"

"Gotta tellya, Mr. Dietz, nothin' that sounds right."

"In what way?"

"Well, just took a report from down south, and it looks like there ain't no action. Zip."

"How do you mean, 'no action'? Specifically."

"Mean just that. Place they're stayin', our people wired in the manager, and he says the Jew's keepin' his head down. Juicin' mostly. Ain't hardly moved all week. And tonight the other one, card scuffler, he's out on a midnight boat cruise, f'Chrissake. Got some twist along. It's like he got his mind on his love life, 'stead of business."

Tacked to the opposite wall was a plaque honoring Dietz's generous contributions to the United Way. He gazed at it. Unconsciously, the knuckles of his free hand rapped the desk. After a short pause he said, "That last game, that was Monday night, was it?"

"Yeah, right. Monday and Tuesday."

"Since then there's been no, ah, evidence of any more scrambling?"

"Like I said, zip."

"And no getting into the wind moves?"

"Not a one."

"This is very strange, Eugene. Not the way it's supposed to be. Not good."

"Don't I know it, Mr. Dietz. Don't stand up, none of it. I think we oughta send our man in right now, you want my idea."

"The two weeks is up, when again?"

"Be midnight, Wednesday."

Dietz studied the calendar on his desk. "Hmm," he said, "five days."

"That's if you wanta let 'em keep on givin' with the shuffle, that five."

"And you think they're going to dime on us?"

"Lookin' that way."

Dietz could hear the anxiety and doubt in his subordinate's voice. Like any effective executive, he listened for such things, took them into account. He was silent a moment, gathering his thoughts, weighing and considering his options.

Eugene finally said, "I can call it in anytime, Mr. Dietz. Tonight, you want."

And Dietz, his decision arrived at, replied quite evenly, "No, no, I think not. Not just yet. What I'll do, I think, is make a trip down there. Business is slow this time of year, I could get away by, oh, say, Tuesday."

"You think that's a good idea, Mr. Dietz? Gettin' yourself in that close?"

"I appreciate your concern, Eugene, but I intend to act strictly in an advisory capacity. Like a, uh, consultant, you might say. This is one closing I want to see done right."

"For a while it went in stages," Caroline was saying, lying on her side, snuggled against him. Her voice was frail, plaintive, but one of her hands described nervous circles, as if to draw figures of ruin and disaster on the air. "There were times—not many— when it was calm, almost serene. Then there'd be an explosion and it would all turn ugly again. A few years ago there was a period when everything seemed to be spinning out of control. That was a very bad time for me, Tim. Hospitals, sedatives, wise psychiatrists. What they used to call, politely, a 'nervous break-down.' "

"And now?" Waverly said. "How is it now?"

"Now it's mostly just numb."

"But there was a time when you loved him. In the beginning, at least."

Caroline considered gravely before she replied. "I suppose so. I don't know. Your memory plays tricks on you, after all these years."

"Not mine. I remember your wedding, I saw you, I was there."

"What you saw was a girl," she said, somewhat impatiently. "A child. Oh, there was the sexual part, in those days. Robbie could be awesomely priapic. I'm sure he still can, though not with the wife, of course."

And remembering also the scene at Jock's hideout condo the other night, a dissolute Robbie sandwiched between his machines of infinite pleasure, Waverly thought how apt it was, *priapic*, how fitting. The sort of word that would roll easily off her tongue. But what do you say to it, a harsh truth like that? You say nothing. So that's what he did, said nothing, lay there allowing his gaze to float around the room, this Royale class cabin of theirs with its beige walls and its gaudy flowered drapes at the recessed window; its couch and chairs strewn with their hastily discarded clothing; its complimentary bottle of champagne, three-quarters gone now, on the table by the bed; and its mirror over the bureau, giving back an image of two melancholy fugitives from life's insults and disappointments and abundance of fractured dreams.

It was Caroline broke the silence. "I'm sorry, Tim, for making you listen to all this."

"I asked." Which was the truth. It was something he wanted to hear from her, wanted to know.

"It's the champagne. Gives me the *vin triste.*"

"You know," he said pensively, "I'm just as sorry. But I confess I don't understand why you put up with it. Why you stay. Your children, you say, but that won't wash. Not in this age. Children go with their mothers."

"Not when the mother's unfit, they don't. Robbie's got a file on me, very thick and very damning. At documentation, he always excelled. There's all those hospitals, shrinks. The drugs I need to keep going anymore, they're on record, they couldn't help my case." She shifted slightly, turning so she no longer faced him. She hesitated, drew in a shallow breath, murmured, "And there've been other men, too. As you might guess."

Once again Waverly was lost for something to say.

"You give up a lot along the way, Tim. You drift."

Who should know better than I, is what he thought, but what he said was, "You couldn't make it without them? Without your kids?" This was the part he needed to settle.

But she said, "I don't know, I don't know," distress rising through her voice. She reached across him for a cigarette, lit it, inhaled deeply. It seemed to steady her some. "Can I tell you a little story? About Robbie, Jr.?"

"Of course."

"He was always a lonely child, stayed close to home, no friends, playmates. Nothing at all like his father. Before we got the place in Hunters Creek, we were living in a small house in Houston. There was a park just down the street, with picnic benches, swings, slides, an old bandshell. Nothing particularly special but, for whatever reason, Robbie loved it, loved that park.

"One morning—he was six, I remember it distinctly—he announced he was going there. A picnic, by himself, all alone. The neighborhood was good, it was safe, it seemed to me a fine idea. Like a gesture of independence. Very encouraging sign. I packed him a lunch, got him started.

"It was summer, a beastly hot day, the way it can get in Houston. I stood in the doorway watching this determined, sturdy little man in short pants and T-shirt marching off to his solitary picnic. So happy and proud of himself. Several times he turned and waved, big wide smile on his face. In Texas, in the summer, we have these gigantic black flies, big as thumbs, the kind that assault you. It was his luck to walk right into a wall of them. About halfway down the block he stopped, and his arms started batting the air, and he started dancing this convulsive jig. He threw his lunch sack on the ground and came tearing back to the house, a swarm of flies trailing him, face all contorted, sobbing, falling into my arms, and crying for me to help him, salvage the day, make things right again. . . ."

Her voice cracked. She sucked in her lower lip, and her eyes misted over, sought the ceiling. She stubbed out the cigarette in the ashtray Waverly held for her. He watched her.

"It was like I was seeing his future unfold in that little scene, Tim. Like it was a metaphor for his life. Or maybe more an augury of what was in store, what might become of him if I weren't there."

Because he had once been a literary man (a thousand years ago, in another life), and because being near her seemed to bring out those buried instincts, and because, finally, her story called to mind a blurred image of his own forfeited son, Waverly was thinking just then of Achilles, of "The sorrow woven into the patterns of a man's life." Prophetic lament. "It's all very sad," he said quietly, and another silence began.

After a while, not long, Caroline said, "This is turning into the wake that photographer warned us about. It's not what I intended, and I'm not going to let it happen. This is *our* night."

And having so declared, she sprang off the bed, gathered up her clothes and purse, and disappeared into the bathroom. The shower sounded. Soon the door opened and she came through it, dressed in her cream silk pants and matching top, sweeping a cascade of hair off her wide forehead. Renewed, it appeared, revived and filled with all the manic energy of a restless driven spirit. Waverly had an idea where that surge of energy came from, but he chose not to remark on it.

"Come on, Tim," she said, tugging at him playfully, "your turn. No more malingering. I'll finish up in here."

When he came back into the room a few minutes later, she was standing before the mirror, applying the final touches: running a comb through her hair, painting on lipstick and eye color, fastening earrings, pulling on a necklace and the diamond-studded tennis bracelet. He watched the ritual, staring intently, as though to lock and seal her features and all her nimble fluttery motions permanently in memory.

She turned and presented herself. "How do I look? Be honest."

"Gorgeous is how you look."

She gave him a smile at once exhilarant and wistful.

He said, "What's next?"

"The casino's next. You're going to teach me how to play cards. Make us rich. If we can't be happy, we can at least be rich."

D'Marco was into his third set of curls, bombing out the reps— four, five—racing the pump—six, seven—taking the burn right down to the belly of his biceps—eight—battling the last ones— nine—clenching his hard jaws, groaning—*ten!* Did it! He set the cambered bar on the floor and dropped onto a bench, arms engorged with blood, heart thudding, breath escaping his lungs in violent gasps. Blitzed, radically. Nevertheless, it felt good, hitting the big steel again. Better than good—sensational. Old Schwarzenegger had it right: getting pumped beat getting laid, hands down, no contest.

Sigurd, slouching against the squat racks, toothpick projecting from a corner of his mouth like a moist needle, looked on with an expression faintly bemused, faintly superior. He waited till D'Marco's breathing returned to something approaching normal, and then he volunteered a word of advice: "Better slow down, chief. You like to blow a nut, end up wearin' one a them trusses rest of your life."

D'Marco tried ignoring him. Lardball. Strutting around the exercise floor in his street clothes, sucking a pick, advancing his value-minus opinions like they were nuggets of rare and precious wisdom. The idiot prince, prince of dumb. Any real hardcore gym they'd of shagged his fat ass right on out of there, long since. Here, Stayin' Alive, Friday night, place almost empty but for a handful of pencilnecks pushing powder-puff weights, wouldn't tax an invalid—here nobody seemed to give a shit.

Sigurd was persistent. "Know what I'm sayin', truss? Like a rupture support? Looks sorta like a diaper?"

D'Marco, still not fully recovered, managed only to produce a surly grunt. The idea of himself ruptured, trussed, diapered, was the kind of idea you'd expect out of Mr. Wizard there, got a spit-bubble opinion on everything. Imagine him, D'Marco Fontaine, in a truss, him with his washboard abs, solid as armor plate, impregnable. (Though on surreptitious fingertip examination they *did* seem to be softening a little. Unless he was imagining it. Maybe he should be backing off from the heavy stuff, least till he got his life back in order again.)

Without a word he got to his feet and went over to the lat machine, set the pin in the plate stack at eighty—nice medium poundage—and commenced a set of pressdowns. He visualized his triceps rippling and swelling, inflating like sausage balloons up the length of his arms. Midway along in the set his muscles began to cramp, suffused by a delicious stinging ache. What are you going to do? Grind 'em out. No pain, no gain. Course this was no way to train either, workout once in eight days, full body at that. Normally what he did was split it up, chest and back first day, legs second, arms and shoulders third, and then repeat the whole process. Six big bombing sessions a week and one day off for good behavior. It was a science, building and maintaining your physique was, and it took mental discipline and dog-ass work. Results were worth it though: living sculpture, pure art.

But no sooner had he released his grip on the bar than Sigurd, hovering near, omnipresent, was at it again: "What's that one for?"

"Tris," D'Marco said curtly. He didn't want to encourage any more chin-dribble conversation.

"What's tris?"

"Triceps, pissbrain. Back of the arms."

Sigurd's mobile tongue shuttled the toothpick to the front of his mouth, balanced it between front teeth. He shook his head slowly, a show of bafflement. "Look like a helluva lot a butt bustin' to me, just to put some bumps on your arms."

D'Marco scowled at him. "Yeah, well, little butt busting wouldn't hurt you any. Maybe get that hippo ass yours through a door without a crowbar."

"Oh, I thought about it couple times," Sigurd said good-humoredly, apparently stung not at all by the remark. "But then I figure what's the percentage, puttin' yourself through it? Sooner or later we all gonna croak, even you, all them muscles or not. Life's too fuckin' short, why sweat it? Enjoy it while you can, is my motto."

"Sounds like something'd be your motto," D'Marco said. He turned away, set the pin in the machine at one-ten (first set went good, might as well go for it—pain-gain principle again), hauled in a great breath, and focusing on the mighty effort ahead, blotting out everything else, grasped the bar and forced it down.

Sigurd, however, oblivious to this heroic contest—man versus the inexorable tug of gravity—kept right on talking at him.

"Take, for instance, this fella I knew up by Lisle. Soaker, real rummy, all his whole life. This was a guy really loved his sauce, even though it was pro'ly killin' him. One day, though, he gets it in his head he's gonna quit—just like that—zap!—chill bird. Takes a vow: turn things around, be a new man."

Already by rep four D'Marco's tris were tightening. Sweat beaded on his brow. His form deteriorated. His concentration flagged.

The cautionary tale wore on:

"Full year he's clean. Proud of himself, but all jittery-actin' too, grouchy, hatin' the world, way your dry drunks get to be. So one morning he's carryin' out the trash and here comes a rabbit barrelin' down the alley, sees him, bites him on the leg."

Rabbits. By rep six D'Marco's focus was irretrievably lost. The one-ten could as easy been a ton.

"Well, guy's pissed, 'course, but he don't think nothin' more about it. Only a fuckin' rabbit, right? Big mistake. Turns out this bunny's got the rabies. Couple days later he comes down with the fever, starts doin' some foamin' himself. Week or so later they find him dead—forgot to tellya, he lives alone. Anyway, he's stone-ass dead. Pretty ripe too, was the way I heard it. So what he done was make his last year shit-miserable, and for nothin', seein' he ends up just as dead. Account of a rabbit. Guy's name was Leonard, I remember right, big fella, bald, always wore a hat—"

Squarely in the middle of a rep D'Marco let go of the bar and the plates went clanging. "God*damm*it, I'm working out here. Can't you find someplace to go?"

Sigurd shrugged. "Got nothin' better to do. Anyway, I never been in one of these sweat palaces before. Always wondered what they was like."

"Now you seen it, why'nt you wait outside?"

"Too hot out there."

"Well quit rapping on me," D'Marco snapped. "I'm trying to stay centered here." He went next to the dumbbell rack, picked up a pair of thirties and began pounding out a furious set of laterals. Even the thirties felt heavy.

Sigurd tagged right along. For a while he was respectfully silent, but eventually, a few sets later, he was moved to observe, "Y'know, we got a lot a your iron-slingers, joint. Jailhouse ladies, most of 'em. I remember this one dude, come in couple months after I did, spick, name of Ramón. Built like King Fuckin' Kong. I mean this was one freaky chili pepper, make even you look like Peewee 'longside him. Mean-lookin' mother too, so everybody figure he had the toughs to do his own time. Figured wrong, though. Spades jumped him, El Rukn gang it was, touched him up good and stretched his lollyhole wider'n your Cal-Sag Channel. Inside a week they had him turned out."

Sigurd's pick was all but disintegrated now. He removed it, examined it, flicked it away. Then he glanced at D'Marco innocently, and with a mischievous lilt in his voice concluded the vignette. "Yeah, wasn't nothin' but a natural-born punk inside that gorilla suit. All them muscles good for was vampin' the spooks."

Okay, that was it, that was enough. Ruptures, trusses, diapers, rabbits, spicks, spades, punks—that was plenty. D'Marco turned slowly, very deliberately, and fixed the grinny face with a steady gaze, fierce and, given the level of his fatigue, filled with his best studied menace. "You got something to tell me here, this little story?"

The grin slackened some. "No, nothin' to tell, just—"

"You suggesting I'm like your greaser friend?"

"Nah, man, nothin' like that. Anyway, he wasn't no friend of—"

"What'd I just say? About you clacking at me while I'm trying to get in a workout—what'd I say?"

"Said don't," Sigurd said, and now, under the weight of that raw-eyed glare, the grin was collapsed utterly.

"And you did."

Sigurd rolled over conciliatory palms, backed away. "Maybe I better wait for you out front there, hey."

In a voice cold, sure, D'Marco said, "Maybe you better. While you still can."

That sent him scurrying.

D'Marco stood with arms folded over his noble chest, watching till Sigurd was certainly, mercifully, gone, and then he returned to his labors. But nothing *felt* right anymore: rhythm off, thoughts wandering, weights heavier than ever, a bone-weariness, mental as much as physical, settling in fast. He pushed himself through a few more listless sets, but none of them were doing any good and he knew it. Finally he gave up in disgust. It was this tangled piece of business throwing him off; get that wrapped and he'd bring things back to normal again, routine. Next week, he promised himself on the way to the showers, next week.

The dealer was riding a serious streak. Six consecutive hands without a loss. When she took her seventh on another natural, third in a row, a thin penciled line of eyebrow arched slightly and a flicker of a smile, whimsical and unapologetic, crossed the lacquered mask of her face. The players' faces, in contrast, were pinched into varying shades of irritation, worry, disgust, and woe.

A hush, compounded in part of disbelief, part silent rancor at the pitiless gods of chance, descended over the table.

Caroline occupied the critical third base. Waverly stood behind her, studying the hands and trying to balance an elementary aces-fives count in his head. Without much success. In blackjack it was tough enough to keep a tally on a four-deck shoe, impossible—for him, at least—when the head was bubbled with drink. "Think of it as units, not money," he whispered encouragingly in her ear, mindful of his own problem, not four days back, with that fundamental axiom of gaming. Physician, heal thyself.

Emboldened by this wise advice, Caroline dismantled her dwindling pillar of ten-dollar chips, stacked five of them in the wager square in front of her, and waited tensely for the next assaultive deal.

The cards came out. She caught an inspiriting ten on the first round, deflating deuce on the second. Dealer showed a three. "Hit it," Waverly said when her turn rolled around.

Caroline snatched a glance at him. "But I thought you stand on these stiff hands," she said doubtfully. She was a quick study but she'd had only the short course in the game.

"This one you hit."

The dealer looked on impatiently.

Caroline signaled for a card, and it was a miraculous nine that fell. She clapped together delighted hands.

"Nice hit," said the dealer dryly and without a trace of enthusiasm. Her eyes were shiny as polished brass, and just as hard. She flipped over her hole card, revealed a six, and dropped a ten on it. Her nineteen total wiped out everyone else and raised a quiet groan around the table.

The player at Caroline's immediate right let out an exasperated wheeze, glared at her. He had a seamed, canny face narrowed by sunken cheeks, a booze-ruined nose, and a shag of unruly dun-colored hair. "Third base supposed to know the game," he growled peevishly. He'd had an eighteen going, a might-have-been push. A peanut player, he'd lost a single chip, ten whole dollars.

"Play your own hand," Waverly said to him coldly.

For an instant they stared at each other across a hostile gulf. The disgruntled player flinched first. He turned away, muttering something about "fuckin' railbirds," but under his breath. Through the next several hands he sat hunched forward in a kind of raging, concentrated sulk, and at the shuffle he got out of his chair and stalked off. Waverly eased into the vacated seat, which felt steamy beneath him. The loser's residual heat.

"What a rude person," Caroline said.

"Yeah, well, you're not likely to find many of your gentle folk here."

A smile spread over her face. "Apart from us," she said.

"That's right. There's us."

To retain the seat, cushion her from any more cretins, who were in plentiful supply, it seemed, he bought a hundred worth of chips and settled in. Recreational play. If there was such a thing for him anymore. Evidently not, for he found himself automatically resuming the count on the next deal, or trying to resume it, with no greater success than before. An accelerated film of cards and numbers, blurry and out of focus, whirled behind his eyes. The rhythmic clatter of slot machines rattled in from the room directly behind them, assailed the ears. Symphony of dissonance. Players came and went, featureless but for their glazed, neurasthenic eyes. In a vacuum of time the game rolled on.

After a while—thirty minutes? an hour? who could tell?—Caroline nudged him and said, "Let's quit now, Tim. It's making me dizzy, all these cards."

The shoe was over half down. If he had the count anywhere near right, the remainder of the deck should be rich in aces and faces. If he had it right. "One more hand," Waverly said, and he pushed out all his chips, eleven stalwart soldiers, a big hundred and ten. Mr. Fearless. Caroline stacked hers in two columns, squared them off, and slid one of the columns into the wager square. Ms. Prudence.

Bets down, here come the cards.

Waverly got one of the tens he knew had to be in there, and then he got a four to go with it. The dealer showed a five. When it came his turn, Waverly held up a flat palm.

Caroline had an ace-six. "What do I do with this?" she asked.

"Double it," Waverly said.

"But I've only got seventeen."

"Still you double."

"Ma'am?" the dealer sighed.

Somewhat reluctantly, Caroline pushed her second chip stack out alongside the first and said "Double down" and another ace was laid on her hand. For Waverly, it was momentarily gratifying to see his tally hadn't been all that far off the mark. For all it might prove.

The dealer rolled over her hole card. A ten. And then with a deft gliding motion she pulled, sure enough, the quashing six out of the shoe. "Twenty-one," she intoned, and scooped in the chips and gathered up the cards.

Caroline looked stunned. Like someone bludgeoned from behind. "What happened, Tim?"

Waverly shrugged. "Sometimes you lose."

She managed a smile, but it was tight, meager. "But all of it? On one hand?"

All of it was maybe three hundred dollars, outside. "Come on," he said. "I'll buy you a consolation drink."

Waverly led her through the dining room and into a small adjacent lounge. All the tables were occupied, but he found seats for them at the bar. He ordered two champagne cocktails, and when they arrived he raised his glass and said, "Welcome to the heady world of gaming."

Caroline touched her glass to his. She took a sip and set down the glass and got a cigarette and fit it into an Aqua Filter and lit it and released a thin band of smoke. All her movements were deliberate, as if she had to think each one through carefully, and she still looked vaguely disoriented, close even to dazed. "How long were we playing?" she asked.

"Almost three hours."

"Three hours. I would have said fifteen minutes. It's so strange."

"How's that?"

"Like an out-of-body experience, a time freeze. And coming back is like waking from a deep sleep."

Though he'd never thought of it in quite that way, it struck him now how accurate she was. A deep sleep. Caroline Vanzoren Crown, perceptive as always. "That pretty well describes it," he said.

"And you do this for a living. I can see why. It's hypnotic. Exhilarating. Even when you lose. Especially when you lose."

"You don't want to make more of it than it is," Waverly said, adopting a sober cautionary tone. "Which is finally nothing more than endless repetition inside of immutable rules and boundaries. Games. After a while it gets to feel quite unremarkable."

"Nevertheless, it's got to be addictive. I speak as an expert on addiction."

"About that, addiction, you may be right. As my partner likes to put it, the gambling fever can get you down and beat you till you're dead. It's the suspense that's the addiction. For all those rules and boundaries, and for all the numbers and cunning strategies you carry around in your head, nobody can ever know how it's going to turn out. Nobody."

"In that, I suppose, it's a lot like life," Caroline said. Her face was bright, troubled, eyes full of a desperate innocence.

"I don't think so. It's just numbers, pure abstraction. It's got no connection with real life whatsoever."

She held up her glass again. "Well, either way, here's to suspense."

Win or lose, it was a night for toasting.

A steward marched into the room and announced the midnight buffet: Setting up right now, folks, ready in twenty minutes. A joyous whoop rose from a party at a nearby table, and they bounded for the door.

"You must be hungry," Waverly said. They had missed both dinner seatings, eaten nothing all evening.

Caroline's face assumed another expression. She gave him a wilting smile and a look that lingered just long enough, by one trimmed beat just long enough, to flash a secret message. "We've got a couple of hours left, Tim. Maybe we can find something better to do."

Helluva way to spend a free night, was how Sigurd saw it. What they coulda been doin' was a little high struttin', throwin' back a few cold ones, maybe even layin' some prime tube, they'd got their shit together, got lucky. Some a your general after hours good time bouncin'. Like any real man suppose to wanta do. 'Stead of what they *was* doin', now the cheese-eater got his boss muscles pumped, which was pullin' into the lot behind the Singer Island Ocean Mall so's he could scarf up a seaweed salad or whatever the fuck it was they passed off as chow at Mother-ballin' Nature's. If it was even open this late, which Flashdoodle didn't know for a fact but which was still okay by him since it was on the way to the port anyhow and since they still had a couple hours to snuff before the boat come in. Maybe (Sigurd thought about saying but didn't), they jammed it, they could find a goddam church someplace, make the Ladies Bible Club meeting, put a head on the night. Comes of teamin' with a little old granny, he concluded sourly. Be a whole different story, it was him pilotin' these overdog wheels and him layin' down the rules.

D'Marco parked at the south end of the lot, in a spot as far away from a light and any other vehicles as he could find. He made a cautious visual sweep of the area: some kids playing grabass in the street behind the mall, here and there a few beach hustlers still on the prowl, otherwise all clear. "Wait here," he said, and he stepped out, lifted the trunk, removed his holstered

.38, and brought it back inside. It was awkward, getting it strapped on in the narrow confines of the car, particularly with his arms and shoulders still tight and achy from the workout, but he managed. Next he wriggled into his sport jacket and checked in the pocket for the blade he'd taken to packing lately. Little extra insurance. Satisfied all the gear was properly in place, he said, "You got your piece?"

"Course I got it," Sigurd huffed. "What'd you think?"

"With you, I never know."

"Now you do, hey, we gonna go grub down that rabbit food or what?"

"Don't talk to me about rabbits."

Sigurd threw up his hands. No talkin' about nothin', Mr. Boiled Owl Shit here.

D'Marco was stalling. His legs felt cramped, almost trembly. His glutes throbbed. Maybe he shouldn't have hit it quite so hard. Layoff and all, even a candyass bombing session like tonight's wiped him out. By rights, he should be feeling that post-workout euphoria about now, that power surge coming on. Nothing was right anymore. Finally he said, "Go take a leak first," and he hauled himself out of the car and with a walk measured and stiff, something close to an arthritic's walk, started across the lot. Sigurd fell in beside him. They turned the corner and headed for the public restrooms on the beach directly across the street from the mall.

What neither of them noticed was the car, a lime-green Olds Cutlass, pulling in just then at the north end of the lot. Its driver was a thickset man, olive-skinned, with eyes remote and empty and unblinking as a reptile's. And those eyes followed them now.

D'Marco had an intense distaste, bordering on loathing, for communal johns. They were seedy places, most of them, dank and foul, breeding grounds for God-knows-what-all kinds of noxious germs. This one was no exception, was if anything worse than usual: rust-flaked sink, paint-blistered walls graced with dreary graffiti, exposed stool bubbling inside a doorless stall, pools of stagnant water of uncertain origin slicking the stone floor beneath the urinals. Also was he repelled by the unwelcome, unsolicited chatter their steamy intimacy seemed inevitably to inspire. When it came to matters of personal hygiene, he wanted privacy, silence. Mercifully, it was empty in here, except of course for monkey-see, monkey-do, who tagged right along and went straight to the sink and scrubbed down his hands as if he were readying them for heart transplant surgery, dried them thoroughly, and then stepped up smartly to a urinal scoop, unzippered his fly, and let loose a torrential splash. As coda, he detonated an explosive blast of wind.

D'Marco hung off to one side, waiting for him to finish and watching the baffling backward procedure. When Sigurd made no move to return to the sink, D'Marco said, "What're you doing, washing your hands first?"

"That's the way I do it," Sigurd said mildly. "Wash 'em first."

"You wash *after*, mutant. That's how it's done. After. Didn't you ever learn nothing?"

"Yeah, but y'see, I got a theory on that."

Immediately, D'Marco regretted this dialogue. And he was the one initiated it. Talk about learning nothing. "Figures," he muttered. "There anything you haven't got a theory on?"

"This one makes sense, you think about it. Good common sense. See, your hands, they all day long been touchin' one thing or another. Who know where they been? You ever catch yourself diggin' the wax outta your ears or a greenie outta your nose? How 'bout if you got a bunghole itch, have to do some heavy gougin'? Or say you had a twat over, play a little stink finger. Places like that, that's where they been, your hands. But take your dick. There she is down there, all covered up in your Jockeys, clean as a whistle. Like it was bandaged, practically. So my theory is you handle the old joy wanger with real special care, real sanitary." He paused just long enough to wink lewdly. "Take care of it and it'll take care of you, hey."

D'Marco laid a flat palm on his forehead. "Do me a small favor," he said wearily.

"You name it."

"Take your fucking theories out of here. Wait outside."

"Sure thing, chief. But you think about what I told you, you'll see that's a theory stands up."

"Out!"

It was a little cooler outside, not much. A small breeze lifted off the surface of the ocean, some relief from the scorch of the day. Sigurd lit a cigarette—might as well get one in while you can, spare the naggin'—and stood filling his lungs with smoke and gazing wondrously into the Atlantic's forbidding blackness, deep and immense. Fuckin' awesome sight it was too, at night. Made you feel puny, like, about as substantial as this thin trail of smoke leaking out of your face and vanishing in the air. Scary, almost, you thought about it: maybe—what?—five hundred feet of sand between you and all that pitching, rolling force and power. Swallow you right up and suck you under, the Big Dude Upstairs took it in His head to raise a serious wind, one of them typhoons or hurricanes or whatever: There goes Sigurd Stumpley, down, down, into the darkness at the bottom of the sea; there goes Sigurd, history. Little poem there. Sad.

There was a sound of footsteps behind him, and he looked over his shoulder in time to catch a glimpse of a stocky figure entering the john. For a fleck of an instant, no more, their eyes met. Sigurd turned back to the ocean, took a deep pull on his cigarette, and tried to recapture some of the cosmic wonder he'd been feeling only a moment ago. But it proved elusive, that wonder, perhaps because the notion of his own death at the hands of capricious supernal forces was too melancholy to contemplate; perhaps because, after a moment's reflection, it occurred to him there was something peculiar in those eyes, something uncommonly chilly, some somber purpose in them; and a sudden alarm went off in his head, and he reached inside his jacket and yanked out his piece and charged through the door.

And came to a lurching halt. Frozen in paralytic shock. His eyes goggled at what he saw: The stocky figure—looked like a wop under the pale light of the bare bulb on the ceiling—in wobbly balance on one leg, knee of the other buried in the small of D'Marco's back, gloved hands tugging a nylon cord cinched around D'Marco's neck; and D'Marco, for his part of it, thrashing wildly, both feet off the floor, arms flailing, hands clawing at air, veins in the throat bulging, face purpling, eyes swimming, mouth widening in the curious appearance of a silent scream. Partnered, the two of them, in a furious dervish dance. And Sigurd their petrified audience of one.

The wop saw him, dropped the cord, and grabbed for the butt of a gun protruding above his belt. Too late. The spell broken, Sigurd lunged, galvanized by a blind terror utterly new to him, outside his experience; and in a wide looping backhand swing, powered by the storm of his fear, he brought the flat of his piece squarely into the wop's face, splattering something, from the sound of it, nose maybe, cheekbone, teeth, something, enough anyway to stagger him, bring on a gushing fountain of blood. Sigurd swung again, forehand this time, connecting solidly with the side of the head, rubberizing the knees. The wop sank onto them, one hand still clutching after the butt of the gun. Sigurd stepped around behind him and with a mighty downward stroke, like a piston dropping, drove the heel of the piece into the top of the skull. Blood squirted from the opened gash. Astonishingly, the wop made no sound whatsoever, other than a kind of wheezy grunt. He shuddered once, then flopped face first onto the stone floor.

Sigurd stood over him, chanting Did it did it did it did it did it. . . . His breath came in abbreviated gasps. Tremors racked his body. Strange stupefying mix of awe and delirium and triumph and relief. Another sensation new to him. And then, remembering his partner, he wheeled around. There was D'Marco, slumped against the opposite wall, his legs crooked under him at tortuous angles, his head lolling against a urinal, his eyes still spinning. His face was chalky, all the purple drained away but for a narrow wine-colored stripe circling his throat, like a necklace inlaid beneath the skin. A damp stain darkened the crotch of his trousers.

Sigurd came over and squatted down beside him. "You okay, chief?"

No response.

"Chief?"

The eyes quit rolling. A dull focus came into them. D'Marco lifted a hand, slowly, as though he were moving it through water, and jabbed a finger in the direction of the fallen wop.

"Yeah, he's out," Sigurd said toughly. "I took him down."

"Drag him over . . . that crapper," D'Marco sputtered, voice a thin sandpaper rasp.

"What for?"

"Do it."

Obediently, Sigurd got up and grasped the inert figure by the ankles and tugged it—felt heavy as a goddam cement bag—across the floor till it lay more or less perpendicular to the entrance to the stall. He had an idea what was coming next, and it didn't cheer him any.

"Shove his fuckin' face in it," D'Marco wheezed.

"Listen, I gotta tellya something, man. I ain't never iced nobody before."

"Now's your chance."

Sigurd gripped the figure at the waist, hauled it partway up, and jerked and twisted till he had the torso drooped over the bubbling stool, arms dangling around the porcelain sides, hands brushing the floor, face an inch or so above the churning water, reddening fast from the spill of blood. He straddled the back. Hesitated. Talking about it, this moment, this act, thinking about it, imagining it, visualizing it—that was one thing. Doing it, he was discovering, that was something altogether different. He turned eyes full of desperate pleading on his partner. "Man, I don't know about this—"

"*Dunk* him!" D'Marco bawled, a thick-tongued squawk.

And so he did. But not without a small struggle, for the figure seemed to come partly to life, the torso jerking and squirming, the arms flapping weakly, like the wings of a crippled bird straining to get aloft, the immersed head rocking back and forth under his quivery hands, an emphatic gesture of no. No.

Soon everything went limp. Sigurd started to rise, but D'Marco motioned him back and fumbled in his jacket for the shank, slid it over to him. Sigurd gaped at it dumbly.

"Pick it up."

"C'mon, hey—"

"Pick it up."

Sigurd picked it up.

"Open it."

It was a switcher. Sigurd hit the release button and a glittery blade fired out one end.

"Now take off an ear."

"Holy fuck, I can't do that."

"Yes you can."

"Fucker's dead, man. Let it be."

"Said do it."

"But why?" Sigurd pleaded. "*Why?*"

"Make a point. People contracted him, they'll know why. Do what I'm tellin' you."

Sigurd stooped over and seized a hank of hair and lifted the lifeless head out of the water. He fit the blade in the hollow behind the right ear. And with his eyes squeezed tightly shut, he drew the knife handle back and down, describing a longitudinal semicircular arc, sawing against tendon tough and gristly as raw meat. When he opened his eyes the side of the head was slick with blood, but the stubborn ear still dangled by a stringy tendinous thread. He hacked at it viciously. Eventually it severed, and the ear fell into the stool, floated on the crimson, bubbly pool. Sigurd released the hair, and the head plopped back into the water. He shrank away, mumbling Jesus Jesus Jesus. . . . He felt as if the very seams of himself were unraveling. He felt faint. Too many new sensations, too alien, bewildering, come too fast. And most of all the stunning recognition that death, harsh and final, really did come with the territory. Astonishing discovery.

It was the D'Marco rasp brought him back: "Get a towel. Wet it down. Wipe off everything you touched, you come in here."

Sigurd swiped a moistened towel over every surface he could recall touching, sink, pisser, walls, stool, everything. The busy mindless chore seemed to help some, settle him down.

D'Marco watched through eyes pared to tiny, dazed slits. The act of breathing evoked guttural noises in his throat. "That'll do," he said finally. "Now gimme hand here."

Sigurd grasped him under the armpits and pulled him to his feet, steadied him against a sudden rush of vertigo. D'Marco fished the keys to the LX out of a pocket, handed them over. "Go get the car. Bring it around. Honk. Move quick, before somebody comes in here."

"You gonna make it?"

"Move!"

Fast as his chunky legs would propel him, Sigurd dashed for the parking lot. He steered the LX into the street, pulled up by the walkway to the restrooms, and gave the horn three short blasts. Immediately, D'Marco came through the entrance, weaving slightly, moving with a tottery shimmying stride, rather like a mechanical windup toy. Sigurd reached over and cranked open the door. D'Marco lowered himself stiffly into the bucket seat. "Roll," he said.

"Where to?"

D'Marco shook his head slowly. "Don't know. Outta here."

Responsibilities, choices, decisions—these were burdens unfamiliar to Sigurd, but not entirely disagreeable either, or unwelcome. It was as if through some magic of reversal he had achieved a moment, however fleeting, however brief, of ascendancy in this peculiar alliance, parity at the very least. As if he had turned a corner in his life, no looking back. So maybe it was worth it, what he done in there, that john. "Go to the Spray," he said, gripping the wheel firmly, all those potent horses underneath him responding to his touch. "Get you straight."

"Whatever."

Sigurd circled the mall and headed back to the hotel. With the door to the room bolted behind them, Sigurd guided D'Marco to the nearest chair and sat on the edge of the bed facing him. "Now how you doin'?" he asked. "Any better?"

D'Marco didn't answer right away. His eyes traveled around the room, slid over Sigurd, came to rest on his own damp crotch. "Christ," he said miserably, "I soiled myself. Christ."

"Hey, man, that's okay. Been me, I'd've dropped a load and a half."

"He took me from behind."

"Yeah, I know. I know. But we fixed his ass good."

D'Marco elevated his chin. "How's my neck look?"

Like somebody took a paintbrush and drew a burgundy-colored line around it, was how it looked, but Sigurd said, "Not so bad, little raw yet."

D'Marco touched at it gingerly. "Think it'll leave a scar?"

"Nah, shit, be gone, day or two."

"You think?"

"Sure."

"Y'know," D'Marco said, a trace of wonder in his croaky voice, "I almost took the thump back there."

"You come close," Sigurd affirmed.

D'Marco stared at him levelly, curiously, as if he were seeing him for the first time. Behind that baffled gaze he seemed to be wrestling with emotions strange and foreign, aberrant to his nature. There was a space of silence. At last he said, "Guess I owe you one, Chubbo."

"Forget it, man. Nothin'. I'm slidin' down the same pole you on, hey."

"Call you Burt, now on."

Sigurd's face creased and wrinkled in sublime joy. A sudden inspiration came to him. "Listen, you think we could bag it tonight? Them marks, they ain't goin' noplace."

"Fuck 'em. I had enough tonight."

"Aw*right!* Tellya what. You wait here. Unwind." His glance fell on D'Marco's stained trousers. "Maybe get yourself cleaned up a little, you can."

"Where you going?"

"Got a surprise for you, chief. This one you're gonna like. Bring you back to life real quick."

"Look at you," Caroline was teasing. "That's what they call a grudging smile."

No denying that. The souvenir photo she held up for his inspection revealed the two of them posed on the gangplank, his face full of tight, strained vigilance unrelieved by the slight tuck at the corners of the mouth, and hers, in contrast, wreathed in an exhilarant smile. "Must be I don't photograph well," Waverly said. "Certainly it's not the fault of the evening. Or the company."

"It's been a beautiful evening, Tim," she said quietly.

"That it has."

In the silence that followed, they seemed to mourn its passing, both of them.

The features of this Caroline, the one examining their like-
nesses, wore a drowsed, stroked-out look, as if she had ascended
to another sphere. A natural serenity softened the eyes. Even the
fluttery hands were still. She contemplated the photo a moment
longer, then slipped it back into her purse.

"You'll want to be careful with that," Waverly cautioned gently.
"Prying eyes, you remember."

"Careful is what I've been all my life," she said, gazing out to
sea.

They occupied chairs by the pool at the extreme rear of the
ship. The sounds of a dying revel reached them from the lounge
on the deck directly above, some feeble laughter, an occasional
spiritless shout, the Calypso trio, with "Lulu" again, but wistful
now, almost desolate: "Lulu gone away. . . ." Walking the song
home, putting it to bed. Somewhere far below them the ship's
propeller churned, opening a whirly seam of foam in the calm
black water. A fat yellow moon hung in a sky splashed with stars
shimmery as a cluster of jewels scattered on the velvet fabric of
the night.

After a while Caroline said, "When am I going to see you again,
Tim?"

"I don't know. I suppose it's really not for me to say."

"Anymore, I'm not so sure about that."

"Well, you know where to find me. I'm not going anywhere."

As though it had just occurred to her, she said, "That game you
asked about? With the Arab? I heard Robbie say they're planning
it for next week sometime. Monday, if they can arrange it."

Monday. And the period of grace expired Wednesday night. It
was going to be a run right down to the wire. And on the other
side of that wire, who could tell? No good trying to look past it,
get there first. "Thanks," he said. "That helps clarify things."

"It was as much as I could get."

"You did fine."

"You're intending to play?"

"More than intending. I'm counting on it."

There was another small silence. Waverly stole a sideways
glance at her. The serenity was gone out of her face. Her eyes,
puzzled, troubled, were fixed on the trail of foam unzipping the
sea in the wake of the ship. Finally she said, "Can I ask you
something, Tim?"

"Ask away."

"Those scars on your body. How did you get them?"

Earlier, lying beside him in the cabin, she had run a finger along one of those scars, looked at him curiously, but said nothing. And he had volunteered nothing. Now he said lightly, making light of it best as he could, "In the argot of the world I inhabit, I got my melon thumped a few times. More than a few, I guess."

"And the trouble you're in now. This game coming up. They're all somehow a part of that world?"

"There's a connection, yes."

"After it's over, the game, then what?"

"After that, I honestly don't know."

She turned and faced him, and in her distressed rising voice there was an echo of the emotional civil war sundering her heart. "I want to see you again, Tim. I *need* to. Once more, anyway."

I want, I need, I must have: Grant me just this one want and I'll be happy, content; well, maybe that one too, maybe one other, one more. What a bundle of urgent wants we are, Waverly was thinking, all of us. And he heard himself replying, "I want the same thing."

And as they sat there nurturing their wants, the ship came through the Lake Worth Inlet, passed under the looming shadow of Peanut Island, and steamed toward the port. "Let's watch," Caroline said, and so they stood at the rail, staring at the garish blaze of lights on shore. The ship eased laterally into the pier, nudged it. Casually, almost as a kind of throwaway mention, Caroline said, "I think maybe I won't be going back to Houston next week. Maybe I'll be going with you instead."

Waverly looked at her searchingly. "You 'think'?"

"That's what I think tonight."

"Even without your children?"

"Even then."

In the depths of those luminous eyes of hers Waverly saw, or thought he saw, realms of vast possibility, infinite hope. He was crowded with feelings for which there were no words. And curiously, when his own eyes scanned the lot behind the port entry building, as they instinctively did, the black Mustang was nowhere to be seen. He felt suddenly as if he had been gifted with a peculiar prescient vision of moving toward some event, as yet undefined, but monumental and inevitable and outside the boundaries of his control, still another surprise ahead in a life full of turmoil and ambushed dreams and terrible, terrible surprises. "I promise nothing," he said.

"Neither do I."

D'Marco was drunk. First time in longer than he could remember, years. Head inflated, skin prickly, face flushed, eyes whiskey-glazed, speech slurred, limbs slack, a lazy warmth seeping outward from his chest to his farthest extremities, scalp, fingertips, toes—no mistaking it, he was surely drunk. In evidence was the seriously tapped jug of Jim Beam sitting on the table beside him, half of Sigurd's—Burt's—surprise. Sitting all squirmy sexy wiggly on his lap, nuzzling his neck, was the other half: Miss Rhode Ass Island, if not this year's then last—some recent vintage, anyway. Look at her: spill of platinum hair, jade green eyes shadowed in violet, round red targets of rouge on cheekbones cut with the precision of a diamond, pouty mouth large and glittery with lip gloss—holy Christ, looked like a rich confection there, three-layer cake drenched in frosting and topped with a puff of whipped cream. Like your wildest, most forbidden, most deeply buried pornographic dream sprung to life. Come true. With a woman, he didn't even want to try remembering how long it had been. Long.

"Ooh, such *muscles,*" she cooed, honeyed voice. One of her hands was inside his shirt, stroking the deep cleft between his pecs; the other clutched at a partly flexed bicep. Spectacular hands she had, the fingers practiced, nimble, sure, the nails scarlet talons. Ball-squeezer hands. Pud-pullers.

D'Marco gave in to her satiny touch, to the delicious, wondrous sensation of being still alive. Instead of dead. He brought the bicep to a tight swelling peak. "Yeah, I got pretty fair set a cannons on me," he allowed modestly, sloshing the words. His tongue felt furry, too thick for his mouth.

"But your neck," she murmured, brushing moist and slightly parted lips over the raw welt, "what happened to it?"

"Uh . . . that . . . uh . . ."

He was rescued from a reply by Burt's voice booming in off the deck behind them, trailed by Maylene's squealy giggle: "Yo, Jake, we havin' any fun yet?"

Without looking over his shoulder—neck still much too tender for that—D'Marco lifted a leaden arm and polished the smoky air in response. "Fun," he repeated. "Yeah, right, fun. Gettin' there. Gettin' close."

"How come he calls you Jake?" asked Miss R.I. "Thought you said your name was D'Marco."

"Nah, it's Jake. Was jus' pullin' your leg."

She licked his ear. "I like D'Marco better," she said. "Sounds so strong. Hard."

Too late to go back on it now. Too bad. For tonight, at least, he was Jake. Sigurd's idea—Burt and Jake. Another of his fuckin' theories. And she was Brooke or Belinda or Brigitte, something like that, something with a goddam *b* in it somewhere. She had her slim elegant legs draped provocatively over the arm of the chair, Brooke-Belinda-Brigitte did. Now she brought one knee up near his chest, exposing even more of both creamy thighs, barely covered anyway by the denim mini already riding perilously high, barely clearing the crotch. "Speaking of leg-pulling . . . ," she said.

Or started to say, for just then Maylene, announced by her vile perfume, came tromping through the slider, proclaiming in hog-caller bray, "Gotta pee." Maylene wore a mini-skirt too, revealing elephant thighs, ponderous, thick, shapeless, and mottled on their backsides with fat bubbles that, in Sigurd/Burt theory, gave away her insatiable lusts. She wagged her head at Belinda (D'Marco had settled on that one, liked the silky melody of it) and said, "You wanna come along, honey?"

"I'll just freshen up a little," Belinda whispered in his ear, and she slid off his lap, ran a meaningful lingering hand over the bulge in his pants, and addressing it directly, said, "Don't go away, now."

The pair of them, elephant and sleek gazelle, a study in polarities, disappeared behind the door to the can.

Sigurd lurched into the room. All the buttons on his shirt were undone. His sun-toasted belly swelled over his belt. A film of sweat slicked his forehead. His eyes were fogged, mouth set in a lop-sided grin, pinch of a cigarette dangling rakishly. In his hand was a water glass full of Beam. With inebriate caution he lowered his rump onto a bed. He said, "So whaddys think so far, big Jaker?"

" 'Bout what?"

"Rhode Island. I give you the straight goods on that one, or what?"

"That one you got straight," D'Marco affirmed.

"Some set a hooters on her, hey. You road-test 'em yet?"

"Yeah, sure, course I did," D'Marco mumbled, though in fact he had yet to make contact with any of the Belinda treasures. Even loosened by drink, some natural reserve, the distancing imposed by the iron edicts of the mythology of his life, forestalled him.

"Tonight's the night, my man," Sigurd declared with a slow-motion wink. "Fuck, suck, and run amok."

D'Marco motioned impatiently at the bathroom door. "What's takin' so long?"

"Give 'em time," said the worldly-wise Burt. "They gettin' themselves primed, way twats always gotta do. Be out, minute. Then it's quick as a wink you're in the stink, hey. Get the job done right." He gulped some Beam. Made a whistling noise through his teeth. His brow furrowed in what appeared to be the effort of thought. He snapped a finger. "Oh yeah, job talk, almost forgot. When I was out on the deck there I seen the mark come in across the street. Squeeze dropped him off. So we still doin' ours. Job, I mean. Little sideline squiffin', that don't hurt none."

D'Marco nodded. A remote corner of his bleared brain took in this intelligence, processed and recorded it, but he didn't say anything. The whole night was so bizarre, so inverted, he didn't want to think about it right now. Didn't really give a fuck, actually. He was grateful just to be alive, still walking around inside his skin. For now, this moment, the one upcoming soon as that door swung open and the Rhode Island vision came gliding through it—for now that was enough. Plenty.

Maylene and Belinda suddenly appeared. And wordlessly, as if on signal, everyone moved somewhere, purposefully and, through D'Marco's eyes, eyes of the unseasoned drunk, at a suddenly accelerated pace, fast-forward blur: there was Maylene, stripping off her blouse and plopping onto a bed, legs twin pillars in the air as she tugged at her skirt; there was Sigurd, fumbling with his belt, dropping his pants and his boxer drawers and falling across her; and there was Belinda approaching him, slipping gracefully out of her skirt and halter top, clasping his wrist and drawing him out of the chair and leading him to the unoccupied bed and reaching behind her and dousing the light, and then drawing him down, down, into a tangle of limbs and a swamp of moist steamy aromas, urging him on, directing him by touch—go here, go there—uttering pleasured yips and crooning, "Now baby sweets honeydip now yes now now . . ."; and there he was, D'Marco Fontaine (or Jake), thinking What've I missed—Where've I been?

Later, he lay on his back, arms flung out, head whirling, senses reeling. Stuporous, numb.

Sigurd's sly, slushy voice filtered through the dark and the silence settled over the beds. "Anybody up for little switch meat?"

Nobody answered.

Sigurd gave it a moment and then tried again. "Y'know how the song go: 'Pig knuckles and rice, / You eat it once and you want it twice.' "

Both girls giggled.

D'Marco heard rustling sounds, felt movement on the bed. Hands pawed at him, groped in secret private places alien hands had never before intruded and penetrated. He was too emptied to speak, or protest. And then a mass of panting flesh descended on him, and astonishingly a fresh surge rose through his loins. He grasped doughy grinding buttocks and the backs of two lumpy thighs, and discovered, to his amazement and utter disbelief, at least one of Sigurd's (Burt's) loopy theories was right after all.

20

Waverly woke early the next morning, hauled by Bennie's roupy snores out of a slumber dream-riddled, unsatisfactory, and brief. Off and on, mostly on, for the next thirty hours he listened to the sotted memories and deepening alarms of a partner sinking fast into a doom-struck torpor, offering sterile assurances where he could, and watching a phone that stubbornly refused to ring. Sometimes, nodding at appropriate junctures in one of the wandering B. Epstein chronicles of the past, Waverly found himself concocting fanciful visions of escape, a bold flight to some remote outpost somewhere outside the reach of shadowy, vengeful shooters, a life with Caroline Crown (make that Vanzoren; his fantasy—why not?) of bland routines, predictable patterns, small happy commonplace problems with agreeable resolutions. Till his eyes refocused on this desolate pouchy fellow rooted to a La-Z-Boy in a corner of a scummy beach apartment, this man by nature and experience possessed of a shrewd, unclouded, elementary, and yes, ultimately benign view of the world, this benefactor and unlikely friend, caught in a cross-hatched web of low schemes and deceits and paybacks none of his own making, and reduced now to inertia and despair—and seeing him that way, Waverly's enchanted vision of another life dissolved like the filmy disjointed imagery of a fantastic dream.

At about two o'clock Sunday afternoon the telephone finally rattled, and Waverly, long past dissembling, bolted off the couch and picked up the receiver on the second ring and heard with a mix of disappointment and relief the blustery voice of Robbie Crown demanding, "Tim, that you?" Waverly confirmed that it was. Robbie told him the game was definitely on. Waverly said fine. Then in a tone studiedly neutral, all the bluster gone out of it, Robbie said they really ought to get together today, run by time and venue and arrangements, details like that, and "some other business." He knows, Waverly thought; Where and when? he asked carefully. Somewhere out of the way, Robbie suggested, where they could pop a couple, talk; away from The Island, he specified. Waverly proposed the Crazy Horse on North Lake. He started to give directions, but Robbie said he knew the place, could be there in an hour. It was settled: three o'clock, the Crazy Horse.

Bennie was dozing. Just as well. One fewer not-so-happy problem to deal with. Waverly scribbled a vague note and left it on the counter. He slipped across the room and lifted the keys to the Seville from the pile of change on the coffee table. Outside, first time in two days, he was assaulted by a corrosive heat, and he had to pause a moment and adjust his eyes against a violent glare of sun in a white sky. Consequently, he missed the prying gaze leveled from behind the partly cracked open door to Oh Boy O'Boyle's unit.

Fifteen minutes later, well ahead of the appointed hour, he swung the Seville into the near-empty Crazy Horse lot. He took a table in a corner by a window. Ordered a ginger ale. It had been a while, three months or more, since the last time he was in here. He looked around. The walls were adorned with Crazy Horse T-shirts and framed photos of nubile young ladies in Crazy Horse tank tops. There was lively piped-in music, but it seemed to have no brightening effect whatsoever on the handful of morose Sunday-afternoon drinkers anchored to their bar stools. None of them looked familiar, or threatening. He thought about rehearsing some responses for this upcoming exchange, but when nothing came to him he gave it up and simply waited.

Shortly after three Waverly caught a fleeting glimpse of the back of a heavy figure passing the window, and from the public man's purposeful stride he recognized instantly it was R. Blake Crown, come to have a little chat. In another instant Robbie was settling his bulk into the chair opposite him. They traded greetings. Robbie ordered a Jack Daniel's, "straight and tall." He asked Waverly what he was drinking, arched an eyebrow at the answer, said, "Whatever turns your motor over," and instructed the girl to bring a fresh ginger ale as well. He told some wicked anecdotes about the Arab, punctuating them with the throaty laugh of a barking seal. His delivery was practiced, staccato. A man with a great deal to say and in a hurry to get it said. He sat with his thick shoulders scrunched forward, a tight, restricted smile stuck on a face burned the color of red clay but with a sallow tinge to it too, fatigue's pasty yellow wax.

Waverly watched and listened, saying very little. The drinks arrived. Robbie took a healthy jolt, straightened his back and squared his shoulders, regarded Waverly steadily a moment. Here it comes, thought Waverly; now, finally, here it comes. He was mistaken.

"That game the other night," Robbie said. "You mind my asking how much you lifted off those boys?"

"Why?"

"Just curious."

"No, I don't mind. It was seventy-five thousand, thereabouts."

Robbie gave a breathy whistle. "Nice take."

"The cards were good to me."

"But you were playing them right, too. Especially that last hand."

"That was the one put me over the top. Saved the day."

"You know," Robbie said thoughtfully, "it doesn't surprise me you're good at cards. You always were a tactician, problem-solver. I remember how you played chess."

"Poker and chess are two entirely different games."

"Suppose they are at that," Robbie said, clearly indifferent to gaming theory. "Tell me, you ever heard of something called the Golden Rule, your profession?"

"Oh yes: Man with the gold makes the rules."

"That's the one. This game coming up—tomorrow night, by the way, eight o'clock, out at Jock's condo again—this one the raghead's got all the gold so he's laying down the ground rules. Which is part of what I wanted to talk to you about."

"For instance?"

"Well, for one thing, he'll only play eight hours at a stretch, one break. Three nights running, is what he wants."

"What else?"

"Stud poker and lowball only, five- and seven-card."

Waverly shrugged. "I can live with those conditions."

"I expect you can. Stud's your game, right?"

Little cunning word play there? Waverly couldn't be sure: The florid face was expressionless, gave away nothing. "That's right," he said. "How did you know? You didn't seem to be paying much attention the other night."

"Jock. He said you weren't too keen on the crazy games."

"Right on that, too. But if they're the only ones in town, that's what you play."

Robbie made a small appreciative chuckle, absent of mirth.

"What's the other part?" Waverly asked innocently.

"Pardon?"

"You said the ground rules were part of what you had to tell me."

Robbie cupped his hands behind his neck and gazed at some point beyond Waverly's shoulder. He let a moment elapse before he said, "Yeah, there's a couple other things I thought we might discuss."

So at last we get to it, Waverly thought. Wrong again.

Robbie said, "You remember it's a no-limit game tomorrow night."

"I understand that."

"Some large dollars likely be changing hands."

Waverly was genuinely puzzled by the oblique angles of this conversation. "That's why you play," he said.

"Sure it is. But the camel jockey, he's got the whole Arabian treasury behind him. Jock, Bulldog, they're millionaires, many times over. I'm thinking your seventy-five soldiers going to be seriously outgunned at that table. Unless of course you've got some other sources to tap."

Waverly didn't bite on that.

Robbie's gaze narrowed in on him slowly, appraisingly. "If that's not the case," he went on, "about those other sources, I mean, then I've got a little proposition to make you."

"What would that be?"

"I happen to have some spare change to invest. Not a lot. About what you got, as a matter of fact. What if I were to buy in with you, put another seventy-five on top of yours?"

Waverly decided it was time for a cigarette. He shook one out of his pack, lit it, followed the drift of smoke with his eyes. "Let me see if I've got this right," he said. "You're offering to stake me?"

"Exactly."

"Why would you want to do that, a nongambler like you? And why me? If you want a piece of this action, why not your buddy, Jock?"

"That's three questions," said the shrewd counselor. "Which one do I address first?"

"You pick."

"Okay, first things first. The sorry truth is, Tim, I'm a little overobligated just now. I need to raise some loot fast—i.e., by next week."

Something else they had in common, Waverly was thinking. He said, "How much loot?"

"Not much. Couple hundred balloons would swing it."

"That's on top of the proposed stake?"

"Correct."

"All right, one question down. Two to go."

"Those are easy," Robbie said. "I'm the one put this deal together. Me. Without me it would be a handful of air. Dreams. Right now I'm about a twat hair away from nailing it down, and it's my 'buddy,' as you put it, who's got me jumping through my own asshole. Good old boy, Jock. After all the pimping I've done for him, this project, he's trying to spin me out of the loop. Man's word's about as valuable as a Salvation Army doughnut." His voice was heating up. Various shades of anger played across his face. His eyes were full of grievance.

"If you owe him money, wouldn't a loan be simpler? And considerably less risky?"

"Aah," he said with a vexed swipe of a hand, "all my cash cows are dried right up. You don't want to hear the details, Tim."

That much was true. He didn't need any more of the Crown family's catalogue of woes. What he had already, that was enough. "So you come to me," he said. "You must be desperate."

"Desperate, guess I'd have to say yes. But I'd have thrown in with you even if such weren't the case."

"Really," Waverly said with some skepticism. Greasing he didn't need either. "Why is that?"

"Remember your Humanities, Calvin College? 'The fox knows many things, but the hedgehog knows one big thing.' One of those ancient Greeks said that, forget which. My thought is the cards are your one big thing. Everything worth knowing about them. Including maybe a little sleight-of-hand."

Waverly stubbed out his cigarette. He looked at him coldly. "You're talking about cheating?"

"It's winning I'm talking about."

"Okay, let me trade quotes with you: 'All life is 6–5, against.' Damon Runyon said that."

"So? What's the point?"

"Point is, when it comes to cards there are no guarantees. Ever. Even if I did cheat. Which I don't."

Robbie held up a flat palm. Stop signal. "Just making a joke," he said, and he fabricated a hearty laugh in evidence. "No offense. I know you don't need that kind of edge. But I'm guessing you *do* need a backup bankroll, and if I'm right, then that's where I come in. That's my proposition."

Waverly did some quick arithmetic in his head. For himself and Bennie he had to come through with at least one-seventy-five. Add to that another two hundred and you were looking at close to four hundred K. Big numbers. But not out of reach in a no-limit game with players heeled like these were. With any luck he could pick up the whole bundle the first night, duck on out of there. Fuck the Arab and his imperious ground rules. Jock too. Just get up and walk away. With any luck. Of course there was always the counterscenario: his seventy-five valiant soldiers snuffed in one small run of bad cards. Pick your scenario. He liked the first one better, but liking didn't necessarily make it so. "Any stakehorse I play for takes fifty percent of the plunder," he said. "And a hundred percent of any loss. If we make this arrangement, that's how it works."

"Just get me those two big balloons by Wednesday. Anything over that, we'll work out something equitable. We got a deal?"

"Deal."

"Sensational. I'll slip you the cash tomorrow night. Oh, you do understand this has to be strictly between you and me. I got an act going here."

"Is that something like an image to preserve?"

Robbie's upper lip curled slightly, parody of a smile. "Something like that," he said. He picked up his drink, which seemed to have been forgotten in the intensity of the dialogue, and tossed down what was left. "Got to scoot," he said. "The sheik summons."

For Waverly it was hard to believe he was squirreling out of this one—the Caroline end of it, anyway—so effortlessly. And yet it appeared to be so. Until Robbie got to his feet and stood there a moment, looking distracted, like a man with something more on his mind, something loosened from the grip of memory and then suddenly recovered; and when it was, Waverly found he was mistaken once again.

For Robbie said, "Oh yeah, one other item, speaking of acts. Yours and Caroline's, it's transparent as a pane of window glass."

He removed a snapshot from a shirt pocket, and with a flip of the hand fluttered it onto the table. Waverly didn't bother to look at it. He knew what it was.

"Couple of happy campers," Robbie sneered.

Quite evenly, though a little short on authority or conviction, Waverly said, "She's coming with me, you know."

"You think so?"

"Yes."

"You're talking trash, old buddy. Old friend. She's going no-where. We've been down this trail before, Care and I. Many a time."

"This time's different."

"Different? Let me give you a piece of legal advice, Timothy. Free. No charge. Same as I gave Care." His eyes sparked danger-ously, and the free advice unspooled off a bobbin of venom. "If she decides to bolt, she can kiss the kids goodbye. For good and all. Her history, running with somebody like you, ex-con, mur-derer, card hustler—in a custody fight I'd turn her inside out and upside down. Punish her. Drag her through so much muck she'd be taking a lease on a rubber room, long-term. So you remind her of that, your next little getaway cruise."

He started to leave, paused, turned, and looked over his shoul-der at Waverly. The facsimile of a smile, long since departed, returned, spread slowly over his sizzled face. "See you tomorrow night, huh? Meantime, you have yourself a super day. Partner."

No more than ninety seconds after Waverly left the Tropicaire Apartments on his way to what would be a most curious meeting, the telephone jangled in a second-floor room of the Sea Spray. At the time that it sounded, Sigurd/Burt was just stepping out of the shower, absently humming some unrecognizable tune; Maylene was sprawled laterally across a bed, deep in the narcosis of a boozy sated sleep, inert as a corpse; and Belinda, the prize of Rhode Island, was sunning herself on the deck. Which left only D'Marco/Jake, prostrate on the other bed, nursing a rhythmically thumping head, a still stinging neck, and various other anatomical parts tenderized by the frisky entertainments of the preceding thirty hours—only him to reach over stiffly and uncradle the re-ceiver and grunt into it something resembling a greeting, a slug-gish and sour-tempered and upwardly inflected "Uh?"

His voice, however, picked up momentum and, given his con-dition, a kind of fevered intensity, and had anyone been listening he could have been heard muttering, "Yeah, when? . . . which way? . . . by himself? . . . how about the other one? . . . yeah yeah, you did good . . . right, keep watching." He put down the phone and swung his legs over the side of the bed, steadied himself for just a fraction of an instant, and then made for the door. Before he got there Sigurd/Burt came out of the bathroom, obscenely naked but for a ribbon of towel strung around his privates, saying, "What's up, man? Thought I heard—"

"Mark took off in the Caddie," D'Marco/Jake barked over his shoulder, "Jew's still there. Get dressed, goddammit, and get your ass out on that deck, cover him." He slammed the door behind him and, fast as he was able, sprinted through the corridor and down the two flights of stairs to the basement-level parking area. In a moment the LX came squealing onto Ocean Avenue. He pointed it north, the direction he'd been given, and passed by the mall and the bunker-like public restroom where, only two nights earlier, he'd very nearly drawn his last breath.

No sign of the Caddie.

At the end of the street he swung left, crossed the bridge, and pulled up at the intersection of Blue Heron and Highway One. Uncertain which way to go next. On an instinct he turned right, and for the next sixty minutes he covered and recovered a good share of Lake Park and North Palm, main thoroughfares first: Silver Beach Road, Old Dixie Highway, Park Avenue, North Lake, Prosperity, RCA Boulevard; followed by residential streets with names such as Jasmine, Laurel, Fair Haven, Gulf, Harbour, Garden Lane; his eyes searching frantically, head swiveling in spite of the raw, abraded neck. But this time his instinct failed him. No Caddie.

On a last hunch he went west on PGA Boulevard through Palm Beach Gardens to the grounds of the PGA National Golf Course, and from there to the condo that was the site of last week's game. Still no luck. Place looked deserted: drapes drawn and not a single vehicle parked in the street out front. For another half hour or so he drove around aimlessly. Finally he just gave it up and returned to Singer Island. And the first thing he saw, coming down Ocean Avenue, was the elusive Caddie sitting outside the Tropicaire Apartments, sunlight glinting off its windows.

During the time he had been gone the three occupants of the room had changed positions. Game of musical assholes. The door to the bathroom was open and Maylene, clad only in bra and panties that looked about a yard wide and twice that measure vertically, stood before the mirror applying paint. Now she was the one doing the off-key warbling. String-bikinied Belinda napped on a bed. Out on the deck Sigurd/Burt, behind his blue blocks, appeared to be gazing across the road, though he also pulled at a bottle of beer.

D'Marco/Jake joined him. "When'd he get back?" he said.

" 'Bout twenty minutes ago."

"Any other action over there?"

"Nope, not a goddam thing. Must be he just went for a little Sunday afternoon drive, hey."

"Anything more out of the manager?"

"Nothin'."

D'Marco/Jake thought about it a minute. But not long. He wagged a thumb in the direction of the room. "Okay, get 'em out of here."

The tone of the command was such that Sigurd/Burt thought it better not to argue. There was a sound of rising voices from behind the glass slider, but D'Marco/Jake didn't bother to look. Instead he kept his eyes locked on the apartment across the street. Soon Sigurd/Burt was back on the deck, mumbling somewhat sheepishly, "Girls was wonderin' if we could spare some change. Y'know, little time and trouble money?"

"Do what you want," was the glacial reply. "Just get 'em the fuck out of here. Now."

And though he was seething with shame, disgust, self-loathing, he felt at least partly redeemed by the certain knowledge he was himself again, D'Marco Fontaine. Jake no more.

PART

FOUR

21

The Arab was a man whose appetites seemed to be writ large in the contours of his soft brown face. Maybe it was in the mouth, a wide cavernous chamber with lips full, red, perpetually moist, perpetually parted, revealing teeth so glaringly white and so even they might have been quarried from marble. A mouth custom-designed for ingestion, consumption. Or maybe the nose: steeply angled, slightly beaked over a gully deep as a watershed beneath bristly nostrils that twitched occasionally, as though they were sniffing after some as yet unsavored ambrosial delight. Certainly it was in the eyes: dark, peering, watery, somewhat protuberant, with a rodent's remote, pillaging cast to them. His hair was coal black and brilliantined to a patent-leather sheen. Billows of flesh cushioned the clefted needle of a chin. Perhaps because of its extrusive quality, that dust-colored flesh was smooth and wrinkle-free, and so estimating his age was all but impossible. Forty, maybe, give or take five years.

And yet he was by no means a corpulent man, for all the puffiness. Soft, yes, but delicate-boned, with narrow shoulders and frail chest tapering into a plump little orb of tummy framed in round hips, propped by slack buttocks and supported on thin planks of legs. Shaped rather like an indolent girl, was Waverly's thought on first meeting him. There was, in fact, a subtle, almost feminine elegance in his gestures and mannerisms, a kind of perfumed languor. Earlier, when introductions went around (conducted, of course, by Jock and in his finest down-home style: "Prince, like you to shake hands with our pro here. Prince Mohammed Al-Fassi, Tim Waverly"), the prince had extended a limp, finger-bejeweled hand as though offering it up for a kiss. With a chilly elevation of chin he peered at Waverly, and in a drag queen's whispery baritone allowed to some small pleasure. And later, before assuming his place at the table, he summoned with his eyes the bodyguard who evidently doubled as manservant and who, in that capacity, helped him out of a pastel-pink linen jacket and drew back a chair.

Now, three hours into the game, Waverly had taken his measure and arrived at the conclusion this Arab, this dandyish prince, was something less than the dangerous opponent whose formidable reputation preceded him. Without a doubt he knew his mathematics, perhaps too well, for he played with a certain mechanical predictability, devoid either of imagination or daring and seemingly oblivious to anyone else at the table, as if the contest were exclusively between himself and the cards, an extended version of solitaire. Nor was he a reckless wagerer, aggressively forcing hands through the sheer weight of his limitless resources. As a result, with just those three hours behind them, Waverly was up over sixty K. The heavy hitter. So far.

Although Jock, possibly out of deference to his titled guest, had managed to stifle some of the nonstop chatter that normally characterized his play, after Waverly's third consecutive win he was moved to remark, "Look like you got your booster rockets on tonight, Mr. Waverly." This observation was delivered in a musky drawl, cornmeal persona still intact. Some constants yet in this world, thought Waverly as he raked in the chips, a nice little haul lifted directly off the prince himself, who backed away on the last card of a low-ball hand.

A couple of other such constants were Bulldog and Buel. The former played with his usual taciturnity, strategies and emotions concealed equally behind the ossified overbit grin; the latter with the same desperate incaution that had brought him to grief only a week before. What poor little B.B. was doing here was anybody's guess. Fulfilling some darkly prophetic, dimly understood, self-abasing need, maybe (Waverly had seen that kind of player, a welcome addition to any game). Or maybe he'd been strong-armed by Jock, since Orton and Demerit had wisely opted against sitting in, though they were present tonight as spectators. Also looking on was Robbie, who, after passing Waverly an envelope full of bills at the door, had discreetly avoided him ever since.

And that was it: five players, three railbirds, and one manservant/bodyguard. No ladies of the night, by fiat of the prince, who preferred his pleasures compartmentalized and who, after graciously absorbing the loss, said in an unruffled voice betokening noble ease under all circumstance, "Nimrod, a cigarette, please."

Like a fearsome genie emerging from a bottle, Nimrod rose off a bulbous couch, whose cushions deflated beneath him on the ascent, and approached the table. He stood four or five inches over six feet, had to go an easy two-seventy. An immense slab of a man, all but neckless and with a square huge head that seemed either to have sprouted from the beefy shoulders or to have been lowered onto them by a crane. His kinky hair was clipped short, with a razor slash part on the left side. His skin was a midnight blue-black. A prominent Neanderthal brow ridge hooded eyes utterly blank. The remainder of the face looked stepped on, the nose flattened, nostrils wide and flaring as a baboon's. In a series of deft moves, each one executed with deliberate precision, as if form were all, he produced cigarette and flame. A hush settled over the table, and every eye in the room (the prince's excepted) followed those moves. Watching him, Waverly was reminded of the Jacktown superdudes he had known, predatory blacks with abundant reserves of brutality, the sort who could come at you like a rockslide, and not infrequently did. Men not to be messed with.

"Also a glass of white wine," the prince directed, and in a flash Nimrod vanished behind the door to the kitchen. Another flash and the wine appeared before the prince, who took a fastidious sip. Nimrod loomed over him, hovering. An image, quite unbidden, came to Waverly: Nimrod turbaned, bare to the waist, scimitar slung from garish pantaloons, palm leaf fan in hand—the Nubian slave ministering to an effete master's every whim. The prince set down the glass, lifted a dismissal finger, and Nimrod returned to his place on the couch.

The game resumed.

Antes in, Bulldog's deal. He called seven-stud, shuffled expertly, and spilled out the cards in a blur. Waverly caught a split pair, ten-nine in the hole, pairing nine up. Sequentially from his left there was B.B. showing a queen, Arab an ace, Jock a six, and dealer sitting on one of his tens. The Arab peeked daintily at his down cards, pursed the moist lips, and pushed in five thousand in chips. Everyone stayed.

For a fourth card Waverly pulled another sweet nine. He felt a momentary adrenal rush: trips, must be living right today. B.B. got the Arab's ace, Arab a meaningless five, Jock a jack, Bulldog a four. Almost imperceptibly, Bulldog nodded at Waverly and said, "Nines driving."

Waverly upped the bet to ten. The Arab glanced at him with passionless distaste, flipped over his cards. B.B. and Jock called the bet. "Dealer folds," said Bulldog. A hint of a scowl, more a tightening at the eyebrows, crossed the upper elevations of his face, counterweight to the static smile. Thus far he was the principal victim, had to be down a full balloon, maybe more. A serious flogging.

Fifth card. Worthless duck for Waverly, big queen for The Big Guy, and Waverly's rightful ten dropped on Jock.

B.B. said twenty thou, winning hand written all over his joyous little face. Curiously, for there was no evidence in his exposed cards of even a flush in the making, Jock called the wager. Must be double-paired, Waverly thought, chasing the full boat, undervaluing the balls of the The Big Guy. Not so Waverly, who turned down his cards. Too much eager luster in B.B.'s pinprick eyes.

Sixth street. Just the two of them left. B.B. was dealt a four, Jock a six, his first pair showing. Puny sixes. Nevertheless, he called B.B.'s bet, which was stepladdering, thirty K now.

Last card out. B.B. studied his hand, but only briefly. "Better make it forty," he said.

Amazingly, rashly, Jock called, saying, "I got me a loaded schooner here, Mr. Beebee, sixes on top a jacks. I'm thinkin' maybe you ain't holdin' all the spot cards you need."

He was wrong.

And that's what B.B. said, squealy voice resonant with ill-suppressed glee: "This time your thinking's wrong, Jocker"; and he rolled over a queens high full house. With his diminutive hands he scooped in the substantial pile of chips. Revenge of the dwarfs.

After another hour of play the prince called for a break. Nobody argues with a prince. He stood while Nimrod slid back his chair, then swayed over to a couch, Nimrod in escort, and eased himself into it. B.B. and Bulldog, joined by Orton and Demerit, headed for the kitchen, Demerit lecturing both players on their blunders. Jock got to his feet heavily, stretched his arms overhead like a man coming out of a none too restful sleep, fired up a Macanudo. Waverly stayed where he was. So did Robbie.

The prince said, "A bit more wine, Nimrod." As soon as his servant was out of the room, the prince remarked, to no one in particular, the three of them generally, "Nimrod, you see, is my good-luck charm." A giggly *heh heh heh* trailed this intelligence.

Nobody seemed certain what to say to that, so Jock, playing at agreeable host, filled the breach of silence with, "Boogie that size charm the socks off you right quick." Signal for Robbie to deliver an obliging gust of laughter.

In a moment the good-luck charm was back, bearing wine. The prince lengthened his ample mouth, laid two fingers on his lips. Recognizing the gestured command, Nimrod instantly produced another cigarette. Once it was lit, he took a position behind the couch, standing with his legs apart and hands crossed over the small of his back in something like a soldierly parade-rest stance.

The prince held the wineglass by its stem. He smoked with a wrist flung back, cigarette aimed at the ceiling. "Actually," he explained, straining smoke between the perfect teeth, "his name is Kanavis. We changed it to Nimrod when he came into my employ. It seemed more fitting somehow. *Heh heh heh.* He comes from—what is the name of your quaint city, Nimrod?"

"Carbondale," was the answer, a low bass rumble, Nimrod's first utterance of the evening.

Jock came over and flopped into a chair opposite the prince. "That right," he said, addressing him directly, doing his best to be cordial though his natural antipathy for all the duskier shades of skin did not conceal well. "Midwestern boy, huh?"

"He is a former professional athlete," the prince went on, as though relating the attributes of a fine breed of animal. "Your American game of football, I believe. What was your team again, Nimrod?"

"Hamilton Tiger Cats. Played in Canada."

Ghetto gunburst seemed to be Nimrod's preferred style of speech. If he had any thoughts on this conversation, himself as its centerpiece, none of them could be read from his impassive face and empty eyes.

"Nimrod is a man of extraordinary physical strength and athletic prowess," the prince declared. "He is also an expert at weaponry. Show these gentlemen your latest toy, Nimrod."

Obediently, Nimrod stepped around the couch and planted himself in the space between Jock and the prince. He opened his jacket, exposing a gun side-holstered to his belt, and from an inside pocket he removed a cylindrical object wrapped in foam and small enough to fit easily in the palm of a hand. He lifted his arm and drew it to his shoulder, posed for an instant like a quarterback cocked and ready to release a ball. And then his wrist snapped suddenly, and with the explosive pop of a discharged rifle the innocuous-looking cylinder was magically transformed into a steel wand two feet or more in length, so polished and glittery it caught the light in the room, sparkled.

"What is it called, Nimrod?" the prince asked.

"Expandable baton," Nimrod replied, adding in the flat tones of someone reading specs from a manual or reciting them from memory, "tempered steel, four sections, twenty-eight inches."

"Give us a demonstration, please."

The foursome from the kitchen, alerted by the whap of the baton, bunched in the doorway, and for the second time that evening Nimrod was the cynosure of all eyes in the room. He executed a series of abbreviated chops, forehand and back, followed by long looping swings, all his weight behind them, whooshing the air. There was in the display none of the Ninja's art and dazzle grace, only a sheer elemental force, as though he battered a phantom adversary relentlessly and without mercy. Apart from the trace of satisfaction that sometimes underlines methodical concentration, his expression gave away nothing, and he kept right on swinging till the prince said mildly, "That will do." Nimrod's battering arm dropped to his side and he bent over and drove the extended end of the baton into the carpet, collapsing it back into its harmless-looking foam-covered handle.

The show was over. Beginning to end, it had all the quality of a carefully rehearsed performance, and whatever was intended as its point, a point was surely made. Something like a smile crossed the prince's face, but in back of that smile was a labyrinth of ambiguous messages. To Jock he said, "Rather impressive, is it not?"

Jock gave a low appreciative whistle and said, "Sure as shit don't want this boy yours gettin' mad at *me.*"

Heh heh heh went the prince.

Waverly got out of his chair and shouldered his way through the dumbstruck group at the door. In the kitchen he searched the refrigerator for a ginger ale. No ginger ale. Another Appelgate ploy? Who could tell. He found a can of Seven-Up and took it to the window overlooking the street. He glanced right, he glanced left, and there at the end of the block, partly shadowed by a tree, but only partly, as if stealth and surprise were no longer of any great matter, was the outline of the black Mustang. Another point made. He turned away from the window and discovered Robbie at the counter, pouring himself a straight shot of Wild Turkey. Out of the side of his mouth Robbie whispered, "How we doing?" Waverly put a flat hand in the air, wiggled it in a so-so gesture. Hope and anxiety, equal parts, etched their way into Robbie's otherwise sullen features, and he was about to say more when Jock appeared.

"How about fixin' me one of them, Robber?"

Robbie dutifully poured.

Jock took the proffered glass, looked back and forth between them slyly. Around a chops-licking swirl of drink he said, "So. What're you boys up to?"

"Just critiquing the game," Robbie said quickly.

Jock fixed his gaze on Waverly. "What do you think of our A-rab, Mr. Waverly?"

"As player or person?"

"Either one. Both."

"He's got a nice card sense," Waverly said. "May be a little too exquisite for my tastes."

"Does come on like a regular sissy, don't he? You'd maybe figure him for a swish, except the Robber here says he goes through the tail like grain goin' through a goose. That right, Robber?"

The Robber, clearly not comfortable at this unexpected caucus, agreed the homely analogy was right.

"Yup," Jock said, mouth stretching open in a grin extremely wide, extremely nasty, "whole troop of our Florida blue-eyed blondes gettin' their knees dirty out to his suite of rooms, Breakers."

Waverly had nothing to say to that. The sexual appetites and proclivities of the Arab interested him not at all. Robbie, evidently even less comfortable with silence, put in, "All those ragheads turn into cocksmen once they get over here."

"Well," Jock allowed judiciously, "all that dick drive don't seem to be servin' him too good at poker. He ain't showin' me much so far. Matter a fact, cards all look to be goin' your way, Mr. Waverly."

"There's a lot of game left," Waverly said.

"Yeah, that's truth. Fat lady don't yodel till Wednesday night." He finished off the drink, cocked his head in the direction of his cash-flow room. "Well, expect we better get back in there. Before he sends that jumbo spade lookin' for us, give another demonstration with the thumper stick."

Twice the deck went around the table, and for Waverly the tickets ran nothing but cold. It rattled him some. And then he took his first pot, a small one, and he settled down, imposed an order on the whirl of odds and cards and numbers spinning in his head, studied the faces for shades of expression, watched the motions and gestures, attended to melody, pitch, and resonance in the voices. He found the rhythm of the game again, and all his fretful heat drained away in the icy focus of concentration. He won some more and then some more after that, hitting miracle hands, do-no-wrong cards falling on him, zinging in the bets when they did, whacking anyone foolish enough to get in his way right into the wall, blitzing them. He had no clear idea how far ahead he was. Far.

The hours passed. Very near the end of the session he got drawn into a three-cornered race with Jock and the Arab. Seven-stud again. Five cards out and not a pair showing anywhere. Contest of nerves. The Arab's queen-jack-nine suggested a possible straight in the making or made, possible split pair or pairs, remotely possible high trips waiting in the wings, waiting to pounce. Possible anything. But his circumspect wagering, a steady five, supported none of these notions. Jock's feeble-looking eight-three-deuce was an enigma. Why was he still in? Had to be some power, real or latent, lurking down below. Waverly was sitting on a hearts four-flush, three of them, jack-five-four, intimidatingly up, the fourth, a seven, in the hole along with another little insurance five. Potential flush, potential low trips—it was a hand with some degree of promise. Also, against these two, of manifold hazard.

Jock had the deal. He laid an ace on Waverly, diamond, no help in either direction. The Arab got an eight, tucking in one end of the straight but still leaving a gap, establishing nothing. Jock dealt himself a pairing three, and the power, such as it was, passed to him. He squinted at Waverly's cards, drawled, "Huh, still could be a flush hidin' down in the cellar." He cast an appraising eye on the Arab's hand. "Possible straight over here." He looked at his own cards, tugged his underlip pensively. Nice theatrics. Finally he said, "These little maggies couple weak sisters up against all that weight. I better check."

Bet to Waverly. Time to test the water. "Twenty," he said, and the Arab called and, without a blink, bumped it twenty. Forty to Jock, who unhesitatingly pushed in his chips, counted out some more, and said, "Let's put another twenty on top of that." Very chilly waters, polar waters. Back to Waverly. Now he had to think about it a minute. The Arab's bump could mean he had the bobtail straight filled in. Jock's re-raise could mean he'd made the trips threes, maybe even a full load. Both wagers were, of course, calculated to sell those notions, but both players, Jock in particular, could be going down the river on bluff and dreams, each hoping to steal the pot on nothing at all. Astonishingly, only one other heart had surfaced, so the flush p.c. was good, not all that far off even.

"Mr. Waverly?" Jock said.

Two words, five syllables. But there was just a faint tremulous ripple under them, not much, just enough to give him away. "I'll call," Waverly said. Hit the flush and he was golden.

Out came the final cards. Waverly peeled back the corner of his. It was black. But it was also a five. Making three of them.

Jock's two weak sisters driving. He bet a reconnaissance twenty, Waverly called, and the Arab coolly raised it twenty. Jock made some perfunctory spluttery sounds but he didn't buckle.

Crunch time. "Put another twenty on top of that," Waverly said, and he slid forty thousand in chips across the felt and into the swollen pot. He glanced over at Robbie, who straddled a chair behind and between Bulldog and B.B., and whose face had gone gray, pinched with alarm.

"Whoa," Jock whooped, "now *you're* doin' the sandbaggin'."

"Deplorable," the Arab said. "Most deplorable." Mocking or in earnest, it was impossible to tell. His lips parted in a viperish smile and he added quietly, "But I don't believe you have anything, sir. I shall raise your twenty by the same amount."

Now Jock hesitated. He shook his head ruefully, tried on an arid grin. "Jesus G. Gawd," he said, "you fellas walkin' me right to the gallows." Nevertheless, he met the two raises: come this far, there was nothing else to do.

Twenty more to Waverly. The once towering stacks of chips in front of him were reduced to a single dwindling pillar. A night's plunder and the greater share of his own and Robbie's stake, and all of it gone to feed this one mammoth pot. Maybe the Arab was looking to spook him with all that money power, bringing it to bear at last. Or maybe he'd made his straight after all, was sucking them both in. Maybe, but Waverly didn't think so. Too hard a sell. No, he didn't think so. He called.

"I hold two pair," the Arab said, displaying his hole cards. "Eights. And Mr. Appelgate's threes."

Jock's grin widened just a crack. "Now ain't that something," he said, "you catchin' my maggies. Only thing is, I got a couple paints humpin' mine." He turned over his cards, revealing a pair of kings backing up his threes; and then he turned to Waverly. "What do you have to say, Mr. Waverly?"

With an effort Waverly held in a huge relieved sigh. "Three-some," is what he had to say, and he laid his two concealed fives face up alongside the third.

Jock's grin stiffened. For a sliver of an instant he looked confounded, stunned. Then, remembering himself, he blustered,

"Look like the pro run us both over, prince. We coulda put our hands together, we'd've smoked him."

"Another time, perhaps," said the prince. His viper smile had never once flickered, but his liquid eyes were narrowed to slits. And they were tacked on Waverly.

Who was just then sweeping in the mountainous pile of chips. Inspiriting take. Certainly he wasn't going to run a tally now, not with those two sets of baleful eyes trained on him, but even split with his shifty stakehorse (who, after a shudder, exhibited the vacant, zombie look of the man delivered out of a deep coma, awed to discover himself sentient, still alive), it had to come close to putting him over the top, near to home free. But as he played through the remaining few hands of the session, just coasting now, treading water, Waverly continued to feel the combined weight of that malignant glare. Now there were two of them dogging him.

22

Shortly before noon on the following day, Gunter Dietz's plane touched down at Palm Beach International Airport. After deboarding and collecting his single bag, he hailed a cab outside the terminal and directed the driver to take him to—here he had to consult a note carefully tucked in his wallet—the Sea Spray Inn on Singer Island. A first-floor, poolside room was reserved in his name, and once the door was secured he unpacked the bag, stripped off his sticky traveling clothes, and showered. It had been a while since business had taken him to Florida, and even though the temperature was soaring into the upper nineties when he left Chicago, it was nothing compared with the blistering muggy heat down here. Happily for him, his stay would be brief: three nights at most, possibly no longer than the day after tomorrow if things went as planned. And it was his intention to see that they did.

Accordingly, after the invigorating shower, he sat down at the phone, laid out the wallet note in front of him, and made the first in a series of calls.

"Yuh," came the rude greeting, barest trace of an interrogative lift pinned to the tail of the grunted monosyllable.

"Who's speaking?"

"Who's askin'?" was the reply, tough, take-no-shit tone.

"Gunter Dietz."

A moment of empty air. Then the voice, gone suddenly servile, near to lickspittle, filled it, after a fashion, with, "Oh . . . This is Sigurd, Mr. Dietz, Sigurd Stumpley. . . . Remember me from up at the Hilton there, Arlington? . . . Wasn't expectin' it'd be you . . . thought it might be my Uncle Eugene. . . . See, I was just gonna punch in with him, let him know what's . . . well, y'know, make a, like, report . . . purr say. . . ."

Dietz let it stumble along, run down. Eventually it did. "Now you can report directly to me," he said coldly. Apart from Eugene, he had revealed his plans to no one, so for all this dim bulb knew he was two thousand miles away. Instead of one floor down. Get to that part in good time. Timing, pacing—in business that's how you spelled success, carried the day.

"Sure thing, Mr. Dietz. Lemme see, what can I tellya? Looks like what they're up to is—"

"Is there someone there called, uh, Frog?" Dietz broke in, consulting the note again.

"Yeah, right, correct. He's here."

"Put him on."

Dietz could hear snippets of a hurried conversation, muffled obviously and unsubtly by a hand covering the speaker. Then he heard, "This is Frog."

"And this is your contractor," he said.

"Okay. What can I do for you?"

Dietz liked the attitude he heard in this voice. Not the slightest cringe in it, none whatsoever. Very cheering sign. Maybe something was being handled properly after all. "You can start," he said, "by telling me the status of your, ah, assignment."

"Not much to tell. Nothing went down over the weekend, and then last night the player went out to the same place he was at before. Bunch of cars out there, so I got to figure there's another game going on."

"What do you know about this game?"

"Nothing. I can't get a line in there. Looks to be strictly cards, though. No sideline entertainment, cheerleaders and like that. Not like last time."

"So it could be serious play?"

"Like I say, no way to know."

"This game, how long did it go on?"

"Most of the night. Player goes over about eight, stays till maybe four this morning."

"And the Jew? Was he with him?"

"No. Jew's keeping his head down."

"Who's on him?"

"I got the manager wired in, place they're holed up."

"That would be the Tropicaire Apartments?" Earlier, when the cab pulled up at the hotel, Dietz had stood in the entrance gazing at the four bungalows diagonally across the road. And the gaudy pink Seville parked alongside one of them, that would of course belong to the kike. So it was exactly as Eugene had described it to him. No surprises, which was how he liked things to be.

"Yeah, that's the place."

"Across the street?"

There was a pause. And then the voice came down the line again, guarded now, wary. "That's right, too."

"And how do you suppose I know that, Frog?"

"Somebody filled you in?"

"Guess again."

"You're here? Florida?"

"Closer even than that," Dietz said. "I'm on the floor below you." He gave it a moment, let the weight of this bulletin settle in, and then he added, "From here on out I'll be directing traffic. Personally. Is that understood?"

"You're the contractor."

Now the voice had a shrug in it. Quick study, this Frog. Another good sign. "That I am," Dietz said. "And what I want you to do now is stay right where you are. Keep them covered over there. I'll get back to you in, oh, say, half an hour. Maybe less. You got that?"

"I got it."

Dietz put down the phone and took a brief time-out to fit the pieces of the puzzle together in his head. Formulate a strategy. It was delicate, getting himself in this close. Risky. About that, Eugene had been right, absolutely. All the same, he was beginning to feel something of a rush, a rising surge. Good feeling. Nothing like a little hands-on action to set the sluggish juices flowing again. Cushioned by layers and layers of insulation, he hadn't been caught up in a down-and-dirty payback like this one was going to be in years. Years?—more like decades. Even a CEO needs to get some grease under his manicured nails now and then. But cautiously, he reminded himself, and from a discreet distance, and with vigilance and extreme care.

With his enthusiasm (make that excitement—call it what it is) thus tempered and contained, he placed the next call. Got another "Yeah" greeting, sloshy and belligerent. Not much to be said for telephone etiquette, this business.

"I'd like to speak with Mr. Ep-stein, please."

"You're doin' it. Who's callin'?"

"Gunter Dietz." It was amusing to Dietz how the mere enunciation of his name could evoke a stunned silence. Gratifying. "You remember me," he put into the lengthening empty space. "I trust."

"Oh yeah. I remember."

"Then you also remember why I'm calling. That is, if you and your, uh, associate have looked at the calendar lately." Dietz spoke slowly, very evenly, stringing out his words, extracting from them all the modulations of menace and bug-squashing contempt. He'd almost forgotten how much he enjoyed this end of it, the build-up, circling in, tightening the noose.

"Listen, wanna tell you, Mr. Dietz, that—whaddya call it?—what we was talkin' about, up to Chicago?"

"Surcharge."

"That's the one. Anyway, we 'bout got it put together for you. Whole package."

"That's splendid, Mr. Ep-stein. Splendid. Particularly since the, ah, settlement deadline is only some thirty-six hours away."

"Yeah, well, we'll for sure have it by then. Could be even little sooner. You want, I can give you a jingle tomorrow."

"This is very encouraging news, Mr. Ep-stein. You see, it's just like I told you. Nothing's impossible. When you've got your priorities right. Right?"

"Priorities. Yeah, right. So. You got a number, I can get to you?"

"Number," Dietz repeated, as though he were measuring the meaning of the word. "No, I think not. I think it's better for me to contact you. This same time tomorrow, say. Review your progress, arrange the delivery. Is that, uh, suitable? Mr. Ep-stein?"

"That'd be real fine."

"Fine. We'll talk again, then. Soon."

Dietz's third phone conversation was conducted in spare, telegraphic, down-to-business tones. No frills, no dance-around nonsense, and in the peculiar shorthand of their trade, which he discovered to his satisfaction came back to him easily, like the lyrics of a forgotten song come back across the years from a departed youth.

"Frog?" he said.

"Speaking."

"All right. Just tagged the sheeny. Tomorrow's squeeze time. Zotz time."

"Sounds right to me. What till then?"

"Round-the-clock on both of them. You stay with the player, your partner—what's his name again?"

"Sigurd."

"Him on the Hebe."

"So how's it going down tomorrow? You going to want any stunts first? I do stunts."

Stunts. For these two marks, gave him all this grief, Dietz liked the idea of stunts. "Depends," he said. "I'll get back to you. Meantime, keep in tight. Crowd 'em. Let 'em know you're there."

"You think they're thinking slash-and-dash?"

"No question. In their dreams. But we're not going to let that happen. Are we."

"Not a prayer."

"Good. I'm in one-o-eight. Anything cute, next twenty-four hours, you buzz."

"You got it."

Dietz's final call that afternoon was made to room service. He ordered a light lunch and also, after debating it, a gin and tonic. Do him good, he decided. He specified Bombay gin. No Bombay. Beefeater, they could give him. Beefeater. You might know, comes of staying at a low-rent dump like this one. But that, of course, was part of the territory, came with the action. Can't have it both ways. And so with a sigh he said, "Okay, Beefeater, then."

Waverly's face was buried in the pillow. He lifted his head slightly, enough to mumble, "Who was it?"

"Go back to sleep. You gonna need it tonight."

Waverly rolled over on the air mattress. With the heels of his hands he ground at rheumy eyes, restoring a clouded focus. He felt something of the druggy numbness that comes of dream-riddled sleep, though if he had been dreaming, the images and the story line—if there'd been one—had both vanished. But they could have been no more surreal than this blurry waking-life vision that greeted him, the gradual locking together of the features and lineaments of this room: the face of Bennie Epstein, anxious, pale, almost bloodless, looming over the counter; a palmetto bug creeping across the floor, miniature armored vehicle on the prowl, animated appetite, search, destroy, consume; the coffee table with a bottle and glass at one end, and alongside them a tube of cigar going in a conventional ashtray, its smoke funneling toward the ceiling on the slow motion tow of the fan; and layering the table's surface like a cluster of green bricks, stacks and stacks of neatly banded bills.

"Come on, Bennie," he said. "Who called? Was it Caroline Crown?"

Dreams. Talk about the slippery borders of dreams. After four days of silence he was coming to wonder if she was herself nothing more than a vagrant image in one of his bizarre and fugitive dreams.

Bennie came around the counter and slumped on the couch behind the coffee table. He retrieved the cigar, stuck it in his mouth, and swept a hand grandly over the money. "Remember how much you brought home last night? Remember that?"

"I asked a question here, Bennie."

"Four-three-o. That's how much. More'n you ever scored in your life."

"Cut up that score with our stakehorse and it doesn't look quite so big."

"Does to me. Give your citizen buddy back his share and all's we're lookin' at's a thirty-five-K leap to Bottom Line City. Thirty-five long. One good home run."

Waverly propped himself up on an elbow and fixed his partner with a steady gaze. "Who called?" he said.

"Dietz. It was Dietz callin'."

"Dietz," Waverly said after him.

"Which is why I'm givin' you a playback on them numbers. So you don't forget where your head's at. Suppose to be at."

"What did he want?"

"Want?" Bennie said shrilly. His hands were roving again, wide emphatic gestures. A sprinkling of sweat glistened on his bald pate. "Jesus. Wants his money, is what he wants. What'd you think?"

"Did you tell him we're almost there?"

"Listen, guy like Dietz ain't givin' no gold seals for almost. He wants it all. He's comin' to collect."

"What do you mean? He's here? Florida?"

"Here, Chicago, don't mean shit either way. Gonna be some-body with his hand out tomorrow—Dietz, somebody else, don't matter who—and whatever we slap in it better add up right. Or we're dog chow, Timothy. Dead meat."

"We may be anyway. Even if the figure is right. You know that, Bennie. You know it."

Of course he knew it. They had lived in the creases of this life long enough, both of them, to understand its ordinances, its deadly rules. He knew it. So did Waverly.

Bennie held one of the green bricks in the air, a visual aid. "Just get me one more of these, thirty-five count, and I'll take care of that part. That part I can handle."

"You're sure about that?"

"Sure as anything's sure."

"Yeah, well, the bills I can't help you with till tonight," Waverly said. "If then."

"That ain't what we wanta hear, Timothy. You won big-time last night. You can do it again."

There were no answers to be threshed from this conversation. A circle ending where it began. Waverly pushed back the sheet and got to his feet stiffly. "I guess we'll just have to wait and see, won't we," he said.

Bennie batted the air with the bills. "Aah, go take your shit, shave, and shower. Go on, dickhead. I'll brew you pot a coffee."

Half an hour later Waverly sat at the counter sipping coffee hot as molten lava. Potent, vile coffee. His air mattress was deflated, stashed in the closet, a lonely concession to order in the otherwise hopelessly littered room. The palmetto bug had advanced across the floor, reconnoitered the baseboard along one wall. Over on the couch Bennie stared silently at the hoard of deliverance money or at nothing at all, no way to tell for sure. His cigar smoke hung on the ceiling.

The phone rang. This time Waverly answered. He could be heard voicing responses, affirmations mostly: "Yes . . . yes . . . I can do that. . . . When? . . . Yes." .

At the conversation's close he turned and faced his partner, who said wearily, "It's the broad, right?"

"Right."

"And you're gonna see her."

"Also right."

"Ah, sweet fuckin' mystery of sweet fuckin' life."

Waverly said nothing. He was in no mood to contemplate any more of life's abundant mysteries.

"This Dietz," D'Marco was grousing, "what's he doing down here, anyway?"

"Shit, I dunno. Watchin' out for his investment, s'pose. My uncle says he's tighter'n a worm's twat."

"I don't like somebody looking over my shoulder, I'm doing a piece of work."

"Maybe he wants to play little smashmouth himself."

"He does, why the fuck'd he contract me?"

Sigurd shrugged. "Dunno that either, man."

"Well, I don't like it."

"What're you gonna do, hey? He's the big bouncer, Dietz. You carry the weight, you call the shots. Purr say."

"Purr shit," D'Marco growled.

Sigurd didn't say anything. Ever since Sunday, since D'Marco (wouldn't answer to Jake no more) dismissed the fluff (which, way things worked out, Dietz showing up, was maybe piece of luck after all), he'd been spiky as a nun two weeks past due her granny. Regular red ass. Not as bad as before the ear-zippin' in the public pisser down the road there, but still plenty sour. Like he was chewin' on his own balls, 'stead of everybody else's, for a switch. So Sigurd figured it was better just to keep a rag in it. For now, anyway. Get this job nailed shut and maybe they'd jump a little gash one more time, before he had to head up north again. That Rhode Island, she'd stiffen old Mr. Roundeye for you. And Maylene—whooee!—ain't a schwantz in this whole wide world gonna hit bottom, that one.

But that was for tomorrow night or the next one, if it even going to come at all. For right now they were parked on the deck outside their room, sweltering in the midafternoon heat, squinting, blue blocks notwithstanding, into a fireball sun bleaching the western sky, popping sweat out of every pore (least he was; D'Marco looked cool; pissed, but cool), and scopin' the marks' place, as directed. Course not a fuckin' thing goin' on. Might as well be standin' watch on a boneyard (which, when you thought about it, is what they was doin', there bein' two kinds of dead: horizontal, in the ground there, and the still-walkin'-around kind, like them poor dumb fucks across the street was).

D'Marco, craning his neck, broke in on these wandering reveries, demanding, "How's it look?"

And Sigurd, mistaking him, hunched forward in his chair, gaped at the Tropicaire bungalow, and said, "What? Don't see nothin'."

"Talking about my neck, dickdip."

Though the wine-colored bruise was fading some, it was still looking plenty splotched and raw, like he'd taken a serious lick off a bullwhip. Could be he was going to end up with a permanent hickey, but Sigurd knew better than to say that, so he said just the opposite of what he was thinking: "Comin' along real good. You ain't gonna have to worry 'bout no scar there, hey."

D'Marco ran a finger along the purple welt, tracing its outline gingerly. "You think so?"

"Oh yeah. Can't hardly even see it no more."

"Tell you one thing," D'Marco muttered darkly, "this goddam sun's not helping it any."

It was the opening Sigurd was looking for. Way he saw it, made no sense at all, both of 'em fryin' out here, doin' the Crispy Critter number when you got a air condition room the other side a that slider. And besides, he had this nagging bit of business yet to attend to. Put off almost a week now, it had to get done, before things started shaking out here. But by now he knew his partner well enough to come at it roundabout fashion, back door. "Sure can't be doin' it no good," he agreed, gave it a beat, and then advanced the notion, "Y'know, maybe what we oughta do is, like, spell each other. Take a little break."

"We got work here," D'Marco said, gruffly but not very firmly, a touch of doubt in it.

"Fuck, man. One pair eyes good as two, this kind a work."

D'Marco didn't immediately reply. His fretful loving finger continued to stroke the abraded neck. Sigurd waited. Matter a time now. Finally D'Marco said, "This break idea. Lemme guess, you want to go first, right?"

"Nope. Other way around. Get that neck yours outta the sun. Before we gotta run you over to the burn ward." Sigurd let him think about that, but not long. "Except I do got to make one call," he said quickly, almost under his breath. "Take me three, four minutes, outside."

D'Marco narrowed his blue blocks gaze on him. "Call?" he rumbled, scowling. "Call who? No more cunts in here."

"Nah, this ain't cunts. This is up to home."

The menacing, practiced scowl softened into a sneer. "Got to check in with Mama, do you?"

"Well, yeah," Sigurd said defensively. "She worries." And with an edge of defiance in his voice, he added, "That okay by you?"

"Make your fucking call. Make it quick."

Put in two hours out on the cooker there and the sudden rush of chill air in the room stabbed you right between the eyes, about knocked you over. Sigurd, momentarily dizzied, plunked his rump on a bed till he was sure he wasn't going to faint, or ralph, and then he pecked out Mom's number on the Touch Tone and after ten beeps or so (probably one of her goddam shows blasting on the TV) got a greeting sounded like a parrot croaking the word *yellow.*

"Mom, it's me, hey. Sigurd."

"Sigurd? Sig, it's you? Where you been? Why'nt you call? You shoulda called. I been worried."

Parrot screech resonated with a blend of joy and the grievances of filial neglect. See, what'd he just tell him out there, D'Marco: You got somebody, a mom, say, you got responsibilities. To her, Sigurd said (and in his own inflections and cadences there was a new swagger, authentic shooter's swagger now, fringe benefit of

the rite of passage icing the other night), "Yeah, well, ain't nothin'
for you to worry about. I been busy, is all, keepin' on top a this
job."

"Where you at now, Sig?"

Where? Dumb fucking question. But he said tolerantly, "Florida,
Mom. Still in Florida."

"When you comin' home?"

"No way to tell for sure," said the weary, toil-worn warrior.
"Won't be long, though. Couple days, maybe."

Mom started in on him: You eatin' right? Gettin' enough rest?
Takin' care of yourself? You got to take care of yourself, Sigurd.... He listened without hearing, voicing reflex assurances
("Yeah ... sure ... I'm doin' that.... Right.") at the occasional
split-second break, Mom catching her wind, in the torrent of ma-
ternal wheeze. What he really wanted to do was tell her how
Dietz was actually down here, Dietz himself, and how he'd just
been talking to him, filling him in on the action, you could maybe
say, more or less. But then he figured maybe that wasn't such a
keen idea either, seeing as how she might spill something to Uncle
Eugene, put him on the horn before presto, doing his patent-
pending ass-dicing number. Sigurd was wrestling with these war-
ring impulses when, just then, D'Marco came charging through
the slider, barking, "Player's on the move," and, pitching him the
keys to the LX on his dash to the door, "Cover the Jew, track
him, he trys to bolt"; and Sigurd said into the phone, "Gotta run
now, Mom."

"But we was just gettin' talkin'," Mom whined.

Sigurd, clutching the keys, another emblem of his accelerating
coming of age, another milestone, said, "Somethin' come up.
Work."

"Sigurd, you watch out for yourself, son. You hear me?"

"Don't you worry none, Mom," he said toughly.

It was a vast and sprawling complex, the Collonades Beach
Hotel was—three hotels in one, actually, the Collonades North
and South linked to the central unit by a bewildering maze of
passageways and breezeways and clusters of satellite bungalows
strung like connective tissue between the three multistoried struc-
tures. And on close inspection it seemed on the perilous edge of
toppling, disintegrating, a glass-and-concrete House of Usher at
any moment about to implode, crumble into powdery dust, settle
into the sand. Vanish utterly, and by the wind only grieved.

Standing at the entrance to the main building, Waverly had

ample time for such melancholy flights of fancy, and other thoughts as well. Twenty minutes (she'd said, somewhat breathlessly), meet you across the street from your apartment, over by that abandoned hotel, I forget the name, twenty minutes. That was easily an hour ago, maybe longer.

And so he waited, shielding himself under the canopy from the implacable sun, a wall of white gold in the cloudless sky. And eventually the Jaguar came tooling down Ocean Avenue and pulled up in the drive. She approached him, smiling meagerly, swaying ever so slightly, elegantly dressed in pink chiffon body blouse, deep cut, and black silk skirt looped by a wide bow belt. Her heels clacked on the grainy asphalt. Sunlight defined the firm planes of her face. Her eyes were hidden behind bronze-tinted Serengeti Drivers. A lady of style and fashion, unmistakably Palm Beach, come to call, bringing with her the fragrances of a delicate perfume and the hint of a scent of gin.

"Late again," she said, rolling over helpless palms.

"It's all right," Waverly said, not much conviction in it.

"Would it do any good to say I'm sorry?"

"It's all right, Caroline," he said again.

"There's this party, reception. For the prince. At the Venetian Room in the Breakers, no less. All the investors and wives were there. Are there."

"Sounds very festive."

"Don't be angry, Tim. Please."

"I'm not angry. Maybe a little baffled by what's going on. Or not going on."

She gave him a tight, strained look, a look contracted with seriousness, doubt. Then, taking his arm, she said, "Let's stroll."

Waverly wagged a thumb at the car. "Cops'll ticket you if they come by. This place is posted, you know."

"Jock's treat," she said with a shrug.

They started down the breezeway that ran the length of the building. At the south end they came on a cobblestone walk, a promenade of shops, dark and shuttered now, leading through the hotel to a grassy, weed-choked courtyard in back. A wrought-iron gate barred the entrance. A sign on the arch above it identified the promenade as the Rue de Paris. Caroline stood gazing at the sign a moment. She began to giggle softly.

"Remember the word games we used to play sometimes? When we were young?"

Waverly looked puzzled.

"Rue de Paris, Rue de toot? Like that?"

Remembering his way back across the chasm of years, he said, "Rue de Vallee."

"Rue de wakening."

"Rue de day," he said, and her face lost its animation and the giggling stopped.

"Let's go on," she said and, still clutching his arm, guided him away.

They walked very slowly, as if to conserve themselves against the wasting heat. The breezeway led them past a paint-blistered bungalow unit and then along the front of the Collonades South. Occasionally, at her wordless direction, they paused to peer through the grimy windows. Here and there a tiny light gleamed from a wall fixture or an ornate chandelier. Some of the corridors were littered with chairs, lamps, dismantled beds, mattresses, assorted trash; others were perfectly clear.

At one of those pauses she said dreamily, "Such an eerie place. Up close this way."

"It wasn't always like this. In its day it was a showcase. Singer Island's finest."

She didn't seem to hear him. "So many ghosts in there," she sighed, as though mourning them.

Waverly looked at her curiously. So many ghosts, yes, and so many human messages to give and receive and decode and interpret. He wasn't sure yet what the message was here, but he had an idea. Figured he would wait, a while longer anyway.

They continued on. This breezeway opened onto a large parking lot, empty and barren as a level patch of moonscape; another sheltered passage flanked the south face of the hotel, leading to the back, and from there to an amoeba-shaped pool, and beyond that to the beach. They turned the corner and walked that way. At the end of the passage was a stairwell covered by a wire mesh evidently intended to discourage trespassers, though from the trampled look of it without much success.

"Do you suppose there's people in there?" Caroline said, indicating the snarled wire.

"It's possible."

"But who? Who'd dare go inside?"

"Vags, dopers, street people. Who knows?"

"But it's so . . . creepy."

"It's a place to crash."

At just that moment a hot puff of wind lifted off the ocean, filled her skirt. She smoothed it down modestly, and around a small golden laugh she said, "There be spirits here. Phantoms."

Waverly was at last run out of patience. "Is that what you came to talk about, Caroline? This ruin of a hotel?"

"No, it wasn't that."

"What then?"

A rush of quick feeling came up in her face, and she turned away from his direct gaze. "Robbie says the deal—his project—is practically closed. Finalized, in his words."

"Really. Good for him."

"He's very excited over it. Almost manic."

Manic, was he. Small wonder, manic. Waverly said, "I expect by now you know he found the photo."

"Oh yes. I was the first to know."

"And that he's talked to me about it?"

"That too."

"Well? Do you have any thoughts on the matter?"

"Thoughts," she repeated, staring out into the deserted parking lot, seemingly gathering them. And after a hesitation she said, "It's all so tangled. He's begging me to stay, keep the family together. Promising to change."

"And you believe that?"

"No, no, no, I don't believe it." Her hands made fluttery circles in the thick oppressive air. "I know better. But it's not easy for me, Tim. Don't you see? He's such a weak man, under all that brass and bluster. Desperately insecure."

"Also mean-spirited," Waverly said quietly. "By your own testimony."

"Mean-spirited, yes, and egocentric and cruel and vengeful—all those things. But about one thing he's right: we have a history, even if it's a wretched one."

"So what is it you're telling me?"

"I don't know. Maybe, finally, there's no escaping your own past after all."

The past again. The worm at the core of every dream is always the past. Who should know better than he, who against all reason had entered that shadowland of memory and grief so many times. So many times. The message he'd suspected he was hearing earlier, peering through a glass into this ghostly relic, this wreckage, was clear enough now. And yet, looking at her this way, at her pained, tarnished loveliness, seeing past it to the restless, spirited girl he remembered, the girl she had been, he was seduced once more by the treacherous fiction of hope, and in spite of his best instincts he heard himself saying, "Friday, on the ship, you said you were coming with me. I have to ask you if that's changed."

"I don't know."

"You've got to decide, Caroline. By tomorrow night things are going to be breaking fast for me. One way or another, you've got to decide. On this one you can't flirt with time."

Her rising hands met her falling face, and through splayed fingers and in a voice pleading, choked with tears, she said, "I *can't* decide!"

Waverly felt a great hollow space opening inside him. "I think that means you already have," he said.

A jumble of emotions seemed to hover over the grave and measured silence that fell between them. And then, as if by unspoken accord, they started back, saying not a word, nothing left to say, a peculiar desolate harmony charging the silence. At the door to the car, unticketed for all his cautions, she turned and from behind the bronze-tinted glasses regarded him with a lost gaze. "Timothy Waverly," she said, and though the tears were gone now, her voice crumbled on a ruined smile.

"Caroline Vanzoren."

"Such a happy coincidence, meeting you again, here, of all places, after all these years."

"Destiny's puns, coincidences. Somebody said that. Something like that."

"Maybe we're not quite done with them yet. Those coincidences."

"Maybe."

"Goodbye, Tim."

Waverly followed the Jaguar with his eyes till it vanished at the end of the street. The hollowness inside him deepened, widened. Draw me a map of the brambled landscapes of the heart. Instruct me in the mysteries of its geography. Read me the riddles of its cryptic, arcane semiology. No maps appeared, and no answers occurred to him. But off to his right, no more than thirty yards up the road, was a quicksand reminder of the other side of his life: the shooter, standing at the end of his own shadow in a slanted beam of crystal sunlight, arms folded across the wedge of chest, lips curled in a wicked sneer, and head shaking slowly, side to side.

Bennie was unsystematically and with a theatric show of irritation stuffing clothes in a bag on the floor. He glanced up when Waverly came through the door and muttered, "Better grab some gear. We gotta move."

"Move? What's going on?"

"Goddam bug day tomorrow."

"Bug day?"

"Yeah, their funeral. Remember?"

Waverly expelled a sigh. "The tenting. I forgot."

"You ain't solo there. You were gone, Oh Boy pops in, says they startin' up first thing in the morning so we got to be out tonight. Nice timin', huh. As if we ain't got enough grief."

About that he was surely right. Of all the petty, messy distractions they didn't need just now, this one had to be a front-runner. Waverly said, "Where's he putting us?"

"Dog pound in back."

"We have to move everything?"

"O'Shithead says no, you want to trust an Irishman. Says that bug gas they pump in here won't hurt your laundry. Just you. Choke you up a little. As in dead."

Waverly sighed again. "So what are you taking, Bennie? That's all I'm asking."

"Takin' enough for a couple days. You better do the same."

"The loot? You got it?"

Bennie gave him a withering look. With his shoe he nudged a small satchel by the bag. "Some of us ain't got our heads totally up our ass."

Waverly let it go by. He was not in a humor to bicker. And anyway it was probably deserved, the way things seemed to be falling out.

Bennie stooped down, zippered the bags, hoisted them, and huffing and sweating, started across the room. "I'm headin' on over. Be sure and lock up here, huh?" The door banged shut behind him.

Waverly stood there trying to consider what he'd need, but his thoughts wandered, scattered. Caroline, Robbie, Bennie, the shooter, the game coming up (less than three hours now, his watch reminded him, got to focus, center), tomorrow night's showdown—too much cluttering his head, too much. He felt spiritless, bleary, almost dazed. He looked around the room. Focus, focus. A change or two of clothes, he'd need, some shaving gear, that should do. He gathered them. The air mattress—don't forget the air mattress. He collected the mattress. And the door, remember the door. He locked it on his way out, pocketed the key.

Minus only the praying tin hands on the wall, this apartment was identical to the one they'd just vacated. A little short on imagination, here at the Tropicaire. Bennie was on the couch, bent over the banded green bricklets stacked on the coffee table, counting them again, as if to assure himself none had disappeared in transit. Waverly deposited his things in the closet and dropped into the La-Z-Boy, set it in reclining position. "You want to wake me in about an hour?" he said. Bennie grunted something affirmative-sounding.

Waverly's eyes fell shut and he dozed, but only fitfully. Bizarre, disjointed images—a batallion of furious palmetto bugs on the march; a barefoot nymph in gauzy silk sheath cavorting through a meadow blanketed in blue snow; an elegant French restaurant peopled exclusively by discriminating diners, every one of them headless; buildings collapsing, consumed in flames—haunted the misty borders of sleep, churned his dreams, jolted him back. After a while he gave it up, hauled himself out of the chair, and changed into slacks and coat and tie, his working wardrobe. He sat at the counter, smoked a cigarette, waited.

Bennie lectured him: "Soon as you're over the hump—thirty-five K is all we're lookin' at, remember—get up from that table and cash in. Split with your chum and get out quick. Rest is his problem. Ain't nobody give a rat's rectum what they think. Fuck 'em. It's our asses on the chopping block here."

More in that vein. Waverly presented a listening face but didn't entirely attend to what his partner was saying.

A little after seven Bennie said, "It's time. You ready to hit it?"

"Ready."

"You straight yet, broadwise? Or do I wanta ask."

"It's looking like I'm straight," Waverly said. "What you'd call straight."

"There's a rosy switch."

Simultaneously, they came to their feet. Bennie walked him to the car. In parting, in a husky, throaty voice, his lardy features twisted in a grimace evidently intended as a confident smile, he said, "Go crack the slab, Timothy. Finesse them chumps. Dazzle 'em. Anybody can do it, it's you."

If ever there was a dazzler, thought Waverly, it's got to be me. But what he said was, "Do my best."

"Do that and you'll inhale 'em."

"Later, Bennie."

About forty-five minutes later, Jock ushered his guests into the cash-flow room and with an oratorical exordium declared, "Gentlemen, let's play poker."

And about eight hours after that, in peroration considerably more subdued, he announced, "Guess that wraps it up for to-night."

The Arab was the big winner, with Bulldog trailing not far behind. B.B. was down some, nothing too serious. It was Jock and Waverly who had been blitzed thoroughly, steamrolled, both of them.

Jock made a twitch of a smile, an exhausted feeble spite in it. "Feelin' sorta bubble-eyed are you, Mr. Waverly?" he asked innocently.

Waverly was gazing at his shrunken towers of chips with a kind of immobilized awe. All of last night's score gone, and a good share of the stake as well. Somewhere in the neighborhood of three hundred and fifty thousand dollars, give or take some change. And all of it gone. "Something like that," he said.

23

"**Y**'know what a fella oughta do," Sigurd was saying, one chili dog down, his mouth bulging with another, "is come up with a real fat bun, wide one, big enough so's you could get two dogs in it. Sorta like your double cheeseburger only the dogs got to lay side by side 'stead of stacked on top each other. Call it a Double Dog. Whaddya think?"

What D'Marco thought was maybe, just maybe, if he didn't utter a word, didn't acknowledge it, the brainless chatter would trail away, soap bubbles in the air. There was a stretch of silence, not long, but long enough to sustain him in this slender hope. He was wrong.

Sigurd finished off the last of the uninspired single dog, sent it down on a wash of diet cream soda, burped contentedly, lit a cigarette, and resumed his creative ruminations. Out loud.

"See, how you'd advertise 'em—on the TV, I mean—is you'd show this dude sittin' at a desk, writin' or pushin' papers or something, whatever it is your regular citizens do at work. Clock on the wall behind him says it's goin' on noon. Everything's quiet, no sound. Then all of a sudden you start gettin' them real quick shots"—he made a series of rapid-fire finger snaps— "flash on the screen—y'know how they do that?—like it's suppose to be his thinkin' they're showin'? You follow what I'm sayin' here?"

Silence wasn't going to do it. "Yeah, I think I can follow that," D'Marco said, staring straight ahead.

"Okay. What them flash shots show is a couple dogs way the

fuck off in the distance—real pooches, I'm talkin' now—kind they
run out to a track, forget the name—"

"Greyhounds," D'Marco said, shooing away the smoke floating
toward him on the turgid air. "Those're greyhounds."

"That's the ones. So anyway, they're tearin' across a, oh, a field,
like, them greyhounds. Your camera keeps goin' back an' forth
between 'em and the dude. He's startin' to get some idea now,
you can see it all over his dumb citizen face. Also you're startin'
to hear this music, real soft at first, but gettin' louder all the time
the dogs movin' in closer. Music goes"—here Sigurd supplied the
melody—"da da dit, da da dit, da da *dit dit dit.* Y'remember that
one, Lone Ranger song?"

"That's the William Tell Overture you're trying to sing,"
D'Marco said. Oddly, he remembered this fact, and this one only,
from a music appreciation class he'd taken years ago, in high
school.

"Yeah, well, whatever." Sigurd had both hands in the air now,
one representing the sprinting greyhounds, the other the cere-
brating citizen; and as his vision unfolded, built to a climax, his
voice rose excitedly: "So the mutts're goin' like crazy, like they
got rockets in their ass, and the dude, he can't work no more, he
got this idea fillin' up his head, back an' forth you go, till finally,
whap!"—the word was punctuated by a slap of the hands—"he
fires outta his chair, goes through the door, down the stairs, out
in the street, barrel-assin' fast as them hounds, maybe faster even,
till he gets to this, like, eats stand, an' then the music, which has
got so fuckin' loud by now it's about to blow your eardrums, it
just stops dead, an' the dude, he steps right up to the stand, says,
'Gimme a *Double Dog!*' Last thing you see is him grubbin' one
down, big shit-eater on his face, like he just got his nuts cracked.
Oh, and maybe he's reachin' down to pat them real dogs, which
somehow just showed up outta nowhere." The heat of invention
had brought him to the edge of his chair. In summation he said
expectantly, "Some idea, huh? Bet you'd make a goddam mint off
it."

Now, finally, D'Marco looked at him, thinking that in twenty-
four hours, maybe less, maybe closer to twelve, he'd never have
to listen to this dribbleshit again ever, rest of his whole life. And
while he was still grateful—as nearly as he understood gratitude—
to be alive, he had to wonder at the mad gods who, out of all the
people in the world, or at least all the people in the business,
which, when you thought about it, was quite a few—anyway, out
of all of them they had to finger this one, Mr. Double Dogs here,

to be the one to rescue him. Strange how things work. Maybe it was a test. Build your character. "Oh yeah," he drawled, "that's a sensational idea you got there, your double dogs."

They were back at their post on the deck, sweltering once again in the dank midday heat. More of the test. The morning had come up gray and thick with a fog that, backlit and thinned by the sun, hung even yet like an orange smudge in the sky. Across the road a crew of workmen, busy and industrious as the bugs they waged a losing war on, were putting the final touches on the Tropicaire bungalow. On the roof a pair of them clipped together the last sections of nylon tarp. Down below another attached to the exterior of the structure a DANGER sign. Still another lugged a tank from the truck to the slit of an opening in the tarp covering the door. The truck itself bore the legend TERMINEX MAN, which Sigurd found vastly amusing. "Terminex Man," he hooted, "that's what they oughta be callin' us."

Even D'Marco could see the humor in that. "That'd be about right," he said.

"Sure look funny that way," Sigurd remarked as, swatch by nylon swatch, the bungalow vanished under the dull gray tarp. "Look like a goddam circus tent, only ain't nobody havin' fun inside."

"That's because the clowns are in the one in back."

"Yeah, well, come tonight their clownin' days is history."

"That's another one you got correct."

A thought, inspired by the tenting, was taking shape in D'Marco's head, but before it could crystallize, the phone sounded on the other side of the slider. "I'll take that," he said, and in the room, into the speaker, he said, "Yeah?"

"Gunter Dietz," was the reply, delivered in an exasperated, syllable-chopping tone.

"What can I do for you?"

"You can start by telling me what's going on over there."

"Tenting," D'Marco said, just a trace of wiseass in it. "It's called tenting."

There was a pause, and then the voice came down the line cold as an Arctic wind: "What the fuck is that, tenting? Where are they? What's shaking down here? I want answers, Frog. No cute games. Answers."

D'Marco figured he'd better ease up. This, after all, was the guy paying the freight. He said, "Tenting's what they do to kill off the bugs. Nothing to sweat, that other business. Marks're in the apartment right behind. We're covering them."

"What about last night?"

"Same as before. Player goes out to the condo, comes in about four this morning. I'm on him all the time. Jew stays home with his head under the sheets. Neither of them peeked out once today."

Since nothing had come of the meeting with the cunt yesterday afternoon, D'Marco decided not to mention it. Why clutter things? If it turned out she was dumb enough to be in tight with those two walking stiffs, show up tonight, then she could take the same fall they were going to. Tough luck, lady. You lose too.

"What's their new number over there?" Dietz demanded.

D'Marco gave him the number supplied by the helpful weasel of a manager.

"All right. I'm going to, ah, nudge them a little. You stay by the phone. I'll get back to you in, uh, five minutes."

It was closer to ten minutes later when D'Marco picked up the phone on its first rattle and, taking a cue from his contractor, said simply, "Frog."

"Dietz."

"So. What do you hear?"

"They're stalling," Dietz said, and now his voice was glacial, full of bottled fury.

For D'Marco, pumped and ready to hit it, sling some moves, this was not cheering news. "Stalling?" he said. "How's that?"

"They want an extension."

"How long?"

"Till morning."

D'Marco felt a sudden relieved rush. "Morning's no problem, my end of things. Midnight, morning, all comes to the same."

"You're missing the point, Frog. They're thinking to chump me. It's in his voice, the Jewboy. I can hear it."

"And what're you thinking?"

"I'll tell you what I'm thinking—no, strike that 'thinking'— what it is we're going to do. Player'll be back out at the game tonight. You stay glued to him. Your partner—what's his name again?"

"Name's Sigurd."

"He covers the Jew. Same drill. But only till midnight."

"What happens at midnight?"

"Midnight he steps across the street and, ah, secures our sheeny friend."

" 'Secures,' " D'Marco repeated. "You mean smokes?"

"No, not yet. This Sigurd just sits on him till the player gets back to the apartment. That's when you move in, muscle him. Then you bring the two of them over here."

"Your room? You want them there in your room?"

"That's right. One-o-eight. Also, Frog, whatever money they've managed to collect, don't forget to bring that along too."

"Listen," D'Marco snapped, "I'm not into skimming. You got any worries that way, you better find yourself another boy."

"Just a reminder, you understand."

"Oh yeah, I understand. Anything else?"

"One more thing. Yesterday you mentioned, ah, stunts, I believe it was. Any further thoughts along those lines?"

"Yeah, I got some good ideas, one in particular."

"What would that be?"

"That tenting going on over there. Bug juice they use, it can be hazardous to your health. Hear it paralyzes you before it takes you out. Not a nice way to go."

For a while there was silence, and then Dietz, very evenly, very judiciously, said, "That might do. But I want to see some squirming first. Those two, they're not getting off that easy. They're going to feel a world of hurt, Frog. Before it's all done."

D'Marco, thinking of all the tools and instruments in his gear bag, the dagger and torch and icepick and pliers and other assorted paraphernalia of his vocation, said, "That we can arrange too."

While D'Marco and Dietz were reviewing their plan for the evening ahead, refining it, working out any kinks, another sort of deliberation, much less focused though no less intense, was going on in the Tropicaire bungalow across the street. "Got to be a crossroader at that table," Bennie declared, concluding a long, rambling and for him uncharacteristically profane monologue, his voice hoarse with misery and fear.

"Face it," Waverly said, "the cards turned on me. That can happen."

"No way! No way a player with your kind of smarts gonna get smeared over like that 'less there's work down. Run it by again. Got to be a pattern in there."

"Why? To what end? We already did this."

"Humor me here, huh?"

Waverly, sapped, bone-weary, was sprawled across the couch.

He watched Bennie pacing furiously, hands slicing the air, the veins in his throat filling, pulsing dangerously, a plume of smoke trailing from the cigar stuck in his mouth. What he really wanted to do was retreat into the groggy sleep ruptured only moments ago by the jangling phone. Forget sleep. "All right," he said. "One more time." He covered his eyes with the palms of his hands, and as he reconstructed, to the best of his blurred memory, the ebb and flow of last night's game, what he discovered, astonishingly, was a glimmer of the pattern Bennie searched for. Faint and inconclusive, but a possible pattern all the same. For the monster pots, the heavy money hands, seemed invariably to come on the Arab's deal and, he remembered now, it was invariably the Arab—cool, assured, impervious to bluff—who scooped them in. But the Arab? Impossible.

Nevertheless, midway into the summary, Bennie interrupted him to say, "He's the one. Got to be him."

"But why? For him that's loose change. He's no Robbie Crown."

"Cheatin' got nothing to do with the size of your bankroll. Cheatin's in the blood. A crossroader don't do it for just the money. It's the buzz he's after, the high. Believe me, Timothy, about that I know."

Waverly thought about it a minute. "Okay," he said, still skeptical, "assuming there's anything at all to this—which is very, very doubtful—then how?"

"How? You're the one was there, you tell me how. What about the deck? You see any edge work, crimpin', high belly strippers, shit like that?"

"Appelgate supplies the decks. And he lost too, remember?"

"Maybe he got the mechanic grip, goes south with a swing card. You watchin' for that?"

"I know that grip. He doesn't have it."

"How about double-teamin', somebody makin' shade."

"Look," Waverly said, patience on the wane, "these are citizens. Assholes, but citizens. Every one of them's got deep pockets. They play for recreation. You're not going to find a cheater in that kind of company."

"What'd I just tell you, 'bout crossroaders? Pay attention. If it ain't the deck and it ain't the grip and there ain't no shade, then he's gotta be usin' some kind a gaff. Nothin' else left."

"Except maybe a run of luck."

Bennie stopped pacing. He cocked his head slightly, and the look he cast on his partner was a look compounded of wonder and infinite pity. "Yeah. Sure. Luck."

Waverly shrugged. "Believe what you like," he said. "But if he is cheating, he's too slick for me. Either way, where does it leave us?"

"Leave us? You're askin' where it leaves us? Suckin' worms is where it leaves us, Timothy, we can't come up with that goddam surcharge by morning. That's what he said on the phone there, Dietz."

"So what do you suggest?"

"Suggest you produce that loot tonight."

"Just like that, is it? Wave a magic wand and a quarter mil appears?"

"You can do it. You come close Monday. If the raghead's scammin' on his deal, back off, donate your ante, zap him on the other hands."

"And if I can't? If the cards don't fall right?"

Bennie went over to the window and gazed out at the tented bungalow across the courtyard. He stood with his hands clasped behind him. A thoughtful posture, meditative. Finally he said, "You could make 'em fall right. You know how to put together a cold deck, deal seconds. Turn that date-picker's game around on him, whatever the fuck it is."

"Come on, Bennie," Waverly said, addressing his back. "I can't do that."

"Can't or won't?"

"Can't. They'd tumble in a finger snap. They may be amateurs but they're not fools."

Bennie didn't turn. For a moment he was silent, and when he spoke again there was an edge of pleading in his voice. "Maybe I ain't gettin' through to you here, Timothy. With Dietz there ain't no middlin'. It's deliver in the morning or catch your own lunch for breakfast. You understand what I'm sayin' to you?"

"I understand. And I'm telling you how it is at that table."

Bennie's fatty shoulders seemed to sag. "Well, you can't, you can't," he said dismally. "So we better start thinkin' on another plan. Do that, I gotta have me a drink." He crossed the room, flopped onto a counter stool, mashed the burnt-out cigar in a saucer, and poured a glassful of bourbon. "You?"

"That's the last thing I need."

He took a long gulpy swallow, peered into the glass. Furrows of doubt pinched his forehead. At last he said, "Okay, here's what we do. You go out there, play till the break, midnight, then you gimme a call, fill me in on where the numbers at. If it's lookin' anywhere near close, I just might be able to cut a deal with Dietz."

"How close is close?"

"Two balloons. Nothing less."

"And if I'm not close?"

Bennie's reply was quick, professional, the accents of rueful experience in it. "Then you blaze outta there. I know them condos. Shooter's parked in front, you leave the car, duck out the back, shag on up to the hotel, call a cab, get to the airport, get in the wind. Don't forget to hold back a little bail-out cash. You're gonna need a nut, you get that far."

"What about you? They've got to be tracking both of us now."

"Try and do the same, I s'pose. Maybe I can twist some cover outta O'Boyle. Have to find a way somehow. I'll give you the number of a fella in Miami. He's okay, standup. If you make it—"

"Heavy on that *if,*" Waverly broke in.

"Yeah, well, if you do, you call him. But give it a couple months first. Better we don't know where each other's at, case one of us gets tagged."

Waverly shook his head slowly. "That's your plan?"

"Best I can do. Get this deep in the caca, it's hurrah for me and fuck you. You're a Jacktown gradu-ate, Timothy. You know that's how it's gotta be."

"I know."

Bennie drained his glass, held up the bottle. "Sure you won't have one?"

Waverly came over and joined him at the counter. "One," he said, "For old times."

Bennie poured. "Could be some new times ahead yet too," he said, gazing at his partner steadily. "Y'never know. Maybe the gods'll be smilin' on you tonight."

Gods that smile. On B. Epstein, and only on him, was it a speculation never outworn. "Stranger things have happened," Waverly said.

They touched glasses.

Bennie's gaze fell away, seemed to turn inward. All his features slackened. "Y'know," he said ruminantly, "next month I hit the big six-o. Sixty years young. Don't ever kid yourself, boy. Life begins at sixty."

Waverly felt good. No accounting for it; tote up the score and it made no sense whatsoever. Here he was, held hostage by forces utterly outside his control. Look at them: Up ahead a showdown game that may, or may not, be stacked; directly behind him, filling the rearview, all pretense of guile or subtlety long since scrapped, the black Mustang bearing the agent of his own death; an escape plan so flimsy (cut and run, it reduced to, don't look back, hope for the best) it had the surreal quality of a Saturday morning cartoon—the innocent deathless Roadrunner, here he comes, beep! beep!, there he goes, exempt from the laws of nature, physics, miraculously survived again; and Caroline Crown, don't forget Caroline, appeared out of nowhere, the past, to touch his life for the twinkling of a moment with the swindle of hope, and almost certainly gone now, and gone for good. All those oblique, slippery forces. Yet in spite of them, in defiance of all reason, he felt good, driving north on Ocean Boulevard, covering the length of Singer Island. Better than good, golden, as if reality had lost all sense of scale and proportion, as if for him there were no such things as defeat and disaster and bottomless grief to be drawn from the neutral air. Timothy Waverly, Roadrunner: quick my wit, keen my eye, fleet my foot. The elevated delirium of invincibility. Bennie's smiling gods.

He turned west on PGA Boulevard, into the misted violet afterglow of sinking sun. And also into reality's first rude intrusion, the line of evening traffic ahead of him worming to a stop at the drawbridge, two concrete slabs of road, rising magically above the Intracoastal Waterway while a slow-motion barge chugged on by. For five minutes, maybe more, seemed like more, he waited. This unwelcome breach in the fanciful bubble of serenity set his nerves on edge. He drummed the wheel impatiently, smoked a cigarette. Finally the bridge descended, the barriers lifted, and the traffic inched forward, gradually accelerated. He checked his watch. Ten minutes to eight. He was going to make it, time to spare. Can't get rattled now.

Except there was another breach waiting in the person of Robbie Crown, planted outside the condo entrance, glaring at him as he drove up the street and pulled in behind the Arab's Rolls Corniche. They approached each other on the walk. Robbie came hurrying toward him, gripped him by the elbow, and steered him back to the car, rumbling under his breath, "Jesus, where you been? We've got to talk."

Waverly disengaged his arm. "About what?"

"What!" Robbie sputtered. "About what happened last night. What went wrong. What you're going to do about it. That's what."

The full face boiled up crimson, looked on the fine point of breaking out in a violent sweat. The jowls quivered when he spoke. The hands swatted air. Shades of B. Epstein, Waverly thought, but then he quickly amended that thought; for apart from their shared agitation and obvious panic, these two sometime friends, or more accurately representations of the two antipodal sides of his strange life, were nothing at all alike. "I lost," he said simply, and he didn't bother to disguise the contempt in his voice. "You were there. You saw it."

"Lost," Robbie said, giving back some of the contempt. "More like stomped on. Punished."

"With cards, nobody writes any warranties. You knew that going in."

"I didn't know you were going to piss it all away. You're supposed to be the professional here."

"Look, I'm not into critiques or recriminations, either one. Last night was last night."

"All right, then, what about tonight? What do you intend to do about it?"

"Go inside and try and win our money back, that's what I'm going to do. Nothing left *to* do."

Waverly was getting mightily sick of these conversations. Everybody a strategist, everybody ready with advice. Let them play the game. He started for the door, but Robbie stepped into his path. "Hold on a minute. We're not finished yet, you and me."

Waverly looked at him narrowly. "What else is on your mind? Besides money."

Robbie didn't flinch. "Not Care, if that's what you're talking about. That one's already settled."

"You're sure, are you?"

"Sure enough."

"Then I think maybe we are finished. You want to get out of my way?"

Robbie didn't budge, but his sneering tone softened some, turned wheedling, lawyerly, honeyed with sweet reason, though with an undertone of desperation too. "Listen, Tim, never mind our other, uh, differences. They're behind us now, forget them. I have. Tabula rasa." A swipe of the air and they were gone, those differences. "You want to score in there," he continued, "so do I. We both need to lay our hands on that cash. And tonight's the flash point. You know that."

Waverly glanced past him. Parked under a tree along the curb at the end of the street was the Mustang, its natural blackness

deepening in the shadows and the falling light. "Don't I though,"
he said.

"So what about those special skills you pros are supposed to
have?"

"What about them?"

"If there was ever a time to use them, it's got to be now. It only
makes sense, Tim. For both of us."

"We've been over this ground before," Waverly said frigidly.
"You already know my answer."

Robbie exploded. "For Christ's sake wake up, will you!" Then,
remembering himself, he lowered his voice. "Everything's on the
block here. Everything. It's the only way."

"No, that's where you're wrong. There's another way. Tonight
I'll win."

"How the fuck can you know that?"

"Call it a hunch," Waverly said, and again he started for the
door and this time Robbie made no move to block his way.

But he was mistaken. The first hour he took several hands,
small ones, but enough to elevate the perilously whittled stake
over the hundred-K mark and make him believe in his hunch.
And then, second hour, he leveled off, losing more often than he
won, just scraping by. Third hour and the plunge began, the long
greased slide, down down down. Nothing seemed to come his
way, or when it did there was someone, always someone, waiting
to pounce, outgun him, put him up against the wall. And not
infrequently, more times than a few, more times than the laws of
probability and chance dictate or condone, that someone was the
prince.

Waverly watched hm. Resplendent in glistening plum-colored
jacket and paisley print silk tie, the prince played with a kind of
effortless tranquillity, attacking and retreating with an uncanny
sense of timing, his brown face stubbornly blank. When he spoke,
which was seldom, there was a dulcet, phlegmatic quality to his
voice, absent utterly of the exhilarating properties of risk and
danger that now and again will kindle the speech of the most
veteran of players. And when he raked in a pot, which was often,
there was a pert, almost girlish edge in the motions of his delicate
hands. His fingers were heavy with rings that occasionally caught
the light above the table with a startling glint. His hair, lustrous
as a coat of freshly laid tar, gleamed brilliantly under the same
overhead light.

He watched the rest of the competition as well, Waverly did,

moving his eyes carefully from face to face. Drummond, Jock—
nothing to be read in their expressions other than the jaundiced
sulk of defeat. Hard losers tonight, both of them. Not so the jubilant little B.B., who was, wondrously, the only other winner thus
far and who, just then, was locked in a serious one-on-one with
the charmed Arab. The game was seven-stud. The Arab had the
deal. But B.B., to all appearances, easily had the better of him
going into the last card. He displayed two pair, jacks over fours,
and from the transparent sparkle in his eye, a boat already floating. The Arab, showing a lonely pair of nines and nothing else of
any weight, called the bets with a calm so passionless it bordered
on indifference. The pot, fed through the first four cards by the
three dropouts, grew like a mutant weed. A big score in the making for The Big Guy.

Except it never happened. The final card came down, B.B. doubled the bet, and the Arab, after a studied hesitation, saw it and
raised him back a sum large enough to capture the attention of
everyone in the room—the three idled players, the three railbirds
looking on from a discreet distance, even the motionless black
figure filling the couch behind the table—and to send a quick
shiver through the diminutive frame of the dumfounded B.B.
There was nothing for him to do but call. He'd had his full house
all along, of course, but it was the fours full. The Arab turned
over three nines and a pair of lowly deuces, permitted himself a
thin smile, and without a word gathered in the chips.

To no one in particular B.B. remarked, "Guess I got whacked
good that time." He was trying valiantly to mask his disappointment, but the corners of his mouth drooped and his eyes swam.
For a moment it seemed he might burst into tears.

"Guess you did at that, big fella," Jock allowed pitilessly.

Waverly thought about what he had just seen. Only a fool would
have bet into the hand B.B. was showing, and the Arab was no
fool. Or a clairvoyant, and he was not that either. Or a cheat. In
less than three hours the pattern was emerging again. A replay
of last night. Bennie had to be right. Somehow, some way, there
was work down here.

The deal had passed to Jock, but before he could shuffle, Waverly said, "Call for a new deck."

Jock arched an eyebrow. His upper lip curled slightly. "You
fixin' to change your luck with a different batch of cards, Mr.
Waverly?"

"Why don't we try it, see what happens?"

"Didn't know you pro*fess*ionals played on superstition. Thought it was all science."

"Whatever works," Waverly said. He looked across the table at the Arab, who regarded him with a smile so amused and faint it might have been practiced before a mirror.

"Robber," Jock directed, "go get me a fresh deck. Bottom drawer of the desk in the study back there."

Robbie jumped at the command, exited the room and returned with the deck. Jock broke the seal, shuffled, and the game rolled on.

Twice the deal went around the table. Same pattern. Whatever the gaff was, Waverly couldn't get a figure on it. The deck was so squeaky clean it could have served nicely at a ladies bridge club. So it wasn't the cards. And the Arab wasn't the only one to score pots off his own deal; Bulldog did it, even B.B. It was mystifying. Also unnerving. Crunch time an hour away, and hand by hand they were grinding him down. Five in a row he tossed in. A quick glance told him the hundred K was slashed in half. At least in half. Finally he caught a promising run in a seven-card lowball game, a pot builder, and found himself, like the hapless B.B., squarely in the Arab's fire path. For it was the Arab, once again, dealing the cards.

Five were out. Waverly showed a seven-three-deuce, and down below he held a sweet ace-five. A hand not all that far off perfect. So far. Good enough to spook everyone else. Everyone, that is, but the poised and patient Arab, who sat on a nine high backed by a six-five. Close, but no cigar. So far.

Wagers down, the Arab flipped them each a card. A pairing five for Waverly, big exposed queen for the dealer. Waverly bumped the bet to twenty thou. No other choice: His pair was concealed, on the surface he was mighty as Godzilla. Even a hard-rock player should understand when to back off. Not the Arab. Unblinking, he called.

Last card down. Waverly peeked at his and though his face revealed nothing, behind it was a dismay as acute as a stab of physical pain. The card was a king. His near-perfect hand ravaged, his strategy in ruins. On one card. But the four showing were still intimidators, and he was run out of options. And almost out of money. He counted out his remaining chips, shoved them in. "Twenty-three thousand there," he said mildly. "Bet it all."

Again the Arab's wettish lips formed the mirror-cultivated smile, and the gaze he leveled on Waverly was deadly shrewd. Knowing. "I shall see your wager," he said, equally mild; and after a nice dramatic pause and in a voice little more than a murmur, he added, "And I must raise it thirty."

Waverly had the dizzying sense of sliding helplessly into a deep sinkhole. He needed space to think it out. No space. "You can see my plate's empty here," he said. "Would you take a marker, if it comes to that?"

The Arab's gaze turned inward, contemplative. He steepled his hands, seemed to consider. The overhead light winked off a ring-weighted finger, and some inner monitor whispered a warning in Waverly's ear.

"Perhaps I could do that," the Arab said grandly, enjoying the moment. "This one time."

"Then I'm in for the ride."

They displayed their hole cards, let the hands speak for themselves. The Arab showed paired fours, but the queen was his highest card. With a certain simpery satisfaction he said, "I believe I defeated you, sir. Most unfortunate."

He reached for the pile of chips, and again the light danced on the ring, and now the monitor set off a siren in Waverly's head and he thrust out a hand and pinned the Arab's wrist to the table. He seized a card and held it over the ring, which gave back a tiny reflection of the card's face. "No," he said, "*this* is what's unfortunate."

A collective gasp rose through the room. The railbirds came to their feet, Nimrod right behind them. "Fuck're you doin'?" Jock spluttered.

"It's called a shiner," Waverly said, voice gone hard with scorn. "Oldest gaff in the game. What you've got here is a crossroader. An oily little cheat."

"Cheat!" Jock bellowed on a flying wedge of spittle. "You're way out of line, Waverly."

"You saw it."

"You're not playin' with your five-and-dime hoods here. Prince is my guest. Let go his hand."

Waverly glanced about, searching for support. Orton and Demerit had faded back against a wall. Robbie's face wore the stricken look of a shock victim. B.B.'s hands twisted in his lap, and he shook all over with a nervous little giggle. Bulldog's protuberant teeth were set in a terrible smile. Jock's fleshy jaw jutted aggressively. No support anywhere in this room. And across the table the Arab fixed him with liquid reproachful eyes. His brown face was on fire. Waverly released the pinned wrist.

There was a sudden sharp pop, and the foam-wrapped cylinder in Nimrod's hand lengthened into the glittery steel wand. He slapped it in his open palm and came at Waverly. The Arab lifted a restraining arm. "Nimrod! No! Not here. Not yet."

Nimrod stopped as abruptly as a trained hound coming to heel, but his free hand clenched and unclenched, a rhythmic fist-making. His eyes were cold as steel spikes. Death in them.

Jock turned to Waverly and snarled, "Get your ass outta here, you sonbitch. While you still can."

Waverly pushed his chair away from the table, stood, and backed slowly toward the door. From the other side of it he heard Jock pleading, "I'm real sorry, prince. That scumsucker got no right to . . ."

And that's all he heard before he took off running. Had he been in the room he would have seen the Arab scorning Jock's apology, and he would have seen him turn to his bodyguard and heard him say in a voice corrosive with venom and wounded pride, "Now!"

After two fidgety, eventless hours out on the deck, Sigurd decided to act on a notion that had been rattling around in his head all evening. He popped inside, made a quick call to room service, and told them to send up a cold sixer. Couldn't hurt none, he figured, couple brews; steady his tweaky nerves. This was some kind of heavy shit coming on, midnight, more responsibility than he'd ever had laid on him in his whole life, and he didn't want to fuck up. Wanted to show 'em all—D'Marco, Uncle Eugene, Dietz, especially Dietz—Sigurd Stumpley had some def moves in him. Do it right and get in tight—that was his motto. Also make Mom proud, that'd be good too, little fringe benefit, like.

He was right about the beer. Back on the deck, sipping at one (but slowly, temperately, and only his third), he was feeling better already, mellowing in the convalescence of the black wash of night. Okay, okay, so his partner might not approve—so what? Fuck him. He wasn't here to bitch about it and he didn't have to know. No harm being done. Nothing going on across the road over there. Everything under control. Fuck him. Anyway, he was borderline bonkers, that D'Marco, had to be your primo candidate for the wig factory.

Take tonight, for a for instance. Earlier, going through his gear bag, deciding on the pieces they'd be using, he'd held up a double-edge shank looked about a foot long—dagger, he called it—and said something about cutting 'em up, making a splatter platter. Then he brought out a goddam blowtorch, f'Chrissake, talked about doing a Shake'n Bake on 'em. Real casual-like, like he was trying to choose between a Bud and a Coors (or a carrot and a cuke, his case). And when he finally handed over the .22 and the silencer, his eyes got all wet and glittery and he said, "Do a tap with one of them and the loudest noise you're gonna hear is the mark's scream." That's what he said. Dr. Frankenfuckinstein.

The way Sigurd saw it, clipping the marks, standing up, that was one thing. But he wasn't so sure about that weird kinky stuff, like the business with the ear the other night. That was straight out of the D'Marco Fontaine twitch house, and he didn't like to think about that.

So he tried not to. He eased back in the chair, sipped beer, and waited, allowing his thoughts to drift along like the ragged coiling clouds skimming across the face of the moon. The very shape of the sky, empty of stars, seemed to shift before his eyes. Sky, clouds, peekaboo moon, sultry night—all combined to cast a magic spell, much as he'd felt that other night, gazing into the immense black void of ocean and contemplating, in his own fashion, the awesome mysteries of fate and chance, and the thin fragile line between life and death.

But a little after eleven these philosophic musings gave way to an urgent summons in his bladder, and though he didn't like to leave his post he figured he better get it taken care of now, before the fireworks show began. In the john he washed and rinsed his hands deliberately, after his habit, and planted himself over the stool, unzippered his fly, and was about to blissfully unstopper the dam and—wouldn't you know?—the goddam phone rang. Nice fucking timing. Unrelieved, he went into the room, picked up the receiver, and pressed it to his ear, and before he could even get out his standard *Yeah* salutation a breathless old fart voice demanded, "You see it?"

"Huh?" Sigurd said with some annoyance. "Who's this talkin'?"

"O'Boyle. Tropicaire. You see it?"

"See what?"

"Lady. Just drove up. Went in the unit there."

"When'd this happen?"

"Just now, like I said. You didn't see it?"

"Nah, I hadda come inside a minute."

"You Frog? You ain't Frog."

"I'm his partner."

"Fella called Frog, he said watch real close tonight, anything funny go on let him know, he didn't say nothin' about no lady, so I thought I oughta—"

"Okay, okay," Sigurd cut in on him, "give it a rest, hey. I got to think here." His mouth had gone suddenly dry, and he could feel his heartbeat picking up speed. Even the sting down below was on temporary hold.

"I do right, callin'?"

"Yeah, you did good."

"You tell Frog, okay?"

"I'll tell him."

"Anything else I should do?"

"Nah, just stay where you are. Keep watchin'. Keep cool."

The instructions were pronounced toughly, evenly, like he knew what he was doing, but Sigurd had to wonder if they were delivered to the manager or to himself. He put down the phone and, tugging at his fly, hurried out onto the deck. Sure enough, there was the Jag parked outside the apartment, same car the player's squeeze drove. So something was for sure going on, something funny, like the freeze dry just said. He looked at his watch. 11:20. Wasn't till midnight he was suppose to make his move. Maybe he should get on over there right now. Or maybe call Dietz. Fucked if he knew: Nobody said nothing about *this*.

He stood there a moment, heart thumping, bladder burning. An agony of doubt and physical distress. And then the decision was taken out of his hands, for off to the right two fingers of light appeared and behind them a car streaking down the road and squealing to a stop alongside the Jag. Holy shit, it was the Caddie, the player. Sigurd looked back up the street, fully expecting to see the LX come wheeling around the corner. No LX. Something serious gone wrong, mistake somewhere. And he knew Dietz frowned on mistakes. So did D'Marco. Seething with manic energy, cursing out loud the wicked luck that laid the burden of choice squarely on him, he dashed through the slider and out the door and down the corridor and down the stairwell, moving stiffly, fast as he was able given the mounting pressure in his lower regions, and attaching the silencer to his piece as he ran.

Not even midnight yet and here comes Mr. Badass tearing through the door like a chased hound. Jumps behind the wheel of the Caddie and takes it rocketing up the street and out onto PGA Boulevard. Whatever was coming down here, it wasn't in the plan. But whatever the fuck it was, D'Marco had no time to deliberate. That was okay. Didn't matter. Been enough deliberating already.

He turned the key in the ignition and pulled away from the curb. He swung onto PGA and, picking up speed, shaved the gap between him and the player easily. No problem there. None. Caddie up against this sweet little tooler of his—no contest. And as his vision narrowed on it, gun-sighted it through the windshield, all the sluggish lethargy comes of sitting on your can waiting three hours or better (three hours?—make that two long weeks) melted right away in the tingly heat welling up out of the pit of his stomach and rising through his chest and charging his limbs and quickening his breath. Same familiar heat he always felt just before a pop. Was nothing in the world measured up to that feeling. Nothing even close.

So intent was D'Marco on the unequal race, its winner and loser foreordained, he never once bothered to glance in the rearview mirror. If he had, he'd have seen a curious sight: a Rolls coming down the road behind him, moving just as fast as he was, swinging in and out of the traffic just as nimbly, a fierce-eyed black man at the wheel.

Quite by accident, it was the drawbridge that rescued him. Rescued?— more accurately bought him a moment of time. The Mustang closing in fast, the feeble escape plan utterly abandoned in the wild confusion of flight, he caught a glimpse up ahead of a tall-masted yacht slipping through the channel. He had a clear run at the bridge, and he floored it and got in just under the falling barrier gate. In the rearview he could see the Mustang grind to a fishtailing stop and swing about in a wide turn, and behind it, unless he was mistaken (for the two slabs of roadway were parting now, rising), the Rolls Corniche doing the same maneuver. So he had to assume there were two of them now, and if he was right, then the shooter would know instinctively where he was headed and the superspade would be keen enough to stay with the vehicle that was clearly tracking him, and if they took a back route down Prosperity and over to Highway One and across the Blue Heron Bridge then he had maybe a five-minute start on them, five minutes at most, no more, maybe less.

All these thoughts swept through Waverly's head, and others as well, but none so dizzying, so chilling, as the thought inspired by the sight of the silver Jaguar parked outside the Tropicaire bungalow. Caroline? Here? Now? Not even the unkindest fate could play a joke so desperately cruel as this one. Yet when he came bursting through the door, there she surely was, perched on a counter stool, coolly sipping a drink; and there was Bennie, chewing up the rug, clutching a glass of his own, scowling, fuming. They spoke in unison, a simultaneous chorus.

Bennie: "Timothy, fuck're you doin' back—"

Caroline: "Tim, I've decided to—"

Waverly silenced them both with a flagging arm. "No talk. No time. They're right behind me. Out out out—now!"

Bennie's jaw dropped. He understood. He slung the glass on the couch and made for the door. But Caroline froze. Waverly crossed the room and seized her by the wrist and yanked her roughly to her feet.

"My things," she said, wagging her head at two bags on the floor in a corner. "What about—"

"Forget the bags. Move!"

She moved. But outside, as he swung open the Jaguar's door, she balked, turned, and gave him a frantic, searching, bewildered look. "Tim, what's happening? Why are you—"

"Listen, Caroline. Don't talk, listen. You're in danger here. Serious danger. I want you to get in this car and drive away. Fast as you can pedal."

"But I came here to be with you," she said, and her stunned eyes were streaked with tears. "Go with you. The way we said."

Waverly hesitated. So much to say. So many messages undelivered. "I know, I know. Maybe we'll make it yet. Another time."

"For Chrisfuckinsake, Timothy," Bennie was bawling at him, squeezing his bulk in under the wheel of the Caddie, "let's roll!"

There was a hollow flat thumping sound and, instantaneously, the sound of the Jaguar's rear window shattering. Waverly jerked Caroline down behind the door, and peeked around it, and in a voice not all that far off a groan he said, "Jesus, we're too late."

For diagonally across the road, no more than fifty yards away, coming at them in a peculiar twittery hop, was the sidekick, the comic fatty, not so funny anymore with a piece in his hands. But just then he stopped abruptly and wheeled around, caught in the headlights of a car rushing toward him.

Waverly stood and pulled Caroline up beside him, and over his shoulder he called, "Come on, Bennie. Run."

"Run where?"

"Over there."

The three of them darted across the street and down the breezeway in front of the Collonades, Waverly in the lead, urging them on: "Run, run." He heard the car come to a squealy halt and he looked back once and of course it was the Mustang. They kept running.

And as they turned the corner at the south wing of the hotel, two more of the hollow thumps sounded behind them. They sprinted along the wall as far as the stairwell in the back, and there Waverly suddenly stopped. He looked around him. Wall on one side, wide empty parking lot on the other, and ahead of them a grassy sweep of lawn and beyond it an expanse of open beach and beyond that the dark silent ocean. Caroline's breath came in great shuddery heaves. Bennie gasped out the words, "Now where?"

Waverly put a foot in the wire mesh covering the entrance to the stairs, forced it down. "Up there," he said. "Nowhere left to run."

About halfway down the street D'Marco stopped running, set himself in a crouch, gripped his piece with both hands, and popped two caps at the figures fleeing through the shadows along the face of the hotel. Impossible to tell if he hit anything. No screams, he didn't think so. He came out of the street—no cover there—and followed the breezeway the length of the building. Again he stopped, flattened his back to the wall, sucked in a deep breath, and graceful as a ballerina, pivoted around the corner, arms extended, elbows locked, the weapon in his hand swaying back and forth like the head of a tranced cobra. No one in the parking lot, no one in the dark passageway ahead of him. He ran to the back of the hotel, paused, listened. There was the sound of footsteps clambering up the stairs directly above him. Also heavy footsteps coming up behind him, and Sigurd's wheezy panicked voice: "You see 'em, man? You clip 'em?"

"Shut the fuck up. Tell me, quick, what went down here?"

"I dunno. I'm watchin' from the deck and outta nowhere the cunt pulls up, then the player. Didn't see you, didn't know what to do, so I figured I better get over there, sit on 'em till—"

"Okay, so there's—what?—three of 'em?"

"Yeah, right, three."

"They packin'?"

"Dunno that either. Don't think so, way they bugged outta there. I'd've nailed 'em too, except you—"

"C'mon."

"Where to?"

"Just follow me, assbag. Move it."

D'Marco took the stairs three at a time. From the sound of it they couldn't be any more than three, four flights above him. No lead at all. Very cautiously, he came out of the stairwell at the seventh and last floor. He heard the footsteps receding down the oceanside breezeway, and then he heard a door cracking open. No more footsteps. Executing the same balletic move, he swung around the corner. Empty breezeway. Empty silence.

Silence, except for the clomping, sounded like a goddam baby elephant mounting the stairs. Worthless fuckup. Preceded and announced by his ragged breathing, Sigurd emerged from the stairwell in a mincing, tiptoeing step. He was about to say something when D'Marco put a flat hand in the air, forestalling speech and movement, both. D'Marco waited a moment, studied the layout, improvised a plan; and then he motioned him forward and in a toneless whisper said, "Okay, they're getting cute here, real cute. What they did was duck into one of those rooms, can't tell which. Sound of it, they're down at the other end of the hall. Here's what we do. You take this end, anything move, blow it over. I'll go down one floor, come up the other end, box 'em in. Then I'm going to hit one room at a time, flush 'em out. All you got to do is cover me from here. You think you can do that?"

"Yeah, sure, course I can do it," Sigurd said, but the conviction was annulled by the chirpy flutter in his voice. His face was shiny with sweat and his body seemed to jiggle all over, particularly the lower half.

D'Marco looked at him narrowly. "What's the matter with you? You better not be going pussy on me here."

"Ain't nothin' the matter," Sigurd mumbled, "I'm set." He sure as shit wasn't going to say anything about his urgent—make that acute—need to piss. Fuckin' bladder felt like an overinflated balloon about to pop on him any second now.

"All right," D'Marco said, starting for the stairs. "Let's do it."

All the way over to Singer Island Nimrod, an able and experienced stalker, kept a wary distance between himself and the Mustang, and when he turned onto Ocean Avenue and saw the action in the street he killed his headlights and pulled up at the curb. He wasn't exactly sure what was goin' on, but he pretty soon got a bulb: Regular OK Corral out there, couple hope-to-dies suited up and bustin' on his punk. That boy got to have some kinda jacket on his ass, just don't click up with nobody. Put a whole new figure on it, them two bounty hunters did, but that was fine, negative wet. They get in his game and they be gone too. Tonight he goin' earn his keep, bring his dustball prince back a boss trophy, like the punk's hand maybe, same one caught Mr. Smooth doin' the nasty.

So he waited just long enough for them two little bros to get to the end of the dark hotel, and then he climbed out of the Rolls and took off after them on a dead run. For a man his size he covered ground fast. In one hand he held a Colt .357 Magnum, in the other the extended steel baton (his own magic wand, you give her a sweep and she guarantee to disappear anything in your path). He did a sly at the corner, peeked one eyeball around it in time to see them bounding up the stairs. He scooted along the side of the building, stopped in the stairwell, got his wind, then followed them up. On the fifth floor he heard somebody coming back down, so he hugged the wall, set to spring. But whoever it was—just one of 'em, he could tell by the step—got off on the floor above and went down the breezeway.

Nimrod thought about it a minute, put it together: one on each end, punk in between, nice little squeeze. Okay, that was cool. Let them do the heavy work, then he strut in and collect the gold star. Treading noiseless as a ghost, he continued up the stairs, but when he came out on the top floor even he, who'd seen plenty, his day, even he was unprepared for the sight and the sound that greeted him: jelly-butt bro standin' there with his back to him, Johnson in his hands, splashin' a Niagara out over the rail. Nice time be leakin' the lizard, nice move, real professional.

Sigurd's stance was wide-legged, flat-footed, hump-shouldered, the very image of centered focus. Aiming his member between two rickety columns of the waist-high guard rail, he fire-hosed the dark void beneath him. A low whistling sigh escaped his parted lips. His eyes roved out over the somber ocean, here and there flecked with white foam from an indolent surf breaking on the beach, but otherwise black as the starless bowl of sky. His face wore the dreamy contemplative look of a man luxuriating in the indescribably blissful sensation of relief long overdue. A band of moonlight poured through a gap in the cluster of clouds, and for an instant, for reasons unknown to him—the night, the sea, the sky?—who could say?—he was dazzled, awed, lost in the boundless immensity of space and the relentless spill of time.

But only for an instant. Something dimly preconscious, more felt than heard, the red alert of an animal in mortal peril, flashed across the synapses of his brain and impelled him to turn. An enormous figure, black, silhouetted in the sheath of moonlight, glided effortlessly toward him out of the dark. His worst nightmare actualized, his fanciful movie come true: *Ride, Muthafucka, Ride.* And as though seeing its approach through the wrong end of a telescope, time and motion and distance blurred, he froze in a paralytic trance of dread, heat jolting in his chest, hands still clutching the still spraying member. And though he couldn't believe any of it was happening, and happening to him, as he gazed, stupefied, at the figure bearing down on him, its steel-pointed eyes stuck in the black face and fixed remorselessly on him, its bulgy arm swinging some long glittery shaft at him in a lethal looping arc, he understood the terrible moment of his own death had arrived at last. In an agony of fright he lurched backward, and he shrieked once as the rail splintered under his weight and his hands released the errant organ, agent of all his calamity, and clawed at air, but only briefly, for a dense velvety fog seemed to rise up to meet him and cushion his seven-story fall.

They had made it as far as the next-to-the-last room in the corridor. Waverly stood with his back pressed to the wall alongside the door. Bennie and Caroline crouched in the corner opposite him, bundled in shadows. Nothing moved in the breezeway. The moon came out from behind a tumbling rush of clouds, and a pale shaft of light slanted through the window and fell across the floor. Waverly searched about desperately for a weapon, anything to serve as weapon. Objects, fuzzy and distorted by the blackness of the room, took on a kind of dim shape: a mirrored dresser, a table, couple of chairs, couple of beds with a nightstand between them, and on the nightstand a lamp. Tubular brass lamp, catching a thin beam of light. He made a stay-down motion at Bennie and Caroline—all communication by gesture now, not a word whispered—and then he slipped over and removed the cobwebbed shade. He knotted the trailing cord around the lamp and, grasping it with both hands, batter's grip, returned to his station by the door.

He waited. Still nothing out on the breezeway—no movement, no sound. And waiting that way, poised in comic, inept ambush behind a flimsy door, the dark humor of the scene, the moment, was not entirely lost on him. Bottom of the ninth, two outs, bases loaded—and the slugger stepped up to the plate, home-run hitter, come to salvage the deadly game. Beware, you shooters! This formidable foe, resourceful prankster, packs a mean and hefty, well, lamp.

A scream, more on the order of a squeal, pierced the silence, followed closely by the sound of splintering wood, followed by the sight of a figure darting past the window, followed by a series of familiar sharp thumps echoing through the corridor. Waverly slid the door open just a notch, just enough to make out the figure stooped over something—impossible to tell what, some shadowed fallen lump—at the south end of the breezeway. A curtain of cloud descended over the moon. He signaled Bennie and Caroline, and they came to their feet and the three of them bolted through the door and ducked around the corner into the north stairwell and went clattering down the steps, Bennie in the lead now and Waverly, still clutching his redoubtable lamp, bringing up the rear.

D'Marco came out on the top floor in time to see one figure leaning over the guard rail and another sailing through the air, arms and legs fluttering in the frantic graceless fall of a broken-winged bird. He couldn't tell for sure who the flyer was, but from the pitch of the scream he could pretty much guess. Pile of goo splattered across the grass seven flights down, that had to be Sigurd. Poor Chubbo. Poor dumb fuck. Never going to be a Burt now.

So what he did was put on his fast shoes and dash through the breezeway, laying down a volley at the figure shrouded in darkness at the other end. It rocked back off the rail, staggered, seemed to do a shuddery little dance, made a guttural noise, and then toppled thuddingly to the floor. D'Marco edged forward slowly, weapon arm extended, rigid. His jaw muscles bunched. A pair of needlenose pliers, unseen but no less real, pinched his nerve ends. When he arrived at the end of the corridor, what he heard was a faint throaty gurgle and what he saw was a mound of flesh reclining face down in a pool of blood and, by the stink of it, piss.

It didn't move. Nevertheless, D'Marco approached cautiously, piece leveled. He put a foot under one beefy shoulder and rolled the inert figure over on its back, fully expecting to discover the player or possibly the Jew, one or the other, tried to pull an end run on them and in fact succeeded, though only by half. But his face registered a blank gape of incomprehension at what he saw: goddam spook, f'Chrissake, couple gushing holes in his chest, snowball eyeballs bulging, mouth ajar, tongue lolling, still fighting for breath, still gurgling. A metal baton about the length of a bat, and a gun, looked like a Magnum, lay on the floor just beyond the reach of the limp outthrust arms. An obvious shooter, or maybe even heat. Jesus, it got complicated. D'Marco stooped down for a closer look. Never seen him before in his life, far as he could tell, since they all looked alike, especially in the dark. Whoever he was and whatever the fuck he was doing here, he was gumming up the game. But not anymore. Trust a spade be in the wrong place at the worst time.

D'Marco laid the silencer-elongated muzzle of his piece squarely between the eyes, gone glassy now with resignation. "This one's for Burt," he said, and he squeezed the trigger and took off the top of the head. A twitching spasm shook the body and ran its course, and the gurgling stopped. He was surrounded by a sudden silence. A moment's thoughtful silence. He didn't know anything about regret; sorrow was an emotion alien to him. Still, he felt a curious vacancy, as if a persistent, nagging, familiar ache had lifted, but too abruptly and with insufficient notice. Better not to think about it. The way he saw it, his obligation was fulfilled, debt paid. So much for partnering. Never again.

Rushing footsteps sounded at the opposite end of the breezeway. He swung around and caught a glimpse of three shadowed figures turning into the stairwell. Okay, back to business. Time to wrap it up. Business he understood. He reloaded the .22, grabbed the Magnum—little extra firepower never hurt—stuck it under his belt, and took off after them in an adrenaline-pumped sprint.

Running, dodging, scrambling, stumbling, cursing, fetching breath in panting gasps, they made it down six flights of stairs and through the rat's maze of breezeway along the bungalow units and down the last flight to the ground floor behind the main building, where Caroline sagged against Waverly and moved her head slowly, negatively, and said, "No more. Can't run anymore." Bennie was no better off. Doubled over, clutching his side, snorting like some barnyard animal, he couldn't find the breath to speak, but even had he been able the message would surely have been the same: No more.

Terror squared. A whole new dimension to the quaint image of blind flight. Waverly looked about wildly. Open breezeway ahead of them; wide swatch of lawn, absent of cover, to the right of them; and behind them a shooter, or shooters, no way to know, coming on fast. Which left nothing but the hotel dining room, vast as a cavern and as impenetrably dark, on the other side of a long wall of glass. He had a speck of an instant. He had the lamp and he had what remained of his wits and that's all he had. He had no choice.

The door was only a few feet down. He gave Bennie a shove and dragged Caroline along beside him, and then he set himself and drew back the lamp and swung. The shattering glass ruptured the silence. He thrust a hand inside and released the bolt and yanked open the door and pushed them through. Near as he could make out there were three, maybe four, files of tables, most of them still with place settings and lantern-shaped candle holders, and still draped with white linen tablecloths. Clusters of round white holes in the dark. The air in the room was musty, stifling, thick with the vestigial aromas of a thousand leisurely pleasured feasts. He heard a shuffle of footsteps out in the breezeway. A wisp of a shadow, barely visible in the murky light of the cloud-smeared moon, crossed the glass. One shadow, one shooter. One was plenty, more than enough. No pleasures tonight, and no leisure.

He steered Caroline and Bennie to a table in the second file directly opposite the door. "Down," he said, and obediently they hunkered down. Bennie's breath came in dry, hawking gasps. A palsied quake shook Caroline's thin shoulders. She stared at him vacantly. He tugged the tablecloth back and partly over them, anchored it with the candle holder and dropped to his knees and started to crawl away.

"Where you goin'?" Bennie said, voice a rasp of fear.

"Just stay down. There'll be shooting. If you can get behind him, run for the door."

"What about you?"

Waverly looked at him steadily, at both of them, this exhausted pair, petrified with fear, innocently tangled in the braided chain of folly and mischance and evil luck that strung together the sorry chronicle of his life. "Don't ask," he said.

Bennie couldn't meet the steady gaze. He didn't ask.

"You watch out for her," Waverly said. "You'll do that for me, right?"

"Yeah, right. Do what I can."

The shadow was at the door. Waverly crept across the floor and ducked behind a table. There wasn't time to put much distance between himself and Caroline and Bennie: couple of tables, maybe ten feet, no more than that. Narrowest of margins. After the first pops he couldn't count on them staying down; one or the other, maybe both, was bound to be spooked. So what he had to do was draw the action—and the fire—his way. The shadow remained crouched by the door, seemed to deliberate. Taking its time, taking no chances, running no risks. Softly, but distinct enough to isolate his general location in the room, Waverly said, "Welcome to the Collonades. Why don't you come on in."

For a prolonged moment there was only silence. Then on a ghost of a chuckle came the reply, "Oh, I'm coming, man, I'm coming. Bet to it." But no fire. Nobody's fool, this shooter.

Waverly gripped the lamp tightly in his right hand. With his left he reached up and lifted a place setting off the table—knife, two forks, a spoon. Handful of silver and a brass lamp. Puny weapons. Now he had a serious choice to make. He could chuck the silver into the row of tables behind him, classic B-movie maneuver, and hope the shooter was keen enough and quick enough to see through it. Or he could create the rackety diversion right here, right next to him, assume this shooter was a beat behind. A hard call, either way. And all of it turned on the unknown: an unknown level of cunning in an unknown adversary.

The door creaked open. On an impulse, a hunch—no, more a wild guess—he tossed the silver straight up in the air. He braced himself, ready to take a backward leap, dodge and run. The silver came clattering down around him, and a silence settled over the room. No movement at the door. No fire. Nothing. Silence.

It lengthened. Till finally a voice, mirthless, wised-up, heavy with scorn, drawled, "Jesus, man, you need new material. Give it some thought. We got lots of time."

Time? Waverly felt curiously like a child again, playing childish games in the dark, propelled by memory and imagination down some magical menacing corridor of time, pursued by specters and shadows invested with awesome powers of prescience, unde-ceived, thinking his thoughts, reading his mind. A fantastic, time-warped game of hide and seek. Deadly game. His legs were pulsing, cramping. And he was run out of strategy and artifice and clever transparent moves. He drew in a breath and bawled, "Here I am, chump, over here," and then he drove his shoulder into the table, upended it.

The shadow came charging through the door, announcing, "Avon calling" and executing a deft acrobatic roll across the floor and laying down a scatter of fire.

Waverly dove to the right. A bullet pinged off a chair next to him, another skimmed just over his head. Someone, he couldn't tell who—Bennie? Caroline?—bolted out from under the table-cloth and scampered toward the back of the room. A sudden wash of moonlight fell through the glass, and the shadow took on form and shape and dimension in a square of the silvery light, and it was kneeling now, both arms lifted and extended, taking careful aim at the figure fleeing into the dark. Waverly sprang to his feet and lunged across the narrow space between them. He had the peculiar dreamlike sensation of running at peak speed, all the stops out, but running through a wet patch of fresh-laid cement. He brought the lamp down across the outline of a collarbone, shattering it. But not before the shooter got off a round. Two shrill cries pealed simultaneously through the night. The shooter slumped forward. His piece rattled onto the floor. One arm dangled limply, the other clawed at his belt. Waverly swung again, caught him squarely across the back. The force of the blow would have flattened anyone else. Not this one. He came up off his knees, agile as a gymnast twirling in air, and speared his good shoulder into Waverly's midsection, plowed him backward, took him off his feet.

Waverly was sprawled on his back, his head wedged against the solid wooden base of a table. And the shooter was all over him, hammering at him with a fist, just one, but that one was heavy enough. Instinctively he crossed his arms over his face in a desperate effort to blunt the impact of the single clubbing fist. Abruptly the pummeling stopped, but a forearm dropped across his exposed throat, the full weight of a body behind it, bearing down on it, mashing out his last gagging breaths. His pinned legs and torso thrashed wildly. His arms flailed the air. Tiny explosions erupted in brilliant starburst patterns behind his eyes, which were swimming up in their sockets now and which fell on a loop of white cloth above his head. He grabbed for it, yanked it, and a candle holder and four sets of tableware came spilling down on them in a tangle of linen. The shooter, undistracted, single-minded, bore down harder. Waverly's tongue seemed to be inflating, filling his mouth. His arms sagged. His hands groped feebly along the floor. One of them, his left, turned over a piece of silver, a fork by the feel of it; and he brought it up in a rolling stabbing motion and drove it into the shooter's face, just below the cheekbone, and then raked it diagonally across the right side of the face, tearing the flesh, ripping a nostril, slicing the lips. The shooter let out an astonished screeching wail, and his arm lifted off Waverly's throat and he lurched backward, shuddering convulsively. Blood squirted out from under the hand that covered the lacerated face.

Waverly sucked in air, gasping and wheezing like an animal run too hard, too long. Exhausted, emptied, he nonetheless recognized dimly he had a sliver of an instant remaining to him and not a bit more. Understanding that, he jammed the fork into the covering hand, puncturing it; and another scream issued from those shredded lips and the shooter, centered by the perfect, exclusive focus of pain, a writing package of pain, grasped at the fork with his other hand, the limp one. Seizing what was left of his instant, Waverly bucked him off and scrambled across the floor and recovered the fallen gun. He trained it on him, staggered to his feet. Now he held the power. From somewhere off in the second file of tables a quavery voice called, "Timothy? That you?"

"Bennie?"

"You okay?"

"Get over here! Quick!"

Bennie hauled himself off the floor and came toward him, holding out helpless palms. "Listen, I tried to stop her but she—"

Waverly wasn't listening. He pressed the gun into one of the upturned palms. "Cover him. If he moves, whack him."

He weaved through the tables in the direction of where she fell. He found her lying on her back in a widening pool of blood. He dropped to his knees and lifted her head gently and cradled it in his lap. Her eyes were open, startled, steep with wonder. Her breathing was rattly and faint. He said, "Hang on, Caroline. I'm going to get you out of here."

Scarcely audible, she murmured, "It hurts, Tim. Hurts really bad."

"Hang on," he said, "hang on," repeating it desperately, as if the force of his words and his will could restore breath, animate slackening limbs, arrest a spirit leaking away on a rushing current of blood, vanishing in the dark. Her lips seemed to move, but he heard nothing. He bent in closer. "What is it, Caroline? What? Tell me."

"We could have had such a time, Tim. You and I. Such a party."

"We will yet," Waverly said, believing not a word of it.

Her lips moved a while longer, producing no sound. A death knowledge filled the wonder-struck eyes. Her expression changed. She sighed a small rueful sigh and her breathing stopped.

For a long, stunned moment Waverly didn't move. He knelt there, his own eyes fixed in a desolate mid-distance stare, her head still resting in his lap, limp in its tangled bed of hair. He was overtaken by the anguished wish to go back, far back, across the gulf of years, and begin this journey over again. And then that universal melancholy wish passed, replaced by a choking rage. He eased Caroline's lifeless head onto the floor, mumbled something, or maybe he didn't, maybe he thought it instead, and rose up and crossed the room.

The shooter was on his feet now, swaying a little, steadying himself against the back of a chair. Somehow he'd gotten the fork out of his hand. His face was glazed with blood. Bennie stood on the other side of the table, keeping a wary distance, a piece in each hand, one of them lengthened by a silencer, one not. Both were leveled on the wobbly figure. Two-gun Epstein.

"He was packin' this," Bennie said, giving the Magnum a slight wiggle. "I patted him down."

"She's dead, Bennie."

"Jesus, Timothy. What can I say?"

"Nothing to say."

Waverly looked over at the shooter. Recognized him as the same one who'd been tracking them these past weeks. He took the Magnum from Bennie and came around the table and gazed at him, as though he were committing the mutilated features to memory. Very evenly he said, "You killed her, you son of a bitch. You know that? You killed her."

D'Marco stared back at him, a challenging thrust to his jaw. He lifted his good shoulder, half a shrug.

"I think you better move away from the chair now."

A fierce light kindled Waverly's eyes, stark contrast to the lunatic singsong that had entered his voice. And from behind him came the B. Epstein voice of reason, caution, prudence: "C'mon, Timothy, you can't ice him. What's the good? We got trouble enough."

Waverly ignored it, repeated the directive.

"Let it alone," the elevating voice of reason pleaded. "We got to get outta here before the steam comes down. Look at him. Ain't no Hollywood in his future, that face. Give him a rap, it makes you feel better."

D'Marco, waiting the outcome of the debate, hadn't moved. Waverly jabbed the gun at him. "I'm not going to say it again." D'Marco took one halting step back and set himself in a defiant stance, or as nearly defiant as his dangling right arm would allow.

"Use your head, Timothy. He's the finger on the trigger is all he is. He ain't the one."

"I understand that," Waverly said. "Which is why we've got one last obligation to discharge." To the shooter he said, "Where's Dietz?"

"Who's Dietz?"

Waverly gave him a look of measuring, summing up. "Think hard. You don't have much time."

"You don't have to go looking for Dietz," D'Marco sneered. "He'll find you."

Waverly shook his head sadly and pointed the Magnum and squeezed the trigger and sent a bullet smashing into D'Marco's left kneecap. The thunderous report and the agonized screams rose, comingling, and echoed off the walls and ceiling of the vast room. D'Marco flopped across the floor like some wriggly snared fish. Waverly followed him, stood over him, tapping a foot and waiting patiently till the screaming abated some. "Try again," he said mildly.

D'Marco croaked out the words, "Sea Spray."

"Room?"

"One-o-eight."

"You're sure? I'll come back, you know."

"It's one-o-eight."

"Very good. You just spared yourself a knee."

"Fuck you," D'Marco hissed, and he might have said more if the butt of the Magnum hadn't banged him on the side of the head.

"General anesthesia," Waverly said to no one but himself, and then he came back to where Bennie stood, slack-jawed and gaping, and said, "We've got to move fast now, Bennie. Take one of those cloth napkins, wipe down that gun you're holding, and lay it over by him."

"This is crazy, Timothy. What you're doin' here."

"Just do it."

"Awright. Awright. You want the piece emptied?"

"Not necessary. He's going nowhere."

Waverly stuck the Magnum in his jacket pocket and grabbed a napkin. He found the fork and wiped it clean. He did the same with the lamp and the rest of the scattered silver. Over his shoulder he called, "Anything you touched, get it all." He moved purposefully, conscious of time slipping away. When he was finished he joined Bennie at the door.

"Here's what you do. Go back to the Tropicaire, check on O'Boyle. If he's up, keep him occupied. Watch him close, he could be in this."

"You're goin' for Dietz," Bennie said. His voice was flat, resigned.

"I'll meet you at the car. Give it ten minutes, no more. I'm not there by then, get yourself into the wind."

"Say it one more time, Timothy. This is puzzle house, what you're doin'. Changes nothing."

"Yeah, well, we do what we do."

Bennie made a defeated shrug. "Ten minutes," he said.

"Outside."

* * *

Waverly came down the first-floor corridor of the Sea Spray, ticking off room numbers till he arrived at 108. He glanced to his right and left. Clear both ways. He removed the Magnum from his jacket and rapped softly on the door. Voice on the other side said warily, "Frog?"

"Yeah, it's me."

The knob turned and the door swung open. Dietz looked at him blankly. Looked past him into the empty hallway. Looked at the gun. "Who're you?" he demanded.

"One of your debtors. Come to settle up."

Dietz, obedient to the thrust of the gun, backed into the room. "You'd be Waverly," he said.

"And you'd be Dietz."

"That's right."

"I understand I owe you money."

Dietz cleared his throat and, putting some menace in his voice, some growly CEO intimidation, as if there were merely a desk between them or a conference table, not a .357 Magnum, said, "That's correct too. You got it?"

Brash move. Ballsy guy, this Dietz. Waverly made a small contrite smile and said, "Afraid not. I couldn't raise it."

"Okay. Give me what you got and we'll call it square."

"But you see, Mr. Dietz, I've got nothing," Waverly explained patiently. "Apart from this," he added, indicating the gun.

Dietz adopted a bargaining tone. "Well, maybe we can work something out," he said, pliant negotiator now.

"You'd extend the deadline?"

"I could do that."

"A schedule of payments, maybe?"

"Yeah, that's an idea."

"Something orderly. Businesslike."

"You're doing business," Dietz said, eminently reasonable, "anything can be arranged." A thin expectant smile creased his lips.

What a curious inverted world you inhabit, Waverly was thinking, rife with curious, shifty games. Very strange. He said, "I don't think so, Mr. Dietz. Not this time."

"Look, what do you want?"

"Want you to step into the john there and lie down in the tub."

Dietz's mouth tightened. The smile, what there'd been of one, vanished. His eyes darted furiously. Waverly made a prodding motion with the gun and followed him into the bathroom. Dietz climbed into the tub and stretched out on his back.

"Come on, Mr. Dietz, you know better than that. Face down."

Dietz rolled over on his stomach and laid his hands flat against the walls of the tub, as if he were holding them back. A man familiar with the position, aware of its special meaning. He turned his head to the side and said, "Your partner—what's his name?"

"Epstein."

"Let me talk to him. We can do a deal." All the color had drained from his face, and all the growl was gone out of his voice.

"Afraid he's not available. It's just you and me."

Waverly filled the sink and pulled two bath towels and a wash-cloth off the rack. He dunked them in the water, wrung them out best as he could with one hand, slung the towels over his shoulder, and stuffed the washcloth in a pocket. Never once did he take his eyes off the prone figure squeezed into the tub, and never once did he lower the piece. "Now you can get up," he said.

"Fuck's going on?" There was a ring of astonishment in the grunted question. A mix of disbelief and hope.

"Up."

Dietz got to his feet stiffly and stepped over the rim of the tub.

Waverly moved back through the door, beckoned him. "Come along, now."

"Where to?"

"You'll see." He got in behind him and poked the Magnum into the small of his back. "Oh, one thing more, Mr. Dietz. I want you to be cool. You know I've got nothing left to lose. You understand that?"

Dietz bobbed his head vigorously, signifying he understood.

Waverly directed him through the corridor and out the side door and across the deserted street. They passed under the Trop-icaire sign, its yellow neon crackling against the black sky. At the entrance to the canvas-draped apartment Waverly said, "You're going to have to get down again. Same as in the tub, only with your hands behind you."

"Listen, we can still—"

Waverly brushed the back of his neck with the muzzle of the gun. "Better just do it, Mr. Dietz."

Dietz got down.

Waverly straddled him and looped one of the towels around his wrists and fashioned a knot. It was tricky, keeping him covered and tightening the knot, but he was dextrous, he managed. With the other towel he bound the ankles. That was easier. He seized

Dietz at the collar and pulled him to his knees. Helped him to his feet.

They stood facing the tarp that covered the apartment door. A sign was pinned to it. Waverly let him read it. He figured it was only fair. There was a certain ceremony to be observed here, a ritual of sorts. Beneath the skull and crossbones the sign announced:

DANGER

FUMIGATING WITH VIKANE SULFURYL FLUORIDE

DEADLY POISON

ALL PERSONS ARE WARNED TO STAY AWAY

A twittery spasm surged through Dietz's body, head to foot, fleet as an electric charge. He rocked back on his heels. He made a peculiar sound, wordless, not particularly loud, not a moan exactly and certainly not a cry, more a sustained catarrhal bleat. Most peculiar sound. But to his credit he didn't beg.

Waverly unclipped two sections of tarp. They fell away, exposing the door. He reached in a pocket, removed the key to the apartment, and fitted it in the door. From another pocket he took the damp washcloth, covered his mouth and nose. He found it difficult to restrain a smile: Timothy Waverly, masked avenger, instrument of divine reckoning, justice. Along with all its muddles and reversals and endless disasters, the low theatrics of his life appalled him. Nevertheless, come this far, there was nothing to do but round things off, restore the varnish of order. So he turned to Dietz, who was still producing that curious bleat, and said, almost kindly, "Just breathe deeply. They say it's easier that way."

He swallowed his breath and pushed open the door and forced Dietz, hopping, inside. A hot blast of clotted noxious air assaulted his eyes and penetrated the wet cloth and stung his nostrils. He gave Dietz a shove, sent him sprawling. Hacking and gagging, he backed out the door, pulled it shut, and removed the key. With the butt of the gun he hammered at the knob, springing it loose in the appearance of a forced entry. It wasn't much in the way of a dodge. Best he could think of. Then he clipped the two sections of tarp together and wiped the clips with the washcloth. And from the other side of those tarps and from beyond that door came a brief muffled howl and some thrashing noises followed by a dwindling wail and something that sounded like a sob and then nothing at all.

Waverly ducked around the corner of the apartment and discovered Bennie behind the wheel of the idling Caddie. He climbed in and Bennie took the car squealing into the street, muttering, "I ain't even gonna ask."

Waverly said simply, "Happy ending to our story."

24

They were pointed north on the Turnpike. Bennie drove as fast as he dared. The cigar in his mouth was gnawed to a moist stub. Exits flashed by. Clouds sailed like smoke across the gradually lightening sky. Waverly gazed numbly at the streak of highway cleaving the landscape in two. There was about him something of the dazed quality of the walking wounded. A desolate sense of bleakness filled his throat.

For a considerable time they rode in silence, each occupied with his own thoughts. Waverly's were wandering, unfocused, not so much thoughts as a confusion of images floating behind his eyes, vivid, antic, bizarre. Predominant among them, arriving like a pulse of dim light issuing through time and space from the corpse of a distant star, was a vision of Caroline Vanzoren Crown. For a while it persisted, that vision, but as the highway unspooled ahead of them it seemed to wane, displaced by a mesh of soiled emotions and vague longings, and also by wistful ruminations on destiny's intricate intersecting orbits, the lengthening trail of violent death left in his wake, and all the multiplying games and falsehoods and fictions insulating his own life.

Without any warning his stomach began to rumble ominously. Bennie's generated a sympathetic echo. Dyspepsia's symphony. Waverly couldn't remember when he'd eaten last. "Dueling bellies," he said, for something to say.

Bennie made a gesture of impatience. "Hey, you're thinkin' chow, put it right outta your head. We ain't stoppin' till we showed this bad-news state our heels."

"Where we headed?"

"Dunno. Outta here. West, maybe. You ever been to Nevada?"

"No. Never."

"Maybe west, then."

"How much are you carrying?"

"Under a nickel. You?"

"Less than a dime."

"Holy fuck," Bennie said, "under a nickel and less'n a dime." He clamped down on the cigar, yellow-knuckled the wheel. "Here we go."